Renaissance Man

M. Garzon

Petal Press Canada

Cover Design by Christina Conway | Dazzle by Design

Copyright © 2013 M. Garzon

All rights reserved.

ISBN: 0988001365

ISBN-13: 978-0988001367

To Lori Connolly and Cassandra Aurora-Garzon,

the best sisters-in-law ever.

Acknowledgments

Big huge thank-yous (with balloons attached!) go to the following:

Foremost and always, to my brothers Lavih and Ilan. I know you're always there to catch me if I fall. And then laugh at me.

My proofreaders Jennilyn Robbie, Brooke Woboditsch, Stephanie Roy, Corenne Taylor, and Sharleen Banning.

Stephanie Binette, acupuncturist and true healer, for keeping my little family healthy.

Teri McTurner, who is the kind of friend who is just as close, no matter the distance between us.

Melanie Pelletier and Jason Hayden, the best neighbors anyone could ever hope for. Thanks for the help with the kids, Mel!

Sommer Christie, Mental Performance Coach

Steve Taylor for answers regarding police procedure in Ontario.

Priya Sarin for answering questions about the legal system.

COTH forum users for generously sharing their knowledge.

Sandridge Saddlery for the loan of the bitless bridle.

For the wonderful cover, extra thanks to Christina Conway of Dazzle by Design for your generosity, patience, and mad photography skills!

Thanks also to our models. On the front:
Thea Lepore, Kyle Armstrong and Wyatt (Play Boy), owned by Tina Filion-Luiten.
Back:
Thea and Aragon (owned by Christina Conway)

Finally, to Holly Hallett and Dunelm Farm for the horses, location, and putting up with the photoshoot circus.

Books in the Blaze of Glory series:

Blaze of Glory
Look Twice
Renaissance Man
Halo Boy
Elina
The Turning Point (short story)
Horses Coloring Book

Other books by M. Garzon:

Awesome Possum
Lemon Squeezy

The Hoofs Of The Horses

The hoofs of the horses! — Oh! witching and sweet
Is the music earth steals from the iron-shod feet;
No whisper of lover, no trilling of bird
Can stir me as hoofs of the horses have stirred.

They spurn disappointment and trample despair,
And drown with their drum-beats the challenge of care;
With scarlet and silk for their banners above,
They are swifter than Fortune and sweeter than Love.

On the wings of the morning they gather and fly,
In the hush of the night-time I hear them go by —
The horses of memory thundering through
With flashing white fetlocks all wet with the dew.

When you lay me to slumber no spot you can choose
But will ring to the rhythm of galloping shoes,
And under the daisies no grave be so deep
But the hoofs of the horses shall sound in my sleep.

One

I stood by the bed, discreetly watching Jaden undress. I wasn't sure why I was being discreet since he was always quite frank in his appreciation of my body, but I wasn't as bold as him. He was standing a few feet away, by the closet. His shirt was already unbuttoned, and I admired the sculpted lines of his chest and stomach. He was at a slight angle to me, not quite sideways, and his expression was thoughtful as he unbuckled his belt and started drawing it slowly through the loops.

I didn't know what happened. All of a sudden there was a buzzing in my ears; a wave of weakness made me sink down shakily onto the bed. I dropped my face into my hands. A second later his arms were around me and I leaned into his welcome warmth. I was trembling.

"*Mi querida*, what's wrong?" His voice was low and worried.

I shook my head slightly against his chest. "Nothing. Just a bit dizzy, for some reason."

"Téa..." Disbelief was clear in his tone, but he kept rubbing my arm soothingly, and I felt his lips press occasionally against my hair. I didn't say anything, since silence seemed the safest policy at this point.

He sighed. He kept one arm around me, but his other hand went to my chin and turned my face to his. He turned the full force of his hypnotic, gold-flecked brown eyes on me — he knew full well that I couldn't refuse those eyes anything. Nor could I lie to them. Apparently, he meant business.

"You saw me taking-" he started saying.

"It's nothing to do with you," I interrupted quickly. I stretched up and met his lips, but although he kissed me back, his usual enthusiasm was lacking. He was careful, almost tentative.

I pulled away with a groan. "Oh, no."

"What?" He looked at me in alarm.

"Don't go getting all analytical and overprotective on me," I pleaded. "I think maybe I'm just hungry."

"When did you eat last?" he asked, frowning.

"I don't know. This morning, I guess."

He seized my hand, rolling his eyes, and scolded me gently all the way to the kitchen. "You're going to have to start taking better care of yourself — how do you expect to keep up the pace you've set if you never eat?"

I didn't bother arguing with him, but settled onto a stool at the counter and watched him move around his loft's small kitchen, something I always loved to do. My enjoyment certainly wasn't diminished by the fact that his shirt was still hanging unbuttoned.

We had a quick meal of leftovers. I was putting the plates in the dishwasher when Jaden spoke from the sink. "Even if you didn't eat all day, I have a strong suspicion that's not what made you dizzy."

I closed the dishwasher and turned to face him. "I don't want to talk about this."

Half his mouth quirked up. "Oh, I'm sorry. Did I give you the impression you had a choice?"

My brows shot up. "Yes, in fact," I said. I stepped nearer and ran my hands down his muscled chest and over his stomach. "You've given me the impression that I *always* have a choice."

I let my hands continue downward. He grabbed my shoulders and pulled me hard against him, and we stumbled toward the bedroom, shedding clothes on the way.

As we fell onto the bed I murmured, "Don't forget I have a curfew."

A low laugh rumbled through his chest. "Are you asking me to be quick?"

We didn't rush, and I had time to relax with my head on his chest afterward, his arms warm around me. It was the first time in weeks I'd even approached happiness.

I awoke with a start. "Oh, crap," I whimpered when I checked the bedside clock.

Jaden reached over sleepily; I gave him a quick kiss on the cheek and jumped out of bed.

"Gotta run, I'm late." Very, very late — it was early morning, and I had to get home in time to feed the horses. Preferably *before* my stepfather noticed I was gone.

2

It was snowing when I stumbled outside, and I frenziedly brushed just enough white stuff off my car so that I could see. I got in, shivering violently and still half-asleep as I maneuvered through the snowy Toronto streets. I relaxed a bit once I got onto the cleared highway, and I felt warmer as my mind roamed over my evening with Jaden. It was the first time I'd seen him since he'd left to play polo in Florida, but he almost hadn't gone at all. I remembered having to convince him.

"Maybe I should stay," Jaden had said worriedly. That was two days after Seth, my twin brother, had left for Spain.

I gently disentangled his hand from his hair and held it between my own. "You need the money," I reminded him. We were sitting on the old tack trunk in the gloomy shed since the barn had been busy with people. Jaden was distressed at leaving me so soon after Seth's departure. I shivered — the shed wasn't heated — and Jaden pulled me more tightly against him.

"I'll be okay, really," I said with more conviction than I felt. I knew that a few weeks of polo would pay for Jaden's final semester of school.

He had gone, in the end, and Christmas had felt less like a holiday to me than it had the year before, when I'd been in Florida with no tree and Chinese food for dinner. Dec and I, still barely speaking, went to Aunt Penny's and Uncle Robert's house for Christmas. The most uncomfortable Christmas dinner ever, as it turned out.

To their credit, the Foster family had never treated us like 'the stepkids'. Even when Dec first married my mom — years before he adopted us — we were held to the same standards as the rest of the Foster clan. They had adopted us too, and from the way they were acting, I wondered whether they were now suffering similar feelings of betrayal from my brother's defection. During the meal, Aunt Penny frequently put her hand on Dec's shoulder, but her stiff manner with me spoke volumes, and the rest of my family seemed ill at ease. As soon as the meal was over my cousin Stacey grabbed my arm and dragged me upstairs to her bedroom.

"Holy crap," she said as she shut the door.

"Yeah," I said tiredly. "Let's hope the New Year brings a new mood, otherwise I might as well go to Spain myself."

"Would you really?" she exclaimed. She looked more excited than shocked at the possibility.

"No," I sighed. "I can't."

I had kept busy over the holidays. I was still too angry with Dec to talk to him much; I blamed him for Seth's absence. Teri, my best friend, was at the barn almost every day helping out. Her pony Picasso had been sold the week before, purchased as a Christmas present for the luckiest little girl ever, and we'd both cried while wrapping his legs with shipping bandages. We had stuffed him full of treats and patted and kissed him before Teri handed over the lead rope to his new owners, but we didn't watch him get into the trailer. That was too hard.

"Are you sure you don't want to go home?" I had asked Teri as she prepared to teach a beginner lesson. The lesson schedule always picked up during holidays.

She shrugged. "I'm okay." Only the way her celery-green eyes refused to meet mine gave a clue to her feelings.

"You're a lifesaver, Ter. I don't know what I'd do without you." I meant it, too. Even though I was positive she'd rather be relaxing at home, away from the constant reminders of Picasso's absence, Teri was here freezing her fingers and toes off because I needed the help. With Seth gone I was stretched way too thin — Gran taught the odd lesson, but the cold was harder on her than it used to be, and Dec was busy with a work project that was behind schedule. Julia was on vacation with her parents, who had decided that a week down south would help her get over the break-up with Seth. I wished it were that easy for me.

"Any big plans for tomorrow?" Dec had asked me the day before New Year's Eve. We were having a simple soup-and-sandwich dinner, and the table felt empty with just the two of us.

"No," I replied. Teri was going out with her family, and my other friends were gone. Even Kabir had stayed in California over the holidays.

"Oh. Well, do you want to do something, just the two of us?" Dec had looked uncomfortable; both of us knew it wouldn't be an enjoyable evening.

"That's okay. Why don't you go out, Dec." I was pretty sure he had plans with Joanne, his girlfriend.

4

On New Year's Eve Jaden called me at ten minutes before midnight. I could hear the sounds of a party in the background, and for a second was transported back to our magical evening of the year before, when all had seemed so right with the world.

"*Corazon*," he said quietly. "Stay on the phone with me until midnight, so I can pretend you're here in my arms." By the time I hung up ten minutes later, after having wished our friend Michele a Happy New Year too, I had felt a whole lot better. After all, this year promised to bring a lot of good things, too.

I came out of my reverie as I pulled into the long, tree-lined driveway to Shady Lane Stables. It was barely dawn, and I hoped fervently that I could sneak in before Dec realized I hadn't come home.

No such luck. He stepped out of the kitchen the minute I was in the door, his expression grim. He didn't say anything, but then his glare said enough. The fact that he was in pajama bottoms and a T-shirt didn't make him any less intimidating.

"I was at Jaden's, and I... well, we fell asleep," I stammered my excuse.

A spasm crossed Dec's face; inasmuch as he knew that Jaden and I were a couple, he obviously hated the thought of us sleeping together. Let alone doing anything else in bed.

"Listen to me, Téa. You may think you're all grown up now, but you're still young, and as long as you're living in this house there are rules to follow."

I felt my temper awaken. "Tell me you're not using that 'as long as you're under my roof' line on me." I had lost my brother to that policy not long before, and the memory was still raw. "We fell asleep. It was an accident!"

"That's what telephones are for! Why didn't you call me as soon as you woke up?"

"I didn't think of it until I was in the car," I admitted, "and then my phone was dead."

He took a quick step towards me, and I tensed instantly, my breath catching. My reaction must have shown because a pained look crossed his face. He stopped, and I watched him breathe deeply for a moment.

"Okay," he said more calmly. I relaxed. "But this had better be the last time, Téa."

"Dec, I don't get it. I'm sorry I didn't let you know, but it's not like I was out with a stranger. This is Jaden we're talking about. You know I'm completely safe with him."

"I don't care," he said obstinately. "I want you home at night. And I'll be having a word with Jaden to that effect, too."

I felt my jaw set, but I knew better than to argue with him now. I trudged upstairs and went straight to the phone in the guestroom. It still felt like Jaden's room to me, since he'd spent so much time in there during our first summer together.

"Hey, it's me," I said morosely when he answered. "I wanted to give you a heads up, Dec's pretty mad. Maybe you shouldn't answer your phone for the rest of the day."

"How mad?" he asked immediately. "Are you okay?"

"I'm fine. But don't let him blame you for me staying out all night."

"Don't worry about me," he soothed, sounding relieved. "I can handle Dec as long as you're all right."

"I'm far better than 'all right'," I told him, smiling. "I had an incredible time with you yesterday. I wish I could stay over more often... though it's not looking too likely."

It was something I'd have to address with Dec at some point, I realized. We owned a family business; who knew how long I'd live here? Until I finished university, at the very least, and maybe a lot longer. And even though I'd still be under 'his' roof, I didn't want Dec telling me how to live my life when I was twenty-five.

Jaden hadn't stayed in Florida as long as he usually did. He was going into his final semester of law school, and I supposed even *his* charm and intelligence had limits — his professors had insisted that he be present for the entire winter term, which had just started for both of us. It was only my second semester of university, and it looked like the workload was going to be even heavier than in the first. On the third day of classes, I crept into a cavernous, almost-full auditorium and found a seat. My neighbor had dark hair and a gangly look, still more boy than man.

"I'm Chuck," he introduced himself. He had an open, friendly smile.

"Tay-a," I replied, pronouncing my name clearly for him. After class, we headed to the cafeteria together for lunch.

"Did we have a class together last semester?" I asked him as we got into line.

"I don't think so, but you do look kind of familiar," he responded. A second later he waved to someone. "Hey, Shannon." A woman with short auburn-and-grey hair and a comfortably round shape joined us. After the introductions were made we found seats together; it turned out we were all biology majors.

"My dad and granddad are both vets," Chuck told us. "But it's gotten so hard to get into vet school that I might be the first generation not to take over the family practice," he said glumly.

"At least your family understands," Shannon said. "My entire family thinks I'm nuts for leaving a steady job at forty years old to go back to school. But being a vet is all I've ever wanted. I figure better late than never."

"What about you, Téa?" Chuck asked.

"Well, my family owns an equestrian center, so I've worked with horses most of my life. Being a vet just seems like a logical next step," I said. I didn't add that it wasn't my first choice since Chuck and Shannon both seemed so anxious to get into vet school.

"Horses, huh?" Chuck looked at me with renewed interest. "We have a mixed practice — small and large animals — and horses are probably the trickiest to treat. For me, anyway."

"Why?" I asked, surprised. Only a few of our horses had issues with the vet.

"I'm not a horseperson." Chuck grinned. "And they know it."

I nodded in understanding. True horsepeople seem to be either born or made in childhood, with the odd individual developing the skills in adulthood. But horses, unlike other animals, can immediately sense whether you 'know' horses or not. Maybe it's because they're such intuitive creatures, or perhaps it's due to their highly subtle interpretation of body language, but whatever the reason, there's no fooling them.

Julia came home that weekend looking more gorgeous than ever, her smoothly tanned skin the perfect backdrop for her tarnished-silver eyes. She traipsed into the barn smiling and chattering to other boarders about her holiday, and I was caught unawares by a wash of anger.

"Téa!" Julia bounced over and hugged me. She handed me a small, satiny bag. "I got you something."

Guilt beat back the anger inside me. "Thanks, Jules. You didn't have to do that." I pulled out a beautiful silver necklace and earrings set with small blue stones. "It's beautiful," I said sincerely.

Julia grabbed my arm and pulled me toward the tackroom. "C'mon, I want to tell you about my vacation!" I had to grin; Julia was as irrepressible as always. Teri showed up soon after and we all headed for the house to warm up.

While I made hot chocolate Julia handed Teri a bag similar to mine.

"I thought it would match your eyes," Julia enthused.

Teri's necklace was gold with light green stones. "Thank you," she said quietly. She gave Julia a quick smile, but I could tell she wasn't happy.

Julia didn't seem to notice, though. "What have I missed?" she asked as we sat down with our mugs.

I looked at Teri since her news was the biggest.

"I've decided not to go back to school," Teri said. "I'm going to become a jockey."

Julia gasped. "But... Ter! What did your parents say?"

"They said it's my life, and they're behind me no matter what I choose."

I felt the familiar stir of envy at those words, even more strongly now than the first time I'd heard them. How much simpler would my life be if I had a parent like that? I'd still have a brother kicking around, for one thing.

"But aren't they worried about you? Don't they want you to get a good education?" Julia frowned.

"Sure, they're worried. They know it's dangerous, and they're not thrilled that I'll be moving away."

"Oh, right, the horses don't run here during the winter," Julia remembered. "Where will you go?"

"New York. The trainer I worked for at Woodbine went there for the winter. How was the cruise?" Teri asked, obviously changing the subject.

"It was amazing," Julia sighed. "Just what I needed. The sun, the ocean, and always lots to keep you busy. There was even a wedding on board one day! It was beautiful, although I'd never get married on a cruise. Not that I can imagine getting married, anyway. At least not until I'm old."

"Why not?" Teri looked surprised.

"I don't know." Julia shrugged. "Committing to spending your entire life with one person? It seems a little extreme."

"But it would be someone you loved," Teri pointed out. They both turned to look at me.

I hesitated. "Well, Jaden wants to marry me, so-"

"Omigod he *proposed*?!" "Why didn't you-" Their stunned exclamations burst forth.

I held up my hands, laughing. "Easy! He didn't propose, exactly." I explained how Jaden had told Dec he wanted to marry me someday in order to convince Dec that we were serious about our relationship.

"How could you not tell us?" Teri demanded.

"It happened right between winning the Royal and getting stalked by Tom Morin, and then Seth and I started searching for our natural father. There was always something more important to talk about."

"More important than the most romantic thing you'll do in your whole life?" Teri seemed delighted at my news.

"Téa, you're way too young to even be thinking about marriage." Julia, on the other hand, was clearly not delighted. "People change a lot during their twenties, and you're not even there yet. You're in university, you're going to meet hundreds of new people over the next few years."

"I don't think it'll matter who I meet, Julia. No one's going to hold a candle to Jaden."

She looked at me carefully. "He is every kind of sexy, but he's not perfect, Téa. Not like you seem to think."

9

I shrugged. "He's perfect for me. It amounts to the same thing."

Our conversation rolled around my head all afternoon, and over dinner that night I told Dec about Teri's plans.

"Being a jockey is no job for a nice girl like Teri," Dec said worriedly.

"She's tougher than she looks," I reminded him. Teri and I were both petite; we faced the same bias.

"That doesn't matter!" he said loudly. "She'll have to work twice as hard as a man to be half as good. There's too much money at stake in racing for anyone to cut her any slack. And besides, it's ridiculously dangerous." He shook his head. "I'm going to talk to her parents. I'm sure they have no idea what she's getting herself into."

"No! Dec, please, this is what Teri wants," I pleaded. "Her parents are supportive. Why worry them?"

He gave me a direct stare. "Because if it were you, I'd want to know. At least then I'd know enough to stop you."

I spun and stomped out, hot with frustration. I knew Teri. As sensible as she was, if racing was her goal then she wouldn't be dissuaded.

When Teri showed up the next day I apologized profusely.

"It's okay," she reassured me. "My parents and I talked about it, and they know what Dec's like."

I mimed wiping sweat off my brow. "What's up with you and Jules?" I asked, remembering her odd expression the day before.

She sighed. "I don't know. Those expensive gifts... it's just so Jules, you know? It would never occur to her that it might make someone uncomfortable. And it was the same with Seth." She looked genuinely angry now. "She was always pushing him to do better in school, make more money, go out all the time. I feel like she drove him away."

I shook my head slowly. "Seth leaving wasn't Julia's fault. It was Dec's."

I was not in a good mood when I went to ride Hades, and it wasn't improved by his greeting. He put his ears back and curled his nostrils, making an angry face. It wasn't really aggression; it was designed to intimidate me, and it was just part of Hades' personality.

"Cut it out," I snapped at him, yanking the halter over his head.

He looked startled for a second before pinning his ears again and shoving me hard with his nose. I staggered backward a step. Out of sheer exasperation, I shoved him back. Now, that's not the way I'd normally behave around horses because they're prey animals and shows of aggression are usually counter-productive. So his reaction surprised me. My shove had barely moved him, but he turned his head back toward me with his ears pricked forward and his eyes bright. He stepped closer to me and dropped his head to allow me to easily clip on the lead shank, looking oddly satisfied by our exchange.

I shook my head as I led him into the aisle. "You're a strange beast, buddy. But I like you." I patted him before cross-tying him. He was unusually well-behaved, standing fairly patiently while I groomed him and put on his tack.

"Don't tell me you've been waiting for me to push you around all along," I muttered as I led him into the arena. "Don't tell Dec, I'd never live it down."

I mounted and we started working. I'd been riding Hades for a little over a year now, and he was like a different horse. The cantankerous, over-excited behemoth who had first arrived at Shady Lane was now a study in controlled power. There hadn't been any magic bullet with Hades; a lot of slow, painstaking work and experimentation had gotten us to this point. He was still going well in the bitless bridle, and Gran had helped me work out an exercise program to develop his back, hindquarters, and balance. I'd worked with him diligently, riding him at least five days a week, and while he still wasn't an easy horse to ride, I couldn't wait for the show season to start.

Teri left for New York the following week, but the pain of her departure was quickly soothed by a visit from Jaden. I hadn't seen him since our accidental sleepover two weeks before. He strode into the living room radiating energy, his brightness almost too big for the room. His eyes locked onto mine the minute he was through the door.

"Dec's not home," I said quickly, moving toward him. I'd just gotten out of the shower and was purposely wearing a thin T-shirt and skirt, very unseasonal attire for January.

11

He reached me in one long step. The shock of relief as his skin met mine was almost painful, and I pressed myself against him as his hands caressed my shoulders, my back, my waist. As my lips found his I was yanked upwards, and I felt my back slam into the wall. It took me a second to miss the impact my head should have made until I felt Jaden's hand behind it. It felt like years, not weeks, since we'd last touched.

After a few minutes, he leaned his forehead on mine. "Your heart is beating so fast," he murmured. "I can feel it against my chest."

"That's 'cause I'm about to have a heart attack," I said. "I can't believe I went without you for so long. *Te quiero*, Jaden." I whispered the last into his ear, and he pulled away with a sigh that was almost a groan, lowering me slowly to the floor.

"Not quite the response I was hoping for," I groused.

He gave a husky laugh and took my face in his hands. "Patience, *querida*."

"You know very well I don't have any."

"When can you come over to my place?"

I thought it over quickly. "Tomorrow." The next day was Monday, meaning I'd have no lessons to teach.

"I have a meeting near Guelph during the day; I can meet you for lunch too."

Chuck was my lab partner, and after microbiology class the next day he walked me to the visitor's parking lot where I was meeting Jaden. We were discussing that week's assignment, our heads bent over a diagram and only half-watching where we were going, so I was caught by surprise when I looked up to find Jaden in front of us, arms crossed over his chest and jaw muscle hard.

"Um, Jaden, this is Chuck," I introduced them uncertainly. I glanced at Chuck; his startled expression showed that he had noticed Jaden's angry posture.

"I remember," Jaden said shortly. But after a second he stuck out his hand, and Chuck shook it gamely. I breathed an internal sigh of relief when he showed no signs of pain.

Chuck continued on his way home, and Jaden drove to a nearby restaurant, saying nothing. We sat down and a waitress came over, but she didn't say anything either, seemingly distracted by Jaden's appearance. He had one long leg stretched out alongside the booth, and her gaze moved from his booted foot up the line of dark denim, along his muscular black-clad body to his face. At the moment, it looked borderline dangerous.

"What can I get you?" she asked breathily. She never looked at me, even while I ordered.

After she left, Jaden leaned back in his seat and considered me. "Why didn't you tell me?" He was composed now, although his eyes were alive with emotion.

I let out a long breath. "We just recently figured it out ourselves, and, well, I had this crazy notion that you might overreact."

He frowned, tousling his hair before he caught himself and reached toward me instead. I took his hand quickly, knowing by now that my touch would calm his choler.

"It upsets me that you don't trust me," he said finally.

I did a double-take. "Pardon me? *I* don't trust *you*?" I said it faintly, uncertain that I'd heard right.

He shook his head in frustration, pulling his hand back. "Damn Foster family curse. If you weren't afraid of Dec, we wouldn't be having this issue."

"I'm not afraid of Dec," I protested. I was frowning in confusion at the sudden subject change.

"Really? You'd go to him with a problem? Would confide in him, admit to mistakes?" He questioned me as though he was cross-examining a witness; my confusion morphed into annoyance.

"No, but that's basic sense, not fear. And anyway, why does it matter?" I asked.

Jaden took a breath. "It matters because it's affecting *our* relationship. We can't run away from it, Téa. The way you relate to the only father you've ever known is going to have an effect on how you relate to me."

I thought about that for a minute. "I don't buy it."

His brows crept up. "It's a widely accepted psychological principle." He was now watching me with that peculiar mix of amusement and exasperation that I'd come to recognize.

13

"I'm not a principle, Jaden, I'm a person. There's more to me than a conditioned response." I stared at him, taken aback at the sudden anger I felt. "Let's talk about something else."

"This discussion is overdue, Téa."

It was my turn to cross my arms over my chest. "Done. Talking." I forced the words through clenched teeth.

I watched him struggle for a minute, his expression one of mingled shock and displeasure. Jaden wasn't used to being crossed. On the polo field he was a star, in law school he was at the top of his class, and in everyday life people simply yielded to his charisma and confidence. This was the problem when everyone listened to you, I thought crabbily.

His expression smoothed. "All right," he said finally.

Lunch wasn't exactly uncomfortable, but I was glad I'd be seeing him that evening so that we could make up properly. I drove slowly through the February snowfall into the city, its lights illuminating the flakes in multiple colors.

Jaden had given me a key to the loft but I knocked quietly before letting myself in. Something smelled good, and I saw Jaden in the open-concept kitchen directly in front of me. At the uncertain look on my face he came over and wrapped his arms around me, and I leaned into his comforting warmth. He held me for a minute before murmuring in my ear.

"You know you're in trouble, right?"

I sighed. "I know. But we haven't been alone for so long. Can't we talk about it later?" I pleaded. My face was pressed against his chest; I didn't look at him.

"Hmm, that has possibilities... we can have angry sex first, and maybe still have time for make-up sex later."

I looked up to find him grinning my beloved wicked grin. He wasn't mad, then. I exhaled in relief and smiled back at him.

"I'm surprised you recognized Chuck. I didn't, it only came up in conversation by chance."

His brows shot up. "Trust me, anyone I see pressed up against you is going to be burned into my memory forever. And at any rate, I suspect my memories of that night are clearer than yours." That was true. I hadn't been thinking very clearly at the party where I'd first met Chuck — then Charlie — almost two years before.

Jaden and I did make love twice that night, but neither time was angry. Instead, both were tender, and humorous, and passionate — in other words, just what I'd come to expect of sex with Jaden.

He only brought the subject up as I was getting dressed to leave. "About Chuck..."

"I have to put up with people ogling you all the time," I said quickly, "and I don't make a fuss about it." Mostly.

The corners of his mouth lifted slightly. "Ogling?"

"Yes. Like the waitress today."

He looked honestly surprised. "I didn't notice."

"See?" I threw my hands up. "You get checked out so often that to you it's normal! And it's not like I can help it that Chuck is in my class."

"Téa." My name came out on a sigh. "It caught me by surprise, I'll admit. But it wasn't his presence that disturbed me so much as your refusal to discuss it."

I grabbed a handful of his blue T-shirt and pulled him closer. "We're discussing it now, aren't we?" I fitted myself against his hard body, reluctant to leave.

He ran his hands down my back and over my bottom, pulling me close. "In a very enjoyable manner," he agreed as he kissed me goodbye.

I explained Jaden's reaction to Chuck the next day.

"That was your *boyfriend*? The maniac who threw me halfway across the dance floor?"

"Yeah," I admitted.

"People couldn't stop talking about it after you left. He cut through that party like a tornado."

That was Jaden, all right. He was a force of nature.

Two

I treasured the two evenings I'd spent with Jaden even more as it became clear that they would be our last for some time. Between school and the barn my days were overflowing, and Jaden was busy too.

On Saturday I taught lessons all day before spending some time gabbing with boarders in the arena's viewing lounge. I jumped up when I saw the time; it was my job to feed on weekends, and I was running late. After distributing the hay I ran into the feedroom and grabbed the large metal grain cart, but groaned when it rolled too easily. It was empty. I sighed. Our stablehand Alan usually kept the cart filled, and when Alan wasn't around Dec did it. I debated briefly. Dec was in the house but he wasn't in a good mood, and I didn't feel like hearing any lectures about my tardiness. I decided I could manage on my own. I pulled out the tubs of vitamins, minerals, and hoof-enhancing supplements from the bottom of the cart. I braced it against a wall so it wouldn't roll and seized a sack of sweet feed — oats, barley and corn sweetened with a touch of molasses — and dragged it to the cart's edge. I fiddled with the always-frustrating string closure; if you pulled the right end it was supposed to come out in one piece, but I usually lost patience before that happened and hacked the bag open with scissors. This time, though, the string pulled out easily with a soft zipping sound. Maybe I should buy a lottery ticket, I thought, since it seemed like this was my lucky day. I wrapped my arms around the bag's middle and heaved. The grain bags were mixed especially for us by our local feed store, and they weighed forty kilograms each, or eighty-eight pounds. Considering I weighed about hundred and five, I was pretty proud of myself for being able to lift them at all. Until I felt the hot bite of pain in my upper back, that is. I watched the grain spill into the cart, cursing internally, until the bag emptied. I lifted the bag tentatively. Yup, there it was again — the screaming muscle between my shoulder blades. I kicked the grain cart's wheel, hurting my toe.

"Dammit!" So much for it being my lucky day. I couldn't afford to get hurt. I had school, I rode every day, and with Seth gone I had a lot more work to do.

By the time I was done feeding my panic had largely subsided, and when Jaden walked into the house an hour later, carrying Chinese take-out, I forgot about my back. We had dinner with Dec and Gran, who had been spending a lot of time at our place since my brother had left.

"Will you stay for the weekend, dear?" Gran asked.

"I can't," Jaden said sadly. "I just came to ride Kermit. Piba's going to have to wait."

I winced as we were clearing the table.

"What's wrong?" Jaden asked.

"Just a little pulled muscle. It's nothing. I'm not even sure where it is."

He positioned himself behind me. "Hold your arm out straight." When I did he took it and pulled it across my chest. With his other hand, he felt his way across my back. "Is this it?"

"Ow!" It felt as though he was pushing his thumb right into my muscle.

He released my arm and wrapped one of his around me, still standing behind me. His other hand began gently smoothing the hard knot in my muscle. I relaxed into his warm touch.

"What do you do when one of the horses pulls something?" he asked.

"Call the osteopath, the vet, or the massage therapist, depending," I replied.

"But I'll bet that for yourself you do nothing at all," he accused.

"Not true — I call you and your magic hands." I smiled at him over my shoulder.

Dec cleared his throat noisily from the living room. "I'm still here, you know." He appeared in the doorway, and Jaden stopped massaging my back and turned me to face him.

"How did you hurt yourself?" he asked.

"It was Hades again, wasn't it," Dec said. "I keep telling you, Téa, he's a man's horse."

"I don't know how I did it," I said, averting my eyes. Lying to Dec was almost second nature, but lying to Jaden was almost impossible.

17

Talking to them at the same time like this was going to make me schizoid, and I quickly changed the subject.

"I'm double-booked for lessons tomorrow," I told Dec. "Can you take one of them?"

"Sure," he said with a sigh. Dec was tired too.

When he was done riding I walked Jaden back to his car. "You don't remember how you hurt yourself?" he asked when we got there.

"No idea."

"Really," he said quietly. He took a step toward me. "You didn't overdo it, or lift anything heavy in the barn?"

"No," I said stubbornly. I took a step back and felt the car door hit my shoulder blades.

"Then tell me something. Why are you backing away from me?"

I opened my mouth, then closed it again as his wolfish grin flashed across his face.

"Busted," he murmured as he bent to kiss me. He broke away to murmur in my ear. "That's the only body you've got, Téa. You need to take care of it, because I plan on holding onto it for the next eighty years or so."

I decided that both Jaden and Dec had a point; I needed to stay healthy and be able to handle Hades, so the next day I went to the gym at school. I got a trainer to help me set up an exercise program, and I started right away. I went home that night feeling stiff but hopeful. My workout didn't seem like such a great idea the next morning when I got up at five a.m. to ride Hades, but I pushed through my tiredness. It was dark out, the arena was cold and Hades cranky, but it was oddly peaceful too, to ride with no one watching and nothing to distract us. By the end of our session, both of us were happy and relaxed, having focused purely on our communication.

I worked it out so that I got up early to ride three days a week after that. It was the only way I could manage since I was going to the gym during the breaks that I had previously spent studying. *It better be worth it*, I thought grimly.

Being busy had its upside — it distracted me from the phantom limb pain of Seth's absence. I missed Teri too, but she and I texted a lot. Seth didn't have a cell phone in Europe so we talked chiefly through emails and online chat, and he wasn't a very regular correspondent. Without Seth around life lost its sparkle, and I was feeling a little too old and responsible when Kabir, Seth's best friend, came home for spring break. Teri managed to come home that weekend too, and Kabir talked us into going to hear his new band, visiting with him from California. They'd gotten a gig at the nearby Wilfrid Laurier University pub.

I went to pick Teri up at her house. We hugged in the entryway before hurrying through the cold to the car.

"How's New York?" I asked as I drove through the dark. Wilfrid Laurier was almost an hour's drive so we had time to catch up.

"It's great. Really hard sometimes — my body is killing me — but I'm so glad I took the chance and went down there. I'm getting lots of rides, and I'll have my bug for a year so I can get good experience during that time." The 'bug' was a weight advantage given to apprentice jockeys to entice trainers to use them.

"How are things here?" she went on.

"About the only thing that's going well is Hades," I admitted. "I miss Seth like crazy, I have way too much work, and I hardly ever see Jaden. I can't wait for summer."

The bar was a pretty typical grungy college place. There was no cloakroom so we piled our coats and purses on a chair, and laughed when we saw that we were wearing almost identical tank tops and jeans.

"There you are!" Kabir descended on us, flashing his dimples and hugging us each in turn. "Wow, it's good to see you."

We were having a drink together, something I still wasn't used to, when Kabir's bandmates showed up, three skinny white guys who made Kabir look even bigger and browner than usual. Kabir introduced us, but the guys soon excused themselves to go set up.

"You look good, Kabir." I smiled at him. He seemed different; his hair was spikier, his clothes trendier, and his manner more confident.

"Yeah," Teri echoed the sentiment.

"Thanks. I still can't believe our boy." He shook his head. "Have you heard from him lately?"

"Yep. He's working part-time tutoring English if you can believe it."
We all laughed, since Seth's spelling had been the subject of more than
one joke.

Kabir put his arm around me. "How are you holding up?" His dark
eyes watched my face in the low light of the bar.

I shrugged and looked away. His arm tightened around me. "Don't
worry, I'll kick his ass for both of us when he gets back."

Kabir tossed back the rest of his drink and went onstage, and Teri
slid into the seat next to me to watch. We'd heard Kabir play guitar and
sing before, mostly quiet ballads or campfire songs when we went to the
local beach. But the minute the first chord was struck we knew this
would be different, and halfway through the song we exchanged a long,
delighted grin. The band had a punk sound and Kabir's vocals as lead
singer were amazing. He bounded over to us after his set, sweaty and
out of breath.

"Who are you, and what have you done with the real Kabir?" Teri
demanded.

Kabir grinned at her. "I like the new guy better." He definitely had a
new aplomb.

"I do too," she said. Her green eyes didn't leave his face, and she
shifted slightly closer to him, looking even smaller next to his bulk.

It was liberating to act like a regular student for one night, but
reality wasted no time in bashing me over the head. At least, that's what
it felt like when I had to get up and teach the next morning, and spring
break meant more lessons than usual. It also gave me more time to
ride, though, and I put it to good use.

My horse Cal was four and I'd stepped up his training, even riding
him in some lessons with my coach Karen. One morning we joined
Julia, already riding Jasmine; Karen had just returned from a three-
week sojourn to the Florida shows.

"How come you don't stay there for the season?" Julia asked
curiously. We were walking our horses through the steamy wraiths
created in the cold air by five sets of lungs.

Karen grinned. "Someone has to stay behind and teach the poor
shmucks stuck in the cold." Her freckled face was relaxed and her
brown hair highlighted by the sun. It looked like she'd had a good trip;

the pressure and expense of showing in Wellington could take its toll on coaches as well as riders.

"How's Cal coming along?" Karen asked.

"Not bad," I said evasively. In truth, work with Cal had stalled, and I didn't know why. My approach to working with different horses always depended on their personalities. With the insecure types, I progressed slowly, building their confidence by allowing them to succeed often. With the overly bold ones, I provided just enough challenges to keep them interested until their skill level caught up to their enthusiasm. The very intelligent ones required variety.

Usually, I was good at figuring out what each horse needed but with Cal, I was stumped. He was nervous but soon bored of repetition. He was so flexible that he moved like an eel, yet he often acted stiff when I was mounted. I felt as though he was constantly seeking reassurance, which for some reason made me impatient with him — and I was almost never impatient with horses. They were in the game through no choice of their own, and as a consequence, I thought they deserved to be treated with as much respect as I could muster. But Cal... well, he annoyed me. And I had to find a way past that or we'd never make a great jumping team.

After we'd warmed up Karen set up a small gymnastic for us to jump. I approached it cautiously, trying not to think about the uncomplicated joy I'd felt when jumping Blaze. Cal jumped hesitantly, as though he was purposely holding back. I patted him for his effort anyways, stifling my frustration.

"He's definitely got potential," Karen said. I looked over at her in surprise — Karen had a great eye for horses, and she wasn't given to false compliments.

Maybe, I conceded to myself, the issue wasn't Cal. Maybe we simply weren't clicking. After all, Cal was the antithesis of Blaze's cheerful insouciance, and I had gelled perfectly with Blaze from day one. I worked hard for the rest of the lesson, determined to push aside my prejudices and learn to work with the horse I had now.

The following evening Julia shuffled into the barn. Her eyes were red and swollen, and her usually sleek hair was a bedraggled mess. I ran over to her.

"What's wrong?" I asked urgently.

"Can we talk in the house?" Her voice was hoarse with grief.

I went and asked Catherine, my unofficial assistant, to keep an eye on things. Then I linked my arm with Julia's and we trudged through the snow to the house.

"D'you want a drink?" I asked as we shrugged off our coats. She shook her head, so I led the way to my bedroom. She flopped miserably onto the edge of my bed and I sat next to her, curling one leg under me so that I could face her. I waited until she was ready to talk.

Finally, she pushed her dark brown hair behind her ears and looked at me. "My parents are getting divorced." Her whole face crumpled as she said it, and she began crying quietly.

"Oh, Jules, I'm so sorry," I murmured. I put my arms around her. I smelled her expensive conditioner and felt her soft cashmere sweater under my fingers, and realized that what I'd always thought of as Julia's perfect life was coming crashing down on her. The Yamamotos had always seemed like a perfectly happy married couple to me, but then again, what did I know?

When Julia stopped sobbing I got up and found her a box of tissues.

"What happened?" I prompted gently as I sat back down.

She blew her nose. "You're never going to believe it, Téa. They said they've been thinking about it for years but they stayed together for me, to give me a stable childhood. As though it won't affect me if they do it now!" She gave me a desperate look. "I feel like they've been lying to me my whole life!"

"Of course they haven't. They love you, they were only trying to protect you."

She shook her head. "Well, it sure doesn't feel that way. Can I stay here tonight? I don't want to go home."

"Sure, you can stay as long as you want," I assured her, patting her back.

I set Julia up in the guestroom. Dec had always been fine with our friends staying over — one of the few things he was lenient about. The next day I couldn't spend as much time with her as I would have liked since I was working. After breakfast she moped around Jasmine's stall for a while, then she helped me turn out some horses, and by mid-afternoon, I hugged her goodbye and she headed home.

"How is Julia faring?" Gran asked at dinnertime.

"She's taking it really hard," I said, worried.

"She's probably not used to dealing with family problems," Dec noted. I suspected that was true.

Jaden made a surprise appearance early the next day.

"I thought you had to study?" I asked, delighted. Gran was teaching the first morning class, so I grabbed Jaden by the hand and towed him to the house. We were barely through the door when I turned and leaned against him, reaching up on my tiptoes and pulling his head down to kiss him. I felt him smile under my mouth.

"I missed you too," he murmured.

I needed another coffee, so we settled in the kitchen and I told him Julia's sad news. He shook his head.

"It's going around. We have some familial drama unfolding as well." He put his hand over mine on the table. "My dad is getting remarried."

"What?" I hadn't even known his dad was seriously dating anyone.

"He's been seeing this woman for less than a year, and suddenly he's in a big rush to get married, because — brace yourself — they want to have a child together." Jaden's grim visage made it clear what he thought of that idea.

"Wow," I whispered. I sat silently.

Jaden went on, his lips pressed into a thin line. "His fiancée already has a four-year-old son, and she's almost forty, so they're trying for a baby right away."

I pulled my hand out from under his and ran it gently up and down his corded forearm. His muscles were hard with tension. "I guess you're not excited about having a much younger brother or sister."

"He has no business having more kids! He did enough damage with us," Jaden growled.

"Who, Peter?" Dec was suddenly in the doorway, frowning.

Jaden gave a jerky nod and explained the situation. But instead of being upset, Dec's expression cleared.

23

"That explains a lot," he muttered. He got himself some coffee and joined us at the table. Jaden and I exchanged a confused look.

"Your dad's been pressuring me to sell the barn," Dec said, as though that made any sense. He took a deep breath. "You know that when he got laid off last year, he took a lower-paying job, right?" He directed his question to Jaden, who nodded. "And he made some unwise investments, which means that he's been living well below the standard he's used to. With a kid on the way, he'll want to bring in as much cash as he can."

"But what does any of that have to do with the barn?" I interjected.

"My dad left the property to all three of his kids," Dec explained. "The business actually leases the grounds from the estate — it was set up that way back when Gran ran the riding school and Granddad had a job. If we sell the property, the profit will be split four ways between Gran, my siblings and me."

I was completely stunned. I sat with my mouth hanging open, incapable of even forming a thought for several minutes.

"What type of lease does Gran have?" Jaden's nimble mind, of course, was already analyzing the situation.

"It's a perpetual lease that's valid as long as one of Granddad's descendants runs the stable. Why?"

"I'm just wondering what kind of pressure my dad can exert on you to sell."

"He can't force us into anything," Dec said reassuringly, his gaze settling on me.

"But... how come I didn't know about this?" I asked. My voice was barely more than a whisper, and I felt unaccountably shaky. No wonder Julia had been devastated, I thought suddenly. It's a shock when you grow up thinking things are a certain way and suddenly you find they're different.

Dec shrugged. "It never came up. You've never asked how the business was structured, and it makes no difference to how we do things day-to-day."

I shook my head slowly to clear it. It seemed to me that we should have been told, but I couldn't say why I felt that way. I only knew that suddenly, I felt a lot less secure in my home.

I stared into Dec's light blue eyes. "Are you planning to sell?" I asked.

He hesitated, and in that tiny pause, I felt my stomach drop. "Not anytime soon," he said quietly. "This is your home. I want to keep it at least until you finish school."

I could hear my breath coming unnaturally fast but I couldn't seem to slow it. I felt Jaden's hand smooth my hair, then move in soothing circles over my back.

"Take a walk with me," he suggested, pulling me from my chair. I balked at the front door. It was cold out, and I didn't want to face anyone in the barn in my stunned state. Instead, I took Jaden's hand and headed for my room.

"Téa," he objected as I tugged him inside. Dec would be angry if he saw, but I couldn't have cared less about Dec's feelings at that moment.

"It's not like I'm going to ravage you," I muttered, closing the door. "I just need a minute to think."

We settled on my bed, and his reassuring arms closed around me. I rested my head against his shoulder and felt no desire to talk. Or move, but a quick glance at my alarm clock indicated that I had students arriving. I huddled closer for a few minutes before pulling away with a sigh.

"I have to go work. Will you stay?"

He nodded. "I'll ride, and then I'll take you out for lunch."

Somehow while I was teaching in the cold indoor arena my brain got unstuck and started ticking over with questions. The only one that really counted, though, was whether I could trust Dec when he said he wouldn't sell.

We went to the tiny town of Julien's only restaurant for lunch. It was a diner-style place, but they made good breakfasts so I ordered an omelet. Neither of us spoke while we waited for our food. It was one of the things I loved about Jaden; he didn't feel the need to fill up silences. Instead, he made them feel special and intimate. He cupped his hands around my cold ones on the table.

The food came, and I finished half my plate before I felt restored enough to speak. "I still don't understand. I thought Gran owned the barn?"

25

"Gran owns the *business*," Jaden explained. "She owns the horses, the tack, and the equipment, but she rents the location. The actual property — the land, house, and barn — belongs to Dec, Penny and my dad."

"Did you know about this?" I asked. "You seem to understand it a lot better than I do."

"I only knew that my dad expected to get a portion of the money if the barn ever sold. I didn't know any details."

"But why would Granddad make things so complicated?"

Jaden shrugged. "He didn't really. It's not an unusual setup for a business; there were probably tax advantages at the time."

I searched Jaden's eyes. The gold flecks floating in pools of clear light brown never failed to mesmerize me, but today I refused to be distracted. "Do you think it's true that your dad can't force Dec to sell?"

He thought about it for a minute. "Up to a point. He could possibly ask Dec to pay him for his share, but the real deciding factor will be Aunt Penny. The two of them could conceivably take Dec to court and force him into selling."

I felt my mouth drop open for about the tenth time that day. "Do you think she would?"

"I don't know, Téa. Stacey will be starting university next year. Faced with paying for her child's education, even Aunt Penny might be tempted."

This was turning out to be the least relaxing spring break ever. I went back to work and moved through the day on autopilot, and woke up the next day feeling less apprehensive. Nothing would be decided anytime soon, I figured, and in truth, I didn't have any energy to spare for worrying.

Two days later I was getting ready to ride when I heard a loud smack. I whirled around in time to see Hades fling his head up and step back to the limit of the crossties.

"Dec!" I exclaimed, striding over angrily.

"That brute tried to take a chunk out of me," he growled. He gave me a hard stare, but I didn't back down.

"That's no reason to hit him," I snapped. Then I gulped. The barn was full, and defying him in front of the boarders was undoubtedly a bad idea.

I watched Dec's eyes narrow at my impertinence. "Get in the house, Téa."

"Okay, but-"

"Now."

I glanced over at Lisa, whose pinto gelding was on the crossties facing Hades.

"I'll watch him," she said quietly. I headed for the house, fuming, and once inside started pacing the living room. Dec hadn't followed behind me, but that wasn't a surprise. It was a tactic he'd often employed when Seth and I were younger; he'd make us go into the house and wait for him, and usually, the suspense was almost as bad as the punishment. Not this time, I thought grimly. I was fed up with being treated like a child, so when Dec came in I faced him squarely.

"What's going on, Dec?" I demanded.

He looked taken aback, but he stepped closer. His light blue eyes reminded me of ice when he was angry, and he was definitely angry now. "I won't stand for insolence, Téa. I still expect you to treat me with some respect."

My heart was starting to pound from his tense proximity. I took a deep breath.

"I didn't mean it like that," I explained. I realized I wasn't looking at him and forced myself to raise my eyes. "But Hades was entrusted to me, and I don't want him getting head-shy." I hurried on as Dec opened his mouth. "I'll teach him not to bite, okay?"

He hesitated, watching my face, but I could see the rigid set of his stocky shoulders begin to relax, and I tried to keep my expression sincere. Finally, he nodded.

I thought about it as I trudged back to the barn. Hades had disliked Dec on sight, and Dec wasn't much fonder of the horse. At first, I'd figured that Hades had issues with men — it wasn't uncommon — but as it transpired, he had liked Jaden and Seth just fine. He was a very dominant horse, and his cresty neck and wide, solid muscling made me think he'd been gelded late, which would give him more of a stallion's personality. That alpha outlook would be enough to cause him to clash with Dec, who expected clear submissiveness from all the horses he interacted with. I didn't know how I was going to get either of them to back down, but they had to learn to live with each other.

"He was a good boy," Lisa said when I got back. Hades pushed her with his nose and she stumbled sideways with a startled laugh. She righted herself and patted him, recognizing that from Hades the shove was a mark of affection. She tucked a strand of wispy blond hair behind her ear as her eyes moved to study me, and I looked away quickly. Her obvious concern left me feeling both embarrassed and touched.

"Is everything all right?"

"Other than the fact that Dec still thinks I'm twelve, great," I said sourly.

Lisa smiled the gentle smile that had soothed many a hurt. "I think Dec is having a hard time letting you grow up. After all, the more he lets go of you, the more he lets go of your mother."

I grumbled about the incident to Jaden when he came over. To my surprise, he smiled.

"That's just his way. It's not that he's treating you like a child."

"He doesn't treat you that way," I pointed out sulkily. Like a child.

"I earned his respect. I stood on my own two feet in the world, made a success of my career, bought a place to live... you'll get there, *querida*. Dec's not easy to impress."

Maybe my performance with Hades that year would impress him, I thought, since Hades was so monumentally improved. We were planning to start the season in the 1.35-meter division — a shade under four and a half feet — but I hoped he'd move up quickly from there. I was thrilled when his owner, Monica, called me with plans to go to the first A-rated show of the year.

"Get back to me as soon as possible," Monica said after we'd discussed it. "I need to make the arrangements and there isn't much time left." As soon as I hung up I bounced to the barn to see Dec, smiling all the way. I found him putting envelopes into the boarder's cubbies.

"Guess what?" I said. "Monica and Neil want me to ride Hades at the Fieldstone show in Massachusetts. Isn't that awesome?"

He frowned. "Hold on. When will you be gone?"

"Um, Friday to Monday of the week after next." I wasn't smiling anymore.

"So you'll miss two days of school just before exams, and you won't take your students to the schooling show that weekend? Weren't some of them planning on it?"

"Well, yes, but Catherine can go with them."

"They're *your* students, Téa," he said impatiently. "They'll want their own coach at a show. And I don't like the idea of you missing school."

I felt anxiety filling me like sludge. "But Dec, this is a big show," I pleaded. "And the prize money's good." Appealing to his financial sense was one of the few things that routinely worked to convince Dec.

"I don't see why you have to go so far — in a month you can go to Eastwood, and you won't miss any school that way. No one else is doing A shows now."

"Everyone who's in Florida is! It's hard enough to compete when I don't get to ride down there; going to Fieldstone may at least give me a bit of an edge," I said.

He shook his head. "I've got a lot on my mind right now. Let me think about it." He turned back to his sorting.

"But I have to answer Monica today," I said desperately.

"She'll wait," he growled.

I knew better than to push him further or he'd say no out of sheer orneriness. Anxiety made me jittery for the rest of the day, and I felt resentment oozing blackly from my cells. I was nineteen years old. I was responsible for my own life, but not allowed to live it as I saw fit. I was responsible for my own career, but not allowed to follow my passion. I felt suffocated, as though the life I was living was a pale mirror image of the one I was truly destined for. Maybe I could never be great, but I wanted the chance to *try*.

I went into the house, hoping a cup of tea would help calm me. I used the boot scraper on the porch to clean my boots before going in. It was shaped like a hedgehog, and you rubbed your boots against the "quills" — tough bristles that scraped the bulk of the mud off. I felt myself sag as I stepped through the door. If Seth were here there would be trails of mud across the entrance floor, his boots would be dropped

29

right in front of the door where they'd be sure to trip me, and his jacket would as likely be on the floor as on its hook. But — after I'd yelled at him or picked up after him, depending on my mood — he'd tow me into the kitchen for his fourteenth snack of the day and he'd make me laugh and think, as I often did, that it was those small everyday moments that made life worthwhile. If only Seth were here, he'd make Dec smile and I'd get my answer right away.

Toward evening I called Jaden. He was still at school and sounded weary. My frustration with Dec poured out, and Jaden listened quietly until I was done. A long pause followed.

"I know you're busy," I said apologetically.

"It's not that, Téa. Don't you think Dec has a point about focusing on school?"

It took me a minute to be able to speak. "I maintained an A-minus average last semester, even with everything else I had going on," I protested. Mucking stalls for a month, finding my biological father, and my twin's growing discontent had been more than minor distractions.

"And I'm proud of you for that. Now imagine if you actually focused *all* your energy on school — don't you think your average would rise to A or even A plus?" he asked.

I felt confused and irritated all at the same time. "You know I can't focus *all* my energy on school."

"You can't, or you don't want to?" He questioned me gently, but my confusion was rapidly dissipating, leaving ire in its place.

"I didn't realize my academic success was so all-important to you," I snapped.

"Of course it's important to me, Téa. We're building a life together."

I felt the sharp knife-thrust of betrayal. "I've got to go," I said, abruptly ending the conversation.

I dropped the phone and held my head in my hands. Jaden knew better than anyone how important my riding was to me. I'd always thought he fully supported my goals, and for him to now question them — to side with *Dec* — left me reeling with confusion and hurt.

Dec relented in the end. It was weird going to a show without any of my friends, although to my relief I wasn't alone with the Donalds,

Hades' owners, because Karen brought a horse too and I drove down with her. It wasn't a show she normally attended because as Dec had said, in early April most people are either resting after Florida or just gearing up for the show season in the Northeast.

Karen's chestnut horse was stabled right next to Hades, and as we went to feed them their breakfast the next morning Karen abruptly halted, grinning.

"You're going to love this," she said, pointing to Hades' stall. Hanging on the metal door of the temporary stabling was a sign with Hades' show name, 'Lord of the Underworld'. I thought it was a fairly pretentious name to begin with, but the sign had so much bling on it that my eyes hurt. His name was written in some kind of glittery red paint, and the whole thing was framed by what looked like rhinestones. It wasn't the kind of thing you ever saw at a conservative Hunter/Jumper show.

Karen went to feed her horse, still chuckling, and I stomped through the fresh shavings of the stall to feed Hades. He wasn't very polite and kept trying to shove his nose into the bucket before I got to his feed tub. I was so busy fending him off that I almost missed it — something shiny at the bottom of his tub. I scooped it out quickly before dumping the grain in and leaving Hades to eat.

"Check this out," I said to Karen, holding out the clear stone I'd found. She raised it to eye level. It was about the size of a golf ball.

"Hello, hello," Monica sang out cheerfully as she arrived. "Oh, I see you found one of my crystals."

"Luckily, because it was in Hades' stall," I told her.

"Well, yes, I put it there. My astrologer said that it would help to clear away his negative energy," she explained.

I stared at her for a minute, dumbstruck. I very carefully didn't look at Karen, who was covering up her laughter with a coughing fit.

Finally, I cleared my throat. "Monica, you can't put crystals in Hades' stall, it's dangerous. What if he had eaten it?"

She waved a hand airily. "Oh, I'm sure he knows better than to eat a rock. Animals are much more intelligent than we give them credit for, you know."

Really? I had no idea, I thought snarkily. I only trained them for a living, after all. "I agree, but I've also seen horses die from colic after eating strange things. Do you really want to take a chance? Trust me, his energy's fine."

She gave a little pout. It looked odd on her since she was in her fifties. She had pouffy shoulder-length bleached blond hair, long magenta fingernails, and matching lipstick. She was wearing swishy wide-legged beige pants and a pink top that didn't flatter her slightly overweight body. She wasn't unattractive, but it looked as though she was trying too hard. She was a very successful real estate agent, so I could only imagine she dressed differently at work.

She handed me her purse. "Hold Taffy and I'll get the rest of the crystals." I didn't understand what she meant until I looked down. It wasn't a purse at all, but one of those shoulder bags people use to carry dogs. A tiny head popped out. The dog had silky long hair tied on top of its head with a ridiculous pink bow, and she quivered with excitement as she looked around with bulging eyes. When I reached into the bag to pat her she licked my hand enthusiastically.

Monica emerged from the stall with two more crystals, and I handed Taffy back to her.

"She's very cute," I said. I meant it — it wasn't the dog's fault that she was carried around in a garish pink bag.

Neil came puffing up. I was surprised to see them this early; they'd rented a condo with some friends. "We're off to do some sightseeing," he said in his usual officious way. "Our friends came a long way to watch Hades perform, so I hope he's ready to impress them."

I swallowed hard. I just hoped we could do at a show what we did at home.

The Fieldstone Show Park was large and impressive, but I tried not to notice as I warmed up before my first class. Spring was in definite evidence and the day was sunny and cool, perfect for riding. In every direction were gleaming coats of chestnut, grey, black, and Hades' own bay. The venue was new to him too, but at least he wasn't plagued by worries of inferiority as I was, I thought. As we strode up to the in-gate, he raised his head and surveyed the course imperiously, making me smile. No, he definitely wasn't worried.

I tried to take my cue from him. After all, I didn't know anyone at this show. These weren't the same riders who had watched me year after year, struggling on unschooled ponies with my hand-me-down riding clothes and used tack. And so, even though everyone around me was wearing custom-made boots and tailored jackets that cost more than my car, I kept my head high.

"Just get around," Karen reminded me before I went in. It was our first real show of the year and Karen had advised me to ride conservatively.

We walked in and I saluted the judge. Then we picked up a canter, adrenaline making my heart hammer. Hades still took a lot of riding, but now that I could direct his massive power, the jumps themselves were easy. The challenge was in getting Hades to listen to my signals because when he got excited he tended to tune me out. I barely noticed the first two fences, the rhythmic *da-da-dum, da-da-dum* of Hades' canter evidence of his relaxed concentration. We came around a corner to a combination of jumps set on the diagonal. There was only room for one stride in between the fences, which was always a challenge for Hades because of his very long stride. I brought my upper body back and deepened my seat, and Hades mimicked me, shifting his weight back onto his hindquarters, his stride shortening automatically. We jumped in perfectly and he was able to comfortably round himself over the tricky second vertical.

"Good boy," I murmured as we landed. One of his black-tipped ears flicked back, listening, and I felt a wave of happiness from him. My fears evaporated, and by the time I left the ring I was smiling broadly. We had a time fault and finished third in the class, and I patted his sweaty neck proudly as we went to collect our yellow ribbon.

We weren't as lucky the next day when the course included a liverpool, which Hades had never seen before. A liverpool is an artificial pool of water under a jump, and they can spook horses, who perceive things differently than humans do. If they don't know what it is, a liverpool may look to a horse like a big hole in the ground, and sometimes the light reflecting off the water can confuse them. To a horse, any unknown is a cause for fear — after all, an alligator could pop out of there!

Hades stopped dead in front of the liverpool. I wasn't taken by surprise since he'd been backing off on our approach. I let him drop his head and take a look before circling around and trying again. He overjumped it massively, nearly throwing me out of the tack, but I grabbed his mane and managed to stay on and finish. Our refusal meant no ribbon in the class, but I was proud of him anyway. Monica and Neil, somewhat to my surprise, were understanding when I explained the situation. And in our final class, we strutted out of the ring with first place.

The buzz over Hades' win preceded us home, and Karen and I arrived Monday evening to find many hands eager to help us unload. Once everything was put away and Hades had magnanimously accepted congratulations, everyone went up to the viewing lounge above the arena. Its couches and chairs were more comfortable than the tackroom. We had ordered pizza to celebrate and everyone pressed me for details while we ate.

"I still can't believe how awesome Hades was," Julia enthused as she settled down with her slice. I grinned at her, happy that I had at least one friend there to share the moment.

"You're on your way to the big time, girl," Karen said.

The excitement in the air was palpable. I felt like I was on the verge of putting Shady Lane on the map — again. I'd been here three years before with Blaze; it felt different now, less innocent, but the excitement was just as real.

Dec came in and helped himself to a slice of pizza. His gaze traveled from person to person, following the snippets of conjecture and excited anticipation about where Hades and I would go from here, but he didn't say anything. When his eyes came to rest on me they held something akin to frustration. Suddenly I wasn't hungry anymore. I put my pizza down, feeling deflated. I couldn't even join in the happy chatter about my own future, feeling as I did that Dec disapproved of it. It hurt — everyone else was happy for me. Why couldn't the people who mattered most stand behind me?

I was silent as I walked to the house with Dec and Karen afterward.

"Make sure you hang your ribbon from the Open class in the barn," Karen said.

Dec stopped dead, and Karen turned toward him with a questioning look. Dec took one lurching step and grabbed her by the shoulders.

"You let her ride in the Open class?" he roared.

Karen's head drew back, but the flash of shock that crossed her face was quickly replaced by a scowl. "Take your hands off me." Her voice was perfectly flat.

Dec let go, but he didn't back off.

"I guess my sister made the right decision." Karen eyed him speculatively.

Dec flinched. He took half a step backward, but his expression was still hard. "You had no business putting Téa into such a big class, especially at an A show."

Karen didn't waver. "You should give her some credit, Dec. That's the class she won."

Dec's glare turned to me, but he didn't say anything so I hurried inside. I called Jaden as soon as I got to my room. We'd been texting steadily during the show, but this was the first time I'd heard his voice since our conversation about school.

"Congratulations, *querida*," he said warmly.

Something inside me unspooled. "I miss you. When can I see you?"

"Not before next weekend, sadly. I could certainly use the stress release."

I laughed. "You don't have to talk in code, Jaden. I know what you're after." We hung up after a long conversation, and I wondered how I could have been so upset the week before. Jaden was the best thing that had ever happened to me. A small difference of opinion couldn't change that.

Three

My joy over the show invigorated me as I faced my final weeks of school, but three days later I was exhausted again. Chuck and Shannon stayed after class one day and we worked on end-of-term projects together.

After a couple of hours, Shannon stretched and checked her watch. "I'm done for today. Let's go to the pub."

"I can't," I said automatically. "I have to get back to the barn."

"Oh come on!" Chuck urged. "I work in my family's vet clinic too, but not every day — what are you, a slave? Be a rebel! Take some time off." He grinned, daring me.

"Fine," I grumbled.

"Nice party face," Shannon said, laughing.

I followed them, smiling. In truth, it would be nice to take an evening off, although the guilt set in almost immediately. I wasn't teaching that night or I wouldn't have been able to stay at school; what I was skipping out on was my own riding. My career, my dream. *It's only one night*, I reasoned. Surely the added relaxation I'd feel would benefit me?

We wandered into the campus pub and doffed our jackets, tossing them onto one of the wooden chairs surrounding a scarred table. We each ordered a beer, something I almost never had. I rarely drank alcohol, and I didn't know what else to order. Plus, it was cheap.

We shared a plate of nachos, and the time passed surprisingly fast as we talked about our professors, courses, and classmates.

"You never told me why you introduced yourself as Charlie the first time we met," I said to Chuck. Shannon had gone to the washroom.

He picked the last piece of nacho cheese off the plate. "I've been called Chuck all my life. I wanted to try something cooler for once."

"Because 'Charlie' is the epitome of cool," I said, poker-faced.

"Hey, no hating the name," Chuck said. His brown eyes were smiling, though, and I smiled back at him. His easygoing manner and

36

lightheartedness reminded me of Seth, and I felt a sharp pang of loneliness for my brother.

Shannon plopped herself back into her chair. She and Chuck began discussing the finer points of invertebrate anatomy, but my brain was buzzing pleasantly and I didn't even try to follow. A minute later I felt my shoulder being shaken. I realized my head was on the table and lifted it slowly.

"You're a regular prizewinning drinker, aren't you?" Chuck laughed.

I blinked as I realized that I'd fallen asleep, then crossed my arms on the table and rested my forehead on them. "One beer and I'm asleep? I'm a disgrace to students," I groaned.

"Actually it was more like half a beer," Chuck said, holding up my glass to show me. He grinned. "I know just what you need. Be right back."

I shrugged and turned to Shannon. "What did I miss?"

She shook her auburn-and-grey head. "Not much. We were just talking about how the reality of university isn't quite what we'd thought. It's so much work — I took out all kinds of loans to come here and I'm getting mostly Bs even though I'm putting everything I've got into studying. Bs won't get me into vet school." She looked worried.

I nodded in sympathy. It was definitely harder to get good grades now than it had been in high school, but I couldn't say I was putting everything into studying. I had other priorities.

Chuck was back minutes later. He dropped a bag on the table in front of me. "You owe me."

"What's this?" I peeked inside and found a can of Red Bull and a small bag of chocolate-covered espresso beans.

"I wouldn't get through a single course without them," Chuck assured me.

It couldn't hurt to try, I reasoned, and broke open the bag of espresso beans on the spot. I passed it around and we each ate a few before saying our goodbyes.

Those chocolate-covered espresso beans became my best friends. They were on my desk, next to the Red Bull, when Jaden came over that weekend.

Jaden picked up the can, his brows rising ever so slightly. "What's this?"

"It's Red Bull. It tastes awful, but-"

He interrupted me. "I meant, what is it doing here?"

I looked at him blankly. "What do you think? I'm drinking it. It helps me stay awake."

He gave his head a small shake. "Trust me, Téa, you don't want to start down the slippery slope of stimulant use."

"How would you know? You're never tired." I sounded a bit petulant even to my own ears. He put the can down and moved closer to me.

"Yes, my energy's all natural. But there's a limit to how much any body can give, and I've pushed those limits in the past. I tried stimulants for a while, and I'm telling you it's not worth it. They'll damage you, and you'll end up crashing harder than if you'd never used them."

"Jaden, it's just Red Bull. We're not talking speed here. Plus, I won't be drinking it long enough for it to be a problem, I just need it to get through exams."

"Well, I need you to stay healthy, so please — no more."

I cocked my head and fixed him with a look. "You're not the boss of me, Jaden Foster."

His mouth pulled sideways, like he was trying not to smile, and he reached past me for the can. He loped out the door and I heard him pouring it down the bathroom sink. I sighed, stifling my annoyance. I didn't have the heart to argue with him, not when I hadn't seen him all week, but I quickly slipped my chocolate-covered coffee beans into a drawer.

I went into a frenzy of studying for exams. The last one was biochemistry, which I'd been dreading, but it went okay and afterward, Chuck, Shannon and I celebrated with expensive coffees and brownies.

I woke up the next morning and stretched contentedly in bed. The sun was pouring around the edge of my white curtains, promising a beautiful spring day, and I had four whole months to devote to nothing but horses and riding. Life was good.

In the afternoon our vet, Kathy, came to check on the pregnant Gracie. While Stephanie brought her horse out, Kathy lugged in a small, heavy-looking grey machine.

"It's a portable ultrasound," she explained. "Do you have something I could set it on?"

I went and grabbed an end table from the viewing lounge and Kathy carefully placed the ultrasound on it. She opened it and lowered a keyboard. The front part of the machine showed a small black screen. I watched with interest as she ran a bulbous wand over Gracie's very full belly, but all that showed on the screen was a grey blur. Kathy repositioned the ultrasound wand, and all of a sudden the amorphous blur coalesced into a shape.

"Oh!" Stephanie exclaimed from her position by Gracie's head.

I went over and took the leadrope from her. "Why don't you go get a better look?"

I stroked Gracie's face gently while Stephanie, Lisa, and various students oohed and aahed over the ultrasound image. To be honest, the thought of another creature growing inside Gracie's body made me feel somewhat sick. Gracie had had the usual ultrasound a few weeks after being bred, but that one had served to confirm the pregnancy and make sure she wasn't carrying twins. Twins are very rare in most horse breeds but when they occur they present a huge problem, because only about one set in ten thousand survive. A mare's uterus isn't designed for nourishing two fetuses, so usually one or both twins will die, and sometimes the mare will as well. We knew Gracie was only carrying one baby, so this ultrasound was more for Stephanie's benefit, as she was worried about the myriad things that could go wrong.

"See?" Kathy turned to Stephanie. "Everything looks fine."

"Oh, I'm so glad," Stephanie said. She was smiling from ear to ear.

Kathy's grin moved to me. I thought it must be nice for her to deliver happy news once in a while, since she spent so much time dealing with illness. "Make sure you keep giving her the supplements I prescribed, and you'll have to start increasing her grain soon. The fetus will take minerals from her bones and protein from her muscles if it has to."

I nodded, and Kathy packed up to leave while everyone else patted Gracie and offered her congratulations.

"This is perfect," Stephanie sighed happily. "We'll have our babies around the same time."

My jaw dropped.

"What?" Lisa whirled around, looking delighted.

Stephanie opened her jacket and moved her hands over her belly in a gesture as old as time. "I'm pregnant too."

I rested my face against Gracie's while the flurry of excitement and congratulations swirled around Stephanie. After a few minutes people wandered off chattering and I felt Stephanie beside me.

"I'll put her away." She took the leadrope from my hand.

"I wondered why you'd breed Gracie when she was doing so well in the show ring," I said. The reason was clear now.

"It was time," Stephanie said simply. "I've been with my boyfriend for years, and I'm thirty-seven. We couldn't wait much longer."

I nodded thoughtfully. I rarely thought about age, but I supposed that for some things, age mattered.

"Well, um, congratulations," I said awkwardly. I found it a bit hard to look at her now that I knew there was an alien being growing inside her body, but that didn't mean I wasn't happy for her.

Work picked up as the weather got warmer, and we officially hired Catherine. The pale girl with the long dark hair had been my student for years, and she was thrilled with her new job as riding instructor. Gran pitched in a lot too, knowing that once the elementary and high schools let out we'd have no time for anything other than lessons and shows.

The first weekend in May was brightened by a visit from Jaden. He stepped out of his car and I bounded across the sunlit parking area to meet him, wishing I could throw myself into his arms. We practically ran to the house; he pulled me inside and had barely closed the door before his mouth met mine. I had just wrapped my arms around him when I felt a presence next to us, and we turned to find Dec watching us with narrowed eyes.

Jaden squeezed my hand. "We've waited long enough, Dec. We're done pretending," he said quietly.

I stiffened, but Dec just nodded. "You're right." When he went outside I turned to Jaden, wide-eyed.

He grinned at me. "What? You didn't think we'd live in hiding forever, did you?"

I sobered slightly. "I don't suppose your mom's had a change of heart?" My Aunt Paloma was dead set against Jaden and me dating, since we were step-cousins. He gave a half-shrug, as though it didn't matter, although we both knew it did.

We headed out to the barn. As we descended the house's wide front steps Jaden draped his arm around me. I faltered, shocked.

"No more pretending, remember?" He squeezed me against him.

I took a deep breath. "Right."

At the barn door I balked, suddenly nervous. Our family had been horrified when they had discovered our relationship, and Dec had sworn us to secrecy until they'd had time to accept the idea. With the exception of Jaden's mom, they'd all grudgingly come to terms with our involvement, but other than family, only our closest friends knew. The students and boarders at our barn had no idea about us, and I was reluctant to meet more disapproval.

Jaden turned to face me. He ran his hands along the collar of my light jacket, from the back to the front, then curled his fingers into it and pulled me against him. He kissed me hard.

"I love you, Téa. We don't owe anyone any explanations." He kept his eyes locked on mine until I gave a small nod, then tucked me under his arm again. I wrapped my arm around his waist and we walked into the barn that way, as though we did it every day.

Dec was in the tackroom talking to Catherine when we stepped in. Her mouth dropped open at the sight of us, and her eyes got round, but after a second she tore them away from us and back to Dec, who barely spared us a glance. My arm tightened around Jaden as we moved into the barn proper. For a second I wished it wasn't a weekend, since it meant the barn was full of people, but then I decided it was best to get this over with all at once.

Alan came down the aisle, pitchfork in hand. "Jaden," he said, nodding. His eyes lingered for a second on Jaden's arm, still curled around my shoulder, and then he smiled at me and went on his way. As we rounded the corner into the boarder aisle there was a sudden hush.

Several boarders shot glances our way, and some were frowning. I felt my face get hot, and it was all I could do not to hide it against Jaden.

To my relief, Lisa came over and began discussing her gelding's diet with me as though nothing unusual had happened.

Jaden excused himself. "I'm going to get my tack," he said. He dropped a light kiss on my head before striding away.

I turned back to Lisa, who didn't look surprised. "Did you know?" I blurted.

She nodded. "I have three teenage daughters, Téa. I know what young love looks like." She smiled at my stunned look. "I've known how Jaden feels about you since the day that poor boy was tearing his hair out, watching Marty buck around the ring with you. But I didn't know whether *you* knew."

"I didn't back then," I admitted, feeling like a bit of a dolt. Maybe all my worrying had been for nothing. But as I moved around the barn that day some of the looks that came my way were less than friendly.

"That wasn't nearly as bad as I was afraid it would be," I said to Jaden after dinner. Dec and Gran had gone for a walk, and once the dishes were done I towed Jaden upstairs, hoping to connect with Seth online. But when I opened my laptop I froze.

"What is it?" Jaden asked from behind me.

"Tom Morin. He tried to add me as a Facebook friend," I said in disbelief. Tom had been briefly obsessed with me the previous year.

Jaden came and looked over my shoulder, his arm wrapping tightly around me as if to protect me from this cyber-menace. "I hope you blocked him."

I nodded but stayed silent. I didn't resist when Jaden pulled me from my chair and sat us both on the bed. He held me against him and stroked my hair. "Don't worry, *querida*. I won't let anything happen to you."

"I'm not worried. I just think it's sad that this stranger who doesn't even know me is desperate to be my friend."

He frowned. "I'm glad he's far away. I start my new job tomorrow, and if the tales are true, articling will consume my life for the next several months. I don't want to worry over your safety when I'll have so little time to be with you."

I had to set the minor drama aside because it was time to go to Eastwood for the two big shows that started off Quebec's summer circuit. The year before I'd lost a mount there when Marty's owner had disagreed with my decision to withdraw his horse from a class. The humiliation still stung, and I was eager to return to the scene and create some happier memories.

I went with Karen, taking turns at the wheel of her car for the seven-hour drive, because Dec didn't want me driving his truck with our big six-horse gooseneck trailer hitched to it. Karen entertained me with stories of the big-name riders' escapades in Florida that winter, and we discussed our plans for Hades and Cal.

"Hey, Karen, what did you mean when you told Dec "I guess my sister made the right decision?" You know, when he grabbed you?" I asked a bit hesitantly. I was in the passenger seat, watching her profile.

She glanced over at me, brown eyes thoughtful. "Dec used to be engaged to my kid sister."

"That was your sister?" I gasped. I knew about the engagement, but no one had mentioned that little detail. "So what happened? Why'd they break up?"

"Well," Karen answered slowly, "there were a few reasons. But mostly, she was afraid of Dec's temper. She didn't want their children to have to deal with it."

"Oh." I looked out the window. I knew all about that.

With all the talking the drive went fast and we got there before the trailer, giving us time to stretch our legs and greet people before the horses arrived.

After unloading the horses and equipment, Dec said hello to a few people before going to get coffee with Karen. He found me afterward, cleaning my boots in front of Hades' stall.

"Karen says she told you I was engaged to her sister," he said. His big, blunt fingers rearranged a leadrope as he spoke, and he didn't look at me.

"Um, yeah," I said, uncomfortable.

He turned his gaze on me. "Look, kiddo, I want you to know that I'm going back to therapy," he said.

"Because of what happened with Karen?" I asked quietly.

He nodded slowly. "I wish I'd gone to therapy before I married Ellie."

I was taken aback. "But you and mom hardly ever fought." And when they did I'd never worried about Dec hurting her; he had never been anything less than respectful toward her.

"I was thinking of you and your brother." His voice was strained. "If I could have rid myself of my father's influence earlier, things might have been different between us. I was nineteen the last time my father hit me, and it was only the last time because I looked him in the eye and told him that the next time, I was hitting back." He paused. "I don't want it to come to that with us, Téa."

The thought was so ridiculous that I cracked a smile. His face lit up at the sight, and on impulse, I hugged him.

I walked Dec back to the trailer. "Drive carefully," I urged him as he started the long drive home. I wouldn't be seeing him for twelve days and was glad to part ways so peacefully.

For the rest of the day, I had a curiously light heart. I'd been angry with Dec since Seth had left, but now I realized he wasn't the only one at fault. It had been Seth's choice, and Dec was genuinely trying, which was the best any of us could do.

My good mood stayed with me, helped by the bright sunshine, and the second morning of the show I was bubbling with energy as I schooled my student Emma on her grey pony Cameo. In addition to Cameo we had trucked Julia's horse Jasmine, Hades, and three of Karen's trainees, so our days started early and stayed busy. I was grateful that Karen's groom had agreed to help with Hades for these two shows because it allowed me to put all my energy into riding.

Finally it was time to warm up Hades for his class. He had done a small schooling jumper class the day before, but it had barely been enough to whet his appetite, and he pulled me all the way to the schooling area. I smelled trampled grass, and the air rang with the sounds of our sport: snorts, pounding hooves, and the hard breathing of both horses and riders.

"I heard you kicked butt down in Massachusetts," my friend Alex remarked as I arrived. I walked Hades alongside Moose, Alex's best jumper. The horses touched noses briefly, acknowledging each other.

"Word travels fast," I said. "Who told you?"

"It was on the forums," he said. He grinned at me. "Don't expect an easy victory here, cutie."

I laughed, but given the way Hades felt victory might, in fact, be easy. There was a bounce to his step, and his attitude toward the jumps had gotten downright cocky.

I moved away from Alex as Karen hurried over to help me school. She was followed by one of her students, a snooty redhead named Brittney who, unfortunately, was riding an utterly fabulous dark bay mare. When Dec had picked them up with our trailer we'd all been drooling at the sight of her.

The ring was busy, with horses of all sizes going in all directions, some jumping, some arguing with their riders, and some just plain not paying attention. The year before Hades would have taken advantage of the chaos to create some of his own, but this year he paid strict attention to me, although he was still as impatient as ever. He was simply more polite about asking to go faster.

Karen set up a tall vertical, since Hades needed to work on getting closer to the base of his jumps. His thrust was so powerful that oxers, wide jumps with two sets of rails, didn't present a problem for him. On our third approach to the jump I made a tight corner, and all of a sudden Brittney was on the other side of the fence, her horse preparing to jump it from the other direction. I was about to turn Hades aside, but he didn't like the other horse challenging him — at least, that's how he saw it — and he flattened his ears back, took an aggressive stride, and jumped, veering only slightly to the side. Out of the corner of my eye I saw Brittney's horse shy sideways, refusing the fence as Hades landed. He pricked his ears and arched his neck proudly, radiating satisfaction, and I couldn't help but smile at his conceit although I felt bad for the other horse and rider.

"You idiot!" Brittney yelled angrily as she yanked her horse roughly around to face me. "Do you have any idea how much this horse is worth?"

"Brittney! That's enough — go trot around and settle your horse," Karen snapped.

She came over to me and patted Hades' neck. "You're something, big guy." She looked up at me thoughtfully. "You know what makes you so good, kid? I've been thinking about it, and I've finally figured it out."

"My raw muscle power?" I suggested, grinning.

"You wish." Karen laughed. "But you've got something even better. Horses love you."

I frowned at her while walking Hades around in a small circle. "That's it? My mad riding talent is not actually a talent?" This wasn't sounding like a compliment to me.

"It's a lot more useful than you realize. How else could a little shrimp like you handle a beast like Hades?"

My smallness had made me the object of much teasing in the past. For most people in North America being petite probably wasn't an obstacle, but since I was doing physical labor a lot of the time, not to mention competing in a sport, my size *did* matter. I couldn't wrap my legs around Hades properly because they were too short, and I had a hard time lifting hay bales and jump standards at home. I had often wished I was taller and stronger, in part to make my work easier, and in part, I had to admit, so that I'd be a more impressive match for Jaden. The fact that Karen — whose judgment I trusted implicitly — felt that my main strength wasn't anything physical was a relief, in a way.

"He takes care of you. He *wants* to make you happy now," Karen went on. "I would never have believed it a year ago, but it seems to happen with all your horses."

Except Cal, I thought, feeling something twist painfully inside me. I pushed the thought away and concentrated on Hades again.

He was still full of himself as he swaggered into the ring, and after our round, I had to admit it wasn't unwarranted. I had always known that Hades had fantastic potential, but I had never suspected how much *fun* I could have with him. Now that his conditioning and self-control matched his confidence I didn't have many worries in the ring and instead got to enjoy the challenge of making decisions and feeling his raw power carry them out. It was exhilarating.

46

We ended up in a jump-off against Alex on Moose, and two other riders. I was relieved that Brittney hadn't made it into the jump-off because she'd been casting evil stares my way ever since the warm-up incident.

I was third to go, which was pretty good — it meant I got to see how two other teams handled the course, and it gave me an idea of the time to beat. I got the weak, shaky rush that signaled a burst of adrenaline as we entered the ring. I hated that I always felt that way right when I needed the most strength, but it was quickly forgotten as Hades lifted over the first fence. I looked left to our next jump while we were in the air and, feeling the subtle shift, Hades obligingly landed on his left lead, prepared to go that way. The combination fence was child's play to him, and as we rounded the corner I saw the perfect distance to our next obstacle. It was a long approach, and I squeezed my legs and leaned forward slightly. Instead of exploding at my request for increased speed as he would have done the year before, Hades sped up smoothly, lengthening stride after stride until we took off as though we were flying. I heard noise from the crowd, but concentrated on the sharp turn to the final fence. Hades dialed back his speed with ease and we landed to cheers and whooping.

I dropped my reins on his neck and patted his wet neck with both hands as he strolled out of the ring. Karen raised her eyebrows at my daring, but it paid off because we won the class.

As I collected our red ribbon I felt a swell of pride. I'd worked for this, worked hard and unrelentingly, and seeing my efforts pay off was sweet indeed. I had just hopped off Hades and handed the reins to Karen's groom when someone spoke behind me.

"Hi, Téa."

I whirled around, sucking in a sudden, painful breath.

Tom Morin stood before me. He kept a normal distance between us, something he wasn't known for, and I cautiously let myself exhale.

"I'm sorry if I startled you. You were really something in the ring." He smiled.

"Um... hi." I floundered. What was the etiquette when meeting your ex-stalker? Although the "ex" part was beginning to look questionable.

"What are you doing here, Tom?" I said finally. I was never much good at diplomacy, anyway.

He looked surprised. "My sister lives nearby. I've been staying with her — why, did you think I followed you? Oh, no, it's just coincidence," he assured me. He looked sane enough, but then again, I had learned that you can't judge by appearance.

"I just wanted to congratulate you on that great horse you've got," he went on. He nodded at me and moved off.

I felt myself go limp.

"Who was that?" Alex asked, frowning. I hadn't noticed him appear.

"Oh, just my old stalker," I said. I was aiming for airy unconcern, but Alex's sharp look suggested I missed the mark.

"Stalker?" he exclaimed.

"Yeah, don't you have one? Anyone who's anyone has a stalker," I said, giving a little wave. I pulled off the nonchalance better this time, and he smiled slowly at me.

"Okay, hotstuff. Maybe we'd better get you a bodyguard," he joked as he walked me back to the stables. Which was exactly what Jaden would think, I realized with a sinking feeling. Only he wouldn't be joking.

Back at our stalls, I felt a little flutter of pride when I saw that my ribbon had already been hung up. Of course, Monica and Neil would get to take it home, along with the rest of the prizes, but I didn't mind. A deep sense of satisfaction stole into me, sifting down and filling all the little holes of self-doubt that had existed since Blaze's death. I could do this. I knew it now.

I checked on Hades, who was contentedly munching hay in his stall. He glanced up with his usual haughty expression, but it brightened when he saw me and he interrupted his meal long enough to butt me with his head. He was clearly proud of himself too.

"You should be, buddy," I murmured, stroking his neck fondly. "You were great out there."

"He really was," Julia said, peering over the door. She wasn't smiling.

"You and Jazzy were good today too." I joined Julia. She shrugged and handed me an iced coffee.

"You're an angel of caffeine delivery. Thanks." I sucked my straw, blissful.

We settled into the folding chairs in front of the temporary tackroom. Julia had been atypically quiet at the show — no nonstop chatter, no dragging me places at the drop of a hat, and none of her usual infectious buoyancy.

"I think I'm bored with showing," she said now.

"Really?" I was startled, although I would have been bored too, showing in the classes that Julia favored. The Hunter classes were too sedate and subjective for my tastes, although I'd ridden in hundreds of them while growing up. "Maybe you just need a change. Why don't you enter the Derby class, or try a competitive trail ride? Something different for you and Jazzy to tackle." We used to joke that Julia had merely to show Jasmine the course diagram and she'd take it from there; I was sure the mare would love to try something new as well.

Julia shrugged again. She was as exotically beautiful as ever, her features the perfect blend of Orient and Occident, but her apathy made her seem smaller somehow.

"My mom's coming to get me tomorrow. My dad's moving out this weekend and she doesn't want to be by herself." Her face was drawn.

"I'll take good care of Jazzy," I promised quietly. It was pathetically inadequate, but it seemed like the only thing I could do for my friend.

My last class of the show was also the biggest — the Grand Prix. It was only the second Grand Prix I'd ever ridden in, and my nerves were apparent to everyone.

"It's like any other class," Karen reminded me as she gave me a leg up onto Hades.

Sure. Except that the fences were huge and I was competing against well-known professional riders whom I had admired for years. No biggie.

Hades had had two days to recoup, and after warming up I felt, if not relaxed, at least less likely to throw up. Julia was gone but everyone else I knew was on the bleachers around the ring. When the gate steward waved me in I took a deep breath and patted Hades' firm neck. He arched it proudly under my touch, and somehow that small gesture made my nerves seem inconsequential. Hades was proud of our team, and so was I.

Since the fences were big I started off carefully, judging our takeoff spots as precisely as I knew how, but Hades seemed not to even notice the increased height, and by the third fence I forgot to be cautious and forgot to be nervous and instead reveled in the feeling of joint flight.

We left the ring to applause, but I barely noticed. Karen met me and shook her head.

"Way to abandon the plan, kid." Then she smiled and patted Hades' shoulder. "But it worked, so you're in luck."

I certainly was, because we won. I'd won my first Grand Prix, and I couldn't stop grinning. I accepted congratulations and gave Hades one of his favorite hard peppermints before reluctantly handing him over to the groom. I felt as though he and I should be celebrating together. Oh well, I thought, I'll feed him more treats later.

I was floating after my win, even laughing with Monica and Neil, who were ecstatic. Their enthusiasm was understandable since the prize money for the class was ten thousand dollars. After chatting with various people I went back to the barn and gladly peeled off my jacket and helmet. I shook out my sweaty hair, then shucked my boots in favor of sneakers and gave Hades a quick rub as he walked past me to his stall.

We had two days off before the St-Lazare show started, but it was in the same place and there was no time to go home. That meant I got two whole days off, with nothing to do but take care of Hades and hang out with my show buddies. I was ready to celebrate. I decided to start by getting some ice cream. I wandered over to the snack-food truck and got into line. The afternoon sun was surprisingly strong for May and I undid a few buttons on my riding shirt, grateful that it was short-sleeved. I was one person away from ice cream when Monica found me, looking flustered.

"Here you are. Do you know where Hades is?"

"He's in his stall."

She shook her head. "No, I was just there and it's empty."

Despite the weather, I felt a sudden chill. *It's nothing*, I told myself as I jogged to the stabling area. Monica struggled to keep up with me, her heeled shoes sinking into the grass. I got to Hades' stall and sure enough, it was wide open and he wasn't there. I spun around and almost plowed into Monica.

"Where could he be?" she asked, breathless.

I spotted Karen's groom coming into the tent and ran over to her. "Did you take Hades back out?"

She gave me a blank look. "Of course not. He's in..." She faltered as her eyes moved to his empty stall.

"Looks like he got out," I said, worried. I turned to the hovering Monica. "Can you go to the show office and have them announce a loose horse? That way people will be on the lookout for him. I'll go search." I grabbed a lead rope and ran out.

At home, if a horse got loose, it usually went only as far as the nearest patch of good grass. In a show environment it was harder to predict, but horses are herd animals and they tend to stay close to their own kind. I began jogging the perimeter of the large showgrounds, looking both inward toward the rings and outward to the open field. On two sides the field was bordered by distant fencing; the third side was flanked by woods, and the fourth led to stables, paddocks, and beyond them, the road. Eventually I slowed to a walk, but the pace of my heart remained quick. I queried people along the way but no one had seen him. It wasn't as though he'd be easy to miss; not only did a loose horse attract immediate attention, but Hades stood out with his flashy white markings. Not to mention that at seventeen hands and about fourteen hundred pounds, he couldn't exactly sneak around.

I heard the show announcer report a loose horse and saw people's heads swiveling in response. Someone was bound to see him, I reassured myself. I saw Monica picking her way back to the temporary stabling, her arms bent halfway up her sides like wings for balance. Neil was with her, and I reached them just as Emma rushed up to me.

"Oh no, Téa I'm so sorry, I knew I should have said something, I knew it!" Tears were streaming down her face, and her nose was running. Her parents hurried up behind her, their faces pinched with concern.

I put my hands on Emma's thin shoulders. "What is it?"

"I saw a man with Hades." She hiccupped.

"It's our fault. Emma told us, but we thought she was mistaken," her mother said. She smoothed her daughter's disheveled blond hair.

I sighed. People didn't listen to kids; I remembered that well enough from my own childhood. "What did he look like, Emma? And where was he?"

We all crowded around her as she spoke. "I don't know... I didn't really look at the man, I was watching Hades."

"I got a quick look," her dad offered. "He was medium height, with brown hair and a potbelly. He had the horse grazing by the trailers." Even now he didn't say 'Hades', I noticed, but I believed Emma. She practically lived at the barn; she'd recognize a horse as easily as she would a person. The description Emma's dad had given could describe a lot of men. I wracked my brain, but stopped in shock almost as soon as I'd started.

"Oh no," I whispered. "Tom."

"Who's Tom?" Monica asked anxiously.

I explained quickly, wishing I'd taken his surprise appearance more seriously. Everyone started talking at once. I turned around and strode toward the area where the trailers were parked; seconds later Neil was at my elbow.

"Where are you going?"

"I'm going to check all the trailers. You should go to the show office and tell them what's happened, and see if they can help us."

"Never mind them," Neil exclaimed, "I'm calling the police." He pulled out his cell phone and dialed 911. I stopped and saw that everyone had followed us.

"I don't think a missing horse would be considered an emergency," Emma's dad said.

"Well, it's not like I know the number for the local police!" Neil retorted.

I left them to argue and jogged through the clumps of trailers. Many were familiar; vans from large stables all over the Northeast, smaller two-horse trailers that must have been local, and a few trailers for hire. During the show season there was high demand for horse transport and some barns made extra money by providing those services. I walked rapidly through the rows of vehicles, but I didn't see anything suspicious. I stopped and pressed the heels of my hands against my eyes, battling a sudden urge to cry. It's too early to panic, I told myself sternly. He could still be here somewhere. A minute later I felt an arm around my shoulders.

I lowered my hands to find Alex next to me. "Do you want to talk about it?" he asked.

I swallowed. "Hades is missing, and it looks like someone might have taken him."

"What?" Alex gasped. I filled him in on the details as we headed toward the show office. He kept his arm around me, and I was grateful for the support. Alex was a dependable friend.

The show office was in a trailer. I climbed the wooden steps and was assaulted by raised voices coming through the open door. Neil, Monica, Emma and her parents, and several show officials were crowded into the small space.

The show secretary caught my eye and sighed with relief. "Oh, Téa. Thank goodness you're here. The police will arrive shortly. I'm so sorry, but this is beyond our ability to deal with. We've never had anything like this happen before, not ever."

I nodded. I'd never heard of anything like this happening at a show either.

"Are you certain he isn't on the grounds somewhere?" an older woman asked. She was tall and bony, and I recognized her as one of the show officials.

"I've looked everywhere I can think of, and someone saw a man with Hades."

"We'll have the announcer describe Hades and ask everyone to be alert for him," she said worriedly.

It would have been so easy. All Tom would have had to do was wait until no one was around and then take Hades out and walk him over to the trailers. He could have parked out of sight of the rings, and no one would have questioned him; in the hustle and bustle of a large show, a man leading a horse wouldn't draw any attention.

Someone came into the office with a question about their classes, and our little group trailed out.

"We'll stay here and wait for the police," Neil said.

"Why don't we go check on Cameo?" Emma's mom suggested, wrapping an arm around her daughter's shoulders.

I exchanged a look with Alex. "Are you done for the day?" I asked him.

"Yup." He gave me a sympathetic smile. "Come on, let's look around some more."

We searched every corner, under the glaring sun outside and in every stall under the shade of the tents; through the permanent stable, in paddocks that Hades might have jumped into, and up and down the rows of trailers. We walked in silence most of the time, Alex's arm occasionally brushing mine. Forty-five minutes later we were sweating, tired, and I for one was miserable.

"Let's get a drink," Alex suggested.

I moped after him to the snack truck. "Thanks, Alex," I said quietly as we got in line. I meant it, too. He could have been relaxing in the shade somewhere instead of searching with me under the scorching sun.

He slipped an arm around me. "Don't mention it. I know you'd do the same for me." His hazel eyes looked straight into mine until I started to get uncomfortable.

"Um, Alex... you know I have a boyfriend, right?"

"Yes." He looked away, and I gently moved out from under his arm. I felt a bit bad for doing it. I'd never gotten the sense that Alex wanted more than friendship before, but I knew I wouldn't be happy if I saw Jaden looking at another girl the way Alex had been looking at me.

We waited in somewhat awkward silence until we bought our drinks — Coke for Alex and iced tea for me.

"I think the cops are here," he commented, gesturing to a car parked by the show office.

We hurried over. The car was white with yellow and black markings, and if it hadn't been for the lights on top I wouldn't have recognized it as a police vehicle. Neil and Monica were talking to two officers in khaki uniforms.

"And 'ow long ago did you remark he is gone?" the middle-aged male officer asked in a heavy French accent. His partner, a younger woman with braided brown hair, looked around the show with interest.

We answered questions for what felt like an hour. Alex excused himself early on, and I tried to smile my thanks. I told the police everything I knew about Tom Morin, noticing Neil's frown out of the corner of my eye. When we were done, the police went to talk to the show's organizers about their security measures. Neil and Monica followed on their heels, but I couldn't take any more of Neil's bluster or Monica's anxiety. I trudged back over to our stalls and slumped down on Hades' tack trunk. My stomach growled, reminding me that I hadn't eaten since that morning and it was late afternoon. I knew I should probably go find some food, but I didn't feel like moving. I might have sat there until I turned to stone if Emma and her mom hadn't arrived.

"We came to get Cameo ready for the drive home," Emma said timidly. She seemed reluctant to disturb my funk.

"Oh, right." I had to get Jasmine ready too, and I got up, relieved to have something to do. Jasmine and Cameo were going home in a neighboring stable's van. I carefully wrapped Jasmine's legs and made sure she had a full haynet ready to go before helping Emma pack the last of her pony's things.

After we'd loaded the horses into the van I said goodbye to Emma. Her mom gave me a solicitous look and a hug, which made a big lump swell in my throat. As soon as they left I went and sat in a corner of Hades' stall. I pulled out my phone and called Jaden. Usually we texted when it was long-distance, but I needed to hear his voice. He listened quietly, making only a few startled exclamations as I recounted the day's events.

"How are you holding up?" he asked when I was done.

"Not great," I admitted. I felt the cool tracks of tears on my cheeks.

"Are you going to come home?"

Until he asked it hadn't occurred to me to wonder. I was supposed to stay for the next show, but if Hades didn't turn up...

"I'm not sure yet," I said, my voice cracking.

"I wish I could join you but I can't take time away from work right now, not when I just started." He sounded frustrated. "Please, *querida*,

55

take care of yourself. Go have a shower, get something to eat, and try to relax a little, okay?"

"I'll try."

"And remember that I love you."

I felt a bit better as I said goodbye, and the shower and food did sound good, so I headed off to find Monica and Neil. Plus, I thought it couldn't hurt to drive around a bit to look for Hades.

I slid onto the beige leather backseat of Neil's BMW. We drove up and down the country roads surrounding the show; we saw many stables and lots of horses, but there was no sign of Hades. I ran into several barns to tell people about him and leave my number, feeling increasingly hopeless.

"Let's go out for dinner," Monica suggested after a couple of hours. I stifled a sigh but agreed politely. It used to be that shows were about my horses, my friends, and the thrill of competition. Lately it seemed that I spent more time with owners than with actual horsepeople.

We went to the motel and showered first. I made an attempt at relaxing under the water but my thoughts were skittering in every direction. Where was Hades? Was he okay? I was worried sick about him, and I couldn't understand why Tom might have taken him. I didn't bother drying my hair, just combed it and left the wet ends trailing on my shoulders.

I would have been happy with fast food, but of course Neil chose a much nicer restaurant. It was a popular rider hangout called 'Mon Village', housed in a large converted farmhouse built in the early 1800s. Huge exposed logs in the walls created a warm atmosphere, and I probably would have enjoyed it under different circumstances.

"Why didn't you tell us about this stalker?" Neil asked bluntly after we'd sat down.

"He's not really a stalker. He's just an unbalanced man who followed me around for a short while. The other day was the first time I've seen him in over a year, and he seemed fine," I explained.

"Well obviously he's not if he took our horse," Neil said impatiently.

"Honey, let's just try to have a nice dinner," Monica placated, surprising me. She patted his hand and he nodded, tight-lipped. They suited each other, in their own way.

The food was great, but dinner was a quiet affair. The motel room felt very empty when I returned, and I got ready for bed although I was so wound up I thought I'd never fall asleep. I had just turned on the TV when my phone rang.

"How are you?" Jaden's velvety voice enveloped me with warmth.

"I feel so guilty," I confessed. "What if Tom took Hades to get back at me?" I couldn't even give voice to my other fear, that Hades might be hurt in some way.

"Tom? Tom Morin?" Jaden's voice was suddenly sharp.

"Um, yeah. Didn't I tell you? Someone matching his description might have taken Hades."

"I can't believe you neglected to mention that," he said, his voice tight. "Are you safe? Is someone with you?"

"Monica and Neil are right next door. Don't worry about me — worry about Hades."

"*You're* my first priority, Téa. When are you coming home?"

"Tomorrow, if nothing comes up." We said our goodbyes and I hung up with a sigh. I understood Jaden's concern, but his protectiveness felt like an extra burden right now.

Four

The drive to the showgrounds the next morning passed in bleak silence. We checked with the show office only to be told there was no news, and while Neil called the police for an update I headed to the stabling area.

"Téa!" Alex came jogging up to me. It was a bit weird to see him in cargo shorts and a T-shirt rather than riding clothes. "I was going to call you — I asked around last night, and one of the grooms thought she saw Rodney with Hades. C'mon, I'll take you to her."

We ran across the field and into the shade of the stabling tent. I saw Monica and Neil out of the corner of my eye, heading our way. The groom was a heavyset girl with a ponytail. She was in a stall brushing a bay horse and spoke to us across the webbed door.

"Like I told Alex, I don't know your horse, but he matched the description and the guy was definitely Rodney. You can't miss that little weasel."

Dread filled me like sludge. "Rodney." I spat the name.

Neil had arrived beside me. "The horse dealer?" He frowned.

My eyes widened in surprise. "Yes. How do you know him?" Neil might own a horse, but he wasn't familiar with the usual horsey circles.

"That's who we bought Hades from."

I fell silent, shocked. Rodney bought and sold horses, but not valuable ones like Hades. Most of the unfortunate souls passing through his hands were bought from auctions, shoddily trained by unpaid teenage girls for a short while, and sold to unsuspecting buyers for several times the money. He got racehorses off the track, horses with lamenesses that could be hidden, and the occasional horse with behavioral issues. The last thought brought me up short. Hades had been a terror when I'd first met him.

"Maybe he decided to take him back," I said slowly.

Rodney was pond scum. He'd tell people he would give them a bargain if they paid in cash and then, weeks or months later, claim the receipt was fake and that the horse hadn't been paid for in full. The trouble was, by that time most buyers had become attached to their horses and simply paid the falsified 'unpaid balance', rather than deal with the hassle of going to court and worrying about their beloved partner being repossessed. Rodney sold lame horses. He took advantage of streams of teenage girls, who did all the work in his barn in exchange for riding privileges. But worst of all, he was cruel to horses, and they often emerged from his barn head-shy and mistrustful. That was something I could never forgive.

We thanked the groom and straggled out. Neil got on the phone to the police while I turned to Alex.

"Thanks," I said gratefully. "I owe you."

"And I'll collect." He grinned at me. "Seriously, I hope you get him back. You're a great team." He gave me a quick hug before turning to go.

"All right, let's pack up," Neil said glumly. "The police don't sound like they're taking this very seriously, and I want to pay Rodney a little visit on the way home."

The five-hour drive seemed to take twenty, and I was on the edge of my seat even though I tried to distract myself by playing with Taffy, Monica's tiny dog. Rodney's barn was east of Toronto, and it was mid-afternoon when we cruised down the quiet, tree-canopied dirt road and pulled into the messy barnyard. Several dogs announced our presence as we walked toward the barn. Monica drew away from them nervously, and I moved closer to reassure her.

The barn was dim, low-ceilinged, and smelled like it didn't get mucked out often enough. We had barely taken two steps when Rodney himself materialized in front of us.

"This isn't a public barn," he said, immediately arousing my suspicions. His eyes passed over me, but I saw the flicker of recognition when he spotted Monica and Neil.

I took another step and looked past him, and my heart gave a sudden leap as a large head appeared behind the bars of a stall.

"Hades!" I yelled. When I started toward him Rodney blocked my way, glaring. He reeked of stale cigarettes.

Hades gave a shrill whinny, staring at me as though I was a lifeline, but when I tried to go to him Rodney grabbed my arm, hard.

"Let go of me, you jerk!" I yanked my arm away, but before I could move Monica seized my hand, looking worried.

"Just wait a minute, Téa," she said, staring at Rodney.

"That's my horse over there," Neil yelled, jabbing his finger at Hades. "And I want him back right now."

Rodney shook his head. "You're wrong, that's my horse. I've had him for months."

"I've got the bill of sale!" Neil shouted. "The one *you* gave me. It says 'bay Hanoverian gelding, seven years old', and I bought him two years ago, and Hades is nine!"

Rodney's pale, watery eyes darted around furtively. "A Hanoverian, huh? Well then, this can't be your horse, on account of he ain't no Hanoverian. No brand." His tone was derisive, but his body language spoke volumes. He was a thief, plain and simple.

Neil's face turned purple. "I'm not leaving here without my horse, you swine," he yelled into Rodney's face. I felt my own blood pressure rising, and my hands were forming fists when two large men appeared.

"Got a problem, boss?" one of them asked casually. Neither of them looked like someone you'd want to meet in a dark alley.

"I don't know," Rodney said aggressively, staring first at Neil, then at Monica and me. "Do I?"

"You'll be hearing from the police," Neil spat. He turned to go, but my eyes were locked on Hades. He stared at me anxiously, and bobbed his head a few times as if asking how I could leave him here. My heart constricted tightly, making my chest ache.

A push from Rodney snapped me out of my daze. "Get moving, girlie." I felt a flare of hatred so intense I was surprised it didn't burn him, but I spun and stalked out.

Neil ranted the whole way home, and Monica wailed, but I stayed quiet, gnawing the inside of my cheek until it was raw. I was worried about Hades. He was a highly trained athlete and needed regular work to stay healthy. I was willing to bet Rodney didn't have anyone capable of riding him properly. And what about his diet, which had been carefully calibrated to meet his needs? My biggest torment, though, was over his feelings. He'd tried his heart out for me at the show, and this was his reward — he was far from home among rough strangers, with no idea why he'd ended up there. For the first time since I'd known him, he had looked scared and upset, and it was almost more than I could take.

Neil and Monica didn't say much when they dropped me off. It was Monday, the school horses' day off, so I didn't see anybody. I trudged into the house and dumped my duffle bag on the floor of my bedroom before sinking down next to it. I didn't know what to do with myself. After the constant press of school, teaching, riding, and work in the barn, I was suddenly directionless at a time when I desperately needed to keep busy. Finally, I texted Teri with the news. I considered calling Julia, but I didn't want to burden her when she was already so stressed. I called Jaden, even though he was at work, but he didn't answer and I left him a short message. Then I got up and turned on my laptop. It was late evening in Spain; with any luck I'd be able to catch Seth online. I didn't see him though, and when I tried to call, my biological father's wife informed me rather coolly that Seth wasn't home.

I went out to the barn, bombarded by thoughts that swooped at me from every direction. I could feel tears coming and slipped quickly into Cal's stall so that no one would see. He gave me an inquisitive look before taking a tentative step towards me. Everything about Cal looked young except for his eyes — those large, deep brown pools radiated wisdom far beyond his four years. He came to me, his soulful eyes alight with compassion, and slowly lowered his head. He blew softly into my hand before pressing his face against my front. The tears flowed, and I choked back a sob. I wanted to throw my arms around Cal but I was frozen in place. The warmth of his face against me was like a mirage, a promise of peace that I couldn't reach. Instead, I whirled and went back into the aisle, wiping my eyes quickly. By the time Alan came around the corner I hoped I looked fairly normal.

"Can I give you a hand?" I asked. Alan was happy for the help, and I spent a couple of hours working before going back to the house for dinner.

Dec was in the kitchen. I'd called him with an update that morning, but he hadn't said much and I approached him a bit warily. When he was stressed he had a tendency to react with anger and start laying blame. He examined my face silently for a minute before surprising me by putting his arms around me. I hugged him back uncertainly.

"I'm sorry Seth's not here," he said quietly.

I pulled back in shock, and he gave me a wry look. "I'm not good with this stuff. Seth always knew how to comfort you."

I nodded slowly, amazed that this was something Dec would acknowledge, let alone express. Then I gave him a small smile.

"You're not doing too badly." I hugged him again, with feeling this time.

We made sandwiches and a salad. We didn't tend to cook much when it was just the two of us.

"What happens now?" Dec asked as we sat down to eat.

I finished chewing my bite of cheese and tomato sandwich before answering. "I'm not sure. Neil's going to call his lawyer because the police said it's a civil matter now that we know where Hades is. A 'property dispute', they called it," I said, injecting my tone with all the disgust that phrase deserved.

"What's a property dispute?" Jaden appeared in the doorway, and I dropped my sandwich and threw myself at him with a wordless cry. He pressed me tightly against him for a minute before letting go in deference to Dec, but his eyes continued to hold me.

"How are you?" he asked quietly.

I shrugged. He steered me back to the table and sat next to me. I filled him in on everything that had happened, and other than reminding me to eat, he remained quiet.

"What do you think?" Dec asked him.

Jaden ran a hand through his hair before answering. "The news isn't good," he warned me, taking my hand under the table. "It will likely take a long time before the case goes to court, and in the meantime, Rodney will probably try to sell Hades. He can make a lot more money on him now that he's well schooled. You'll have to try to get an injunction to prevent Rodney from selling him before the case is settled."

I tried to tamp down the buzz of panic I felt. "I should go online. I'll post Hades' picture everywhere, on social media and all the horse forums — some forums even have a 'stolen horses' section. I'll tell people not to buy him from Rodney."

Jaden shook his head. "You can't do that. Accusing Rodney of stealing Hades is libel."

"But he did steal him!"

"It has to be proven in court before you can say it."

"Don't get all lawyer-y on me," I snapped.

His hand moved up and down my back. "I know it's frustrating, *querida*, but I don't want you to get in trouble over this."

"It's ridiculous," I grumbled. "That weasel stole a horse and I can't even warn people?"

"Not in public, and not in writing," Jaden specified.

Dec gave him a thoughtful look. "Why don't you take this case, son? I bet you'll be far more motivated than Neil's lawyer, and you understand the horse industry."

"Would you?" I exclaimed, feeling suddenly hopeful.

"Of course I would. I'll have to clear it with my boss first since technically it would be her case — I'm still articling. But I'd be happy to work on it if Neil agrees."

"I'll call him right now." I jumped up and dashed to the phone. Neil agreed readily, grumbling that his own lawyer hadn't even called him back yet.

"It's convenient to have a lawyer in the family," Dec said, smiling. He clapped Jaden on the shoulder and retreated to his office.

I loaded the old dishwasher while Jaden finished clearing the table. We tried to watch TV for a while, but I perched tensely on the edge of the couch with my knees bouncing up and down.

"Let's go for a walk," Jaden suggested. As we went down the wooden porch steps the balmy spring evening seemed to mock my worries, and moving around did calm me somewhat. Jaden took my hand, and we waved at some boarders riding in the main ring before starting down the trail that led away from the barn. As it turned out, there had been virtually no fallout from the revelation of our relationship to the boarders and students. All that angst, and in the end only our family had truly objected.

"Do you think Hades is okay?" I worried aloud.

63

"I'm sure Rodney will take care of him. The better he looks, the more money he can ask for him."

I flinched at the reminder. "How long will it take before we get him back?"

He hesitated. "I'll be honest. It could take several weeks. Some property disputes last even longer — years, in some cases. But not in this case," he hurried on at the dismay on my face, "I'll expedite it in any way possible."

I nodded, swallowing down the lump in my throat. I could feel Jaden's eyes on me as we walked, and suddenly I felt myself being tugged sideways. We wove through the trees, Jaden pushing aside undergrowth. We weren't on any kind of trail that I could see.

"Where-" I started.

"Shh." He turned and pulled me hard against him. His firm lips found mine as one of his hands curved around the back of my neck. His other hand was hot against the skin of my back, and as I parted my mouth and felt his tongue, his hand slid down under the waistband of my shorts. He squeezed my buttock, and I made a sound that might have been a moan. All of a sudden he released me.

"Hey," I complained.

He grinned as he pulled his shirt over his head, revealing his perfect torso. Even though we'd been together for almost two years, I was still obsessed with Jaden. I'd never gotten over the fact that someone like him — so beautiful, so good, so successful — was actually interested in me. I'd long since memorized every aspect of his body: the way his hard stomach dipped into little hollows toward his hips. The way his warm hands, with all their polo calluses, felt as they slid over my skin. The way the sharp angles of his face were unexpectedly softened by the white heat of his smile. And his smell... it was nothing external, nothing he put on. It was the scent of his very flesh, as intoxicating to me as catnip. I couldn't get enough of being close to him. No matter how often we made love, I was ready for more–I sometimes wondered if I was turning into some kind of addict, if I had a problem that I wasn't even aware of. Not that I would have cared if I did.

He spread his shirt and jeans out on the ground before lowering me on top of them. Then he covered me with his body, wearing only his boxers. I could feel his hardness pressing against me as he kissed me again. I wrapped my arms around him and wound one leg around his.

"Come inside me," I murmured in his ear.

"There's no rush," he whispered back, his lips moving to my neck before continuing downward.

"Says you," I grumbled. I buried my hands in his hair, relishing the feeling of his hot skin sliding against mine. His mouth was on my breast, and his hand slid up my inner thigh, past the leg of my shorts, and snuck past the edge of my underwear. I bit my lip as his finger slipped smoothly inside me. Two can play that game, I thought as I ran my hand down his washboard stomach and into his boxers. He groaned against my chest as I enveloped him.

"You're right, why rush?" I teased.

He pulled away from me just long enough to tear off my shorts, and then he was back, his mouth on mine as he filled me inexorably with his heat. He took his time after that, bringing me to the edge many times before we finally tumbled over, gasping. We lay in a heap, catching our breath in the darkening twilight. I savored the sweet, fertile smells of the Earth reawakening. The air was thick with birdsong.

"It's a good thing there aren't any bugs," I mused.

"Yes," he agreed, nipping my shoulder. "No one but me is allowed to bite you."

"Not that I'm complaining, but was there a reason you decided to seduce me in the woods?"

He hitched himself onto one elbow and gazed down at me. "I wanted to take your mind off your troubles," he admitted. He gave a rakish grin. "Did it work?

I smiled back. "I didn't think of Hades once. If we could make love nonstop until he's returned, I'd be fine."

We got up and started tugging on our clothes. "I wish I could stay, but I have to be at work in the morning," Jaden said.

We walked back leisurely with our arms around each other. When we got to his car he held me tightly and gave me a passionate kiss goodbye, ignoring Stephanie and Lisa, who were standing outside by their cars. He brushed my tousled hair out of my face.

"Try not to worry." His honey-drop eyes beseeched me.

As his car disappeared from sight I trudged into the house, picking brush out of my hair and straightening my clothes. I was afraid it was going to be a long night.

As it turned out, that night was the least of it. Two days later not much had changed; Jaden was trying to find a legal means to prevent Rodney from selling Hades, but we were no closer to getting him back. Meanwhile, I was losing my mind from inactivity and distress. I'd been scheduled to be at the show, so I had no lessons lined up. I rode Cal every day and took over some lessons that Dec was supposed to teach, but there wasn't enough work to keep me from obsessing over Hades. I'd talked to Julia, who was sympathetic but distant, and Teri, who commiserated with me over the phone. On Wednesday I finally connected with Seth on a video call.

"Where the heck have you been?" I demanded irritably as soon as I saw him.

He gave me his usual affable smile. "Gee, I've missed you too, Sis."

Before I could explain my bad mood, I heard the sound of childish laughter and two little girls suddenly appeared onscreen. One of them immediately crawled onto Seth's lap while the other leaned close to the camera, momentarily obliterating my view.

"Climb up here," I heard Seth say in Spanish. His Spanish had gotten quite good since he'd been in Spain, although his accent was different from the Argentinean one I was used to, which sometimes made it hard for me to understand him.

"Hola Téa." Carolina giggled. She was six, the elder of the two. She was bright and outgoing, as opposed to four-year-old Nelia, who seemed quite shy and was only beginning to speak to me. They both had lots of wavy dark hair and smooth olive skin. A stranger would never have guessed that the blond young man next to them was a relative.

I made an attempt to talk to my half-sisters for a while, but our conversation was stunted and they soon ran off. I never knew what to say to young kids, since I was rarely around them. Seth watched them go with a smile before turning back to me.

"Okay, what's wrong?" he asked.

He'd noticed right away, of course. I cried a bit as I told him, but I didn't mind so much with Seth. His blue eyes darkened with concern as I spoke.

"Aw, crap. I'm sorry, Sis." He leaned closer to the camera. "What are you going to do?"

"There's nothing I *can* do," I complained. "Jaden's basically told me to sit on my hands and wait."

"Exactly what you're best at," Seth joked. He paused for a minute. "I have some news too — I'm taking off."

My heart leaped. "You're coming home?"

"No, no... just leaving here. I'm going to travel for a bit."

"But why? I thought you wanted to get to know Alfonso and the rest of our family."

He shrugged. "And now I know them. It's time for me to move on. I feel like a fifth wheel around here, and Alfonso and I aren't getting along that great. I'll miss Carolina and Nelia, but I've told them they can come visit us in Canada when they're older."

I struggled not to show how hurt I was that Seth didn't want to come home. "Okay," I said slowly. "Where will you go?"

"On a tour of Europe. I've met some great people over here and we're going to travel together."

"By 'people' do you mean 'a girl'?" I asked suspiciously.

He laughed. "Some of them are girls. That's not why I'm leaving, though. Will you tell Dec for me?"

"Sure." I sighed. Seth and Dec had hardly spoken since my brother had left home five months before to live with Alfonso, our newly-discovered biological father.

The week wore on, but rather than gradually relaxing as I'd hoped, I found myself getting increasingly wound up over Hades' absence. Karen and Teri texted me daily. I knew they were trying to make me feel better, but their missives only reminded me of my impotence. Night became my enemy as sleep refused to visit, and I took to prowling the house and grounds in the dark. The tension had become a constant pain by Friday when I drove to Toronto to meet with Neil, Monica, and Jaden at his office. I was looking forward to gaining some relief.

It was my first visit to Jaden's new workplace. The law offices of Sisto, Goldberg, and Hwin were downtown, and I circled the block twice before opting to park in a paid lot. I hurried into the glass-fronted building and took the elevator to the eleventh floor. The doors whooshed open almost silently to reveal a semi-circular receptionist's desk, behind which sat a woman who was so primped and polished she barely looked real.

"Um, I'm looking for Jaden Foster?" I told Mannequin Girl.

"Oh yes, you must be his one o'clock. Right this way." She rose smoothly and glided down the hall, then showed me into a room that held a table and chairs before disappearing.

Monica and Neil were routinely late, so I stepped into the doorway to look for Jaden. I spotted him right away. Even though I knew he worked here, it gave me a jolt to see him standing there in a suit and tie, looking cool and professional. Next to him was a slim woman in a sage-green suit. She was tall, even without the three-inch heels she was wearing. I couldn't imagine wearing shoes like that to work all day, but I had to admit that, combined with her rather short skirt, they made her legs look very long. She had honey-blond hair in an elegant twist on the back of her neck, and she was nodding seriously as she listened to Jaden speak. She put her hand on his arm and pointed out something in the folder he was holding.

I felt a quiver in the pit of my stomach. I trusted Jaden, of course, but I hadn't realized he was working with women like this, polished and well-educated women. Then again, I hadn't really devoted any thought to it. When they headed my way I scurried back inside the room, wishing I'd worn something nicer than the sandals, jeans and stretchy girl-T I'd picked out. Jaden had a gift for being at ease anywhere — on a horse, in a kitchen, at swanky parties, and now, in an office. I wasn't as much of a chameleon as he was, and I felt distinctly out of place.

Jaden smiled at me as he dropped his papers on the table. He came over and kissed my cheek.

"This is Téa," he introduced me to the blond woman. "London, my boss."

London gave me the once-over as we shook hands. She didn't seem impressed. From close up she looked older than I'd first thought, maybe in her mid-thirties.

Monica and Neil were ushered in by Mannequin Girl, and after introductions were made we all found seats around the table. London sat next to Jaden, and I sat at the end so that Monica could be next to Neil. I shivered in the air conditioning as we all looked expectantly at Jaden. He'd gotten his hair cut; the golden waves were all snipped off, leaving his hair straighter and darker, in keeping with his new job and, I supposed, his new life.

"Well, here's where things stand," Jaden said. "Rodney's been charged with theft and we've filed an injunction to prevent him from selling Hades."

"We have two years' worth of bills, not to mention his Equine Canada passport and breed registration papers," Monica said. "Isn't that enough proof that he's ours?"

"It appears the registration papers may have been falsified," London said. "Or maybe they belong to a different horse."

"It's too bad they weren't DNA testing back then," I mumbled. Everyone turned to look at me. "They take DNA samples at the Hanoverian foal inspections nowadays," I explained. "But they didn't nine years ago." I had a troubling thought. "Since he's lying about Hades' identity, don't you think Rodney might try to sell him anyway, even with the injunction?"

"That is a possibility," Jaden admitted. "But it's the best we can do for now. The horse is in his barn."

"Don't tell me that 'possession is nine-tenths of the law' crap is actually true," Neil exclaimed.

"For our purposes, yes," Jaden said. "Since Hades is in Rodney's possession it's up to us to prove that he doesn't belong to him."

"But Rodney only has him because he stole him," I protested.

"*Allegedly* stole him," London corrected. I glared at her.

"Well, can't we get him back in the meantime?" Monica asked. "Don't the police seize stolen property?"

"Not when living creatures are involved. The system's not set up to care for them," Jaden explained.

I zoned out while everyone discussed what would happen next. From the sounds of it, we wouldn't be going to court for weeks, possibly months, so this year's show season would be a write-off. Even if we won the case in the end, Rodney might surrender a different horse to us, having illegally sold Hades in the meantime. And if we did eventually get Hades back — and my hopes weren't high — who knew what state he'd be in? I rubbed my temples. I couldn't believe this was happening.

When the meeting was over I dragged myself miserably back out to my car. Jaden had said he'd be working over the weekend, so I didn't have the prospect of his company to look forward to, and now that I'd seen the kinds of women he worked with I had an entirely new source of unease, one that I didn't have any emotional energy to deal with. I pushed those thoughts aside and on the drive home considered how to save both Hades and my riding career. I tried to look at the situation from every angle, but all the views were equally bleak.

I remembered that when I'd first seen Hades my immediate impression had been 'Clydesdale cross'. Not that he was in any way clunky, and he didn't have a Clyde's high knee action or the feathering on his legs. It was more his coloration, the full wavy tail, and the big head with its white stripe that made me think of those fine draft horses. It had never occurred to me to wonder at the lack of the distinctive Hanoverian breed brand. In any event, it didn't matter to me whether he was a registered Hanoverian, one who hadn't made the cut, or something else altogether. He was a fantastically talented horse with a personality and a half, and I missed him.

I called Jaden the next day. "Why do you have to be at work on a Saturday?"

He sighed. "London did me a favor by taking a horse theft case. It's not the type of thing the firm would normally handle, and I have to make up for the hours I'm putting into it."

My resentment flashed over into guilt. "Oh. Sorry."

"It's fine, *querida*," he said warmly. "I want to get Hades back for you. It's unfortunate that it's going to take a while."

"Isn't there anything else we can do?" I pleaded desperately.

"Not legally."

"Can't you come to Rodney's with me? Maybe if you talked to him-"

"I can't do that."

I remembered the impotent rage I'd felt at Rodney's. Jaden's anger would be far more effective, but also far more dangerous.

"Are you worried? About... losing your temper?"

He didn't say anything for a minute. "A hundred times I've wished you hadn't seen me fight last year," he murmured finally. His tone was bleak. "My temper has nothing to do with it. I can't speak to Rodney directly because I'm working on a case against him. I'm required to communicate with his lawyer."

"Oh. Sorry. I didn't mean-" I was instantly embarrassed.

"It's okay," he said tiredly.

Alex texted me soon after. *People are talking about Hades on the COTH forums.*

The Chronicle of the Horse, or COTH for short, was a popular magazine with an active forum on its website.

I don't know how to tell you this, Alex went on, *but they think if a horse is stolen, the thief would sell him or move him far away as fast as possible.*

It made sense because if Rodney tried to sell Hades in Ontario or Quebec he'd be recognized. But if Hades were sold in the US or Europe, he might prove impossible to find, and Monica and Neil would lose any hope of getting him back.

I put down my phone feeling worse than ever. I should have been competing at the St-Lazare show that weekend. Instead, my body coiled itself into ever-harder knots. I kept as busy as I could — I taught lessons, rode, helped turn out and feed, and generally avoided being alone with my thoughts, but by the time Seth called on Sunday morning I was in a veritable state.

"I just wanted to give you my new cell phone number since I'm taking off today," Seth said. "How are you doing?"

I simmered silently for a minute before I blew. "Freakin' awful! That's how I'm doing. I'm sick of this happening, do you hear me? SICK OF IT!"

There was a long silence on the other side of the ocean before Seth chuckled. "Well don't hold back, Sis. Tell me how you really feel."

I gusted out a sigh. "It's just... I can't believe this. It's as though Fate is stomping on my dreams at every turn. First Zac got sold. Then Blaze died. Then I lost Marty — every time I finally have a winner, I somehow lose him. I can't take this happening again, Seth, I just can't." My voice broke, but I didn't cry. I was too angry for that.

A pause. "What are you planning?" he asked suspiciously.

I swallowed. "Nothing. There's nothing I can do." I didn't usually lie to Seth, but he was too far away to be of help. There was no point in worrying him until my plan was a *fait accompli*.

I spent the rest of the day feverishly preparing. I needed a trailer, but I couldn't take ours. I couldn't risk the noise waking Dec up, and his bedroom window overlooked the spot where his truck was parked. I also wanted to drive something less easily recognizable, since Dec's pickup had 'Shady Lane Stables' written on the side. I mentally ran through all the people I knew with horse trailers. I didn't want to involve any friends in this because the fewer people who knew about it the better, so acquaintances from other barns were out. I finally realized the polo club was my best option. People trailered in horses every weekend for matches. The trailers were frequently parked overnight, and I was willing to bet the keys were often left in the trucks.

I formulated my plan as carefully as possible, while trying to ignore the voice in the back of my head that was screeching that this was the stupidest thing I'd ever done out of a long list of very stupid things. I went outside and moved my car to the far end of the barn, instead of in front of the shed where I usually parked. Then I tried very hard to act natural for the rest of the day.

"Try to eat something, dear," Gran said at dinnertime. I looked down and realized I'd been moving food around my plate for a while.

"Jaden's pushing to get this into court as soon as possible," Dec said. "There's no point in worrying about it in the meantime."

Of course Dec wasn't worried. He'd had mixed feelings about Hades since the beginning. I forced myself to sit through the rest of dinner so as not to arouse suspicion, but afterward, I cloistered myself in my room.

Dec knocked on my door at ten. "Do you want me to do the bedtime check?"

"Yes, please. I'm tired," I replied. I got into bed fully dressed and went over my plan. There were about a hundred things that could go wrong with it, but it was the best I could do. I wished Seth were here. He'd grumble about what an idiot I was, but when he was done complaining he'd help me. At least then I wouldn't be alone. I was dying to text Teri, but I thought it would be better for her if she weren't involved.

Dec usually went to bed by eleven, but at eleven-thirty, I could still hear the TV on downstairs when I opened my door. I groaned. Of all the nights for him to stay up late. It was a quarter to twelve before I heard him and Blue, his dog, come upstairs. I wondered how long it would take them to fall asleep. I was jittery, and every minute felt like ten. I checked my bag one more time. Penlight — check. Phone — check. Courage — well, I was hoping some would materialize when I needed it.

I pulled on my hoodie and crept down the stairs, feeling like a cliché because I was dressed head-to-toe in black. I was carrying a pair of black Mary Janes in one hand. They weren't exactly the best style of shoe for what I had in mind, but they were the only black ones I had that were rubber-soled. I let myself out of the house carefully before slipping them on. I cringed when I started my car; it sounded deafeningly loud. I drove very slowly down the gravel drive, not waiting to see if I'd woken Dec.

After pulling onto a dark side road near the polo club I parked the car where I hoped it wouldn't be visible. I got out and stood for a moment, absorbing the sounds of the dark country night. I heard crickets and frogs and the odd mysterious rustle. It was too early and too cool for the cicadas yet. I took a deep breath, turned on my penlight, and headed through the woods. I soon wished I'd brought a bigger flashlight because it was pitch black in the woods and I had very little idea where I was going. The sky was overcast and there was no moonlight, which I supposed I should be thankful for, but at the moment I was feeling a bit too creeped out by the dark forest to muster any gratitude for the gloom.

I was grateful when I stumbled into the openness of the polo grounds. They seemed brighter in comparison to the black forest, and with the help of the distant lights from the house, I could see the outline of several trucks and trailers. I hurried toward them as quietly as I could. I opened the door to the first pickup, my heart beating so loud I was afraid it would wake the horses in the nearby barn. I could never be a thief, I thought. The stress would kill me. Then again, I realized with a start, I was kind of stealing something right now. Only it was really more like borrowing. I searched the truck with my penlight but didn't find any keys. Darn. On to the next truck. When I opened the door the cab light came on, and almost immediately I heard barking.

"Oh, crap," I whimpered. The dogs at the polo club knew me — I wasn't afraid of them, but I was terrified they'd wake someone. I shut the door quickly, vaulted into the back of the pickup, and lay down. I could hear the dogs coming, and I was hoping that when they didn't see me they'd go away. Then I heard a voice. Damn.

"There's nothing here." The words were in Spanish, and I recognized the voice. I froze in the truck bed, but a second later I heard whining and paws scrabbling on the paint.

"Téa?" Mateo's face appeared above me. I sat up, face flaming, my heart still playing percussion.

"Hey," I said lamely. Mateo crossed his arms, rested them on the edge of the truck, and waited. I sighed. "I guess you want to know what I'm doing here."

"That would be nice," he agreed.

"I need a trailer. I can't use ours, and I can't explain why, and now you're going to send me home-" I ground to a halt. I was dangerously close to crying.

"Why do you need a trailer?"

"I told you, I can't tell you." I sniffled.

"Come here." He reached over and helped me climb out of the pickup. He rested his hands on my shoulders and studied my face for a moment; now that my eyes had adjusted I could read the expression on his, too. It was concerned. "If you want my help, you will have to tell me something."

I brightened. "You'll help me?"

"Perhaps."

So I told him. I explained my entire hare-brained scheme, and when I was done his brow furrowed.

"This sounds dangerous. Are you sure it's wise?"

"Not one bit. But I have to do it anyway."

He nodded, understanding. "I wish I could go with you, but I am not alone this night. Summer is waiting for me." He glanced back toward his apartment. "I will be right back." He jogged off and returned a minute later with a set of keys. He handed them to me and pointed out a two-horse trailer hitched to a smaller pickup. "Take that one. Good luck."

I flung my arms around him. "Thank you," I said fervently.

He patted my back. "Be careful."

I drove slowly down the polo club's driveway with the headlights off. When I got to the road I checked the time. Almost one a.m. It was later than I'd hoped because my destination was almost two hours away, but at least phase one of my plan had worked, thanks to blind luck and Mateo's kindness.

The drive was numbing, although it went faster than expected since there was no traffic. The highway was well-lit, but once I exited I squinted tensely through the windshield, afraid to miss a turn in the dark. I'd plotted my route online, and the printed map was stuffed in my bag, but everything looked so different in the dark. After driving a few miles I realized I must have missed a sign somewhere and turned around, cursing. I drove slower this time, peering at every opening, and finally found the road I was looking for, the sign largely obscured by branches. When I found the address I drove past it and parked in a pool of darkness. I leaned my head back against the seat and took a few deep breaths. *You can do this*, I encouraged myself. *You* have *to do this*. I got out of the truck, closing the door as quietly as possible, and pulled the strap of my messenger bag over my head and onto my shoulder. I lowered the trailer's ramp, cursing when the metal creaked loudly in the stillness of the rural night. Then I headed for the barn.

Five

I walked down the shadowed road on legs that were shaking from adrenaline. When I got to the small paddock separating the barn from the road I paused. I didn't want to go up the driveway in case there were motion-activated lights. I felt my way carefully around the far side of the paddock. There was room enough for a person and horse to get through between the fence and surrounding bushes. I turned and looked toward the trailer; from my vantage point, it was obscured by trees which meant it wouldn't be visible from the house, either.

I headed for the barn, creeping stealthily. Most barns are kept unlocked at night because it's important to be able to get in quickly in case of emergency. Security consists mainly of lights and barn dogs. Dogs were surprisingly effective deterrents, but you can't keep aggressive barn dogs at a public stable. They were kept for their bark, not their bite. I peeked around the corner and saw the dog I'd noticed on my previous visit, chained to his doghouse as he had been then. I gave mental thanks that I'd remembered him as I pulled a steak out of my bag and unwrapped it before rounding the corner. He barked once before noticing what I'd flung at him. Then he grabbed the steak and disappeared into the doghouse with his prize.

I turned and felt my way slowly into the barn. My heart was thundering so loudly in my ears that anyone could have snuck up on me. Once I was well inside I clicked on my penlight and shone it into the stall where I'd last seen Hades. The face that blinked back was grey.

No no no no, I screamed inside my head. Could Rodney have sold him already? I swallowed back my panic and went down the aisle, shining my tiny light into each stall. I hadn't gone far when I heard a deep, urgent nicker. I spun around. Hades was straining against the bars of a stall at the far end of the barn. I ran over and slipped inside.

"Come on buddy, we have to be quick," I whispered to him. I yanked the halter I'd brought out of my bag and pulled it onto his head. The lead rope was already attached. We took two steps out of the stall and I froze. Shoes. Dammit, why hadn't I thought about how much noise metal shoes would make on a cement floor? Maybe because it was a sound I heard every day, a good, familiar sound in the context of normal daytime activity. But here in the stygian stillness, it was deafeningly, frighteningly loud. I wracked my brain quickly. I could search the barn for something to tie around Hades' hooves, but every second I delayed increased my chances of getting caught. That steak wouldn't last forever. I decided to chance it.

"Try to tiptoe," I muttered, pulling Hades forward again. I winced with every step he took, but we made it out of the barn without hearing anything unusual. I turned quickly toward the path around the paddock, grateful for the darkness that swallowed us up. Hades was crowding me, almost stepping on me, and I realized he was nervous too.

"It's okay, baby," I murmured, patting him. "You'll be home soon."

A dog started to bark. Not the outside dog; this sound was coming from inside the house — Rodney's house. I broke into a jog and Hades gamely trotted next to me. I kept him at the road's edge so the clatter of his shoes wouldn't be so loud, but in any case, it couldn't compete with the crashing of my heart. When we got to the trailer I jogged up the ramp and was brought up short when I hit the end of the lead rope. I turned around.

Hades was planted on the road, four legs wide, tossing his head up and rolling his eyes.

"Not now," I whimpered. I went and stood next to him and patted his neck. "Come on, buddy, you've never been afraid of trailers before." I tried walking up the ramp again. Hades didn't move. Dammit, I thought. Impotent panic made tears run down my face. Of all the stupid ways for us to get caught, Hades refusing to load had never entered my mind. Then again, he was a very big horse, and he might never have been in a two-horse trailer before.

I put my arms around his head. "Please, Hades, please, just trust me," I implored. My tears glued us together, cheek to cheek. I tried again, holding his halter with one hand and stroking him continuously with the other. He followed me hesitantly, squeezing into the tight space, and I tied him quickly before jumping out and running to raise the ramp. Then I ran for the truck, leaped in, and started driving.

I didn't care where I was going at first. I was moving away from Rodney's, shaking with terror. I gripped the wheel as though my life depended on it and tried to slow my breathing. I couldn't afford to hyperventilate. Clearly, I wasn't suited to a life of crime. I kept expecting a commotion to break out behind me, sirens or screeching tires and speeding headlights, but all was calm and after a few minutes my shaking eased and my panting slowed. I started to pay attention to where I was going, and I found a road leading back to the highway. I drove very slowly because Hades wasn't wearing any leg protection, and if he lost his balance in the trailer he could step on himself and do real damage with his metal shoes.

I felt almost dozy on the drive back. I hadn't slept all night, and it was five in the morning when I finally approached home. The sun would be rising soon; I had to move fast. I parked on the road, out of sight of the house, and quickly lowered the trailer's ramp. I went to the front and climbed in through the small door to untie Hades. He gave me a small push with his nose and pricked his ears forward.

"Yeah, I'm happy to see you too," I murmured as he backed slowly down the ramp. I walked him up our driveway, less careful than I'd been at Rodney's. Maybe it was because I knew Blue's hearing wasn't good, or maybe I was just too tired to care. A few horses whinnied greetings as we came in, but mostly it was quiet. I quickly put Hades in his stall.

"Sorry I can't give you any hay, it would look suspicious," I said as I closed his door.

I jogged back to the trailer. My legs felt rubbery but I forced myself to keep moving. I drove to the polo grounds, fast this time, wanting to get there before the grooms were up and feeding the horses. I parked the trailer — leaving the keys in the ignition — and was driving my own car home as the sun poured itself like molasses over the horizon.

I was careful to park back at the end of the barn before I dragged myself inside. I slunk upstairs, dropped my shoes on the floor, and crawled into bed with all my clothes on, giving a sigh of deep gratitude as my head sank into the pillow. Thank goodness it was Monday; Alan would feed and there were no lessons to teach. I could get a few hours of sleep.

As if. Just over an hour later there was a knock on my door.

"What?" I mumbled hoarsely.

"We're feeding this morning, remember?" Dec's voice.

No, I didn't remember. "Why?" I groaned.

"Alan has a doctor's appointment. I'll see you in the barn."

I did some imaginative cursing as I rolled out of bed and stumbled to the bathroom. At least I was already dressed. Ten minutes later I trudged out to the barn. Now that I was awake my mind was working furiously. I'd counted on the fact that Alan would be the one to discover Hades and tell Dec. I'd even been practicing my 'surprised look' when they told me. Even though it couldn't happen that way, for some reason I felt it was important that Dec see Hades first, so once the hay was thrown down I started feeding in the school horse aisle.

"Téa!" Dec's shocked exclamation came a minute later. I strode quickly around the corner and froze. It wasn't entirely an act; I was so exhausted that the night's events felt a bit like a dream. Then I ran into Hades' stall and flung my arms around his neck. He curled his head around me and nudged me, whickering low in his chest, *huh-huh-huh-huh*. I turned to face Dec, keeping one arm around Hades, and wiped the tears from my face. They weren't an act either — I was overjoyed to see Hades home.

Dec frowned. He looked from me to Hades and back again. "Do you know something about this?"

"Me?" I let my eyes go wide. Okay, now I was acting. "What do you mean?"

Dec's pale blue gaze assessed me carefully. I struggled not to look away, suddenly wishing I'd changed out of my ninja clothes.

"I mean it's awfully convenient that he just turned up back in our barn, don't you think?" he asked.

I traced the velvety contours of Hades' nostril with my fingertips for a minute. Then I shrugged. "I guess I was wrong. Rodney's obviously more chicken than weasel."

Dec's brows rose ever so slightly. "You're saying you think he brought Hades back?"

"Well, sure. Who else? He must've been scared to go to court — he is a crook, after all. He probably has a record, and he wouldn't want people to know that, it would be bad for business." I realized I was starting to babble and clamped my mouth shut. I gave Hades one last pat, marveling at his patience — he hadn't pulled away from me once — and stepped out of his stall. "I guess we should finish feeding."

"I'll be right back." Dec headed outside. I waited until he was out of sight before creeping to the door and peeking out. Dec had the door to his pickup open and his head stuck inside. Probably checking the odometer, something I'd never even thought of when making my plans. He closed the truck's door and strode over to where the two trailers were parked. He walked carefully around both of them, looking for some sign they'd been used.

As he turned toward the barn I ran back to the aisle, keeping my head down. I went to pick up more hay, and Dec snagged my sleeve as I passed him. I swallowed hard before turning to face him. Several emotions were playing over his face: suspicion, relief, worry, but in the end, a small smile won out.

"I'm happy for you, kiddo."

I grinned at him, and we resumed feeding. Dec was shooting me some strange glances, but he had chosen to believe I wasn't involved, which was a huge relief. If he thought I was responsible for taking Hades he would have felt compelled to punish me, and that would have been problematic for both of us.

The question of how to tell Jaden was much trickier. In order for the whole thing to seem natural, I should be running into the house to call my friends and happily announce Hades' return, with Jaden being at the top of my list. The trouble was, I was no good at deceiving Jaden. Dec and I finished in the barn and headed for the house. I was dying for some coffee.

"I guess I should call Monica and Neil," I said, hiding a huge yawn.

Dec nodded. "You'd better let Jaden know too, so he can stop the court proceedings." He watched me battle another yawn. "We're lucky things ended this way. It wouldn't be good for Jaden's career if his girlfriend committed a crime."

I gave him a startled look.

"I was afraid you might assault Rodney the next time you saw him," Dec explained.

"Right." I couldn't imagine Dec not exploding if he knew the truth, and yet... well, maybe I shouldn't look a gift horse in the mouth.

I was surprisingly hungry and had two eggs, toast, and two cups of coffee before I felt ready to tackle the phone. I quickly texted Teri and Julia with an update. Then I called Monica, and had to hold the phone away from my ear as she shrieked at the news. I took a deep breath before dialing Jaden's cell.

"Is this a bad time?" I asked hopefully when he answered.

"For you, never," he said warmly. "How are you?"

"Great, actually," I said brightly. "Hades is back. Rodney returned him last night."

"*Rodney* did?" He sounded astonished.

"Well, it must have been him — we went to the barn this morning and Hades was in his stall. Who else could it be, right?" I gave a nervous laugh.

Silence at the other end. I could almost hear the ticking of his mind turning over. "Téa, tell me you didn't have anything to do with this." The warmth was gone, replaced with steel.

"I didn't have anything to do with this," I repeated obediently with my fingers crossed.

More silence. "Well, then. I'll see you tonight."

"I... but... okay." What could I say, that I'd rather not see him for a few days, until I could act unruffled?

I took it easy during the day, deciding not to ride, and even managed to have a short nap in the afternoon. After waking up I had a hot shower, and I felt almost human again by the time boarders began showing up for their evening rides. By nine o'clock only Stephanie and Lisa were still in the tackroom with me. They had been thrilled by Hades' return, and our conversation was lively — until Jaden stepped into the room. He shot me a tight-lipped look and the room went quiet. I turned and busied myself with arranging my bridle in a neat figure-eight so I wouldn't have to look at him. His footsteps closed in; all the little hairs on the back of my neck stood up before I felt his hand settle there, sliding under my hair. His touch was gentle, almost feathery. It wasn't the firm, warm contact I was used to, and I realized with a start that he must be controlling himself carefully. He didn't say a word, his light touch directing me out of the tackroom, into the feedroom, and onto the ladder to the hayloft. He let go while I climbed, and closed the trapdoor quietly before turning to face me. His eyes blazed into mine, but the rest of his face might have been stone. He was in emotional lockdown mode, trying to keep his temper in check, with only the tell-tale twitch of a jaw muscle hinting at the effort he was expending.

I sighed. There was no point in continuing to lie to him since he obviously hadn't believed me.

"I didn't have a choice, Jaden."

"You didn't have a choice but to commit a major crime? What about having some faith in my ability to get Hades back, that wasn't a choice for you?" His voice was carefully controlled too, but his hands clenched into fists at his sides.

"It's not stealing to take back what's yours!" My voice, on the other hand, was already rising. I'd had an overload of adrenaline and a dearth of sleep, and I felt dangerously close to snapping.

Puzzlement crept into his expression. "Tell me something. Have you ever asked yourself what you're willing to risk to achieve your goals?"

My answer was immediate. "Whatever it takes." The look on his face — startled and displeased — made me think that I should have added the caveat, 'as long as it's not illegal or immoral', but it occurred to me that rescuing Hades might fall into one of those categories, in some people's estimation.

"Do you have any concept of the danger you put yourself in? Did you go there alone?" He stepped closer; his eyes were burning so brightly that I had to look away.

"Yes," I admitted.

I snuck a glance at him. He was grabbing his hair with both hands. "My God, Téa! Anything could have happened! What if you'd been caught? You could have been shot or beaten up — didn't you think of *anything* beyond your insane impulse?"

That stung because I thought I'd planned things pretty carefully, considering. "I'm not as helpless as you seem to think," I snapped. "I can take care of myself."

"Oh, really?" His eyes narrowed for a split-second, and then he was pushing me backward. I fell onto the hay bales and he landed on top of me, pinning my body down with his. He grabbed my wrists and pushed them into the hay above my head. Our bodies had been fitted together in many different ways, but not like this — I'd never truly felt his solid, unyielding weight against my entire length. I couldn't move. I could barely breathe.

"Explain to me how you would 'take care of yourself' in this situation," he demanded. His stare bore down as hard as his taut muscles.

"Are you done?" I growled.

In answer, his mouth came down on mine, but I turned my face away furiously. He pulled us up as swiftly as we'd gone down. He started brushing hay off the back of my body with more force than I thought was strictly necessary, and I jerked away from him. I was shaking, not with fear but with anger. In truth, I'd tried very hard not to think about what might happen if I were caught because I couldn't afford to let fear stop me. I'd pulled it off; I didn't want to be reminded of the horrible things that could have happened.

"You can pull away from me now because I'm *letting* you. But against a grown man who actually wanted to hurt you, you *would* be helpless." He said it almost sadly.

Fury rose within me like a cobra strike. I sprang at him, hands upraised and ready. I was almost upon him when his stance registered. He didn't move, but stood passively with his arms at his sides. I tried to stop my forward momentum and stumbled awkwardly into him. He caught my shoulders to steady me, but let go as soon as I was upright. His face was turned downward and slightly to the side, not meeting my gaze.

I stared at him, confused by the rapid change in his attitude. He hadn't tried to defend himself, and there was something so vulnerable in his posture.

"Jaden... I was going to... to..." I stammered, unable to form the words 'hit you', shocked at how wrong they felt in my mouth.

He swallowed before raising his gaze to mine. "It's no less than I deserve, after what I did." His voice was a rough whisper, his eyes tight. I saw it then — under the veil of anger, there was real fear.

I moved closer. "My love, it's okay. You were afraid for me. I understand."

"Yes," he whispered, "so afraid that I almost hurt you myself."

I placed my hands on his chest and ran them upward, over his broad shoulders and down his arms, until I could slip my hands into his.

"You didn't even come close to hurting me physically." I hesitated, trying to find the root of my flash of temper. "I'm used to being underestimated. I'm small, I look young, and I'm a girl. What hurt is that I'm not used to it from *you*."

A shudder passed through him, and he grabbed me in a tight embrace. I felt his heart, beating unusually fast, and knew I'd honestly scared him.

"I'm sorry I worried you," I mumbled against his chest. "If it's any consolation, I doubt I'll ever steal another horse."

He groaned. "What am I going to do with you?"

"I have some ideas," I murmured, pulling his head down to mine. We ended up back on the hay, but he was gentle this time, conciliatory. After a minute he sat up, pulling me with him, and leaned back against the fragrant green stalks behind us. He guided my head onto his shoulder; his other hand looped under my knees and pulled my legs across his lap. A deep sigh escaped him.

"I still can't believe it. You are-"

"Enterprising? Determined? Resourceful?" I suggested.

"I was looking for something along the lines of 'unbalanced'."

I pressed my face into his shirt for a minute, inhaling his beloved scent, before pulling away to search out his eyes. "Jaden, what else could I do? After everything I've gone through, everything I've worked so hard for, how could I have done any differently?" I spoke quietly.

His expression was pained. "You could have *told* me, for starters. I could have gone with you. Better yet, I could have gone in your place."

I was incredulous. "Oh, sure. Because after you said you couldn't even *talk* to Rodney, I should've assumed you'd want to commit a crime." I shook my head sadly. "You're a lawyer now. I wasn't about to risk your job."

"Better my career than your life," he growled.

"It wasn't-" I bit off my argument and took a deep breath. "Let's not fight, okay?" I said softly. I was still shaken by the surge of fury I'd felt towards him. He wrapped both arms around me and rested his cheek against my hair, seeming to sense my thoughts.

"Okay. And I'm truly sorry for using my strength against you, *querida.*" He paused, then went on in a strained whisper. "That's something I swore I'd never do, and I'll never do it again."

His sadness created a choking ball in my throat. I brushed my lips against his neck and strove for lightness in my tone. "*Never?* That's a shame... there are times I really, really like feeling your strength against me."

He made an inarticulate sound, and then my face was in his hands, his lips were moving against mine, and I got to appreciate all over again the things I loved about his strength.

After Jaden left I inventoried my feelings. I found relief that he knew the truth, and happiness that Hades was home and safe, but no pride in what I had done. I regarded myself as honest — okay, I lied to Dec sometimes, but given Dec's personality that was almost inevitable. Even though I'd felt justified in doing it, taking Hades like a thief in the night left me feeling queasy. Even after the fact, though, I couldn't think of another solution, and I resigned myself to living with the guilt. It seemed a fair price to pay.

Seth made a video call from somewhere in France a few days later. His expression was brighter and his smile wider than I'd seen in quite some time.

"I guess traveling agrees with you," I commented approvingly.

"I'm having a fantastic time," he agreed. Then he sobered. "What's happening with Hades?"

"He's home. I kind of stole him back."

He sat in stunned silence for a minute before breaking out a grin. "Holy horse thief, Batgirl."

"Do you think I did the right thing?" I asked. Only to Seth could I admit that I had doubts.

He pursed his lips. "Well, why'd you do it?"

The question surprised me, but I gave it some honest thought before answering. "Partly for Hades; he was so scared and confused... I couldn't leave him at Rodney's." I paused. "But I also did it for me. I've worked too hard and given up too much to have it stolen away."

Seth nodded. "You always did know exactly what you wanted, even when we were kids. And you've never been afraid to go for it. You're running true to form, Sis — I think you did the right thing, for you. Crazy, mind," he smiled widely again, "but right."

I blew out a breath I hadn't realized I was holding. "Thanks, bro."

We talked about his travels for a while, Seth making me laugh as he always did, and afterward, I meandered downstairs feeling better than I had since Hades was taken. I went in search of a snack and found Gran in the kitchen with Dec. She was putting the kettle on.

"Hi, Gran." I went to the cupboard to find cookies to go with the inevitable tea. I leaned against the counter and nibbled one. "Seth's in France. He says hi," I relayed.

Dec just grunted, but Gran said, "Oh, lovely. I do miss that boy."

I snuck Blue a piece of tea biscuit when Dec wasn't looking. "I've been thinking — maybe we should get another dog. Blue's too old to be a guard dog anymore, and Hades getting stolen has made me think we need some more security around here."

Dec raised his thick eyebrows. "Since when do you worry about security?"

Since I'd started having nightmares about Rodney stealing Hades back, that's when. Aloud I said, "Haven't you heard about the tack thefts in the area?"

Dec looked thoughtful. I knew he was aware of the thefts, but he shook his head. "We don't have time for a puppy, Téa. You're always at school or shows, and I've got too many contracts coming up."

"We could adopt an older dog," I suggested. "Shelters are full of adult dogs looking for homes." There was a time when Dec had wanted another Australian Cattle Dog.

"Now's not the time, Téa." He exchanged a look with Gran that made the breath freeze in my lungs.

"Are you going to sell the barn?" I turned to Gran, too scared to guard my expression. She patted my shoulder, but her eyes went to her son.

"We've been discussing it," she acknowledged. "Peter needs the money, and Stacey's been accepted to a college in the U.S. so Penny could certainly use the extra income as well."

My heart started kicking inside my ribcage. "But... but..." I didn't know what to say. My words didn't seem big enough to hold my objections.

"Nothing's decided, and I'm still against it," Dec reassured me. I drew in a breath. He was against it. But for how long?

Jaden's graduation from law school was that week, and as always, I enlisted Julia's help to find a dress. I didn't have much time or patience for shopping so I was relieved when she said, "I'm sure I have something in my closet. Why don't you come over and play dress-up?"

I drove to Oakville right after feeding the next morning. Gran had helped, having stayed overnight yet again. I wondered morosely if she was trying to maximize her time in the house before it was sold but then forced my thoughts to change direction.

Julia greeted me at the door with a smile. That would have been surprising enough, given that she wasn't a morning person, but her mood had been so somber of late that I impulsively hugged her, glad to see her gloom lifting. We went into the large kitchen, all granite and dark wood, for coffee to fortify us before traipsing up to Julia's bedroom.

"You're looking better, Jules," I said as I plopped onto her white bed.

She looked over her shoulder as she opened her walk-in closet. Her face was partially obscured by her long dark brown hair, and her slanting grey eyes glinted with a hint of her former mischief.

"Well, it might have something to do with the fact that I met someone." She disappeared into the closet and came out minutes later with an armful of dresses. She dropped them on the bed and peered at me. "You, on the other hand, look like hell."

"Gee, thanks." I laughed. "Hades' disappearance took about a decade off my life."

"Well, try to get some sleep," she urged as I pulled on the first dress. It was ivory-colored and felt like silk. "Makeup can only do so much."

I nodded. "I want to look good for Jaden's graduation." I hesitated. "We're going through sort of a weird time."

"Weird how? Are you fighting?"

"No... just adjusting to new lifestyles, I guess." Which was true enough; Jaden had an office job for the first time in his life, and I was busier showing than I'd been in years. But the whole truth was that there had been a subtle strain between us ever since he had overpowered me in the hayloft, and I wasn't sure why. I had forgiven him completely, but I got the sense he was still disturbed by the fact that I hadn't told him of my plans to steal Hades. Or maybe it was the theft itself that bothered him. I couldn't say, because the only time I had brought it up his reply had been a curt, "It's done, Téa. Let's leave it be."

Julia shook her head. "Take that off," she said, gesturing to the dress. "If there's making up to be done, then I have the perfect thing." She ignored the pile on the bed and skipped back to the closet, emerging a second later with a bright red, satiny number. "I thought you'd want something a bit more conservative for a graduation, but trust me, when you show up in this Jaden will be tripping over himself to make things right with you."

I slithered into the dress somewhat doubtfully. I'd been planning on something more sober, especially considering that I'd be among family. But when I saw myself in the mirror none of that seemed to matter.

"I have to wear this," I whispered. My straight brown hair hung slightly below my shoulders, and I swept it out of the way to better admire the dress. The fabric hung above my knees and was held up by spaghetti straps. It molded itself to my figure, which had improved thanks to the working out I'd done. I turned and admired the best part — on the back of the dress there was a circle of fabric missing, so that my back was exposed from just above my butt to the bottoms of my shoulder blades, and reaching to the sides of my waist.

"Uh-huh." Julia grinned. "You'll need something to cover yourself for the ceremony — here, try this." She held up a light grey blazer. I shrugged into it and looked again. Perfect.

"Thanks, Jules. So who's the new guy?" I asked as I undressed carefully.

"His name is Al," she said. "He's older, a financial analyst, and he's been so good to me."

"How old is 'older'?"

"About Jaden's age, I guess — twenty-five or so."

"I'm happy for you." I was, too. I thought I'd feel resentment on my brother's behalf but found that I didn't, because Julia had been so down of late that it was a relief to see her smiling again. On the drive home I thought guiltily that I hadn't done much to help my friend get over her sadness. It wasn't only that I'd been busy, either. The truth was that after a while, I had thought that Julia was overreacting. Okay, her parents were getting divorced, but it wasn't like she was going to be shuffled from house to house, a fate many of my friends had endured in childhood. She still had two parents who loved her. From where I was standing, that seemed like a pretty good deal, and I felt bad for not being able to empathize better.

The convocation was held in a venerable stone building with massive pillars across the front. Its oddly rounded shape gave the impression that a giant pebble had been dropped among downtown Toronto's sleek modern architecture. Dec and I rushed in slightly late because he'd had trouble finding parking — or rather, he had insisted on trying to find street parking, and there wasn't any. We found Aunt Paloma and Uncle Peter and settled into our seats, trying to be quiet. I glanced from Dec to Uncle Peter. They were both wearing suits, and it increased their resemblance. Uncle Peter caught my glance and nodded without smiling. Then he turned and spoke to the woman next to him, and I realized she must be his new fiancée. I didn't have time to register more than her general appearance — dark-haired and attractive in a generic way — before my attention was called to the ceremony.

The only graduation I'd ever seen was my own high school graduation. There was more pomp and ceremony at this event, and it was certainly longer, but I didn't find much difference until Jaden's name was called. The rush of pride that made my eyes sting and throat tighten wasn't something I had felt at the end of my time in high school.

After the ceremony, we went outside to wait for Jaden and avoid the crush. It was overcast, and the heavy city smells of hot asphalt and exhaust fumes made the air feel thick.

"This is Christine," Uncle Peter introduced his fiancée. "And this is Paloma, Declan, and my niece, Téa." He gestured to each of us in turn while I frowned. I was the only one whose family connection had been specified, and it made me suspect that Uncle Peter hadn't told Christine of my alliance with his son.

Jaden came out with a laughing group of his friends. He tore himself away, and I admired his graceful, ground-covering stride as he joined us, smiling. His mother got to kiss him first, of course, and then Uncle Peter and Christine, who Jaden had already met. Dec gave him a hug and thumped him on the back.

"I'm proud of you, son," he said gruffly.

Jaden turned to me. My overwhelming joy for him pushed me forward, but something in his face pushed me back, and we ended up sharing only a brief, awkward hug. I pulled away shaken, wondering what had just happened. Granted, we were careful not to flaunt our love around his mom, but this felt like more than an attempt to spare Aunt Paloma's feelings. Our family members were discussing plans to go for lunch; I hazarded a glance at Jaden and found his gaze upon me. Strain was evident in his face. This shouldn't be happening, I thought, frustrated. This should be a day of unadulterated joy for Jaden, but somehow our relationship drama was tainting the moment. Again.

I followed Dec mindlessly back to the truck, barely hearing his muttered complaints about the price of parking. I hunched quietly in the seat during the drive. The restaurant had been Uncle Peter's pick. It was at the top of a high-rise; the elevator doors swept open with a soft chime to reveal a hallway flanked by a glass wall looking down about thirty stories. The restaurant itself was muted, the dark colors brightened by the almost limitless view from windows on all sides.

Dec and I were the last to arrive, and I noticed that neither of the remaining seats was next to Jaden. Oh well, I thought, resigned, I suppose his parents deserve to have him to themselves today. Jaden stood up when I arrived, and he pushed my chair in for me as I sat, which I was embarrassed to realize I rather liked. I felt his hand on my shoulder and a moment later, his voice was at my ear.

"I'm sorry about earlier," he murmured.

I twisted to look up at him. His eyes held regret, and I covered his hand with mine for a second before he returned to his seat. Aunt Paloma stiffened at our exchange, and I noticed Christine looking on with interest. Then I looked again, startled. There was a small dark-haired boy climbing onto her lap — her son, no doubt. I hadn't seen him at the graduation and I wondered where he'd come from. He picked up the knife from his mother's place setting, and she immediately took it out of his hands and placed it out of reach. He started trying to fish ice cubes out of her tall water glass with a fork.

"How's your new job?" Jaden's mother asked him. Her eyes were darkly luminous, and she was immaculately groomed for her son's big day. By all accounts, she had recovered fully from the cancer she'd suffered the previous year. Christine kept shooting nervous little glances her way. I wondered whether she was intimidated, meeting most of Uncle Peter's family — including his gorgeous ex-wife — all at once like this. Aunt Paloma, on the other hand, was treating Christine with polite interest.

"It's going well-" Jaden started to reply. He was interrupted by a thud and startled exclamation as the boy knocked over the water glass.

"Tristan!" His mother moved Tristan into the chair next to hers. "Please, just sit here quietly. Sorry," she apologized to the table at large, wiping up water with her napkin. Jaden helped her until a waiter swooped in.

"Kids will be kids," Uncle Peter said heartily. Jaden's eyes narrowed, but he didn't look at his father.

"So you're enjoying it, then?" Aunt Paloma said when everyone had sat down.

"Yes-"

Tristan started banging on the table with a spoon. His mother quickly took it away from him and began rummaging in her purse while Jaden told us about his new position. "It's a very good firm with a lot of opportunity for advancement."

Christine gave Tristan a scrap of paper and a pen, and she and Aunt Paloma shared a conspiratorial smile.

"I'm glad you're finally starting a real career," Uncle Peter said.

Aunt Paloma bristled like a hedgehog. "Jaden's time was no less valuable when he was playing polo."

"In your family's eyes, maybe," Uncle Peter said dismissively. "But I didn't spend all that money on private schools for him to waste his life being a jock."

I felt my jaw drop open. Jaden had been the polo equivalent of a rock star, one of the best in the world. "Jock" was an insult to that kind of achievement.

"How can you say that?" I demanded.

"Téa," Dec warned.

"Dad," Jaden sighed.

"I'm hungry!" Tristan yelled. "Hungry hungry hungry!"

There was a startled silence punctuated only by Christine's shushing, and then we all began to laugh. Dec got up and found a basket of rolls for Tristan. Jaden caught my eye, his face still touched by laughter, and I felt a spongy softness spreading through me.

Our food arrived. Dec had ordered a steak done so rare that it was almost mooing. He closed his eyes as he savored the first bite, and I smiled, happy to see him enjoying it. I had thought he'd be worried about the prices in this place, but he showed no sign of anything but appreciation. My own mushroom pasta was divine too, and for a few minutes, the only sounds were of cutlery and Christine's quiet comments to her son.

"So," Uncle Peter said once our hunger had been dented. "Are you putting the old homestead up for sale soon?" He looked at Dec expectantly.

I dropped my fork. I stared first at Uncle Peter, acting as though this was an everyday conversation, then at Dec. He finished chewing and wiped his mouth before giving his brother a direct stare.

"I don't think this is the right time for that conversation, Peter."

"Well, when is the right time? You've been putting me off for months."

A rhythmic *thud, thud, thud,* shook the table.

"Don't kick the table, honey," Christine told Tristan. Uncle Peter threw the boy an irritated look.

Aunt Paloma leaned forward. "Would you like to learn to count in Spanish?" She smiled at the boy, and Tristan nodded shyly.

"Téa's still in school," Dec told Peter. "All her income comes from the barn, and mom's still too invested to let it go."

"Mom should be moving to Florida at her age, not handling horses anymore."

Tristan, having apparently learned enough Spanish, bolted out of his seat and started circling the table at a run.

"Tristan!" Uncle Peter snapped.

Jaden reached out one long arm and caught Tristan around the middle in mid-flight. He pulled the wriggling bundle onto his lap.

Uncle Peter leaned close, his face taut with anger. "You do NOT run in a restaurant, do you understand?" The boy drew back, wide-eyed.

Jaden's arm wrapped around the small shoulders. "He's just a child," he said quietly. "It's not fair to expect him to hold still for so long." He smiled down at Tristan. "Hey, big guy. Do you like airplanes?" At the boy's nod, he got up and led Tristan by the hand toward one of the wide windows, presumably to spot some planes. Christine's eyes followed them, her expression soft.

"You have a wonderful son," she said to Aunt Paloma. I noticed she didn't include Uncle Peter in her statement, and I wondered if she was angry with him. I would be.

I was just finishing my pasta when Jaden and Tristan wandered back. "Would you like to see the view?" Jaden asked quietly. I very carefully didn't look at anyone else, but rose and accompanied Jaden to the restaurant's front door, keeping a respectable distance between us. As we stepped into the glass-sided hallway I blew out a breath.

"Yes," Jaden agreed, taking my hand. We strolled down the hallway. Jaden walked right next to the glass but I hung back a bit. It looked like a really long way down.

He stopped once we were around the corner, out of sight of the restaurant's door. The hallway was deserted.

"Great progress we're making with our family," I commented.

He passed a hand over his face. "They're priceless, aren't they? Maybe we should elope."

"Okay," I joked, "but not this weekend, the Classic's at Palgrave."

His face fell. "Oh. A group of us are going out to celebrate graduation — I was hoping you'd come."

"Sorry." I was, too. It was warmer in the hall, and I slipped off the blazer I'd been wearing. Jaden took it and slung it over his shoulder. "I'll do my best to make it up to you," I promised, looping my arms around his neck. His hands went to my hips and he pulled me to him before sliding his hands over the silky fabric. When he got to the bare circle of my back he paused.

"Oh. My. Lord. What are you doing to me?" His mouth came down on mine, and his lips worked insistently while his hands explored the contours of the dress, returning again and again to the bare circle.

"I thought you'd like this dress."

"Like it? It's all I can do not to tear it off you," he growled against my lips. "Red is definitely your color." He stopped kissing me long enough to turn me around and survey the dress's back. I felt his hands, hot on my skin, and reached up to lift my hair out of the way.

"You've certainly gotten stronger. I can see the muscles in your back move."

I shrugged, enjoying the feeling of both my muscles moving under his touch, and his appreciation of them. "It's important for me to be able to keep up with Hades."

Jaden turned me back to face him. He wore his trademark wicked smile. "It's also damn sexy." He set about proving his words, but he soon took a step back, holding my shoulders and breathing hard. "I'm going to need a minute before we go back in there."

When he was composed we walked back into the restaurant. He kept one hand on the bare skin of my back, and when I paused, intending to put the blazer back on, he simply gave a small shake of his head and kept walking. He sat me in my chair and draped the blazer on the back before returning to his own seat, ignoring the icy silence from his parents. Dec raised his eyebrows at me, but he didn't look perturbed.

As we said our goodbyes Uncle Peter gave Dec a meaningful look. "We'll talk soon."

I didn't have time to grill Dec for more answers because I left for the Palgrave show the next day. I brought several students, along with Hades and Cal. It was usually a good show, and I was looking forward to it, but it rained all through the first day. I rode my horses wearing a large poncho which also served to protect my saddle.

Cal had been to a few schooling shows, but nothing as large or impressive as this. He craned his neck in interest at all the new sights, and I walked him all over the grounds, getting him used to the atmosphere. Our biggest problem was that he was an unusually gregarious horse, and he thought every one of the hundreds of new horses on the grounds should be his friend. I had to constantly remind Cal that he was here to work with *me*, not play with other horses.

After I'd put Cal away, damp but clean, I saddled Hades and headed back into the drizzle. Days like this made me question why I loved competing. At horse shows you were sometimes cold and sometimes broiling, and sometimes both on the same day. You ate bad food and didn't get enough sleep, and spent lengthy periods of time waiting interspersed with periods of frantic activity. It was insanity, really. All for those brief, luminous moments when you and your horse understood each other completely, your bodies danced in flawless harmony, and you hopefully did the job better than anyone else that day.

Hades hadn't been himself since he'd returned from Rodney's. He seemed physically healthy, and I had hoped that a simple return to his usual routine, diet, and friends would set things right, but he was unmistakably tense.

I let him walk calmly around the grounds before heading for the schooling ring, mulling over his mood. I was sure that Hades hadn't been started properly as a youngster. Fortunately, the days of thinking in terms of "breaking" a horse were long past for most people. Reputable trainers no longer used the violent methods of our predecessors, choosing instead to teach their young horses steadily from birth, forming a relationship of mutual trust. Naturally, some trainers were better at it than others. Hades might be dominant on the ground, but under saddle, I had come to realize that much of his behavior was defensive — he was protecting himself based on bad experiences he'd had as a youngster. Maybe his size and general pushiness had led his riders to be too rough with him, but whatever the case, it had taken well over a year for me to coax him into relaxing. He had offered me his trust bit by bit, and I had given mine in return, riding him as kindly as possible. The sense I got now was that his trust was shaken. Maybe someone had ridden him badly at Rodney's, or maybe it was simply that I hadn't been there when he'd needed me. In either case, I couldn't hold it against him, but only hoped that time would convince him he was safe again.

Horses are the most generous of creatures. I sometimes think they must find us deeply strange — we put cold metal bars in their mouths, we strap all kinds of bizarre equipment onto their bodies, and we ask them to leap over obstacles that any sensible creature would go around. Yet they humor us with good grace, giving us their all, and even love us despite our perplexing and often onerous demands.

I discussed my worries with Karen over dinner. We were a big, noisy group: Karen's three students — including the obnoxious Brittney — and her groom, plus the three students, two grooms and one boarder from our barn. We'd gone to a local family-style restaurant and sat at adjoining tables, frequently leaning over to talk to one another.

"Hades isn't himself," I said as I started on my salad. A side effect of the increased competition I'd been doing was that I was making an effort to eat better.

"You know him better than anyone," Karen reminded me. "What do you think is wrong?"

I hesitated, wondering whether she would dismiss my suspicion. *She's not Dec*, I reminded myself. "I think he was scared by what happened at Pépinière."

Karen nodded thoughtfully. "If that's all it is, he should get over it after a show or two."

After dinner, we organized the ride back to the motel. Emma's parents took three girls with them and Melanie, a boarder, took the rest. I had my own car since Palgrave wasn't far from home, but I didn't take any passengers. I had decided to head back to the showgrounds, unable to shake the anxiety I'd been feeling. Maybe Hades' tension was rubbing off on me. He had been microchipped days after his return, so his identity would never again be in question, but Rodney didn't know that and I couldn't help but worry that he might try again. I'd even discussed it with Jaden before the show, although he hadn't been concerned.

"It was a crime of opportunity, Téa, and he's lost the element of surprise. I doubt that he'll go near Hades."

Maybe he wouldn't, but I was uneasy all the same. No wonder Hades was acting funny, I thought as I parked the car. At least it had stopped raining, but the air was so damp I felt like I was growing mold. I went to see Hades and said hi to him. He was chewing hay and barely acknowledged me, so I worked my way down the row of horses. I paused in front of Cameo's stall. The pony had to raise her nose up high to reach over her stall door, and I smiled as I patted her grey cheek and fondled her silky ears. She was such a sweet thing.

I was headed two rows over to check on Karen's horses when a voice stopped me in my tracks. Rodney. He was walking outside the barn with another man, and he seemed to feel my gaze because he turned and saw me. He held my stare for a minute before swaggering up to me, leaving the other man behind.

"Well, well," he sneered. "Funny how you seem to have found that horse."

There's nothing to be afraid of, I told myself fiercely, but my heart was rabbiting inside my chest. I tried to smile sweetly. "I guess you were right all along, Rodney — it was a case of mistaken identity. *Our* horse was safe at home."

His rodent-like face twisted with fury, but he spun and marched off, forcing his companion to hurry to keep up. I put a hand to my chest as though I could soothe the galloping beast inside. I was shaking, and I chided myself for overreacting. Nothing had happened beyond the exchange of a few words. I looked around. The showgrounds were fairly quiet at this hour. Darkness was approaching, and grooms would soon appear to do night checks. Security guards would be in place overnight, but there was no way I was leaving now.

I went back to the car and dug an old sleeping bag out of my trunk, kept there for emergencies such as this. It was still too early to go to sleep, so I dumped it in the tackroom we were sharing with Karen's barn and checked on her horses.

"Hey," Alex called from down the aisle. I wandered over as he fastened a stall door. "You look like you've seen a ghost," he remarked.

"Worse. I've seen a fiend." I explained what had happened.

He gave a low whistle. "It's like you're in a suspense novel."

"Yeah, only it's a lot more fun when it's fiction." I relayed my plans to spend the night.

"Why don't you stay in the camper with us?"

"It's a nice offer, but it would defeat the purpose of me staying to guard Hades." Not to mention that Jaden had not been overjoyed the last time I'd stayed with Alex.

"Well, we have a cot you can use in the stall if you want." Now that was an offer I couldn't pass up. We squelched across the wet grass to the trailer, and Alex carried the cot back for me. After looking at how much space Hades took up in his stall, we decided to set it up in Cal's stall instead.

"Well, goodnight," he said after I'd unrolled my sleeping bag. He seemed reluctant to leave me there.

"Goodnight. I'll call you if anything goes bump in the night." As his footsteps faded I sat on the cot and pulled out my phone. I called the motel to let everyone know I wouldn't be back, and then I called Jaden.

"What?" he exclaimed when I'd covered the situation. "Téa, you can't spend the night in a temp stall. It's rainy and cold out."

"I'll get a horse blanket if I need one."

"It's not safe! Have you alerted the security guards yet?"

"What can I say? If I tell them Rodney once stole my horse, it'll raise the whole question of how I got Hades back. You're the one who told me you can't accuse someone without proof."

He made a frustrated sound. "I don't like this. Maybe I should drive up there."

"And what, stay in here with me?" I sighed. "Jaden, you have to work in the morning."

"I'm going to be up half the night worrying about you anyway."

"Don't! Look, Jaden, you're right — I'm cold, and I'm a bit nervous, but this is my life. Grooms sleep in tackrooms all the time. I'm staying

98

right here." I was getting angry and it showed in my tone. I'd called Jaden for comfort, but instead he was adding his fears to my own.

He started to say something but apparently thought better of it. It was his turn to sigh. "Are you sure you're safe?"

"They've got security here, remember?"

"Call me at the first hint of a suggestion of trouble. Even if you just get lonely."

I felt my face soften in the darkening stall. "Okay." Then, because I wanted to hear his voice a bit longer, I went on. "Something's up with Hades. He's been upset all day and I don't know why." That was one of the best parts of my relationship with Jaden; we could discuss our horses for hours, and neither of us ever got tired of it.

"Why don't you try using your gift to find out what's troubling him?"

I squirmed uncomfortably, even though I was alone and no one could have overheard. Cal turned his head to look at me inquisitively. Jaden was the only one who called my oversensitivity a 'gift', but then, he was the only person who knew about it other than Seth, who laughingly called it my superpower.

"It's not like I can read his mind," I almost whispered. "At most, I'll be able to tell how he's feeling right now, while he's safe in his stall."

"Any insight is better than none," Jaden said. "You can try tomorrow while you ride him as well. You don't take full advantage of your ability, *querida* — it could give you an edge."

I smiled at his confidence and wished him goodnight. When I got up and unzipped my sleeping bag, Cal came over to investigate, poking his nose into the bag and trying to look under the cot until he almost tipped it over. I moved him out of the way and climbed in fully dressed, zipping the bag up all the way. Cal's ears went on full alert and he gave a small snort at the sound of the zipper.

"It's just a zipper, silly." I lay my head on my arm. A pillow would have been nice, and I toyed with the idea of going to find a sweater in my car. Too much trouble, I decided. Cal came closer, his shape indistinct in the now almost-full dark. He wiggled his upper lip in my hair, then moved his nose over my face and blew softly.

I stroked his face, my hand gliding effortlessly over the super-fine hairs. "G'night, buddy." I was glad I was sharing a space with him and not Hades. While Hades wouldn't intentionally hurt me, he was not only larger but a lot less careful than Cal.

My horse went back to his hay, and I closed my eyes, suddenly sleepy. Nighttime sounds washed over me; crickets and frogs sang melodies punctuated by the rustle of horses and occasional, quiet voices in the distance. As my body relaxed my mind began to wander. Remembering Jaden's suggestion, I opened myself up to the feelings around me. The sensation was hard to describe — it was as though I was throwing the doors to my chest wide open. At the same time I tried to keep my mind as blank as possible, although my concern over Hades and fear of Rodney's return did flare up intermittently.

It was sometimes hard for me to tell whether an emotion was my own or not, because I felt it by experiencing it. Context was usually an important clue. Nervousness washed through me, and I began tensing up. Was this my fear *for* Hades, or his own fear? I breathed deeply, allowed my muscles to relax, and examined the emotion. As I sampled it again I realized it couldn't be mine; it was too raw, too unfocused, too... young. It was like a child's fear of the dark. And it wasn't Hades. My eyes sprang open and I turned my head to peer at Cal in the gloom. His silhouette stood stock-still, head raised, ears swiveling and alert for danger. I heaved a frustrated breath. What did he have to worry about? Now I was no closer to deciphering Hades than before.

"Go to sleep, Cal," I murmured, and proceeded to take my own advice.

Six

It was a long night. Every kick, whinny and unidentified sound woke me up, and at one point I was shivering so hard that I got up and went to the tackroom for a wool cooler to layer over the sleeping bag. The horses woke up at dawn, so I followed suit, stretching and yawning until my jaw cracked.

I checked on all the horses before visiting the Port-o-Potties. I needed coffee, stat, so I approached a girl who was braiding a horse a few doors down from Cameo and asked her to keep an eye on our horses. I drove to the nearest coffee shop, got a large coffee and settled at a table with a sigh. I called the motel and told my crew I'd feed so they wouldn't have to hurry, but the grooms were already leaving to go braid their horses, so after texting Jaden — *I survived* — I went for a much-needed shower at the motel.

If the night had seemed long, the day was even longer. I was stiff and tired from the night before, Hades was jumpy, and I was too busy. Emma had brought another little girl from our barn to help groom her pony, and I'd brought Erin, one of my students, but it wasn't enough. Hades needed a full-time groom to himself because I had to spend time coaching, as well as riding other horses. On top of that, Melanie interrupted me with questions and requests for help at every turn.

Karen shook her head. "She's not good for your rep, that one. I have a requirement at my barn that anyone who comes to shows has to be in training with me."

That would probably be a good idea, I thought. We wanted to make showing accessible to all our riders, but Melanie only took the occasional lesson and her Thoroughbred mare, Asia, was a bit much for her to handle.

The sun was trying to peek out when I rode Cal into his first class. It was a training class and the jumps were small: three-quarters of a meter, or about two foot six. Since Cal was only four, he had much to learn before we jumped courses of any size. There was an entire four-year-old jumper circuit that I didn't participate in because I didn't want to jump Cal that high yet. Four was barely adult for a horse, and Warmbloods like Cal tended to mature later than other breeds. If I didn't overwork him now he could still be jumping when he was twenty, so I was determined to keep our progress slow and steady, despite the pressure to do otherwise.

"Number 241, Renaissance Man," the announcer called, and I felt a slight thrill at hearing Cal's show name in public for the first time. I walked into the ring rather than trotting, in order to give Cal time to look around. There was so much for young jumpers to learn beyond the physical act of jumping: how to handle different types of footing, how to recognize particular kinds of fences and jump them appropriately, how to stretch out into a gallop one second and the next, compress their bodies tightly like an accordion, all while their lungs are pumping and their hearts are pounding and adrenaline is blurring everything into a haze of excitement.

Since horses are prey animals, cooperation at speed is usually a difficult thing for them to master — to a horse, adrenaline and running mean "escape the predator!" Most of all, they had to learn to trust and work in tandem with their rider, no matter what mood they woke up in, even if they had a small undetected ache or pain, and regardless of what scary and distracting things were taking place just outside the ring. Those strenuous physical, mental, and emotional demands were the reason that horses rarely made it to the Olympics before their teens.

And it all starts here, I thought as I asked Cal to canter. He sprang forward immediately; I couldn't fault his obedience. As I lined up our first fence I strove to block out thoughts of what I'd felt from him the night before, but it began again, the buffeting of doubt and unease keeping rhythm with his strides, although this time it was interspersed with moments of excitement. I tuned it out as best I could and focused on the mental aspects of our ride — I calculated distances and carefully planned corners and rebalanced Cal in plenty of time for lead changes. He jumped a careful round, clean but slow, and we walked out while I tried to smother my frustration.

I took a breath to calm myself and patted Cal's flame-colored shoulder. His body was smaller than Hades', and his neck was slimmer, but his ears were quite far away from me and he was still growing. The most important difference between them wasn't size, it was attitude. Even when Hades had had rider issues, his attitude toward the jumps was always, "Let me at'em." I was beginning to wonder if Cal had what it took to be a jumper.

Hades' big classes weren't until the weekend, and the Donalds were coming to watch. I didn't know what to tell them about their horse's fretfulness, and I was apprehensive. The only wealthy horse owner I'd ever dealt with was Marty's, and that hadn't ended well. I decided not to say anything before Saturday's class because I figured Hades might turn out to be fine, although my gut disagreed. Sure enough, he was distracted during our class and had two rails down, keeping us out of the ribbons.

It was finally warm and sunny, and I walked around on Hades to cool him down before going to find his owners. I jumped off, feeling a slight jar in my ankles, and slowly pulled the reins over Hades' head. I didn't meet the Donald's eyes until I had to.

"What happened out there?" Neil asked. There was a frown on his face.

I took a deep breath. "I think Hades is still upset about being stolen."

Neil looked skeptical. "You can't tell me the horse remembers that," he said.

"Actually, horses have very good memories," I told him. "And look at it from his point of view — he went to a show and tried really hard, he knew he did well, and next thing he knows he's taken to a dark place he doesn't like, with none of the comforts of home and no friends to turn to. Small wonder he's nervous."

"Oh, poor Hades." Monica's hand flew to her mouth, but Neil seemed unconvinced. He was a medium-sized man with a deep tan and grey hair that was almost gone on top. He was also the only man I'd ever seen — other than rap singers — who wore a heavy gold chain. But he owned a very successful import business and I supposed he hadn't made all that money by being dumb.

"Well, what do we do about it?" he asked.

I looked around for Karen, but she wasn't in sight. Then I squared my shoulders. As much as I might want someone to back me up right now, especially someone more experienced and credible than me, these were my clients. As Karen had repeatedly told me, learning to relate to clients was as much a part of being a successful big-name rider as dealing with the horses.

"We start off by giving him some time." Hades chose that moment to rub his face against me, almost knocking me over. So much for dignity. I recovered and scratched him, trying to find the itchy spot under his bridle. Monica smiled.

"Hopefully after an uneventful show or two, he'll realize there's nothing to worry about and be back to himself again," I continued.

"And if he isn't?" Neil asked.

I hesitated. I honestly didn't know what I'd do if Hades didn't get over his fear. "I don't know," I admitted. "But I'll do whatever it takes to make him feel secure again. I've been sleeping in the stall next to him this whole show."

"What?" Monica exclaimed. "You can't be at your best if you don't get a good night's sleep."

Neil, however, nodded approvingly. "I like that kind of dedication. All right then, we'll hope he's better tomorrow."

Hades placed fifth in his class the following day, which was enough to reassure the Donalds. I, on the other hand, didn't feel any better. Hades hadn't been himself, I'd simply ridden him more carefully and compensated for his preoccupation.

After the Donalds left we started preparing for the trip home. When everything was ready I took Hades out to graze, and Erin took Cal. Holding Hades wasn't very relaxing; he seemed to feel that the best patches of grass were always two steps further away, and he made a beeline for every puddle because he loved to paw in them.

"Oh no you don't," I chided, on his third attempt to drag me into water. "You can't get your shipping bandages all wet and muddy." Brittney threw us a contemptuous look as she flounced past. She'd been doing that during the whole show unless contempt was her habitual expression, and it irked me to no end that she'd beaten me in my last two classes.

When Dec arrived there was a flurry of activity as we loaded first equipment, then horses into the trailer.

After the last horse was in, Karen turned to Dec. "You said you had stalls open, so I'm sending a boarder your way. She's a bit of a handful but I'm sure you can handle her." She grinned at him.

His return smile was the genuine smile of old friends. "As long as she pays her board, I can handle her."

"Oh, I promise you board won't be a problem. She's the only child of a woman who made a fortune in business before deciding to have a kid almost as an afterthought. The mother is still CEO of her company and works crazy hours even though she's in her sixties. She's given her kid lots of money and few rules, and you can imagine the result."

Dec nodded and glanced over at me thoughtfully. I'm not sure why, since I'd been raised under opposite conditions.

"Her name's Brittney," Karen went on, and I groaned. Great. I was going to have Attitude Girl in my own barn. That thought, combined with the mediocre results I'd gotten with my horses, made my drive home a somber one even though my students had all done well.

Returning I felt, as always, the expansion of my heart as it caught sight of the gently rolling green hills of home, but even that wasn't enough to shake my mood. I pulled into our long driveway well ahead of the horse trailer, and gladly got out of my car and stretched in the soft evening air. If only I could see Jaden I'd feel better, but the next day was Monday and he'd have to be at work. I wandered into the house for a drink before the horses arrived. I was kicking off my shoes when I sensed movement.

"Surprise," Jaden said quietly.

"Oh!" I whirled around and fell against him in one motion, my arms constricting around him like a vise. I nestled my face into his shirt as a low laugh rumbled through him. His arms closed around me, pushing out my grim thoughts and holding in the wonderful feelings that flooded through me at his touch.

We said nothing for several minutes, our mouths being otherwise occupied. I was vaguely aware that I was sweaty and disheveled from the show, but I couldn't quite bring myself to care as his hands ran over me, drawing thrilling trails.

"I thought you had to work tomorrow," I murmured finally.

"I missed you too much to stay away." He cupped his hand to my cheek as we heard Dec's truck pull in. He sighed. "Come on, I'll help you unload."

Jaden didn't stay long. I hadn't seen enough of him lately, and his absence was scooping out a hollow inside me, albeit a smaller, less painful one than the cavern Seth had dug.

I groaned when I rolled out of bed at five to seven the next morning. I pulled on sweats and stumbled to the barn to find Dec already serving hay.

"We should get someone else to feed on Mondays," I grumbled. It was the horses' day off, but even though I didn't have to teach I still had to get up to feed, thus losing my only possible chance to sleep in.

"Gran and I have been feeding on all the days you're at shows," Dec pointed out. "And you know Alan needs the extra time in the summer."

I grabbed an armful of hay, the stalks scratching my arms. "Maybe I can get Catherine to come in," I mused.

"Do you plan to pay her to come in for one hour?"

"Oh. Right." I sighed and kept feeding, still feeling put-upon. One day a week to sleep past seven in the morning didn't seem like too much to ask, did it?

After feeding, Dec made coffee while I toasted some English muffins for us. I told him about the show and he updated me on happenings at the barn, and we sat down companionably while we ate. I smiled at him suddenly, feeling closer to him than I had for a long time. He grinned back and patted my hand before getting up and heading for his office.

After breakfast, I threw in a load of laundry and decided to catch up with my friends. My text to Teri drew an immediate response.

Guess what? I'll be at Woodbine in July, yay!

I gave a happy little hop in my room. Woodbine racetrack was in Toronto, just an hour away. Next, I texted Seth, and then Julia since it was too early to call her. Finally, I called Jaden.

"I was so happy to see you yesterday," I said once I'd ascertained he wasn't busy with work.

"Likewise. I'm going to spend the weekend at your place. Can you ride to the polo club with me on Saturday?"

"Oh." My entire body slumped in disappointment. "I'll be at a show next weekend. We're leaving Thursday."

"Again?"

I checked the much scribbled-on calendar on my wall as I spoke. "Yes... in fact I'll be gone almost every weekend," I informed him sadly.

I felt tension mushrooming at the other end of the phone. "Really. Well, when am I supposed to see you?"

"I could come to your place tonight," I suggested.

"I'm working late." Frustration had crept into his tone.

My mind flashed to a sudden image of his attractive boss, London, with her hand on Jaden's arm. "Why is your boss making you stay late again? I thought you weren't doing anything important at work."

"You're familiar with the phrase 'paying your dues'? That's what I'm doing. I'm the lowest man on the totem pole, and even after I'm fully qualified I'll have the least experience. Long hours are part and parcel of this career," he explained patiently, even though it wasn't the first time he'd warned me about his demanding schedule.

"So I won't see you for a whole week?" I asked in a small voice. It seemed like an impossibly long time.

His tone warmed by several degrees. "I'll find a way to see you, *querida*, even if I have to track you down at the show."

I wasn't exactly in a sunny mood the next morning, and it wasn't helped by the arrival of Brittney. Brittney, and her entourage. She waltzed in surrounded by three friends whose heads swiveled around as though they'd never been in a barn before. I was on my way to turn Cal out but I lingered in his stall for a minute to watch them.

Alan, friendly as always, introduced himself and showed Brittney to the two freshly bedded stalls that awaited her horses. "You'll like it here," he assured her, "folks are nice."

Brittney barely glanced at the stalls. She didn't smile, just let her eyes travel disdainfully around the aisle. My fingers tightened around the cotton leadrope, and Cal nudged me.

"Hold your horses," I muttered to him. I led him into the aisle. "Brittney." I nodded to her, determined to at least try to be civil. She was a client now, after all. Her eyebrows rose, but she didn't respond. I saw her turn to one of her friends and whisper something as I went outside.

Brittney's horses arrived soon afterward, swaddled in so many bandages, blankets, and neck protectors that it was hard to see any bits of horse peeping out. I recognized Salsa, the gorgeous bay mare Hades had almost jumped on. The other horse was a light grey gelding with legs like pillars and a kind face. Brittney led Salsa into a stall while the van driver took the grey. Brittney closed the stall, leaving her horse fully dressed, and looked around.

"Where are the grooms?" she demanded.

"What grooms? We're not at a show," I said absentmindedly. I was occupied with admiring her horses.

"You mean you don't have grooms for the barn?" The look she gave me was almost panicked, and I suppressed a snicker.

"Um, no. We all take care of our own horses."

Her eyes widened for a second, but she soon managed a sneer. "Well, I suppose it's to be expected in a hole like this. I'll get my own groom." She turned to the knot of girls who were clumped in the aisle. "Alicia, come help me," she ordered. She began removing Salsa's bandages, and the black-haired Alicia sprang over to help.

I had turned out two more horses by the time Dec strode into the barn. He smiled at Brittney with his hand outstretched, his pale blue gaze assessing. "Sorry I wasn't here to meet you when you came in. I'm Dec Foster. Welcome to Shady Lane."

I expected Brittney's usual distasteful response, but she dropped the blanket she was holding and shook Dec's hand, smiling prettily.

"Mr. Foster, it's so nice to officially meet you. I remember you from Pépinière, of course."

I gaped at her. She hadn't given any indication of noticing us when Dec trailered her horse to that show.

"Call me Dec, please."

"Okay, Dec." She tilted her head slightly and toyed with a lock of her chin-length red hair. My eyebrows were edging toward my hairline at the sudden change in her attitude, but I gave a mental shrug, pulled on my cap and headed outside to teach my first lesson of the day. To my relief, Brittney was gone by the time I finished.

"Thanks for the new boarder, she's a peach," I told Karen sarcastically when she came in the next morning.

Karen grinned. "Isn't she though? I've never been so happy to see someone move out of my barn. I'll miss her horses, though. Especially Keeping Time."

I spun to face her, suddenly alert. "Keeping Time? You mean *the* Keeping Time?"

"The one from the winning team at the Pan Am games? Yup, that's the one. I wondered if you'd recognize her."

I felt the twist and pull of something ugly inside of me. Jealousy, anger, and frustration roiled together in a dark brew. How was it fair that someone like Brittney, who'd never done a day's work in her life and who wasn't even a halfway nice person, ended up with a world-class horse that everyone had expected to see at the next Olympics? I felt my mouth press into a tight line as I marched over to Salsa's stall.

"I thought she looked familiar," I muttered.

Karen joined me. "It's an honor to have a horse like that in the barn. George over there is no slouch either — he won the Nation's Cup at Hickstead four years ago."

My jaw dropped open, shock momentarily releasing its tension.

"Her mother gave me a budget and told me to find Brittney the best horses I could within that amount," Karen explained.

"An amount big enough to run a small country," I guessed.

"Pretty much." Karen's shrewd brown eyes settled on me. "She's not a bad rider, Téa. She's put in the hours, but... you're better. I don't want you to go wasting your energy on jealousy. I've seen the damage that can do to a person."

I looked away from her, struggling to quell the protests that swelled inside me. I had worked tirelessly for what felt like my entire life to get to this point. And what did I have to show for it? A talented but extremely complicated jumper whose owners could decide to replace me at any moment, and a young horse of questionable ability who I could barely afford to compete with. A backbreaking job, long hours, and strained relationships. It was hard not to feel that I'd be better off with a rich parent buying me an experienced, uber-trained horse who could teach me the ropes.

I felt Karen's hand on my shoulder. "I know it's hard, kid, but you've learned things that Brittney will never know. You've *had* to. And someday those things will allow you to beat her."

My morale was down to my ankles as I went to get Cal ready to ride. I found his stall empty.

"Alan, did you put Cal out? I told you I was riding him this morning, remember?" I tried to mask the edge of annoyance in my voice. I didn't want the extra work of cleaning Cal up if he'd rolled; there were still a few muddy spots from last week's rain.

"Sorry, I forgot." Alan appeared in a stall door. "That new girl's horses have got my routine messed up."

"Messed up how?"

"Well, I normally turn out in order, but I'm not supposed to touch'em — her groom is gonna turn them out."

I hadn't thought Brittney was serious about getting her own groom for the barn. I trudged outside to retrieve Cal, shaking my head. He was waiting by the gate, and when I clipped on the leadrope I was preoccupied — okay, maybe fuming was more accurate — so it took me a minute to realize that something was amiss. My horse's first step jerked me back to full alertness as his head bobbed down next to me.

I stopped and turned to him. "Crap." I cursed silently as I noticed the raised foreleg. I squatted down next to him, prepared to examine his leg, but the cause of his limp was immediately apparent — he had lost a shoe, and with it, a sizeable piece of hoof. The shoe was dangling crookedly from one side of his foot, and I picked up his hoof to pull it off, not wanting the now-exposed nails to do any further damage. I tried to pry off the shoe the way our farrier had taught me, but I couldn't do it with my bare hands. I lowered Cal's hoof gently back to the ground and looked around. We were at the gate to the large grass paddock right in front of the barn. To my right were the driveway, the shed, and our square, red-brick house. Right in front of me was a wide path that led to the main riding ring and two turnout paddocks, and beyond, the trail into the woods. The barn was just to the left, but as my eyes scanned the normally-busy area I didn't see a soul. Karen must have joined Dec for coffee, her usual habit, and it was a bit early for students.

"Alan!" I tried calling. No response, other than Cal turning to look at me questioningly. I stroked his face. "I don't suppose you'd stay here if I went to get pliers, would you? You'll mess up your foot if you walk on it." I had just decided to move Cal the short distance to the fence and tie him when a familiar car turned into the driveway.

"Gran!" I called in relief. Gran hurried over right away; she would have known immediately that something was wrong from the way we were standing immobile by the gate.

"Cal threw a shoe," I explained when she got close enough.

"Not to worry," she consoled us, patting Cal briskly. "I'll be right back." A minute later she had Cal's hoof between her knees and was expertly prying his shoe off, and I thought how lucky we were that Gran, despite her white hair and thickened figure, was still strong and healthy.

We walked slowly back into the barn, and I was putting Cal on the crossties as Karen came in. "Cal threw a shoe, and a chunk of his hoof went with it," I told her glumly. "His feet were in perfect shape. How could this happen?"

Karen and Gran both turned incredulous looks on me. "How many times have you seen this kind of thing, Téa? You know better than to ask that question." Karen's response stopped short of being severe, but it was clear she wouldn't stand for me feeling sorry for myself, and somewhere inside me — although I refused to acknowledge it at the moment — lurked the knowledge that she was right. Injuries were an unavoidable part of life. I heaved a sigh as Karen bent over Cal's foot, already deep in conversation with Gran about possible treatments.

"I'll call the farrier," I mumbled.

After we'd ascertained that Cal had no other injuries I brought him back to his stall. A girl wandered by as I stepped out. She was in her twenties, thin, with lank brown hair.

"Hi, uh, I'm looking for Brittney's horses? I'm Elise?" she said timidly. Even her name sounded like a question. I wondered how this mouse of a girl would fare working for Brittney, but I showed her where

Salsa and George were stabled and she went right to work, greeting them with obvious familiarity.

I was expecting Julia since we were having a schooling session with Karen, but she hadn't shown up by the time I was done preparing Hades. I was pulling out my phone to text her when I heard her bell-like laugh coming from the tackroom. She emerged a second later, encumbered by all her supplies and followed by a bemused-looking man. Julia dumped her tack and slipped an arm through his before leading him over to meet me.

"Téa, this is Al," she said. She gazed meltingly up at him.

I wiped my hand on my pants before shaking his and thought I detected the hint of a wince. Al had hair like a crow's wing, light brown skin, and intense dark eyes.

"It's a pleasure," he said. He was wearing designer labels from head to polished toe. I wasn't normally one to notice such things, so I figured it must be unusually obvious.

Our lesson began and Brittney arrived and hopped onto George, who Elise had been hand-walking around the ring. I watched horse and rider throughout our lesson and had to admit they were impressive. George flowed over the jumps and acquiesced instantly to all of Brittney's commands. There were none of those split-second differences of opinion that sometimes characterized my rides with Hades. Julia rode well too, although she kept glancing over at Al, which earned her a rebuke from Karen. For his part, Al seemed more absorbed by his phone than by Julia.

We were walking on a long rein discussing our show schedule when the silver lining to Cal's injury struck me. Hades was only entered in one class, on Sunday. I'd been planning to spend four days at the show because of Cal and a student.

"Karen, would you mind schooling one of my riders at the show? The one who's leasing Winter?" After Seth left Dec had expected Winter to be used as a full-time school horse, but I couldn't bear to see his willing nature eroded by so many inexperienced riders, so I had arranged a lease as soon as I could. He was the perfect mount for Erin, who was a tentative, though competent, rider.

I texted Jaden before I'd even finished putting Hades away.

112

I'll be waiting with open arms on Saturday. I had barely pushed 'Send' when Hades' teeth closed next to my phone with an audible snap. He didn't like phones or anything else that drew away attention that was rightfully his.

"Cut it out," I told him, but I wasn't angry, and the glint in his eye said he knew it.

There was always work to catch up on, so I found ways to keep busy over the next two days. The farrier came and reassured me that the damage to Cal's hoof looked worse than it was. He filled the hole with epoxy, reset Cal's shoes, and Cal was ready to ride, though we'd have to minimize the jumping for a couple of weeks.

On Friday evening I went outside to wait for Jaden. A light drizzle silvered the sky. It wasn't unpleasant after the heat of a June day, and I sat on the rarely-used chairs on the covered porch, breathing in the smell of ozone and feeling content. Jaden's car came down the road a little fast, and I smiled at his hurry. He parked by the shed and ran to the house; I met him on the steps. I melted against him like honey in the sun, his embrace the only thing keeping me from leaking through the planks. Where I'd been content, now I was overflowing; the skies were brighter, the world in sharper focus, and my heart so light it threatened to float me off the porch. Jaden stood on a lower step than me, making it easier for our lips to meet, and I took full advantage, holding his face in my hands as my mouth played with his. He made a sound deep in his throat and pulled me tighter against him, so tight I could hardly draw breath. I found myself wishing we were someplace a lot more private, wearing far fewer clothes. After a minute his lips skimmed across my cheek to my ear.

"We're getting wet." He kissed the spot right below my ear and I shivered. "Let's get you inside."

We toweled each other off in the powder room, laughing, and tumbled into the kitchen.

"It's good to see you," Dec greeted Jaden. They chatted while I got us drinks. I had hoped that Dec would go to his girlfriend's house, as he often did on Fridays, but he settled obstinately in his living room recliner. It was okay, though. We watched a bad movie together, and when I curled into Jaden's side on the couch Dec gave only a cursory glance in our direction. After night check — which included several delays in dark corners — Jaden went to sleep in the guestroom. I hadn't thought anything could be more frustrating than the confusion of our first summer, but now I *knew* what I was missing. This was definitely worse.

The following morning we tacked up Piba and Kermit, Jaden's horses, and started along the trail to the polo club. The air smelled fresh after the rain, and the sun caught sparkles on leaves and branches. The multihued greens of early summer surrounded us as our horses' hooves thudded quietly on the damp earth.

"Are you sure about this?" I asked, watching Piba's chestnut ears. Jaden was leasing his horses to Mateo for the polo season.

"I should have done it sooner. The season started a month ago and they're not even fit enough to play a full match," he responded. He patted Kermit's neck, his straight brows furrowed in concern.

"Why didn't you have Jen ride them? Or me?" Jennalyn was Jaden's long-time groom and friend.

"You already had more work than you could handle, and Jen's going to naturopath college, remember? She has a part-time job in the city."

"Oh, right." I looked over at him; he was lost in thought, his long body following his horse's movements with unconscious grace. "You're not going to *sell* them, are you?" I asked with sudden anxiety.

He shook his head, but it seemed more a gesture of uncertainty than negation. "I don't want to, Téa, but I can't rule it out, especially in Piba's case. I won't have enough time for them for the next few years, and keeping two horses is expensive."

A ripple of surprise passed through me. I didn't think I'd ever heard Jaden complain about the cost of anything before, in fact, I'd hardly ever heard him talk about money. I realized with a start that I had no idea what his financial situation was like. I nudged Piba closer to Kermit and took one of Jaden's hands off the reins, holding it securely in mine.

"Don't lawyers make a lot of money?"

"Some do, eventually. But not in the beginning when they're articling as I am." He gave me a curious look. "Don't you know how much polo players earn?"

I shrugged. "I have no idea."

His entire face suffused with tenderness. He pulled our horses to a halt and used our joined hands to tug me forward. He kissed me, gently at first, but his hand soon went to the back of my neck, and his kiss turned deep and searching. A fluttering started in my belly and moved outward, and a moan built in my throat. Piba danced sideways suddenly, breaking our contact.

"Oops," I gasped. "I think I squeezed her." Piba tossed her head in disapproval. "Sorry, girl." I patted her and turned to find Jaden's molten eyes fixed on me. I gulped. I knew that look.

"Come," he said hoarsely. He pushed Kermit into a canter. Luckily we were close to our private copse, and minutes later we were rolling on the grass, tugging off each other's clothes with frantic haste.

It took a while for our breathing to slow. Jaden shifted so that I was lying on top of him, my head on his shoulder. He brushed his hand over my hair, from my crown down to my shoulder.

"I miss being close to you," he murmured.

"I can see that."

"I don't just mean sex — although you may have noticed how much I missed that."

A tingle swept over me. "Um, yes." I had one hand around his strong shoulder and I pressed my face into his neck, wishing I could stay there all day.

"*Querida...*" His voice was husky. "Have you ever thought about moving in with me?"

I stiffened. Jaden felt it; his hand moved soothingly up and down my back. He waited for me to speak. Of course, I'd imagined living with Jaden someday, but that was sometime in the amorphous future.

I cleared my throat. "You mean, soon?"

His hand continued its calming travels. "I know you can't move now, but what about next winter, when you're in school?"

I raised my head to see his face. I could feel my own, tight with confusion. "My love, I can't be away from the barn, you know that. My work is here, and my horses... besides, Dec and Gran need me."

Conflicting feelings tugged at me; joy at the thought of truly being with Jaden warred with my desire for the life I'd been fashioning. I rolled off Jaden and got to my knees. I began straightening my clothes, not looking at him.

"Téa?"

I re-buttoned my breeches, still avoiding his eyes. I was caught off-guard by the wound he'd just inflicted. He'd done it unwittingly, and yet there it was, throbbing in my solar plexus.

"Hey," his low voice spoke near my ear. He kneeled next to me and wrapped one arm around me. His other hand ran down my arm to my hand, which he gripped tightly. "I don't mean to push you. If you're not ready-"

I shook my head, horrified to find tears forming in my eyes. The man I loved had offered to share his life with me, and I was going to pieces. What was wrong with me?

"It's just... very sudden." I turned my face to his. "You surprised me, it's a lot to think about."

He put his palm to my cheek and rested his forehead against mine. "Take all the time you want." A moment later he pulled away and grinned. "Okay, time's up. We're overdue at the polo club." I returned his smile as he heaved me to my feet. There was a tiny flicker of panic in my chest, but I quelled it firmly.

The ride to the polo club went quickly. Jaden gave me an occasional searching look and I tried to reassure him by acting natural, which wasn't hard with his warm presence at my side. We dismounted outside the main barn and were immediately surrounded.

"It's about time," Jennalyn teasingly chided Jaden, taking Kermit's reins from him.

"*Hola, muñequita.*" Mateo gave me his usual two-cheek kiss before similarly taking Piba from me.

We were swept into the barn as part of a chattering, happy group, and we spent the next hour seeing Kermit and Piba settled into their new digs.

"I emailed you everything I could think of," Jaden told Mateo, "but call me if you have any questions. Kermit's pretty easygoing, but Piba can be quite particular. It may take her a while to accept you."

Mateo held both hands up in a very Latin gesture. "She is female. It is to be expected."

They laughed while Jennalyn and I shared an eyeroll. I watched Jaden and Mateo stroll down the aisle, heads together in conversation, and marveled at their newfound camaraderie. It gave me the warm fuzzies.

"Oh, how the mighty have fallen," said a snarky voice behind me. Warm fuzzies gone. I turned to find Sharleen standing behind me with her arms crossed. "He thought he was the king of this place, and now not only has his handicap dropped to *six* — to match Mateo's — but he can't even support his own horses anymore. It's sad, isn't it?" The last, sneering question was addressed to me, but it was Jennalyn who answered.

"There's nothing sad about it," she snapped. "It's his choice. He's a lawyer, for pity's sake, not a hobo."

"Yeah, 'cause the world desperately needs another lawyer," Sharleen said. She sashayed her curvy figure down the aisle. I clutched Jennalyn's arm, chilled by sudden worry.

"Jen, what if Sharleen is mean to Kermit and Piba? Is she Mateo's only groom?"

Her brows drew together. "I didn't think of that. We'd better talk to Jaden. And Mateo."

I hurried after her, relieved that she shared my concern. We found the guys outside, leaning on a fence and talking polo, Jaden's golden brown hair a few inches above Mateo's wavy black. I exchanged an uncertain look with Jennalyn before speaking; I didn't want to upset Mateo by insulting his groom.

"Jaden, Mateo." I hesitated before blurting out the rest in a rush. "Sharleen hates me, and she's always had a mad crush on Jaden but now she's just mad, and I'm afraid that she'll... well, what if she isn't nice to Jaden's horses?"

Sharleen disliked me because I was Jaden's girlfriend, but I wasn't sure whether the men were aware of that, and when neither of them said anything for a minute I felt warmth creeping up my neck as a blush threatened to embarrass me. Then Jaden heaved himself away from the fence and wound his arm around my waist.

He faced Mateo. "What do you think?" he asked in Spanish.

117

Mateo's dark eyes moved to me and they crinkled up at the corners as he smiled. "I cannot imagine Sharleen would behave this way, but I promise to watch carefully. In fact, why don't we go speak with her now?" This last was directed at Jaden.

I squeezed Jaden's hand. "You're the best guarantee that she'll be good to them. Go flirt with her. I give you full permission."

He bent and brushed his lips quickly against mine. "I'm going to stay for the afternoon. Is it okay if Jen drives you back?"

I agreed since I needed to get home. I was confident that Jaden would be able to charm Sharleen sufficiently to change her attitude.

"They'll probably end up downright spoiled," Jennalyn agreed.

Back at the barn, I helped Jen bag some feed for Jaden's horses so their stomachs wouldn't be upset by an abrupt transition to different food.

"Do you want some coffee?" I offered as she threw the bag into the back of her car.

"Sure." She smiled. "We haven't talked in ages, there's lots of juicy gossip."

I got us coffee and we settled at the old pine kitchen table while we talked. She updated me on naturopath school, which she loved, and news from the polo club. I admired her unusual yellow and grey eyes as she spoke.

"Say, Jen, how much money do polo players make?" Jaden had very effectively distracted me from asking him earlier.

"The pros? Well, it depends on where they play, but most of them make six figures at least."

I gaped at her, but she wasn't done. "I think Jaden was making almost a half mil. Of course, by now he'd-"

I choked on my coffee. Jennalyn hurried around the table to pound me on the back.

"As in, a half a million? *Dollars*?"

She sank into the chair next to me and gave me a strange look. "Haven't you guys ever talked about this?"

"It never occurred to me to ask."

"But... haven't you noticed that Jaden's kind of a big spender?"

I thought about it. I knew he owned a loft in the trendy Queen West area and that he drove a nice car. He always insisted on paying for things when we were together, but I supposed I hadn't put the pieces together. I recalled our time in Florida the year before; we'd eaten in restaurants almost every night and Jaden had bought me several relatively expensive gifts. I thunked my forehead with the heel of my hand.

"I'm an imbecile," I stated.

"No, you're not. You don't care much about money, that's all. That's a nice thing, Téa."

I walked Jennalyn out to her car and hugged her goodbye, but my mind was elsewhere. Maybe I didn't notice the trappings of money, but it wasn't true that I didn't care. In some ways, I felt as though money — or rather, its lack — had defined much of my life. My whole family had always had to work hard, but I was affected in particular because I competed in a sport that sucked vast amounts of wealth into a seemingly bottomless vortex. The Donalds had spent over two thousand dollars the previous week to spend four days at a local, provincial-level show, and once a horse started competing internationally the costs spiraled accordingly. It was my lifelong dream to be able to afford to participate in the sport I loved.

I rode Hades and got ready for the following day's show, and my brain gradually stopped whirling. After all, Jaden's previous income didn't make much difference now. He bounded into the barn that evening thrumming with energy. He grabbed me in the aisle and bent me backward to kiss me, and his happiness was so infectious that I didn't even worry about who could be watching. When he let me up I noticed the mild sunburn across his sharp cheekbones and straight nose.

"I don't think I've ever seen you sunburnt before," I commented, recalling his normally-bronzed skin.

"I've never spent so much time indoors before. It felt great to be back on the polo field." His satisfied sigh was proof enough. "I rode Piba and Kermit one last time." His words gave me a twinge, but I told myself it wasn't really the last time. How could it be, when riding them made him so happy?

Jaden went to the house to help with dinner while I finished packing my tack trunk. His energy transformed the dinner table; the quiet mealtime I'd been sharing with Dec was now a lively four-way conversation since Gran joined us too.

"I'd like to come to the show tomorrow," Jaden announced. "It's been far too long since I've watched you."

I agreed enthusiastically.

"I was supposed to spend the day with my mom, so I'll bring her with me." Much as I loved Aunt Paloma, this news dampened my enthusiasm a tad. Gran was spending the night, and she stayed in the guestroom as she always did.

"Take Seth's room," Dec told Jaden after we'd done the bedtime check. They glanced at me simultaneously and I nodded my assent, but had a sinking feeling as I wondered how long Dec would keep calling it 'Seth's room'.

"Now this is a civilized time to go to a show," I commented as we loaded Hades the next morning. Usually, show mornings began before dawn, but since our class wasn't until the afternoon I'd had time to help feed the horses and have a leisurely breakfast myself.

Dec drove, hauling our two-horse trailer, and I was glad. Even though Hades was wrapped in cotton up to his eyeballs, it made me nervous to drive such a valuable horse in such a small trailer, even when I wasn't stealing him.

When we arrived I greeted my barn mates and undressed Hades, watching him carefully for signs of stress. Since he was looking around in his usual regal manner I left him to eat and went to watch Julia ride. I found Al at the ringside and made halting conversation with him, trying in vain to find some common ground, but he seemed evasive and uninterested.

"Look who finally decided to show up." Alex strolled up to us after Julia had collected her ribbon. He mussed my hair playfully; I swatted his hand away.

"Someone had to come and put you in your place," I said, grinning at him.

We all headed back to the stabling area. I was looking forward to getting out of the sun's glare.

"How was the show, Jules?" I asked.

"It's been fun, but I missed you. Al stayed with me yesterday so I wouldn't be lonely." She peeked at him as if in gratitude. My eyes narrowed. "Sorry I can't stay to watch you ride, T, but I'm going to a party with Al," she went on apologetically.

"Have fun." I waved her away just as Jaden and his mom arrived. Aunt Paloma hugged me, and Jaden gave me a chaste kiss on the cheek before helping me get Hades ready. As always, I could feel Aunt Paloma's eyes burning through me whenever Jaden was near, but when it was time to warm up I brought my attention back to my mount. I'd greeted the Donalds earlier and I was peripherally aware of them watching, but I soon tuned them out also.

I reached forward and patted the large reddish-brown neck in front of me. Hades' glossy black mane bounced with each springy step, and his ears flicked attentively back and forth. He seemed alert but relaxed — at least, as relaxed as Hades ever got. A slight squeeze of my legs was my signal for him to trot, his rhythmic one-two motion perfectly steady.

"I'm glad you're back to yourself again, buddy," I murmured to him.

And he was. He handled the course as though he'd never had a nervous moment in his life, and only Alex and Moose did it faster than us. For once, I was thrilled with second place.

Alex rode next to me as we exited the ring with our ribbons. "Way to put me in my place." He winked. As we dismounted Jaden stood back and let me speak to the Donalds first, sharing our relief that Hades was back in full form.

"Congrats on that, by the way," Alex added as the Donalds left. He slung a friendly arm around me. Out of the corner of my eye, I saw Jaden's jaw flex. His mother frowned at his reaction, and I wriggled quickly out from under Alex's arm as Jaden stepped forward.

"You were wonderful," he said, but his eyes were tense and he wasn't smiling. I felt my teeth press together.

"Jaden, you remember Alex?" I made an effort not to sound aggravated. Jaden gave Alex an appraising look as they shook hands, Alex looking up several inches to meet Jaden's eye.

"You're Téa's cousin, right?" Alex said genially.

Jaden opened his mouth. His eyes flickered over to his mother. "Yes, I am."

My irritation grew. One of these days we would have to start acting like a couple around Jaden's mom, although I supposed a horse show wasn't the ideal environment for the drama that was sure to ensue. But then Hades shoved me, reminding me I had to tend to him, and my good mood returned in a rush as I turned to hug his sweaty neck and lead him off for a wash.

I was home for three days before going to the next show. This one had no classes for Hades but several low jumper classes that would have been ideal for Cal, but since I didn't want to jump him on his patched-up hoof, I left my horses at home and brought a handful of students instead. We returned four days later, rumpled, tired, and victorious. Emma and Cameo had won their first Championship, and Erin and Winter had gotten ribbons in the Low Adult division. I'd driven home twice — over two hours each time — to ride my horses, and late Sunday night I was grateful to crawl into my own bed.

I rolled over and stretched the next morning, happy to be waking in my sunny bedroom. Until I realized it was too sunny. I grabbed my clock — seven forty-five. I stumbled to the bathroom and then hurriedly yanked on shorts and a T-shirt before running to the barn. As I skidded into the aisle Gran looked up calmly from behind the grain cart.

"You're up. Declan wanted to let you sleep, he said you looked tired, dear."

"Oh." I stood there nonplussed. This had never happened before.

"You might as well go start the coffee," Dec added, coming around the corner. "We're almost done here." I turned back to the house, yawning and rubbing my eyes but feeling pleased.

Seth messaged me online that afternoon.

What gives, Sis? You don't write, you don't call...

I spluttered uselessly for a second before a reluctant chuckle bubbled up.

Yeah, sorry about that, I'm so irresponsible and BAD at keeping in touch. I was being facetious since Seth couldn't afford many international calls on his phone, and I emailed him regularly to no avail. We chatted online for an hour; he was in Ireland and had gotten a job at a stud farm.

I'll be staying here for a while, so you can call the farm if you need me, he wrote as he signed off.

If I needed him? I needed him every day, but since I couldn't tell him that I told him to stay out of trouble and send pictures.

When Julia arrived the next day I was surprised to see Al clinging to her like a burr.

"Doesn't he have a job?" I asked her when we had a moment alone. We were in the aisle, grooming our horses.

She paused in combing Jasmine's mane. "He took the day off to be with me. He's great that way; even when we're not together he calls me constantly. I've been staying at his place almost every night."

I absorbed this news. I thought it was awfully soon for Julia to be staying over at Al's place all the time, but then again, it probably took her mind off her parent's divorce.

"Well, Kabir's back for the summer — do you want to all get together later?"

"Sorry, I can't. Al and I have plans." She looked honestly disappointed, so I let it drop with a vague sense of disquiet. Cal turned to me as if wondering at the holdup, and I resumed my brushing of his fox-colored coat.

We were tacking up when loud voices angled around the corner, precursors to Brittney and two new girls. They didn't acknowledge our presence as they came in.

"Sorry about the bargain-basement barn," Brittney said, waving her hand dismissively at the boarder aisle. "My trainer's really amazing but her barn's an hour and a half away from our new house. Mummy doesn't want me driving that far."

They swept past me on their way outside. I looked around, feeling peculiarly stung. There was no doubt that Brittney was a snob and her assessment was therefore automatically suspect, but her flippant remark troubled me.

After riding Cal, I walked around and tried to view our property objectively, as an outsider would. The warm, polished wood that made up the barn's interior was chewed and worn in several places, and the cement aisle showed a few cracks, but overall it didn't look bad. When I got outside, though, I noticed signs of wear that I simply hadn't seen before. The matching beige barn and shed were faded, and the navy paint on the door and window frames was peeling. Our 'white' fence boards were mostly grey, and weeds grew in tall profusion around the buildings and paddocks. It used to be Seth's job to mow the grass, but Dec didn't have time to do it and I didn't know how to use the mower attachment on the tractor. Well, they were small things, I thought. Cosmetic things that didn't affect the horses' safety, but that perhaps gave the false impression that we weren't taking care of things.

I found Gran in the barn feeding the midday hay. "How come we don't have flowerbeds like we used to?" I asked her. Cal tried to snatch a mouthful of hay from her as she passed, and I pushed his nose away quickly, knowing he'd get scolded. Gran expected good manners of everyone.

She tossed the hay into Gracie's new double stall and turned an incredulous stare on me. She planted her hands on her hips. "Why don't we have flowerbeds? You and your brother let the ponies treat them like a salad bar, that's why! What wasn't eaten was trampled. It was too much bother to constantly replace them."

"Oh, right," I said meekly. Now I remembered.

She shook her head with a rueful smile. "Why the sudden interest?"

"I thought it would be nice to plant a few things. I'd do the work," I said hastily. "But I don't know anything about it, like what to plant, or how."

Her blue eyes sparkled. "Well, then. I'd be delighted to direct your labors."

Seven

The next day brought a surprise visit from Joanne and Dana, commonly referred to — by my friends at least — as 'the Beiges'. Joanne was Dec's girlfriend, for reasons that remained a mystery, and Dana was her blob of a fourteen-year-old daughter. They shuffled cautiously into the barn, still tentative after several months.

Dec turned away from his discussion with Alan and strode over to give Joanne a peck on the lips. His smile was light, relaxed, and I felt the usual small irritation at their exchange, like the prick of cat claws barely hooking skin.

"We wanted to surprise you," Joanne said. Light glinted off her glasses as she spoke. Dana gazed around dully and didn't say anything. I was mildly shocked that Joanne would consider the idea of surprising someone; she struck me as the type who'd spend a week planning a visit to the grocery store.

"I'm glad you did. Let's go to the house. Dana, why don't you stay here and help Téa?"

My head whipped around. "But I'm teaching a lesson soon. I won't be able to keep an eye on her," I protested. Dana could only be a hindrance in the barn; she didn't know enough to keep out of trouble and I didn't want to spend the day babysitting her.

"She's not a toddler. She can help you with odd jobs." Dec held my gaze for a minute, long enough to convince me not to argue with him, before ushering Joanne out. I suppressed a groan as I surveyed Dana. I could have her clean tack, but it would take so long to teach her how that it wouldn't be worth it, especially since she could damage it if she did it wrong. She couldn't sweep the aisle because I didn't trust her near the horses with a broom; she could inadvertently spook them. She couldn't groom or turn out... a light clicked on in my head.

"Come with me." I got Panda — named for his black and white coloring — out of his stall and led him outside. He was our oldest and gentlest school horse, so I felt safe in handing Dana the leadrope.

"Panda needs to graze, and we need the grass shortened. Don't let him step on the leadrope, don't get it wrapped around his legs, and watch your toes — he's heavy."

It was such a good idea that after I'd finished teaching, I had all my students take their horses out and hand-graze them while I went to relieve Dana of Panda's leadrope.

"Geez, I was out here so long," she complained.

"It's a nice day," I said. "Can't you enjoy it?" It was, too. Small white clouds scudded across a baby-blue sky and a breeze kept the heat at bay.

"But it's so boring to just stand there with a horse, and he was pulling me all over the place."

I bit my tongue. I was itching to tell her to run and find her mommy — in just those words, too — but I suspected that Dec wouldn't be happy with the interruption.

"All right, we'll do something else now." I walked Panda into the cool of the barn while fending off his attempts to wipe his gooey green mouth on me. Then I went to forage in the shed, Dana tripping over my heels the whole time. A rush of memories funneled into me as I searched the shed's dim interior. I could almost feel Jaden against me, taste the salt of his skin on my tongue... I regretfully wrenched myself back to the present. I handed Dana a scraper and a wire brush, armed myself similarly, and set out to tackle the barn's window frames. An hour and much whining from Dana later, we'd only scraped the flaking paint off three windows and I was sweating and frustrated.

"C'mon," I said, tossing my tools onto a nearby bench. "Let's get a drink." In fact, it was time for lunch, and I was relieved to find Dec and Joanne in the kitchen making sandwiches.

"What did you two do all morning?" Dec asked as we sat down.

"We started scraping paint off the window frames so that we can repaint them," I said.

Dec's eyebrows went up a fraction.

"Okay, maybe I should've talked to you about it first-"

"It's not that, Téa — I'll need to budget for enough paint. Although it probably is a good idea to spruce the place up a bit." He chewed

126

thoughtfully. Joanne smiled at him, a private smile that made me think there was more going on than I knew.

My project had to be temporarily abandoned for another four-day horse show. I hadn't seen Jaden in almost two weeks and was grateful when he said he'd come meet me there.

"I can only come on Sunday. London's got a big case so I'll be at the office on Saturday," he said.

"Nice to know I'm less alluring than a bunch of files." Not to mention London.

"Trust me," he purred, "you're far more alluring than anything here, and as soon as I get a minute alone with you, I'll prove it."

That happy thought would have to hold me for a few days, and I wouldn't have time to miss him overmuch. Along with Cal and Hades, I was bringing several students, and Julia and Brittney were coming too.

We worked together to unload and set up at the show. Emma bounced around with excitement; she wore a feed tub as a hat and various equipment dangled from her coltish body. Her dad had placed a limit of two horse shows a month, partly because of the expense and partly because he didn't want to spend every summer weekend traveling to shows, and Emma chafed at the restriction.

It was the Canada Day long weekend and the show was a popular one. Hades won his warm-up class on the first day, raising my hopes that he was well and truly over his bad experience. I took particular satisfaction in beating Brittney, who came in third with Salsa. Brittney's face was sour as she dismounted and tossed the reins to Elise. I grinned, even though I had to take care of Hades myself. Erin was helping, but she couldn't handle Hades on her own.

"Why didn't you hire a groom in the spring?" Karen demanded in exasperation as I took off Hades' open-front boots. "You know how hard it is to find one during the season."

"I thought I could manage the way I usually do, I guess." Which meant doing most things myself and getting my students to help at the bigger shows. Clearly not an option anymore.

"You're not on the Trillium circuit anymore, kid. You need a full-time groom, and that horse can't be handled by just anyone." She gestured to Hades. "Besides, the Donalds can afford to pay someone really good to help you."

That was true, although I found myself perpetually reluctant to increase their already monumental expenses. I supposed I wasn't yet accustomed to the vast sums they were spending.

Once Hades was comfortable in his stall I set off with Julia in search of a cool drink. We were ambling back, contentedly sipping iced cappuccinos, when we passed Brittney and Alicia, the black-haired girl I remembered.

Brittney gave me a disdainful look and turned to her friend. "I didn't think showing in that color breeches was even still allowed," she said, loudly enough for me to hear.

I felt my face flame, but Julia's was ice-cold as she retorted, "It's too bad you can't buy some talent to go with your trendy new breeches." She looped her arm through mine and strolled casually toward the stabling as though nothing had happened. Sometimes I wished I had even a fragment of Julia's cool confidence. My best comebacks tended to come to me sometime the next day.

I was still hot with embarrassment as Julia dropped into a folding chair in our tackroom.

"I wish 'Brittney' wasn't such a common name," she groused. "Every time I hear it all I can think about is Seth with that blond bitch."

I frowned at her language. It made her sound harsh and angry, two words that I wouldn't normally use to describe my friend.

"*I* wish I knew what she has against me," I said, frustrated. "What did I ever do to her?" I plunked myself onto a tack trunk.

"Maybe it's jealousy," Julia suggested.

"Yeah, right. Even my breeches are outdated, remember? Brittney has everything. What could she possibly be jealous of?"

Julia tilted her head as though studying me. "You have a dad, for one thing, and she doesn't. Plus, people know that you've gotten to where you are through talent and hard work. But Brittney... she's had to work to learn to ride like anyone else, and I'm sure she's taken falls and had her share of blisters like the rest of us. But when she wins people say, 'If I had an expensive horse like hers I'd win too'. She'll rarely get credit because people think her success comes from her mom's money rather than the effort she herself makes."

"Pfft. If that was my biggest problem in life, I'd take it."

Julia's grey eyes seemed to darken. "You know, I've had the same issue. I may not be rich like Brittney, but I've been on the receiving end of that 'your problems aren't important because you've got money' attitude, and it's bullshit, Téa. Everyone has problems."

I blinked, taken aback by her vehemence. Then I felt the sour curl of shame. The truth was, I *did* feel that Julia had it easier than me, and I knew that Teri did, too. Teri had started working at the racetrack at seventeen, and I'd been working in our family stable since childhood. Julia was twenty and had yet to get her first job. We did sometimes envy her, but we loved her more.

"Look, Jules, I'm not saying that Brittney doesn't have problems. Just that she's-"

"A red-haired she-devil?" she guessed, grinning.

"With her very own pitchfork."

Jaden and Al both showed up on Sunday, along with Monica and Neil, who were thrilled when Hades won another Grand Prix. I felt like the girl on the moon afterward, every step lifting me three feet into the air as I went to the snack bar with Jaden, Julia, and Al.

"I'm so proud of you," Jaden said quietly as we sat down. I beamed at him as best I could while chewing my fries. I *was* trying to eat healthier foods, but I figured a Grand Prix win merited a few French fries.

"I hope Monica and Neil give me another bonus," I said when I'd swallowed. "I need a new raincoat." Brittney's snide comment had made me self-conscious about my appearance at shows, and I didn't want to keep wearing my old poncho on rainy days.

"Don't you get the prize money when you win?" Al asked. It was the first curiosity he'd shown about our sport. "How does that usually work?"

"The horse's owners pay all the expenses, like entry fees and transportation. Professional riders charge a fee per class they ride in. In the jumper divisions, riders normally get a cut of the prize money, but I don't always."

Jaden frowned.

"So what's your incentive to win?" Al asked, puzzled.

I just looked at him. It was Julia who said, "You don't know Téa. She wants to win like she wants to breathe."

I smiled my thanks, and she squeezed my hand briefly. Al looked uncomfortable for some unfathomable reason, but his curiosity seemed satisfied. He and Julia excused themselves soon after.

Jaden moved his chair closer to mine. "Why doesn't your contract cover prize money?"

"When Hades first arrived it was for training, so the Donalds signed a simple board and training contract. When I started riding him at shows I told them my riding fee. It wasn't complicated, it didn't seem worth drawing up a contract for."

Jaden looked at me carefully. "Did you pick an industry standard amount? The same amount other professional riders are charging?"

"Well," I hedged, "I think it might be a bit lower. I'm just starting out as a pro and he's such a phenomenal horse."

Jaden placed his hand on the side of my face. His thumb gently stroked my cheekbone. "Don't undervalue yourself, Téa. Your interests need to be protected. Why don't you go online and find a rider agreement, and we'll customize it?"

I kissed the inside of his wrist. "Dec's right. It *is* convenient to have a lawyer in the family."

Jaden surprised me by announcing he was coming to my place. "I want to spend Canada Day with you." It took a long time to pack up, drive home, and settle the horses, but I fell into bed feeling that all was right with the world. I was doing work I loved and looking forward to a day off spent with my sweetheart. The only thing missing was Seth, but he'd sounded so happy in his last few messages that I couldn't help but be glad for him.

Jaden fed the horses with me the next morning, and we spent a few leisurely hours at home before heading for the July First festivities in a neighboring municipality, since my own town of Julien was too small to host much in the way of a celebration. It was a hot, sunny afternoon, the very essence of summer. Children ran around sticky with cotton candy and cried when they dropped their ice cream. People played Frisbee and ball, and delighted screams carried over the green field from the rides set up nearby.

We listened to the outdoor concert for a while, sampled some gourmet popsicles, and even went for a ride on the Ferris wheel. I clutched Jaden's hand tightly at the top, and he laughed as he tucked me firmly into his side.

"You ride an animal fifteen times your size at speed over huge obstacles, and you're afraid of the Ferris wheel?"

"I'm not *afraid*," I corrected. "I'm just not... unafraid. At least horses have a sense of self-preservation."

When it got dark we lay on our backs on the sun-warmed ground to watch the fireworks. I breathed in the midsummer smells of crushed grass and bug spray, mingled with the exciting scent of fireworks. My head was pillowed on Jaden's arm, our bodies touching along the length of my side, and if I could've bottled that feeling I'd label it 'bliss'.

Afterward, Jaden needed caffeine since he had to drive all the way to Toronto after dropping me off. We stopped at a coffee shop, blinking in the bright light after the darkness of the car.

"I hope we get to spend more days like this one," he said as we sat down. "I'm going to do my best to keep my weekends free. Is there anything special you'd like to do next time?"

My heart dropped. "Oh. Jaden, I'm only here for another week. Then I... I'm going to Quebec for three weeks." I looked away, berating myself even as I did so. It wasn't as if I was confessing to a crime. I was following my dream — a perfectly valid, legal dream. Jaden's groan reminded me of why I couldn't meet his eyes.

"Again? Why so far, and for so long?"

"The Bromont International is a three-star event, the points count toward *world* rankings. And there's a national-level show right before it, and it's too far to come home in between."

I peeked up at him. His hand was sweeping through his hair, frustration etched in every line of his features.

He rested his sinewy forearms on the table and leaned over them. "You know, I know guys who complain their girlfriends are too clingy."

"You want me to be clingier?" I asked, confused.

131

"I'd like to be able to spend time with you without making an appointment a month in advance."

"Jaden, I'd love to spend more time with you, but it's the middle of the show season! You know what that's like." My own frustration began to swell.

His tawny predator eyes didn't release mine. "No, I don't, actually. Polo isn't the same. We may travel to tournaments occasionally, but it's possible to spend most of the season at one club."

"But..." I cast around desperately for an anchor point. How could we have had such a monumental misunderstanding? "I haven't been hiding some deep dark secret. You *knew* I was going to be showing a lot this summer."

He exhaled heavily, and his body softened. He reached across the table, and I grabbed his hand like a lifeline. "I knew you'd be competing a lot. What I didn't know was how much traveling that would entail." His eyes reached into mine. "I *miss* you." His last, fervent whisper sliced through me. It smarted, and yet a warm glow spread from it all the same.

Jaden's admission wasn't the only thing that made me reluctant to leave. Gracie's foal was due soon, and I very much wanted to witness the birth. Dec had installed a video camera in the corner of her stall so that we could monitor Gracie from the house. He promised to send me video of the foal's arrival if I missed it, but that wouldn't compare to being there. Stephanie's belly was getting noticeably larger also, but she was prepared to jump in her car and race over as soon as her horse went into labor.

I patted Gracie's neck as I led her, lumbering and slow, to the grass paddock early one morning. "Please keep your baby in until I get back," I entreated. I knew it didn't work that way, but it couldn't hurt to ask, right?

I made a detour to the house for a couple of chocolate chip cookies and wandered back to the barn just as Lisa and Melanie arrived together.

"How do you stay so thin when you eat chocolate chip cookies for breakfast?" Melanie exclaimed.

Lisa shook her head at me. "Those cookies were meant to be a snack, you know." She had delivered them fresh-baked the day before. I gave her a guilty smile and turned out two more horses before giving in to her urging to get a real breakfast.

Dec was already pouring coffee. "I wanted to talk to you." His pause was enough to alert me that this wasn't regular breakfast conversation. "We'll have to find a new beginner horse soon. Maybe you can put the word out while you're at the shows because Sebastian's parents want to buy Panda." At a spry thirty years, Panda was our most dependable school horse. Almost all our students had their first few lessons on him, and he was wonderful. He slowed down when he felt his riders losing their balance, and he did his best to interpret their unclear and often contradictory cues.

"But... but..." I was standing by the kitchen table, stuttering with shock. "We can't sell Panda! He's a part of the family." I was aghast at the very suggestion; it was something we'd never done in the past. Gran's old horse had been thirty-five when she died and hadn't done any work in years. She'd been well taken care of until the end.

"Things are tougher now with your brother gone," Dec explained. I noticed his reluctance to say Seth's name. "And all your traveling has an effect, too. We have to pay more for help."

I brought the conversation back to Panda. "Sebastian and his brother are young now, but what happens in a couple of years when they want to gallop and jump? They'll overwork him, he could get hurt."

"Their parents will watch them. We're lucky that someone is willing to provide a good home for Panda at his age."

"It wouldn't *be* his home — this is his home, he's lived here for twenty years!" I was having trouble forming an intelligible sentence. I couldn't believe that Dec was serious about this.

"You see, this is why you'd never make it in this business, Téa," he said angrily. "You're not tough enough."

Okay, that was too much. "I've been working my butt off in this barn day in and day out for ten years!" I yelled.

"It takes more than that!" Dec said loudly, slapping his thick palm on the table. "This place is a business, and sometimes you have to make hard business decisions. We can't keep all our old school horses in

133

cushy retirement, not when we have the option of someone else taking on the expense. And what about when one of the boarders falls on hard times and can't pay her board? You'd have to sell her horse to recoup the money — would you do that?" He gave me a stony look for a minute before answering his own question. "No, you wouldn't. Face it, Téa, this business would chew you up and spit you back out if you had to do more than teach and ride."

I spun and left the room, and Dec didn't stop me.

I had tried to cram all my lessons into the few days that I was home, so I spent eight hours in the baking sun, teaching and breathing in the dust stirred up by multiple hooves. My voice was raspy when I trudged into the house at dinnertime.

Dec and I eyed each other warily.

I got a glass of water, drank it in gulps, and cleared my throat. "Can you at least wait until I get back before making any decisions about Panda?" I faced Dec across the counter and tried not to sound like I was pleading. "You weren't going to sell him anytime soon, were you? It's only July, and he'll be in full work at least until September." 'Full work' being a relative term.

His sky-blue eyes seemed to warm infinitesimally. "Okay."

I sighed in relief before collapsing at the table. I was teaching again after dinner; the longer days meant more hours to ride outside, but despite my tiredness, I felt reassured. Dec would wait, and in the meantime, I'd think of a way to keep Panda home where he belonged.

The heat continued that week, suffocating and unrelenting. We dug out two large old box fans and placed one in each long aisle of the barn, and we only turned horses out during the early and late parts of the day. When the heatwave hadn't broken on the third day we canceled the midday lessons, and I began taking horses out of their stalls and running cold water from the hose over them before returning them, soaked but cooler, to their stalls. Most of them loved it. Cal kept sticking his face under the spray, and Panda gave a deep sigh and dropped his nose almost to the floor as the cool liquid washed over him. I did Gracie at three-hour intervals, worried about the effect the heat might have on her and her baby. She did seem particularly listless, so at lunchtime, I called Gran.

"I'll be right over," she said promptly.

Dec, Alan, and I were relieved to see Gran stride briskly into the barn, looking inexplicably cool in long beige shorts and a short-sleeved lilac blouse. She met us at Gracie's stall and stepped in with confidence. Gran had far more experience with foalings than Dec, and while I'd seen one foal born and did possess some theoretical knowledge, I didn't trust myself to judge whether Gracie was okay. Gran patted her and spoke to her quietly. She took her pulse and watched her breathing before running her hands over the protuberant liver-chestnut belly and bending to peek underneath it.

"Why, she's waxing up," she said, straightening with a smile.

"Oh!" I exclaimed. 'Waxing up' referred to the beads of colostrum, the all-important first milk, appearing on the mare's teats. "Should Stephanie come?" I could barely restrain myself from jumping up and down.

"There's time yet," Gran said. "It may be a day or two before the actual labor begins; she isn't showing any other signs."

"I'll let her know it's coming." I skipped to the tackroom, where I'd left my phone so it wouldn't get soaked during the horses' showers. After sharing a squeal of excitement with Stephanie I called Jaden.

"I wouldn't want to miss that. I'll be over right after work," he promised.

I waded through the sultry air to check on the horses that lived outside. I leaned my forearms on the baking fence board while I watched them for signs of distress. They seemed fine, clustered in the shade of the run-in shed and the few trees by the fence's edge, but I felt unsettled. The fine hairs on my body were reaching outward. The utter stillness didn't feel calm — it felt like that split-second silence between indrawn air and a scream. I scanned the skies to find roiling steel-grey clouds overhead, and I turned quickly to make my way back to the barn. The wind hit just as I made it there, blinding me with hair blown into my face despite my ponytail. Dust swirled in eddies as I trotted inside.

"Looks like a storm's coming," I commented. Dec and Gran were in the tackroom, assembling supplies that we might need for the foaling.

As if to underline my words, wind whistled through the open tackroom door, causing Gran to exclaim as rolls of gauze bounced to the floor. We'd been keeping all the doors and windows open to catch every wisp of air. I could hear stamping in the barn along with the rising wail of the wind.

"Let's close a few things up," Dec suggested. The air was still hot despite the fact that it was now moving rapidly, and I closed the windows in the horses' stalls reluctantly. By the time we were done, gusts were howling down the aisles through the open doors, carrying dust, leaves, and debris with them. The aisle connected to the indoor arena was the worst since the opening at the far end of the arena was a large garage door. I ran to lower it while the wind snatched at my clothes and hair. My glimpse outside showed trees swaying like dancers and grass flattened against the ground.

I secured the door and blinked the dust out of my eyes as I trotted back into the barn. Dec and Alan were shutting the remaining doors, leaving the barn stuffy, dark and oven-like. A few horses circled their stalls nervously, upset by the noise and voltaic energy in the air.

"It's so hot — can't we leave the doors open a bit?" I asked.

Dec and Alan exchanged a worried look. "We can try, as long as we stay inside to keep an eye on things," Dec said finally. I began to open the double-wide door that faced the main ring; the wind tore it from my hands and it crashed into the barn's side with a bang.

"Are we getting a tornado?" I was getting scared. Tornadoes weren't unheard-of in our area, but they were relatively rare. A small one had touched down in a neighboring town a few years before, but I had never experienced winds this strong.

"Don't know," Dec said tersely, "but we should close things up and go to the house."

"I don't want to leave the horses," I protested.

"I need to check the weather reports and I'll feel safer with you in the house," he insisted. "You too, Alan. Mom, come on," he called toward the tackroom. Gran joined us and we secured the door. Dec took Gran's arm on one side and I took the other, and Alan clamped his hand on my other arm before we headed for the house, chained together like daisies. My eyes were streaming by the time we got inside.

"I'll make us some tea." Gran bustled off to the kitchen while I washed my hands and face in the powder room, grimacing at my disheveled state in the mirror.

When I got back to the kitchen Gran was setting out tea and a plate of scones. Alan was on the phone with his family. I poured myself some tea and was adding milk when Dec appeared, looking worried.

"Well, there's a tornado watch in effect," he announced as he dropped into his chair. Gran passed him the teapot before rising to answer the phone. From her assurances, we could tell it was a boarder checking on her horse.

We spent a tense afternoon listening to the wind howl and answering calls from worried boarders and students. Jaden called regularly also; they were getting high winds in Toronto, but no tornado warning. And then, just before feeding time, the power went out.

"This'll make feeding fun," I muttered.

"You're not coming," Dec said firmly.

"I want to check on everyone. Besides, you can't go by yourself, what if something happens to you?"

"We'll all go," Gran decided. Alan had left earlier to rejoin his family, and had called to let us know he'd arrived safely. There was no way to finish cleaning the stalls in this weather.

We linked arms again and leaned into the gale. It felt like a long journey to the barn, and once inside even Dec, with his massive strength, had to strain to shut the door. We set off in different directions; the barn had two long aisles connected by two shorter ones. Its many windows ensured that it was normally bright in the daytime, but the sullen skies weren't letting much light through today. I made a beeline for Gracie's stall. She was restless, pacing only to stop and listen, ears pricked and head high, to the bumps and shrieks outside. It was impossible to tell if her agitation was due to impending motherhood or to the weather.

Dec went into the hayloft with a flashlight. I was glad it wasn't me; I found it spooky in the dark when I was alone. We took our time feeding, trying to calm and reassure each horse as we went. Most didn't seem unduly disturbed, to my relief. A horse can easily get hurt by panicking in a stall. We gave them all some extra hay so they'd have a distraction overnight.

Our own dinner was eaten cold and by candlelight. I didn't eat much, too unnerved by the rattling of the windows and the occasional loud thump as something struck the house. The image from the camera in Gracie's stall transmitted video to Dec's laptop, but we didn't want to run his battery down by keeping it on, so we checked on her every hour. After getting eyestrain reading next to flickering candles for a while, I went to bed, setting my phone to wake me an hour later since I was determined to keep checking the foal camera. The fourth time I hauled myself out of bed, Dec's laptop was dead. I didn't know if there was a way to pick up the transmission with mine, so I decided to go check on Gracie in person. I yawned as I pulled a hoodie on over my PJs, then I went outside.

Grit assaulted my bare legs and I was tugged and buffeted by the air, but it wasn't as strong as before. After finding the flashlight in the tackroom I clicked it on and took a quick walk around the barn to make sure that the weather hadn't caused any injuries. Beyond looking annoyed at being woken, all the horses seemed fine. When I got to Gracie's stall she was lying down. I tried to be discreet in running my flashlight over her, not wanting to startle her into getting up, but it was immediately apparent that she wasn't having a nap — she was having a baby. Her flanks were drenched with sweat and she was groaning.

"Oh, sweetheart, are you okay?" I asked. I clutched the bars of her stall and pressed my face against them. I wanted to go in and pat her, reassure her, hold her hoof — anything I could do to help, but I was afraid she'd be upset by my intrusion. Gracie was usually very friendly, but even the most docile mare can become nervous or aggressive when giving birth. I didn't blame them; it was such a vulnerable time for them, a fact they felt all the more keenly because they were prey animals.

"Hold on, I'll be right back with help." What help we could offer I didn't know, but I dashed back through the windy dark to the house, light bobbing from the flashlight still in my hand. The wind slammed the door behind me and I spun, breathless, to find Gran already dressed and in the living room.

"It seems we had the same idea," she said, "but you should have waited-"

"The baby's coming!" I gasped, interrupting her.

She brightened. "Oh! Go wake your father. I'll go out straight away." I took the stairs two at a time and crashed through Dec's door without knocking.

"Dec! The baby's coming!" I yelled.

"Mmpf." A muffled grunt. Dec woke up like a hibernating bear — slow and grumpy.

"Gracie's having her foal!" I ran over and jumped on the end of his bed. "Get up! Come to the barn!"

His eyes snapped open. "Okay, okay."

I leaped down and ran back to the barn, hoping that Gran had found another flashlight. I skidded around the corner to see that she had done better; she was holding a large, battery-powered lantern that we used in the tackroom at shows. She handed it to me.

"I'm going to check on her," Gran murmured. "Hold the light up but stay in the doorway." She opened the door and I got my first good view of Gracie. She was lying prone, with her head stretched forward and one foreleg pawing the air. Gran went to her head, murmuring softly all the while. At her approach, Gracie stiffened suddenly. She raised her head.

"It's all right, dear, we don't want to disturb you," Gran soothed. She kneeled down and stroked Gracie's face. After a minute Gracie let her head drop back into the shavings. Gran made her way slowly to Gracie's tail. She moved it aside, but nothing was visible yet. She had just rejoined me when Dec came hurrying in.

"Well?"

"Nothing yet," Gran said calmly as she shut the stall door.

"Shouldn't we leave that open in case we need to get in there fast?" Dec asked.

"Very little should be done fast at a foaling. It's more important that Gracie feels as though she has some privacy. It will make her feel safer."

That made sense. In the wild, a mare would look for a private spot away from her herd when it was time to give birth. And because it was an extremely vulnerable time for mother and baby, Nature had arranged to make the birth of foals relatively quick. Labor was short, foals could stand soon after being born, and run alongside their mothers, however ungracefully, within hours.

"Oh! I have to call Stephanie," I exclaimed. Then I clapped a hand over my mouth, remembering that I should be quiet.

Dec and Gran exchanged a look. "We can't ask a pregnant woman to drive through a windstorm at three in the morning," Gran said.

My brow furrowed. "Well, I'm going to get my phone so I can video it for her, at least." I jogged to the house. It was surprisingly dark without the security light from the barn's roof. Once in the house, I hesitated. Okay, Stephanie was pregnant, and the weather was bad, but she'd waited for this foal for eleven long months. In her shoes, I'd at least want to be informed and have the option of attending.

I used the kitchen phone, which was so old it worked even when the power went out, unlike our cordless ones. Stephanie didn't answer her phone, which wasn't surprising, so I left her a message before retrieving my cell phone and jogging back to the barn. I was already tired and nothing had happened yet. And nothing did, for what seemed like a very long time. We stayed in the aisle and waited, trying to be unobtrusive when we glanced into the stall. Dec went and got us chairs from the viewing lounge.

"I thought foaling was supposed to be fast," I said, worried. "Shouldn't we call the vet?"

Gran shrugged. "It's her first foal, and she's not straining noticeably yet." She glanced over at her son, leaning back with eyes closed in a folding chair that seemed too small to support his wide frame. "I was in labor with Declan for thirty-six hours." She said it as though it was a fond memory, and I shuddered. I couldn't imagine it, nor did I want to. Dec's eyes had opened, and he looked even more uncomfortable than me.

Gran shook her head at the pair of us. "Don't worry, the vast majority of mares and foals do just fine on their own."

Gracie made an *unh* sound deep in her throat, and we all shot to our feet.

"Oh!" I exclaimed softly, remembering to keep my voice down this time. There, clearly visible despite the dim light, was a tiny foot. And then I blinked, and it was gone. I turned to Gran in alarm.

"It's all right," she whispered, patting my shoulder. "She'll push it out again." I pulled out my phone and began recording, and Dec held the lantern up so that the near half of the stall was softly illuminated. Gracie seemed beyond caring what we did, completely focused on her internal struggle.

The hooflet reappeared, followed by another. We let out a collective breath. A properly positioned foal is born like a diver, with its two forelegs extended and its head resting on its knees. Seeing two hooves was the first sign of a normal delivery. The head came next, just where it should be, and then, in a rush, the body slid out. We waited. Both of them, mother and baby, lay without moving.

"Are they okay?" I said uncertainly.

Gran was watching the foal intently. "As long as the foal's breathing, they're fine. Gracie's just resting." I stared at the foal and was rewarded by an upward jerk of its ribs. It was clearly breathing. A minute later, the head moved, the little nose turning upward as the baby struggled to raise its head.

There was a lull, although the foal continued to move occasionally, reassuring us. About twenty minutes later Gracie seemed to decide it was time for action. She gave a concerted push, then heaved herself to her feet. She turned around slowly and stepped toward her baby with her head lowered, blowing softly through her nostrils. She nuzzled the small wet face before inspecting the rest of the baby's body. Then she gave a low nicker. It came from deep inside her chest — right from her heart, I thought, because it was different from any other sound I'd heard her make.

Dec's heavy arm went around my shoulders. "Now that's a beautiful sight."

I nodded, unable to speak. From the husky tone of his voice, I knew that Dec was touched by the moment also. It surprised me a little.

My phone was dying, and Dec left to get his. We didn't want Stephanie to miss seeing the foal stand for the first time.

"Your mother and Dec wanted to have a baby, you know," Gran said. Her white hair was resting against the stall bars, and she didn't look at me. "They were trying. You could have had another brother or a sister."

I had vague memories of my mom saying something about it. I wondered why Gran would bring it up after all this time, but then supposed it was a consequence of watching the birth.

By the time Dec got back, Gracie had licked the foal all over and was nudging it gently with her nose, encouraging her baby to get up.

"What time is it?" I asked, stifling a yawn.

"Four-twenty," Dec said. If the foal didn't stand within an hour or so after being born, we'd have to call the vet, because it was important for it to nurse shortly after birth.

The foal seemed to know something was expected of it. It had rolled onto its chest with its ridiculously long forelegs stretched in front of it. We couldn't tell what color it was in the dim light, only that it was dark. It braced two of its wobbly stilts and gave a little heave with its hindquarters. Gracie whickered her encouragement, and the three humans held their collective breath. The foal pitched face-first into the shavings. It gave a startled snort, which seemed to startle it further, as if it never expected that kind of noise to come out of its own nose. It lay there, eyes wide and legs akimbo, for a minute. Gracie moved to her baby's rump and gave it a nudge. The foal made another effort, then another, and suddenly scrambled to its feet and stood there, swaying. I suppressed a cheer.

"It's a boy," Gran said quietly.

There was a new determination on the colt's face as he took his first shaky step, looking like the world's cutest daddy longlegs. He tumbled to the ground, but regained his feet more quickly this time and stood, legs stretched wide. Gracie moved so that she was alongside him, nose to tail, and that was all the encouragement he needed. An ancient instinct came to guide him, and he bumped his nose along Gracie's belly until he found what he was looking for. He started nursing.

I turned to Gran, beaming. "He's okay now, right?"

"The signs are all good. He's a fine, sturdy little fellow," Gran said, dabbing at her eyes.

"I'm so glad you're here, Gran." I was somewhat in awe of her. She'd been so calm and steady throughout the whole thing. "How do you know so much about foaling?" I knew there had been very few foals born at Shady Lane.

"I've told you my father used to raise horses back in England," she reminded me. A wistful smile accompanied the memory. "He bred some very fine eventers. Dec's horse Corin was the great-grandson of my father's favorite mare."

I was somewhat stunned that I hadn't known this and ashamed that I hadn't shown enough interest to ask. Gran wasn't the type to talk about her history unless prompted. I resolved to ask from that point on. There were pictures in the house of a younger, slimmer Dec competing all over North America on an almost-black horse.

I turned to Dec. "What happened to Corin? Why did you stop riding him?"

"My dad sold him so that I'd focus more on school."

I gasped. He said it so matter-of-factly, but I wasn't fooled for a minute. No wonder he rarely talked about Corin and had given up riding so abruptly. To have your dream pulled out from under you like that had to be heartbreaking.

"That's awful," I murmured.

"That's life, Téa. Things change." He strode down the aisle, ending the conversation, but was back a minute later with a bucket and a handful of other supplies.

"Some lukewarm water and electrolytes for Gracie," he explained, "and iodine for the colt's umbilical stump."

After that was attended to, Gran went to make Gracie a warm bran mash. "It will help keep her gut moving until she's eating normally again," she explained. "Why don't you go in and meet the new addition?"

I looked up at Dec, who smiled and waved me into the stall. I went to Gracie first and stroked her neck. The hairs were stiff with dried sweat.

"You were amazing, sweetie. He's beautiful," I murmured. Then I went and knelt slowly in front of the foal. He pricked his ears — surprisingly big on his tiny face — and regarded me with interest. He had milk on his lips and large, intelligent eyes. He blinked his impossibly long lashes and tottered toward me.

"Hi." I smiled as he pushed his soft little nose against first my cheek, then my hair, sniffing deeply. I stroked his coat, which was fluffy where it had dried but still damp in places. We gazed into each other's eyes in wonder. I couldn't believe how utterly enraptured I was by this little creature I'd just met. The colt's weariness quickly overcame his fascination, and he collapsed into a tired heap on the shavings. I gave Gracie one last pat before quietly closing the stall door.

I stretched, noticing that I could see better as light began to filter through the windows, pulling me out of the fairy-tale fog of the past few hours. I was still wearing my PJ shorts and hoodie. The air inside the barn was warm but uncomfortably close, and since Alan hadn't finished cleaning the stalls there was an ammonia smell. We normally prided ourselves on keeping the stalls clean and the odor to a minimum. Gran was especially insistent about it, and I'd heard her and Dec have several semi-heated discussions about the cost of shavings versus the horses' health.

Gran returned lugging Gracie's bran mash in a red bucket, and Dec quickly took it from her and went to feed Gracie, who stepped carefully around her sleeping baby to go eat.

Gran took in my appearance. "Let's get ourselves some breakfast, and you some clothes."

The thought of coffee perked me up. We were all tired, but it wasn't the pale, dragging weariness I'd felt while I was in school. This tiredness came with the satisfied sense that, for this small moment in time, all was as it should be.

And then we stepped outside.

"Oh, my," Gran said.

Dec passed a hand over his face. "Looks like it's going to be a long day."

The pale light of dawn revealed the effects of the windstorm. The main riding ring in front of us was missing several fence boards, and jumps were scattered around, some of them evidently broken. We walked around slowly in the early-morning chill, opening the rest of the barn doors to let the fresh air in. The calm that now prevailed was an eerie contrast to the scene: large branches were strewn everywhere, there were ragged gaps in the fencing, and litter dotted the landscape.

We checked the pasture that Jaden had built two years before, which luckily turned out to be intact. That was a relief because we had put the pasture horses in the arena overnight, with temporary water buckets and hay, but they couldn't stay there for any length of time.

"I need some coffee before I can tackle any of this," Dec grumbled. But as we rounded the corner of the barn we stopped dead.

"Uh-oh," I said. Dec swore, a rare indulgence for him. The stately old elm tree that stood beside the shed had split and crashed through the shed's roof. I couldn't believe we hadn't heard it, but then the storm had been awfully loud.

Gran patted his shoulder. "Come, now. We'll all feel better after some food. We're fortunate, really, that the only major damage seems to be to the shed."

She was right, I thought. Now that the shock of the mess was wearing off, my happiness over the foal stole back into me.

I'd never been so glad to see a cup of coffee. Dec's mood remained grim, but Gran and I chatted cheerfully over breakfast. We were just finishing up when the house phone rang.

"I just got your message!" Stephanie said breathlessly. "I was waiting for your call but I fell asleep. How-"

"Congratulations," I said. "It's a colt." I was grinning from ear to ear.

Stephanie shrieked, and I could hear her yelling, "It's a boy!" to someone in the background, presumably her boyfriend. "How is he? And Gracie?" she asked.

"Both fine. He's a beautiful baby, Steph." I swallowed, feeling emotional.

"I'll be there was soon as I can. Thank you, thank you!"

There was a small, reluctant smile on Dec's face when I turned around. "At least something good came out of last night," he acknowledged. "Better put some clothes on, kiddo. We've got work to do."

We started by feeding the horses, but someone had to keep an eye on the foal too. We had to make sure he passed the meconium — the first, dark stool — and that he continued to stand and nurse. Gracie, too, needed watching, so Gran took on that job, being the best equipped. After the horses were fed, Dec and I inspected the pasture and run-in shed more carefully before putting the outdoor horses back into it. Then came clean-up duty.

We got gloves, empty feed bags, and tools, and started picking up debris and fixing fences. Alan arrived, but he'd have his hands full with cleaning that day so he could only help Dec with the heavier lifting that I couldn't manage. Dec's eyes kept going back to the tree on the shed, but we both knew we had to get things picked up on the ground first so that lessons could resume and horses could be turned out. The show horses that were very fit, like Hades, required daily turnout on top of their work or they could hurt themselves through sheer excess of energy. We had already made calls to cancel that morning's lessons, but Dec planned to fix the main ring in time for the afternoon classes.

"We can do the smaller paddocks tomorrow," he mumbled around the nail he held between his lips. I was holding a fence board while he hammered.

My heart sank. "Um... remember I'm leaving tomorrow." I was headed for the big Quebec shows.

Dec turned and stared at me for a full minute. Then he turned back to the fence and started pounding again, noticeably harder. Guilt tore at me, but there was nothing I could do. The trip had been planned for weeks.

To my relief Stephanie appeared at that moment, her boyfriend hurrying after her. She waved gaily at me before being swallowed up by the barn.

"I'm going to go talk to Steph," I excused myself. I took his grunt as assent.

I got to the stall in time to see Stephanie slip inside. She hugged her mare's neck, neither one moving for a long moment. Then Gracie turned her head deliberately towards her foal, looking pleased with herself. As well she might.

Stephanie eased herself carefully onto the shavings next to the sleeping colt. He was lying flat on his side, his legs taking up a silly amount of space. She passed a hand lightly over the dark fluff of his coat, over and over, looking mesmerized. I craned my neck to look at

Stephanie's very tall boyfriend, who stood beside me. He seemed as happy as Stephanie and I snuck away quietly, smiling.

When I stepped back outside my smile vanished. There remained so much clean-up work to be done, and I was already limp with fatigue.

"I have to cancel my afternoon lessons," I told Dec as I shuffled up.

He wiped the sweat off his brow with his forearm. "We can't cancel today on top of yesterday, we'll lose too much money." Worry pinched his features.

"But I have to ride Hades and Cal, and pack for the show-"

"Then you'll have to skip your usual preparations!" His nostrils flared, and his fair skin reddened. "Who do you think I keep this place going for, anyway? Do you think I'm doing it for my health? If I worked at my consulting business full-time I could keep normal hours and have time to spend with Joanne, but because you and my mother are hell-bent on keeping this place I'm out here with no sleep and less patience, fixing fences for the thousandth time, and all you can think of is running off to another show!"

I felt as if he'd struck me. Worse, even. I'd always thought I worked hard and did my share to keep the family business afloat, but apparently, I was wrong. Tears stung my eyelids; I wanted to flee, to escape to some quiet corner to sort through my surging emotions, but I held fast. A knee-jerk reaction would only make things worse, and in any case, I didn't have time for that luxury. I swallowed hard and grabbed some nails and a hammer. I could feel the weight of Dec's gaze as I moved to the next section of fencing and started hammering. Pounding something felt good, but my hands were blistered by the time Gran came to get us for lunch.

"I ordered the lumber," Gran said as we sat down. "It should arrive this afternoon. We're lucky that Emma's a boarder, Mr. Tremblay put a rush on our order." Emma's parents, the Tremblays, owned a local hardware store.

"I should cancel some lessons, Dec," I said quietly. "Even if I don't ride my horses, I won't have time to help you if I'm teaching." I kept my eyes on my plate as I spoke.

"Canceling a few days at the show would be a lot more helpful."

My head snapped up and I gawked at him, aghast. "But... I can't do that. It's paid for, and the van's reserved, and the Donalds..." I trailed off, unable to even begin to express everything that was wrong with his suggestion.

"Lessons are our bread and butter," Dec said sharply. "You know that. Going to shows without bringing students only benefits *you*, not Shady Lane."

"But if I make a name for myself-" I began.

"It doesn't change anything," he interrupted. He shook his head impatiently. "Most of the kids who come to us aren't looking to be A-circuit stars." I clamped my teeth together to hold in my retort. Dec was already on edge; I wouldn't get anywhere trying to argue my point now.

Gran looked back and forth between us and raised one white eyebrow, an expression I sorely wished I could mimic.

"Declan, surely you're not suggesting that Téa's reputation as a rider is meaningless," she chided. "You know that people will seek out a winning trainer."

"And winning at shows will ensure our barn is always full," I added.

"The barn's full now," he pointed out, frowning.

"But it's not earning at full capacity," I said quickly. This was something I'd been thinking about. "If more stalls were taken up by horses who were also in training, or whose riders were also students, we'd make more money from the same space. And a more winning reputation would mean we could charge more for lessons, and get nicer school horses that we could take to shows."

"Hmph," Dec snorted. "And what about our old school horses? After the fuss you kicked up over Panda, are you going to tell me you'd be willing to sell them?"

I looked away from his challenging stare. Okay, so maybe I hadn't worked out all the details yet; I still thought I had the beginnings of a good plan. I had thought that I was planning for the future, Shady Lane's as well as mine, but now worms of doubt were wriggling through me and causing me to question my motives, on top of everything else.

I ended up keeping two lessons and canceling the rest, a fact that I was even more thankful for when Jaden showed up shortly after lunch. He found me teaching in the main ring.

"I came as soon as I could," he said. "I had to stop in at work this morning."

My grubbiness and tiredness felt magnified by his immaculate suit and clean scent, but he didn't seem to notice. He drew me to him and hugged me for a long minute, ignoring the gaping faces of my students.

"I'll go help Dec," he said over his shoulder as he left the ring. My entire body felt lighter after our exchange.

When I finished teaching I went and had a shower. I looked longingly at my bed while I pulled on a clean tank top and jean shorts, but I couldn't take a nap. Not after Dec's comments that morning about 'who he was keeping the place going for'.

I found Jaden next to the shed. He'd changed into work clothes and was holding a chainsaw in one hand. He put it down at the sight of me.

"Now I'm the one who's dirty." He chuckled as he embraced me. I felt him pressing his face into my wet hair; it probably felt good in the afternoon heat.

"What can I help with?" I murmured.

"We're about to cut the tree into sections and toss them down," he replied. "I'd rather you stayed away from that, but I have been waiting for you to introduce me to the new foal."

Jaden was enchanted by the foal. He kneeled in the clean shavings and let the small creature nuzzle and sniff him before getting up regretfully. He joined Dec in tackling the tree and patching the shed's roof while I continued mending the fences. Alan stayed late and fed the horses so we'd have more time to spend on repairs. I took some time to lunge Hades also; he had far too much verve to be kept in a stall for an entire day, and I didn't want an excess of springiness to cause him to hurt himself in the van the following day.

By the time we sat down to dinner it was late and dark, but the most pressing repairs had been made. The shed roof would have to be properly redone, and one of the paddock gates needed replacing, but overall the stable could function.

"You're going to have to hold off on your painting project," Dec told me as he helped himself tiredly to potato salad. "We won't have the money for it after all these repairs. We used to have a small emergency fund but I used it to redo the roof on the house two years ago." He sighed, and Gran patted his hand.

It was so late after we ate that I went to do the bedtime check. I also had to re-check my trunk to make sure I'd brought everything for the show. I still had clothes to pack, but the tack and equipment were more essential, and I'd been so tired while doing it that I'd basically flung everything I could think of inside, rather than working from a list as I usually did.

After adding a few forgotten items — my helmet would come in handy — I collapsed on top of my trunk. Jaden had gone out to his car; he reappeared and sat next to me. He handed me some papers which I stared at blankly.

"It's your riding contract," he prompted.

"You lawyered all over it," I said in dismay, noting the neat lines of red text in Jaden's handwriting. I'd thought the rider agreement I'd found was fine — simple, basic, and unlikely to scare off owners.

He put his hand to the side of my face and turned it gently toward him. "I'm trying to protect you," he reminded me, "and as usual, you're not making it easy." He leaned in. I placed my hand on his firm stomach and ran it around to his back as his mouth brushed my temple, then my cheek. I was already losing patience; I locked both arms around him and tugged him toward me. I felt his throaty chuckle as his lips finally moved onto mine. His hand slipped under my legs and he scooped me into his lap without breaking the kiss. I was all for getting carried away, but after a minute he pulled away, sighing.

"You're exhausted, you need to get up early, and I have to be at work tomorrow. We'd better go to bed."

"But I'll be away for three weeks," I reminded him plaintively.

"I'm aware of that," he said shortly. His face hardened as he looked away.

I hesitated before putting my hand to his face. "Please don't be mad at me," I said in a small voice. "Everyone else already is, and it's hard enough for me to leave without remembering you like this."

His gold-flecked eyes swung around and locked onto mine. His gaze burned into me as his body began to thrum with restrained passion. "You're going to be awfully tired tomorrow," he warned.

I nodded. He stood, still holding me in his arms, and strode purposefully to the feedroom before placing me on the ladder to the hayloft. I scrambled up, not wanting to wait another second, and the trapdoor had barely shut before we were entwined and falling together onto the hay.

Eight

The next morning was predictably brutal. Brittney's groom loaded her horses, I loaded mine, and after making sure Hades and Cal were comfortable I climbed into my car and prepared for the long drive.

"Good luck, and enjoy yourself," Gran said. She handed me a paper bag. "I made you a snack, but you'd best get some coffee before you go too far." Her blue gaze lingered on my shadowed eyes.

"Thanks, Gran." I grasped her hand in gratitude for a moment, relieved that at least one member of my family didn't resent my leaving.

It was a long drive, most of it flat and uninteresting. I kept the radio cranked up to stay awake, took regular infusions of caffeine, and made it to Bromont in record time. The Bromont showgrounds were gorgeous, set on rolling green hills next to a lake and surrounded by mature forests, but I wasn't in any state to appreciate them. Karen had texted me our stabling information, and as soon as I arrived I grabbed the old sleeping bag from my trunk, unrolled it in the darkest stall corner I could find, and fell instantly asleep.

I was awakened by a snort at close range. My eyes opened slowly and traveled up a long chestnut nose adorned by a stripe and crooked snip. Cal.

I sat up and patted him groggily. Karen grinned down at me. "Afternoon, sunshine. Do you plan to come get the big guy anytime soon?"

I scrambled up, dragging the sleeping bag with me, and went to collect Hades. My head was still cobwebby with sleep, and I blinked in the bright light. Hades came off the trailer in a clatter of metal, and once down he pranced around me in a circle, snorting. He was decidedly feeling the effects of his day off. Brittney jumped dramatically out of the way although Hades was nowhere near her, and Karen shook her head.

"You'd better take the edge off him before you put him away or he'll destroy the stabling," Karen advised.

I figured I might as well familiarize myself with the showgrounds at the same time. I'd never been to Bromont before, although I'd seen the facilities on television and in magazines. After tacking up I spent a leisurely hour riding Hades all over. We inspected the cross-country course (I was very tempted to try out a few of those jumps), rode around the perimeter near the woods, and found such important locations as the snack bar and bathrooms. The late-day light drenched us in gold as we ambled back, both of us in high spirits.

My first ride proved to set the tone for the show. I loved having my own car and not being dependent on owners or my coach for transportation, and I loved that, other than classes and caring for my two horses, my time was my own. Some days I hung around the show, but others I drove into town. There I'd walk around, window-shop, listen to French being spoken, and revel in my anonymity. At home, there were constant demands on my time and Julien was far too small a town for me to wander unseen. And then, every time I realized how much I was enjoying myself, I'd feel guilty for the work I'd left behind. Dec's words kept coming back to me, making me wonder precisely how much of his life he felt he'd given up for Seth and me. Had he really wanted to leave the horse business behind and make his living as a consultant? If so, had he simply been biding his time all these years until we were grown so that he could finally follow his own dreams? It didn't seem likely to me — Dec wasn't the self-sacrificing type — but I thought that if my mother had asked it of him, he would have done it. The idea left me cold with horror. To think that all those years Dec had been living a life that was his second choice, all for us. We certainly hadn't always been grateful for it.

Most of the time thoughts of home were easily kept at bay. I wasn't overly busy with only two horses, but I cared for them diligently and spent many happy hours hanging out with the other riders, talking tack, training, and general gossip. Alex had arrived and was a regular fixture at my side. Unfortunately, it turned out that wherever Alex went, Brittney wanted to be.

"Dude, what's with your not-so-little shadow?" I asked him over lunch one day. We were in his trailer, eating sandwiches and enjoying the air conditioning.

He grinned, hazel eyes twinkling. "Haven't you noticed? I'm like catnip to the ladies."

I refrained my rolling my eyes. "Suure... I can barely control myself right now. But Brittney seems a little obsessive."

"I think she's dated every other straight guy on the circuit. I'm the last holdout, which I suppose makes me particularly tasty." He waggled his eyebrows suggestively.

I laughed, trying desperately not to snort apple juice out my nose. When I'd managed to swallow I leaned back against the upholstered bench.

"You remind me of my brother," I said fondly. "He always makes me laugh at the worst times too." Or he did, I thought, feeling the familiar rake of pain. It wasn't as sudden or sharp as it had been in the beginning, this missing my twin, but it could still hurt me. Like ripping a scab off the same wound, over and over.

I meant it as a compliment, but Alex seemed less than excited by the comparison. "C'mon," he said, getting up. "Let's see if we can dodge Brittney long enough to ride."

Alex got out his new horse, a quick, smallish roan mare, while I got Cal. Alex's groom took over readying his horse and he came to help me.

"When are you going to get a groom?" he asked as he dusted off Cal's already-clean coat.

"When I can find one who can handle Hades," I groused.

"When she can afford one, more like." Brittney strolled up and smirked at me.

"It's like she's never heard the words 'politically' and 'correct' used together before," I mused to no one in particular. She was so completely blunt it was almost refreshing. Almost.

Brittney turned to Alex, her smile going bright and her eyes wide. "Mummy's having champagne and canapés in the tent after the Grand Prix. You'll come, won't you? Everyone will be there."

Alex glanced at me.

"Oh, you should go, Alex," I urged him, hiding my smile. "*Everyone's* going." Either sarcasm was lost on Brittney or I was beneath her notice because she left happy. Alex watched her go.

"Maybe I could do worse," he said, shaking his dark head thoughtfully. "When she was dating Kent Barnsworth she flew to all of his shows and had a catered lunch delivered every day."

"Seems like a high price to pay for lunch." I smiled at him. "I think you can do better."

Alex was funny and nice, if shy, and Brittney was obtuse and grating. And although I supposed it didn't matter much, they didn't seem like a good physical match. Alex was a lithe five foot eight or so. Brittney was a bit taller, and bigger too, her build tending to stocky. She had that porcelain skin that redheads sometimes have, and blue eyes that would have been pretty if they weren't always looking down her nose at things.

I wondered why I didn't remember Brittney better. When she was mounted I had a sense of having seen her before, because to a rider, another rider's position and style are as distinctive as a face. Maybe I didn't know Brittney well because for two years after Blaze died I hadn't competed much in the higher jumper classes. And in any case, I'd never been part of the wealthy 'in' crowd of juniors that were seen as the up-and-coming riders.

Cal did well in his class that day, placing second after an easy, stress-free round, and I relayed the news proudly to Jaden from my motel room that night.

"Have the Donalds signed the contract yet?" he asked after congratulating me.

"Um... not quite. I haven't found the right time to ask them."

"It isn't complicated, Téa. You give it to them, they take some time to read it, and then they return it to you signed. You need to do this, you deserve better than you're getting."

"I'll do it tomorrow," I promised.

The next day was the Open Jumper class, the first big class of the show for Hades and me. It was a chance to see how I'd fare against the competition on Sunday when I'd be riding in my first international Grand Prix, a thought I'd been studiously avoiding all week. Karen had felt that we were rushing Hades by entering him in the international class, but Neil had said, "Nothing ventured, nothing gained," and since it was his money and his horse, I had reluctantly agreed. I remembered seeing a clause in the new contract about being involved in decisions about class entries and resolved to bite the bullet.

Before a big class, I would withdraw into myself, creating a quiet little bubble from which I hated to be pulled. Before I could get too far into that state, I found the Donalds. They were in the spectator tent with some of their new horse-owner friends.

"Hi," I said wanly.

"There you are! I hope you're feeling good — we're expecting big things today, big things!" Neil said.

I nodded weakly, wondering why I was so nervous. I thrust the contract at Monica. "Um, I forgot to talk to you about this. We should probably have a contract, you know, for both our sakes," I mumbled. "You can take your time reading it." They both looked at me blankly, Neil suddenly quiet. I turned to go. "I'll see you later."

I strode quickly back to the barn, feeling a measure of relief. At least I'd given it to them.

I put the conversation behind me as I got Hades ready. Competition in the Open Jumper class would be stiff; many of the international riders were using it as a warm-up class for the Grand Prix in two days' time. Hades knew that something was up — horses are excellent mood sensors — and pushed me repeatedly with his nose, as though that would snap me out of my nervousness. Finally, I shoved him back, and he pricked his ears, apparently content that he'd done his job and cheered me up.

"Thanks, buddy," I said, smiling despite myself. Karen gave me a leg up and I went to school, now focused entirely on my nonverbal communication with Hades. It was constant and subtle, and consisted of no more than the tightening of a muscle or shift of my weight. Even the direction that I looked in affected my horse. Of course, communicating my intentions was one thing. Getting Hades to actually *listen* was another. Most of my early conversations with him had gone along the lines of:

Hades: Ooh, I see a jump!

Me: Slowly, now. Let's-

Hades: A good gallop will get us there.

Me: Easy boy, we need-

Hades: I got this!

Me: Oh crap.

Hades liked to be asked, not told, but we were now competing at a level where split-second decisions had to be made and there was no time for negotiation. He had to trust me enough to accept the decisions I made for both of us, and I was proud that we had reached the point where he would do that.

Our warm-up went well, and Karen walked me to the in-gate. She had walked the course with me earlier, pointing out elements that would be more challenging for Hades, but what I'd mostly noticed was how very big everything looked. The fences were five feet tall and, in some cases, over six feet wide. My hands were sweaty inside their dark gloves. When our turn came I patted Hades' neck and trotted in briskly, trying to fake a confidence I didn't feel.

Hades had confidence to spare, and as we flew over the third fence — an enormous Swedish oxer — I realized again how little size mattered to him. His hooves were thundering, the sun beat down on us, there was dust in my nose and blood drumming in my ears, but I felt myself smiling.

We were third in the Open class, and I was ecstatic. Of the riders who finished ahead of me, one was a well-known German man and the other was an American woman I'd been watching on TV since childhood. She was riding a new horse, not the famous grey she'd ridden to glory at the Olympics, and I was still in complete awe of her. When she smiled at me as we exited the ring I was almost too overcome to smile back.

I took extra pains with Hades, taking him for a long cooling walk, giving him a thorough shower, and rubbing him with liniment. I bandaged his legs for the night and straightened up, groaning, to find Alex, Karen, and a few other friends clustered at the stall door.

"Well, come on," Karen said, grinning. "You've got to get cleaned up so we can take you out to celebrate."

We went to a local restaurant where we talked, laughed, and rehashed the class in detail from every possible angle, including analyzing the inevitable cell phone footage that several people had shot. Alex and Moose had had a rail down and been out of the ribbons, but he seemed less worried about it than his mom did. Karen's other students were with us too, a stick-thin woman in her forties who dominated the Amateur divisions and a perpetually nervous junior with braces on her teeth. They had never paid me much mind, but tonight they smiled tentatively and shot admiring glances my way. It was odd and unnerving and flattering all at once.

The ease with which Hades had handled the Open class gave me confidence for Sunday's Grand Prix. Powder-blue skies heralded the day, and the energy built steadily as the time grew closer. Monica and Neil came to see me as I was preparing. I wished they wouldn't always do that because it drew me out of my little focus-bubble, but they were the horse's owners and they had a right to see him.

I reached out to stop Monica as she was about to feed Hades an apple. "He can't eat that now," I said regretfully. "You can give it to him after the class." Hades, having seen the treat, snorted and threw his head up in frustration at having it taken away. Karen tried to soothe him as I put on his saddle.

"Sorry, but I think having you around is making him a bit nervous," I said.

"He should be nervous, there's a hundred grand in prize money riding on this class," Neil said bluntly.

Not to mention it's a World Cup qualifying event, I thought to myself. "Being nervous won't help him," I explained. "It will only make it harder for him to focus. Maybe we can see you after the class?"

The Donalds wandered off. Karen rolled her eyes, and I finished tacking up thoughtfully. I hadn't realized the prize money for the class was quite that much. The hundred thousand dollars would be divided amongst the winners, so even finishing in sixth place would likely yield a significant amount of money.

There had been no mention of the contract since I'd given it to the Donalds and I decided I'd bring it up right after the class. A few thousand dollars would help enormously in making repairs at home. In fact, I could spend part of it on paint and flowers, I thought. That would make Dec happy. I was getting excited at the possibilities when Karen brought me back to earth.

"It's time to go." She headed for the warm-up area. I worked Hades away from the other horses for a while, making sure he was attentive to me. He'd gotten increasingly buoyant at the show, almost inflated with his own power. I didn't want to discourage the feeling, but I needed to remind him that I was leading this dance.

When I joined Karen by the jumps I stopped dead. "Oh my God. That's Eric Lamaze." He was doing a relaxed canter around the schooling area on a mouth-wateringly gorgeous chestnut.

"Yeah, he's in your class," Karen said absently. "Why don't you start with the white vertical." She pointed it out.

I froze. "I can't ride in a class against Eric Lamaze," I squeaked. I thought I might be hyperventilating.

Karen frowned up at me, shading her eyes with her hand even though she was wearing sunglasses. "What are you talking about? Why not?"

"Because... he was World Champion and he won gold at the Olympics and... and..." *And he's my idol.*

Karen gave me a level look. "And wouldn't you like to do all those things?"

I swallowed hard and gave a small nod.

"Then go jump the vertical," she snapped. Years of drilling kicked in, and I complied immediately. Karen was harder on me than usual, keeping me moving and testing my reflexes, but we didn't school for long. Hades needed his energy for the ring, and by the time we got to the in-gate I'd come out of my momentary panic.

It's like any other course, I reminded myself as we went in. Hades seemed to agree, and he put in a clean round, earning us a spot in the jump-off. Alex and Moose were in it too, as was Eric and the American rider from the Open class. I went last, which was lucky — I knew exactly what score I had to beat. I cut a corner too sharply and we had a rail down, but I was so proud of Hades that as we walked out of the ring I fell forward onto his neck and wrapped my arms around him.

"Nice ride." I thought I recognized the accent and straightened up quickly to find Eric Lamaze smiling at me.

I gulped. "Thanks," I said in a tiny voice. He winked at me, and I let Hades wander off, bemused. I pinched my arm repeatedly. Yup, I was awake.

We won fifth place, and after congratulations had been accepted and most of our well-wishers had dispersed, I turned to the Donalds. Karen was feeding Hades peppermints so I had my hands free.

"Did you get a chance to look at that contract?"

"We haven't signed it if that's what you mean," Neil said. "It seems kind of strange to get something like that in the middle of the season, just as the horse starts winning."

"Oh. Okay. Well, look — it's usual for a jumper rider to get a share of the prize money." At Neil's frown, I hesitated. "The thing is, I'm spending thousands of dollars to bring Cal along because I can't go three weeks without riding him, but I've got no students here and I'm losing all that teaching income. Right now I'm making more money from grooming Hades than riding him." I'd been charging the Donalds the normal daily fee for a groom but I'd been doing the job myself. "I want to keep riding your horse, but I need to be able to make a living, too," I explained.

Monica wouldn't meet my eye, and Neil pursed his lips. "Well, it may be a moot point, anyway," he said, "because someone's offered to buy him."

"For ten times what we paid for him," Monica added coolly, looking at me for the first time.

Oh no. My heart started racing, and my hands shook. I'd handled this all wrong, I realized. I'd asked them in the wrong way, at the wrong time, and now I might pay for my novice mistake by losing everything I'd worked so hard to gain. Some dim corner of my brain — the only part that wasn't panicking — registered that my suspicions were confirmed. The Donalds had paid Rodney a price that seemed high to the low-end horse dealer, but which was far, far less than Hades was currently worth. No wonder Rodney had succumbed to temptation. I hadn't seen hide nor hair of him during this show, a fact which contributed considerably to the happy time I'd been having. Until now.

My breathing was shallow, almost a pant. I felt Alex come up beside me and was glad of his friendly presence at my shoulder.

160

"Who?" I asked.

"That lady right over there." Monica indicated an older, expensively dressed woman under a tent. "Her daughter rides with Karen as well, I suppose you know her. Brittney?"

My gasp must have been audible because I felt Alex's hand squeeze my arm. I turned away, stunned. I wanted to march up to Brittney and scream at her, to demand to know why she would do this to me when she already had everything she could possibly want. But I restrained myself. It would be childish and unprofessional, and it would make me a laughing stock. Horses got sold all the time, I reminded myself. It was part and parcel of this life. But no matter how I lectured myself, my chest was so tight that I could barely breathe, and my eyes burned with the effort not to cry.

I collected Hades from Karen. She gave me a concerned look, but I shook my head. I couldn't talk about it now, and Karen wasn't the type to pry. She'd wait until I was ready to tell her. Hades was cool but he needed to be showered, groomed, and bandaged, and I was grateful for the familiar, soothing tasks to keep me occupied.

I walked Hades through the lengthening shadows. The heat of the day had passed, and we were almost back at the stabling when Alex jogged up next to me. He had just opened his mouth to speak when Brittney stepped out of the tackroom. She gave me a supercilious look and Alex rounded on her.

"What the hell, Britt! Why are you buying Téa's horse out from under her? You don't need him, you're barely keeping Salsa and George busy!" Alex's black brows shadowed his eyes. It was the first time I'd seen him angry.

She gave a careless shrug. "He's a good horse. If it wasn't me, it would be someone else. Let's face it, *she* doesn't have the money to make it in this sport."

"You-"

"It's okay, Alex," I said quietly.

He subsided and Brittney flounced off.

"You should be at the Grand Prix celebration," I reminded him.

"You're the one who placed in the class. *You're* the one who should be celebrating."

I didn't answer. I had never felt less like celebrating. Brittney's words had stabbed deep because they were true. Making it in this sport took guts and commitment and the willingness to suffer pain, but it also took good horses and lots of training and years and years of traveling and campaigning. And that took money. And I didn't have any, nor did I have very high hopes for acquiring some. Some people made it to the top the way I was attempting to — by riding other people's horses, but the drawback to that was having little control over your career. And, as I had already discovered, you could lose everything at a moment's notice.

Together we finished pampering Hades and put him in his stall with some hay.

Alex wrapped an arm around me. "I'm sorry," he said simply.

"Thanks." My head was down, staring at the shavings. After a minute I felt Alex's other hand take mine, and his head rested against my crown.

"You should go to Brittney's thing," I murmured.

"After what she did to you? No way," he said vehemently.

"I need some alone time," I said. I extricated my hand gently from his. "Go. Eat canapés. Drink champagne. It wouldn't be right to deprive all those women of your catnip essence."

He gave me a long, conflicted look before leaving. I turned to Hades with a sigh.

"What do you think, big guy? D'you want to go graze?"

"I'd rather get a real dinner."

I spun so fast my vision blurred. "Jaden!" I leaped into his arms, my face fitting into his neck and my legs wrapping around him as though that's what they were made for.

He held me tightly for a moment, saying nothing. I felt him swallow before he spoke.

"You and Alex appear to have gotten quite friendly in your time here."

A wave of chagrin rolled up my spine. I untangled myself and slid to the ground, and he let me. "How long have you been here?" I tipped my head back to see his face.

162

The tilt of his eyebrows made me realize I'd asked the wrong question. "Did you really think I'd miss your first international class?" His voice was quiet, and he sounded almost... hurt. That was the proverbial straw. I fell against him, shaken by sobs even as I tried to explain.

His arms closed around me immediately. "Shh," he murmured. His hands rubbed my back. "You don't have to explain now." His voice was strained, rough with emotion, causing me to cry anew at his assumption.

"No," I hiccupped, "Jaden, Alex is just a friend, he was only comforting me."

"For placing in your first-ever FEI class? How thoughtful of him." There was a harder edge to his words now, and his body reacted accordingly.

I shook my head against his chest and started wiping my eyes.

"Look, Téa, I knew this was a risk," he said tiredly. "We never-"

"*What?*" I demanded. I drew back and stared at him.

His eyes widened slightly, but he went on doggedly. "You're constantly traveling. We rarely see each other, and you're sharing intense experiences with your peers. It would hardly be surprising if you developed feelings for one of them."

My mouth fell open. My hands dangled loosely by my sides. I was so stunned that I stayed absolutely silent for a minute, watching emotions dance across Jaden's beautiful, tortured face. And then, finally, the day caught up to me, and I started laughing. I laughed even harder than I'd cried, folding my arms across my middle and bending over in an effort to catch my breath.

"Téa," Jaden said. I glanced up; his face held a mixture of annoyance and amusement. "Let's get some food, and then maybe you can share the joke."

I shook my head and straightened up. "I'm not hungry for food," I said hoarsely. I locked my eyes onto his, seeing the spark of my own desire ignite there. He grasped my hand tightly and led me quickly through the gathering dusk to his car. We spoke only when he needed directions to the motel, and the mood darkened with the skies as he brooded.

I stayed by the door while Jaden turned on the small bedside lamp, leaving the rest of the room in darkness. The light threw shadows across his angular face and pooled in his eyes, making them glitter.

"Come here." It was an order, not an invitation, and he didn't look welcoming.

I straightened my spine and advanced into the small sphere of light.

"Do you see this?" I held up my left wrist, upon which dangled the delicate silver bracelet that Jaden had given me. "Every night before I go to sleep I kiss this bracelet goodnight and pretend it's you. Friendly is all I'll *ever* be with anyone else."

His fingers closed over the bracelet and my wrist; he tugged me forward and used his other arm to press me hard against his body. "I never thought I'd be more scared than when I was watching you jump that course," he muttered, "until I saw Alex with his arms around you."

"I can explain-"

A small smile twisted his lips. "It will have to wait."

Our lovemaking was hard and fast, and I was sprawled across Jaden's chest in a contented daze when my stomach growled. Jaden got up and pulled me out of bed, and after a quick shower, we drove through the dark until we found a small Italian restaurant.

After we'd ordered he reached his hand across the table, and I grasped it in both of mine, feeling suddenly, overwhelmingly grateful for his presence.

"Tell me everything," he invited. And, as usual, I did.

A frown shadowed his face as I spoke, his hand tightening around mine. "Téa, this is precisely why I said you needed a contract in the first place. Why didn't you get it signed?"

"I asked them to, but... well, they haven't done it yet. And I didn't want to insist." At Jaden's uncomprehending look I struggled to explain. "I already lost Marty. The horse world is small, and I don't want to get a reputation for being a hard rider to get along with. Competition for horses is fierce, and Hades is so good, I didn't want to lose him."

"And yet you may lose him anyway, without having gained any of the benefits the contract would have afforded you. Including, I might add, protection against such a sudden loss."

I stared at the tabletop while despair welled up inside me. Jaden's long fingers stroked my forearm.

"I'm sorry, *querida*," he murmured. "Frustration has made me blunt."

I met his eye thoughtfully. "Speaking of frustration," I said, recalling my own. "How could you jump to conclusions like that with Alex? Did you think that as soon as I got a bit lonely and found a cute face nearby, I'd cheat on you? If you think so little of me, why would you even *want* to be with me?"

He winced at the word 'cheat'. "I don't think that." He leaned toward me and paused for a moment, choosing his words carefully. "I only wonder, at times, whether you realize the full value of what we have. You're young, and this is your first serious relationship-"

"I don't live in a bubble, Jaden. I have friends, I read. I know that what we share — what we *are* — is special."

"And yet, when I asked you to live with me, you were not delighted."

Our food arrived, defusing the slight tension, and the conversation turned to lighter things as we ate. Afterward, we drove back to the showgrounds to check on the horses. We walked hand-in-hand through the cool purple night. I nodded at a security guard before going in to check first Cal, then Hades.

"I'm glad you're not sleeping in a stall anymore, at least," Jaden grumbled.

"Someone *should* be sleeping here," I groused. "He got a ribbon in a World Cup qualifier." I closed the stall door and looked morosely over it at Hades.

"Well, it won't be you," Jaden said, stepping up behind me. His arms snaked around me and he pulled me back against his chest. "I have plans for you," he whispered in my ear.

"Then it's a good thing Karen's husband is in town for the weekend, isn't it?" I twisted in his arms and caught his surprised look. "I'm sharing a room with her, remember? Lucky for you, she's gone to his hotel for the night. But don't you have to work tomorrow?"

"I'm going to take a day off." I thought there was something grim about his face as he said it, but in the gloom, I couldn't be sure.

The show wasn't running on Monday, so after feeding the horses I spent a relaxed morning with Jaden. We went for a walk around the lake and had a picnic lunch before returning to the showgrounds to lunge my horses and let them graze. I was in the tackroom hunting up a second lunge line for Jaden when Alex stopped by.

"How'd it go last night, catnip?" I grinned at him.

He shrugged. "It would've been more fun with you there."

Jaden strode in. His presence seemed to fill the small space, and his arm went around me possessively before he dropped a kiss onto my startled mouth. Jaden was quite demonstrative — I had his Latina mother to thank for that — but he was clearly marking his territory.

"Jaden, you remember Alex?" I didn't know whether I was more angry or amused.

The guys nodded at each other. Alex was pale with shock, and I half-reached for him in concern.

"Are you okay?" I asked.

Alex tore his eyes away from Jaden and stared at me in consternation. "I thought... I mean, isn't this guy your cousin?"

I felt my stomach sink. "Not by blood," I said carefully. "We're only related by marriage."

"But you're still *related*." He started backing out of the tackroom, a look of frank horror on his face.

"Alex, wait-"

Jaden's fingers tightened around my shoulder, preventing me from following. I turned my face up to him, distraught.

"Let him go," he said quietly.

"You did that on purpose," I whispered. I felt hollow.

"It wasn't my intention to hurt him." His gaze was so sincere that I wrapped my arms around him and rested there, suddenly spent by it all.

Jaden left after an early dinner, and I cocooned myself in the motel room with a bag of popcorn and the TV remote for company, prepared to watch enough comedies to keep the doldrums at bay. The thought of losing Hades was like a splinter in my brain, and it was all I could do to keep my attention diverted. I'd barely made a dent in the popcorn when there was a knock at the door.

I brushed crumbs off myself before opening it to find Neil Donald standing there. My heart gave a kick. "Is Hades okay?"

"The bugger tried to bite me today, so I'd say he's feeling fine," Neil said with forced joviality. I narrowed my eyes in suspicion.

"Here." He thrust an envelope at me. "Regardless of what happens with the horse, this is yours. I think it covers all the shows."

As soon as he left I ripped open the envelope. Inside was a check for almost five thousand dollars. I staggered to a chair and dropped down limply. I examined the back of the check, then the front again, before noticing the scrawled notation, 'Prize money – rider's share'.

When the shock had worn off enough I bounded to my feet and called Jaden. "Guess what?" I babbled the news excitedly while pacing the room until his lack of surprise aroused my suspicion. "Did you do something?"

"I met him for a short, friendly conversation. That's all," he assured me. "I left on very good terms."

I should probably have felt indignant that he'd meddled in my affairs, but I didn't. He'd merely done what I'd been too cowardly to do for myself.

"Thanks," I said quietly. I did a brief happy dance around the room before the splinter snagged again but, although I tossed and turned much of the night, I had to admit that small slip of paper helped soothe my distress.

My nerves went right back to jangling after Monica called the next morning.

"The potential buyer would like to try Hades out today," she said, stressing the word 'potential' as though that made things better. "Around three o'clock, all right?"

Rage swept through me. "It has nothing to do with me, does it? So you can do it anytime you like," I responded tersely.

"Oh... well, I thought you'd be there," Monica said uncertainly. "You're his trainer."

"Sorry, I have plans for the day." Plans to not kill anyone, which might be dashed if I were around Brittney when she touched *my* horse.

I threw my phone on the bed with an inarticulate growl.

Karen gave me a mild look. "Bad news?"

"Brittney's trying Hades." I spat each word as though they tasted bad.

"And I take it you're not planning to attend?"

I just looked at her.

She sighed. "It's not smart to burn bridges in this business, kid. Even if the Donalds sell, they could get another horse someday."

I sagged onto the bed. Karen was right. I knew it, and I knew that I was acting immature. Horses were a business, as Dec was always reminding me, and I had to start thinking of them that way. But I simply couldn't do it. Horses were my *life*. Every thought I had of them was shrouded in layers of emotion. To me, Hades was a friend and partner with whom I'd traveled across rough, unknown terrain. We had bonded through mutual discoveries and learned interdependence. There was no dollar value for that.

I set aside my despair and went to ride Cal and let him graze. At home he got time outside every day, loose in a paddock, which gave him a chance to just be a horse.

Most modern horses' lives are so very unnatural; instead of spending all their time meandering and grazing, they spend twenty-three hours a day confined to a small space — about the equivalent of a large closet for a human. When they're taken out to be ridden or worked, every footstep, turn of the head, and change of balance is micro-managed. They can't even scratch an itch on their backs if they want to. It was so vital to their physical and mental well-being to have some small moments of freedom, and although some show horses were deemed 'too valuable' to be allowed such interludes of sanity, it was something I'd never want my horses to do without. Unfortunately at shows turnout was impossible, so instead, I took them out on a leadrope and let them graze. It wasn't the same, but it was a pleasant break for them.

When I brought Cal back Hades looked at me expectantly. I hesitated. Of course, he wanted to go out, but I didn't want to ride him — I wanted Brittney to get the full impact of what she was in for. And if I was being honest with myself, for once I didn't want Hades relaxed and happy.

Hades gave a nicker.

"Oh, all right," I muttered.

After Hades had grazed I went in search of a late lunch. Alex was leaving the snack bar, dressed in breeches and a T-shirt.

"Hey, catnip," I greeted him.

He gave me a preoccupied look but didn't stop. "Hey. Sorry, I've, uh, got to go," he muttered.

I felt myself droop. I didn't need any additional worries that day, but I felt quite sure that Alex's new attitude was due to Jaden. I sighed. I could have used a friend that afternoon.

I debated going back to the motel, but when the time came I couldn't do it. I ended up spying instead. When Brittney arrived I skulked in the shadows of an empty stall in the next row. Brittney herself went in to get Hades, which was a surprise. Maybe Elise had the afternoon off. A moment later she staggered backward — Hades had probably shoved her, as was his wont.

"Hey!" Her yell carried to me.

Hades flung his head up, and it looked as though his ears were pinned. Yelling offended him. Brittney turned and started trying to lead him from the stall. He took a few steps before planting his feet. She turned and gave the lead shank a jerk. Hades rose immediately, rearing high above her. She stumbled backward and a *thunk* carried clearly through the calm air.

I ran over. I rushed past Brittney, whose mother was helping her up, and slowed only as I stepped into the stall.

"Easy, buddy," I murmured. Hades' head was still high, his eyes rolling. I was suddenly convinced that the experience had reminded him of Rodney's. I couldn't have said why; maybe it was the anxiety that poured off his body. "You're all right, baby," I said tenderly, stroking his neck. I made no attempt to grab the lead rope, just kept rubbing his neck and shoulder until he lowered his head and gave me a small nudge.

"There you go," I crooned. When I rubbed his forehead he dropped his head further. "Oh!" I exclaimed. Anger surged up inside me, but I backed away calmly before stalking out of the stall.

"Good going, Brittney. You made him cut his head!"

"*I* did! He's a maniac," she yelled at me. Brittney's mom was fussing over her while Monica and Neil looked on in concern. Monica tore herself away and came over.

"Is it bad?" she asked, peering into the stall over my shoulder.

"It doesn't look too deep, but the vet should look at it. The poll is a sensitive spot — it's a bad area to hit." The cut was on the top of his head, between his ears, but my main concern was the possibility of a head injury.

"It looks like we'll have to postpone," Neil told Brittney apologetically. "Next time we'll get him tacked up for you, okay?"

Brittney shot me a venomous look before taking her mother's arm and marching off. She passed Karen on the way.

"What did I miss?" Karen asked. As Brittney's trainer, she would normally have been present while Brittney rode a potential new horse, and I wondered whether her late entrance was intentional. I was back at Hades' side, moving his halter away from the cut and probing gently around it for signs of swelling or pain while I gave Karen a rundown of the event.

She sighed. "You know, if you'd gotten him ready this wouldn't have happened. She never tacks up her own horses anyway."

I'd been having the same guilty thought, and I stayed with Hades until the vet came. When I led Hades out of his stall he rolled an eye suspiciously at the vet, who climbed onto a mounting block for the examination.

"It is far from the heart," the vet said cheerfully in a strong French accent. After quickly cleaning it, he stuck an oddly-shaped bandage over the wound. "To keep out the dirt."

"He has a jumper class tomorrow," I said anxiously. "Will he be okay to compete?"

"*Mais oui*," he reassured me. "It does not even require stitches. If his behavior changes, call me."

"So, I'll see you tomorrow?" I asked Monica and Neil awkwardly. Neither of them looked happy, but they nodded.

"Let's go get some coffee," Karen suggested. We left Hades crunching a carrot and took Karen's car to Tim Horton's. I got an iced cappuccino since the day was humid and hot, but Karen stuck with her regular black brew. I watched as she dumped a small mountain of sugar into it.

She leaned back in her seat. "Mike thinks I should cut down on sugar," she said. Mike was her rarely-seen husband. "But I've already quit drinking. Sugar and coffee are the only vices I've got left." She grinned at me, and I smiled back. Our relationship had changed over the past year; she was still a demanding coach and mentor, but she treated me as an adult now, and as a friend.

Her brown eyes assessed me. "What are you going to do about Hades?"

I was startled by her question. "There's nothing I *can* do," I protested. "He's not my horse."

"Your actions still have an effect, Téa. Look at what happened today. You could choose to make this transition as smooth as possible for Hades and be as helpful as you can to the Donalds, or you can fight it every step of the way. It won't change the outcome, but it will change how everyone sees you, and whether they'll want to deal with you in the future."

Her words were spoken matter-of-factly, but I hung my head, ashamed. "You're right. I just... I don't want to lose him." My voice broke, and I cleared my throat, embarrassed. "I told you about not having a contract, right?" Karen had returned to our motel room during my brief post-check happiness.

She repositioned her sunglasses on her short, sun-streaked brown hair and sighed. "I've seen it before with riders just coming out of the junior ranks. So many will work without a contract because they feel that if they refuse, there are twenty more just like them lined up to take their place. But in your case no one was lined up for Hades — he was a monster."

"They'll line up now, though," I said miserably.

"Maybe." Karen eyed me thoughtfully. "How long has it been since anyone else got on him?"

I rolled my eyes. "Neil wanted to ride him about a month ago, but I talked him out of it." Yet another reason a contract would have been smart, I thought ruefully. "Um, I guess it's been almost two years."

"Well then, Brittney may be in for a rough ride. I tried to change her mind, you know," Karen said gently. "She's a strong rider, but she doesn't have your light touch, and that's what Hades likes."

Nine

Hades seemed perfectly normal the next day, but I checked with the vet anyway before preparing to ride. When the vet laughed and called me a mother hen I felt confident that my horse was fit for his class. It wasn't a big one because I was saving his energies for the next Grand Prix on the last day of the show.

We breezed around the course and won the class. "Uh-oh," Karen said as we emerged from the ring. "Looks like his cut opened up."

I walked Hades to a quieter area and dismounted. Maybe he'd rubbed his head on something — though I hadn't noticed him do it — because the bandage was gone and the cut had reopened slightly. A small trickle of blood flowed into the white stripe on his forehead. His face was sweaty and the blood had smeared, making it look much worse than it was, but the cut itself looked fine.

I gave him a reassuring pat. "Let's get you cooled off." I started walking.

"Speaking of which," Karen said, falling into step next to me, "I may have found you a groom." She motioned a woman over to us. Blond hair fell in curls to her shoulders, and she looked at Hades before she did me. I liked that.

"My, he is a big boy, isn't he?" She turned and held out her hand and I halted Hades to take it, meeting friendly blue eyes. "I'm Tania."

"Téa."

Tania smiled. "Oh, I know who you are. Do you want me to take him?" she offered. I hesitated, but then figured this was a good test.

"He's a bit of a handful," I warned, handing the reins over. I stood still as they began walking. Hades turned his head to look for me and planted his feet when he realized I wasn't coming. Tania tried to encourage him forward, and he gave her an irritated shove.

"Can I push him back?" Tania asked. I appreciated that she checked first.

"Sure thing — he kind of expects it, in fact."

Tania gave Hades a little push. "Come now, none of that. Let's get you cleaned up, and then you can have some nice hay," she said in a no-nonsense tone. Hades pricked his ears, gave one last look at me, and followed her.

I grinned over at Karen. "She might just work out."

"She's very good. We're lucky she quit her last job."

I showed Tania where everything was and then helped her take care of Hades. Afterward, we went to find the Donalds and I introduced Tania as a Hades' new groom. They were pleased that we'd found someone, and she left amongst handshakes and congratulations. I turned back to the Donalds, uncomfortable. They were thrilled with our win that afternoon, although the class hadn't yielded much money, because it boded well for Sunday's class with its one hundred thousand dollar purse.

"Monica, Neil," I said, making myself meet each of their gazes in turn. "I'm sorry about the way I've behaved. The next time Brittney or anyone else comes to ride Hades, I'll be there to help."

Monica's face softened, and I reached out to pat Taffy, ensconced in today's zebra-stripe bag with matching bow. After a minute Neil nodded.

"I have to tell you, though, that if you wait until next year, you could get a lot more money for him," I said. "We're just starting to see what he can do. Once he's winning consistently you'll have your choice of buyers."

Neil passed a hand thoughtfully over his balding head. "I think we'll be hanging on to him for at least a little while."

Relief made my steps light for the rest of the day, even though Alex barely nodded at me when I passed him. I was still feeling good the next morning as Tania helped me tack up Cal, but apparently, my sunny outlook wasn't shared by all. There seemed to be an odd mood prevailing on the showground, and several times I noticed people put their heads together and whisper as we walked by.

Karen was at the stable when I got back from riding.

"Was there a memo to be moody today?" I asked her as I hopped off. I had barely pulled the reins over Cal's head when Tania materialized.

"I'll take him," she said cheerfully.

"I could get used to this." I took off my helmet and caught sight of Karen's face. "What?" I asked warily.

She sighed. "You're going to see it sooner or later." She handed me her phone. An image filled the screen; it was a close-up of me riding Hades, with a shock of blood bright against his white forehead. Someone had snapped it as we were coming out of the ring. Hades' nostrils were wide as he caught his breath, and his head was dropped in relaxation, but it could also look like weariness, I realized. He was dark with the sweat that had spread the small amount of blood. The caption on the photo read "CruelTea". Clever and cutting — to anyone who didn't know that my name was pronounced 'Tay-a'. I could just imagine how bad it would look on a computer, with the image ten times larger.

I lifted my eyes helplessly back to Karen. "Where did this come from?"

She shrugged. "It's making the rounds of the forums. People are complaining that our sport's gotten enough bad press lately, what with insurance scandals and drug scandals — you remember that show pony that died? They're saying this makes us look bad."

"Yes, but I would *never*... I mean, how could anyone think this was intentional? What possible advantage could I gain from injuring my horse's head?" I was almost whispering, limp with shock.

She answered slowly, thinking it through. "It's the impression it gives, that we're willing to compete at all costs, even if it injures the horse. The animal rights groups would be all over this if they saw."

"But... but..." It was all so surreal. I was speechless.

Over the next few days, all over the showgrounds, I'd see people look at their phones then throw me dark looks and mutter amongst themselves. The riders who knew me joked about it, knowing that I'd never hurt my horses for any reason, but there were plenty of people who didn't know me at all. I started walking everywhere with my head down.

"This too shall pass," Karen reminded me on Saturday. She patted my shoulder. "By the next show, everyone will have forgotten about it."

I doubted I would, though. I was obsessed with finding out who had posted the picture and spent all my free time online on my phone, browsing through horse forum pages and Facebook links, trying to find its origin.

On Saturday I prepared Cal for his last class under turbulent skies. Tania gave me a leg-up as Alex arrived, accompanied by Brittney, of all people. He looked up at me sadly.

"Hey, Alex," I said quietly.

"I would never have thought it of you," he said. His voice was soft. At my puzzled look, he went on more loudly. "That picture of Hades? It looks bad for all of us."

"What? Alex, you of all people-" I protested.

"Don't even bother, Alex," Brittney said, slipping her arm through his. "She's not worth it." She led him away, and he didn't look back.

I blinked back tears. Tania frowned up at me in concern. "Are you okay?"

I nodded before plodding slowly down to the schooling area. Cal seemed to sense my mood, because he was skittish and distractible in his class, leaving us in fourth place. Alex won on his new roan mare, which lowered my spirits even further — if nothing else, I at least wanted to beat him.

It drizzled on Grand Prix morning but the rain stopped at midday, leaving the air as thick and warm as flannel. I thanked my lucky stars for Tania and stayed hidden away as much as possible, not wanting the hostile atmosphere to get me down before my class. Hades was apparently the only one unaffected by the mood, and we finished a respectable eighth. I stripped off my helmet and jacket and wiped sweat from my brow as soon as we'd collected our ribbon.

"It's time to go home, big guy," I said as I fed him a peppermint.

Monica came mincing over in her impractical shoes. "Aren't you staying for the party?" She was all smiles.

I shook my head. "I can't. The van's leaving tonight, and I have to be home to unload the horses." The van would be arriving at about two in the morning, and it wouldn't be fair to ask anyone else to stay up waiting for it.

I said my goodbyes. In truth, I was anxious to get home. I'd had a wonderful time at the beginning of the show, but I missed Jaden, I was

176

growing homesick, and I couldn't wait to escape the judgmental stares that I'd been bearing for the past several days.

I woke up automatically at feeding time the next morning, even though I hadn't set my alarm. I considered rolling over and going back to sleep, but I wanted to see everyone so I stumbled out of bed. I could always have a nap later, I consoled myself, yawning.

I found Dec in the barn. He gave me a one-armed hug while balancing three flakes of hay on the other.

"Nice to have you back, kiddo. I didn't expect to see you up this morning."

"You should have stayed in bed," came a voice from inside the feedroom. I caught Dec's smile from the corner of my eye as I broke into a run. Jaden met me in the doorway; I plowed into him and he caught me up, laughing.

"What are you doing here?" I asked breathlessly. I covered his face and neck with kisses.

"I played polo yesterday, and stayed over to see you," he murmured into the nape my neck.

We fed quickly, and the three of us returned to the house together. Jaden and I walked hand-in-hand.

In the kitchen, Dec sat down with a sigh. He rubbed his face with both hands before glancing at me. "Could you get me some coffee?"

I took one step before Jaden's hand on my arm stopped me. He pulled me back to his side.

"Téa got home in the middle of the night, Dec. She's tired." He was frowning.

Dec gave him an exasperated look. "Yes, she got home from three weeks of taking care of two horses, living in motels and eating in restaurants. During which time Gran and I took care of thirty-six horses, taught lessons, fixed all the damage from the storm, and got our own meals."

I moved again. "It's okay-"

Jaden propelled me gently toward my chair. "I'll get it," he said quietly. "Can I get you anything?"

"I'd love some coffee too." I smiled at him and turned to Dec with the expression lingering on my face. "I'm glad you got everything fixed up. I thought of you. I missed everyone."

"Even grouchy old Dec?" Jaden asked, placing coffee mugs on the table.

"Even him."

Dec leaned forward, smiling, and patted my hand. "We missed you too, kiddo. Gran and I watched your Grand Prix rides, you know. You made us proud," he said. His voice turned gruff at the end. I'd talked to Gran on the phone before my classes, and knew she'd be watching, but I hadn't known Dec would be too.

Gran bustled in and headed straight for the counter. "I made muffins, we can have them for breakfast."

Gran must have spent considerable time here, I realized, if she'd been teaching, cooking, and helping with the cleanup. I felt a twinge of guilt and jumped up to help her. I sniffed the muffins; they were strawberry rhubarb, made with the rhubarb that proliferated behind our house. Jaden was pouring juice for everyone and I got the plates.

I closed my eyes in contentment as I took my first bite. When I opened them Gran was watching me with a pleased look from across the table. Over breakfast we caught up on news and rehashed the two rides they'd seen.

"Oh, that wall!" Gran exclaimed. "It's dreadful how small and light they make the blocks these days. Why, in my time, that would have been considered an unfair obstacle."

"If you'd kept him more collected going to the in-and-out in your second class, you wouldn't have had a rail," Dec observed. "You just don't have the strength for him, honey."

Ah, the joys of family. I turned my small, satisfied smile to Jaden, sitting next to me. The look he returned to me made the breath catch in my throat. I'd definitely been away too long.

I walked Jaden to his car right after breakfast. "I'd stay, but I've taken too much time off," he said. He gave me a mock stern look and slipped his hand around the back of my neck. "I expect to see you this weekend. No excuses." He pulled me forward and gave me a lingering kiss, a promise for the weekend.

I wandered happily into the barn. I loved Mondays, our day off. I turned Hades and Cal out in adjoining paddocks, since they had formed an unlikely friendship at the show, and went to see the foal. He was steadier on his stilt-legs, and toddled over to see me as soon as I'd stepped into the stall. When I sank onto one knee he pushed his velvety nose into my cheek. I felt sure he remembered me. Stephanie had named him Smoothie, which I thought was funny considering he'd been born on the stormiest day in years.

I had a shower and started on my massive pile of laundry, waiting impatiently for afternoon, when Teri was coming to visit. My muscles were sore, and I did some stretches before making myself a sandwich. Dec was in Toronto and Gran had gone home, so I went outside to join Alan at the picnic table for lunch. Teri's car pulled in minutes later.

"Ter!" I dropped my half-eaten sandwich and jogged over as she got out of her car, and we traded a joyful hug. It always felt a bit odd to me to hug someone my own size — she felt so small.

She joined us at the picnic table and we chattered excitedly for a while. She looked amazing, strong and sun-kissed, and I told her so.

"I love being a jockey," she agreed. "But enough about me, what about you? You're a Grand Prix rider now — not too shabby." She nudged me playfully in the ribs.

"Yup, I'm so hot that none of the other riders will even talk to me," I said wryly. Teri knew about the debacle with the picture, of course. I'd texted her, Julia, and Seth regularly from the show.

"Yeah... about that." She pulled her phone out of her purse and touched the screen briefly. She handed it to me silently, her face suddenly grave.

I was looking at a Facebook page with the now-familiar picture of Hades. It didn't say 'shared', but that wasn't proof of anything. When I checked the time and date my heart started pounding. It had been posted minutes after my class. I looked at Teri.

"It was posted in at least three places almost simultaneously," she said. Her celery-green eyes were worried, but I detected steel in her voice. "I'd bet money that's the original poster... and check out the name."

I glanced back at the picture. The Facebook user's name was "BritNeigh". She had a cartoon as a profile picture and no personal details listed, but my hands shook with anger.

"Dammit," I almost yelled. "What the hell is wrong with her?"

Teri shrugged one shoulder. "She's an asshole. I think it's a genetic condition."

I gave her a reluctant grin. "It's got to be the same Brittney, right? I mean, what are the chances?"

"One and the same. I asked around."

"Well, that does it," I said, jumping up, "she's getting kicked out of here."

I was still incensed when I told Dec about it that night, pacing back and forth beside his desk. "We've got to kick her out," I finished angrily.

He closed his laptop and leaned back in his chair. "Hold up there. She's boarding two horses and she's Karen's student. We're not evicting her because you had a squabble."

My brows knit together. "A squabble? Dec, she's trying to ruin my career. She's been nothing but miserable toward me since she got here."

He spun his chair toward me suddenly, one hand braced on the desk, tense. "Your *career*? You're getting too old for these childish fantasies, Téa. Yes, you're doing well this year, but you need to start thinking of riding as an extra-curricular sport. You're going to get a real career — one that you can still do when you're sixty, one that pays a regular salary and that isn't dependent on your puny physical strength."

"Riding *is* a real career," I insisted.

Dec shook his head. "How can you say you want to stay in this business when can't even put your personal feelings aside? Do you think we can afford to turn away clients just because you don't like them?" His arctic blue gaze was sharp and unmoving. I felt myself backing down, feeling the edge of his temper.

"But..." I trailed off.

"Are you sure your problem with Brittney isn't jealousy?"

I gaped at him, my agitation suddenly eclipsed by a piercing pain running the length of my sternum. Even Dec thought Brittney was better than me. My own father.

"No," I said hoarsely, "it isn't." I clutched my composure like a shield and left the room.

We left it at that. I taught and rode all week, and when Brittney showed up I avoided her as much as possible.

At times I wondered what kind of person Dec would be if he'd followed his own path instead of going to school as his father had dictated. Maybe he wouldn't be angry and frustrated so much of the time; perhaps he'd even consider bending his own strict rules. Now that was a Dec I wished I could have known.

My spirits couldn't help but rise on Saturday because I would be spending the whole day with Jaden. I'd endured a dressing-down from Dec about how I was shirking my responsibilities — weekends were our busiest time — but even that couldn't dent my mood. I took special pains getting ready that morning, blow-drying my long-again hair and applying makeup. I slipped into a flowered blue sundress, grabbed my rarely-used 'good' purse and skipped out the door in my white sandals. When I got to Jaden's I bounded up the stairs; I had barely knocked when the door flew open. I was immediately tugged into his arms.

"Look at you," he said after a minute, holding me at arm's length. "Your cheeks are rosy, your eyes are sparkling, and your lips..."

I never found out how my lips looked, because Jaden's covered them at that moment. His hot hands moved down my back, from my shoulders to my bottom. He squeezed it, pressing me against his hardness. Then he pulled away, letting out a long, unsteady breath. I opened my eyes slowly.

"We have to go," he muttered. He ran his finger slowly along my collarbone, making my skin tingle. "The next time we spend the day together, we're not leaving the house," he vowed.

"Remind me again who we're seeing?" I asked as we climbed into his car.

"My buddy Colin. I went to high school with him but he's been living in Chicago the past few years. He and his wife just had a baby."

"He has a baby already? And he's your age?"

Jaden gave me an odd look. "He was a year ahead of me in school, and I think his wife is a bit older than him. Late twenties is not an unreasonable age to be having children, Téa."

I felt the prickle of sweat breaking out all over my body. "My mom always told Seth and me not to even *think* about children before we were thirty."

He smiled gently at me. "*Querida*, your mom was not only very young but single and without a career when she had you. If she'd been surrounded by a loving family and had a good income, her outlook might have been different."

"Maybe. But then she still wouldn't have fulfilled her *own* dreams, the things she wanted to do for herself before she began living for her kids."

Jaden glanced at me with interest. "What did she want to do?"

"Travel," I replied promptly. "She wanted to see the world, and she wanted to be a teacher. Instead, she got pregnant at twenty, dropped out of school, and spent the rest of her life working long hours in various stores to support us."

He reached across the gear shift and took my hand. "You rarely talk about her," he murmured.

I shrugged and looked out my window. It had been five years since my mom died. I felt as though I should be over it, but I wasn't. Jaden laced his long fingers through mine and squeezed gently.

I turned back to him with a wobbly smile. "Well, at least this afternoon should be interesting." We were going to watch Teri race at Woodbine, and it would be my first time seeing her in action.

We got to the condo and took the elevator. Jaden's friend Colin, a beefy football-player type, opened the door. After the introductions and obligatory back-pounding Colin led us into a sleek, ultra-contemporary living room. The only splash of color among the blacks and greys was one of those bouncy baby chairs, incongruous on the living room floor.

"This is Mandy." Colin introduced me to a tired-looking woman dressed all in grey sweats, as though to accessorize the room.

"And this is Cameron," Mandy said proudly, indicating the sleeping baby in her arms. I sat in a chair while Jaden settled on the couch next to Mandy. Colin made a brief foray into the tiny kitchen and returned brandishing glass bottles of Perrier. He handed us each a bottle before plopping onto the arm of the couch.

Colin took a swig from his bottle. "So! I can't believe you're at Sisto, Goldberg, and Hwin." He punched Jaden lightly on the shoulder and looked past him to his wife. "This guy was trouble with a capital T in high school, but somehow he always managed to come up smelling like roses." He turned his grin to Jaden. "Must be nice to have a dad with clout."

Jaden shrugged and sipped his water before bending forward to inspect the baby. I frowned. I knew for a fact that Uncle Peter had had nothing to do with Jaden's hiring.

Seeing Jaden's interest, Mandy turned and held out the baby. "Here," she murmured. To my surprise, Jaden immediately put down his bottle and took the small, white-wrapped bundle. Mandy looked across them and shared a smile with her husband.

I watched Jaden cradling the infant. He looked surprisingly comfortable. He softly brushed the downy tuft on the baby's crown, his face wearing an expression of such sweetness that I felt my insides melting.

He looked up. "Would you like to hold him?"

I practically jumped back in panic. "No! I mean, no... thanks, anyway. I'm not much good with babies." That wasn't an outright lie, but in fact, I had no idea how I might be with babies, because I'd had very little exposure to them and had never held one.

Jaden gave a knowing smile and came to stand next to me. "You won't break him," he murmured. He transferred the baby smoothly into my arms, positioning me just right before putting a hand on my shoulder. I sat frozen, afraid to move lest I jostle the tiny, fragile thing. Colin and Mandy looked on with those sappy, doting smiles that only new parents can manage.

"He's beautiful, isn't he?" his mother sighed.

"Um, yes," I murmured politely. Privately I thought that Cameron — and all babies for that matter — looked very much like alien life forms with their hairless heads, toothless, drooling mouths, and spastic movements.

Jaden thankfully took Cameron back from me, suppressing a smile, and I heaved a sigh of relief. I was sweating as though I'd just jumped a course.

"I didn't know you loved babies so much," Jaden commented once we were back in the car. He was clearly amused.

I shot him a glare. "Why did you make me hold it?"

He shrugged one shoulder. "Babies are a part of life, Téa. It's an experience everyone should have." He glanced at me thoughtfully, one hand resting on the wheel. "You're so good with the kids at the barn, it didn't occur to me that you wouldn't like babies."

"That's different. At the barn they're on ponies, I know what to say to them in that situation. Babies are so... strange."

Jaden threw his head back and laughed the warm, carefree laugh I loved, and it struck me how little I'd heard it that summer. He reached for my hand. "Aren't you even a little bit interested in babies?"

Sure, in a car-crash sort of way, I thought. The kind where you can't help looking, all the while thanking your lucky stars it isn't you. That seemed a bit harsh to admit, so aloud I merely said, "Not really. Being a mom is all about cooking and laundry and cleaning up messes. In other words, things I'm not interested in doing."

"I think it's about more than that," Jaden said.

"Maybe on an abstract level. But practically speaking, you basically become a domestic robot and servant to your kids. And," my voice dropped to a whisper, "I'm not sure I even like kids."

"I'm fairly confident that you would like our children," Jaden said drily, the corner of his mouth twitching up. I was mildly annoyed that he wasn't taking my feelings of doubt seriously, and I mulled over his words as we made our way to a Thai restaurant for lunch.

"Were you and Colin good friends?" I asked after I'd started on my Pad Thai noodles. Colin seemed different from Jaden's other friends.

"Not particularly, but we've always kept in touch. I'll probably see more of him now that they're back in Toronto, especially once the nanny starts next week."

"They're getting a nanny? But... that baby looks really new." I found it jarring that anyone would hand over the care of so helpless a creature to a complete stranger.

"Well, yes. Mandy has to go back to work."

"So they're paying someone else to raise their child for them? Don't you think that's kind of selfish?"

"Selfish?" I could tell he was honestly shocked.

"Yes. They're treating their child like some sort of... I don't know, convenience. Something they'll spend time on when it suits *them*."

"It's not that black and white, Téa." He had traveled from shock to the border of irritation. "Mandy can't simply stop working, she has a career to think of. And it isn't only the amount of time you spend with a child that matters — it's the quality."

"Says the man whose own mother arranged her schedule around her children." I was getting fired up without even knowing why. "I know more about this than you, Jaden, because I *was* that kid. The one who got to see her mother for an hour at the end of the day, when we were both tired and frazzled and all we did was eat a quick dinner, shower and go to bed. There was nothing quality about that time."

"What about weekends?" he asked quietly.

I shrugged. "Weekends were for laundry and grocery shopping and cleaning the house. And, sometimes, for activities for Seth and me. But don't forget my mom worked in retail, so when we were young weekends sometimes meant more daycare."

He nodded, thoughtful. "That was a difficult situation for you, but a nanny is different from daycare. I went to school with lots of kids who had nannies and they turned out fine."

"But you had your mom, and you turned out spectacular," I pointed out.

"In your completely unbiased opinion." His eyes grew soft, and the corners of his mouth curled up slightly. "I'll admit, I would prefer it if our children never needed a nanny." My entire body stiffened. Children were not something I'd ever seriously thought about, but nothing about the idea seemed appealing.

I twirled a long noodle slowly around my fork. "So, you want children, then?" I didn't look at him as I spoke.

"Well, yes, someday." His hand covered mine, halting my fork. "I'm not talking about next week, *querida*." I peered up from under my lashes to meet his concerned gaze. "Come on, let's go watch some racing," he said.

I forgot my discomfort when we got to the racetrack and met Teri's parents. The Macleods were also watching their daughter race for the first time, and we made our way to seats close to the rail. I was surprised at how crowded the spectator stands were on a cloudless summer weekend and wondered if it was always this way.

Teri wasn't riding until the fifth race, but we couldn't see her because she was confined to the jockey's room. The first four races sped by, and then it was Teri's turn.

"Hurry, you're going to miss it," Mrs. Macleod said excitedly, pulling Mr. Macleod into his spot at her side. He had gone to place a bet on Teri's horse. Another procession of lean, long-legged Thoroughbreds jogged out, topped by splashes of colorful silk-clad jockeys. I spotted Teri right away, dressed in green and white. She was in the number three position, which meant that once her horse was loaded into the starting gate he had to wait for four more horses. Some horses got very wound up in the gate, but Teri's mount appeared to be waiting patiently. The bell rang, the gates sprang open, and horses burst forth onto the dirt.

"And they're off!" exclaimed the announcer.

The horses were on the far side of the track, so their hoofbeats weren't loud in the air. In my head, though, all was different. My memory responded to the sight of those surging bodies with a burst of sensations — the sharp scent of sweat, the drumbeat of hooves pressing against my eardrums, rubberized reins pulling hard against my sore arms, and the rhythmic rocking of my body, drunk with glorious speed.

As they came around the turn into the homestretch Teri made her move. She was on the rail, two horses back from the leader. Her dark bay colt opened up his stride and swept easily past the horse in second place. He gained steadily on the leader; the finish line was about eight strides away and the roar of the crowd rose as Teri's horse pulled ahead. Jaden, the Macleods and I were on our feet, cheering loudly. Teri's colt stretched further, pushing himself, his hind feet landing, then his front ones, then, in seeming slow motion, he crumpled toward the ground, his nose hitting the dirt, his body flying over his head in an awkward, impossible somersault. His body bounced against the track as a stream of horses parted around him and galloped past, the jockey's faces stark white. The crowd's roar had turned to shrieks.

186

There was a loud ringing in my head. And then I heard Teri's mother scream, the sound ripped from her very soul.

Mr. and Mrs. Macleod rushed toward the rail. Jaden strode forcefully behind them, and I stumbled in his wake, gripping his hand with all my might. We were stopped at the rail by a security guard.

"I'm sorry," he said, blocking the Macleod's path. "You can't-"

"That's my *daughter*. That's my baby!" Mrs. Macleod wailed. She was a small, round woman, but she grabbed the front of the security guard's shirt and shook him. He didn't stop her. Mr. Macleod was frozen and blank-faced beside her. Jaden stepped forward and put his arm around Teri's mom.

"Come on, Marie. Let's go find out where they're taking her. We'll go to the hospital."

I stared in horror at the track, where Teri's horse had lurched to his feet. One of his forelegs was grossly misshapen, and he was shaking so hard I didn't know how he could stay on his remaining three feet. My heart was a spongy mass jammed into the base of my throat; I couldn't breathe past it. I was balanced precariously on the edge of hysteria, but at that moment the ambulance arrived. We watched as Teri's small, limp form was lifted onto a gurney and loaded inside. Mrs. Macleod was making noises like a wounded animal. Tears were streaming uninterrupted down my cheeks.

The security guard had been talking on his radio. "They're taking her to Sunnybrook Hospital," he said in a choked voice. He placed a dark brown hand on Mrs. Macleod's shoulder. "I'll pray for her."

Jaden herded us all back through the large building and into the parking area.

"I'll drive," he said, glancing at the Macleods. I took Mrs. Macleod's soft hand and we hurried together. The parking lot seemed ten times bigger and it took an age to find the car, but finally, we were inside and Jaden was speeding through traffic. My pulse was loud in my ears, and my brain played the same thought on a repeating loop: She has to be okay. She has to be okay. I couldn't get the image of the injured horse out of my head, standing wide-eyed and trembling, his leg dangling uselessly.

By the time we'd gotten inside and found a nurse who could answer us, Teri was being prepped for surgery. We couldn't see her. Teri's parents went to the admissions desk to fill out forms while Jaden and I found chairs. The air conditioning was on high in the waiting room, and I was soon shivering in my sundress.

"I'll go get you a sweater," Jaden offered. I shook my head and slid closer to him on the hard plastic chair. When I rested my head on his shoulder he wrapped both arms around me. He didn't seem cold, although he was only wearing a thin T-shirt.

My phone beeped. *Where are we meeting up later?* It was Julia. I'd forgotten our plans to meet with her and Al.

Can't. At hospital. Ter had an accident. I texted back quickly. There were pictures of crossed-out cell phones posted around the waiting room, but several people had phones in their hands so I hoped the prohibition was against actual calls. My phone rang immediately; I muted it and hurried to the exit to take the call.

After explaining the situation to Julia I realized I'd better call home too since I didn't know when I'd be back. I choked out an explanation to Dec.

"Oh my God," he breathed. "How is she?"

"We don't know," I whispered.

"Will she live?"

I stayed silent. The fact that I couldn't answer that question blocked my throat completely.

"I'm coming up there," Dec said. He hung up. I trailed slowly back to the waiting room, shivering violently at my return to the cold. Jaden was bringing coffee for the Macleods, who had arrived in the waiting room, and he handed them each a cardboard cup before turning and enfolding me in his arms.

"Come to the cafeteria with me." He kept his arm around me as we walked, and I vibrated constantly against him. He detoured to the gift shop. I didn't even notice what he was doing until he handed me a sweatshirt. I pulled it on gratefully and rolled the long sleeves up until my hands showed.

We got coffee at the cafeteria. Jaden got a muffin too, but it sat untouched between us.

"When I think of you galloping at the track..." he trailed off hoarsely, but his eyes, as they met mine, were fierce.

"That was almost three years ago and I haven't done it since," I reminded him.

He passed a hand through his hair. "Which is fortunate, because I think I would explode if you did."

I frowned. "Jaden, let's not make this about me. This is about Teri, and it was an *accident*."

We went back to the waiting room, where I sat next to Mrs. Macleod while Jaden paced the halls. Mr. Macleod seemed to be in some kind of shock; he didn't say a word, just sat and stared unseeingly at the wall in front of him. Every now and then Teri's mom would pat his knee, but he didn't seem to notice. The Macleods had always seemed like the most happily married of all my friends' parents, always chatting to each other companionably. It was hard to see them like this.

"Where's Tim?" I asked suddenly. Teri's older brother should have been here, helping his parents.

"He went to the West Coast for work," Mrs. Macleod whispered. "I don't know if I should call him. If he needs to-" Her voice cracked, and she started crying quietly. I patted her shoulder, feeling useless.

Julia rushed in, and I jumped up and hugged her tightly. When I let go she sat next to Mrs. Macleod and held both her hands.

"How is she?" Julia asked.

Teri's mom drew a shaky breath. "She has a few broken ribs, and one of them punctured a lung. Her spleen's ruptured and will probably need to be removed. Other than that, we don't know."

Julia turned haunted eyes on me.

"Take a walk with me," I suggested. Once we were out of earshot I told her the rest. "Ter didn't regain consciousness between the accident and the hospital. That's got the doctors concerned." We found Jaden and together returned to the waiting room.

The waiting was interminable. Dec arrived; he gave me a hard hug before going to sit with Jaden.

Finally a round-faced, middle-aged woman in scrubs came to find us. "I'm the traumatologist who treated your daughter," she told the

Macleods. "She came through surgery well, considering the damage. She's in recovery. You should be able to see her in a couple of hours."

We breathed a collective sigh of relief and moved to another floor to await Teri's arrival. When she was finally wheeled up a stern nurse blocked our way.

"Family only," she snapped.

Teri's mother seized my hand. "We're her parents, and this is her sister."

I stood at the foot of the bed as Teri's parents each took a side. They murmured to her and patted her gingerly. I swallowed hard. There didn't seem to be much left undamaged. Her nose was broken, her eyes were swollen and discolored, her right arm was strapped tightly to her body, while the left was hooked up to an IV.

Teri opened her eyes slowly. "Don't cry, Mom." Her voice was weak and raspy. Teri's mom cried harder, and her dad came and led her to a chair. I moved to the bedside.

Teri blinked at me groggily. "I must look like crap for you all to be so freaked."

"You might have to blow off the pageant this weekend," I admitted.

"How's the colt?"

I hesitated, wondering whether I should lie. "I think his racing career is over," I said finally. I reached across the bed and took her undamaged hand. It felt cold and small, but she squeezed my fingers weakly.

The nurse came in and shooed us out. Jaden and Dec were leaning against the wall; they straightened up expectantly as we spilled into the hallway.

"She's awake," I said. Jaden took my hand and I leaned against him, needing the support. Dec hugged Teri's mom and shook hands with her dad before we headed for the exit. Teri's parents were staying.

"I tried to tell them not to let their little girl be a jockey," Dec groaned when we were around the corner. He spun suddenly and grabbed me by one arm.

"Do you see what happens when you won't hear reason?" he demanded, shaking me. It wasn't a particularly gentle shake, either.

190

"Hey!" Jaden wrapped his arm around me and pulled me from Dec's grasp. "Ease up, Dec — she just saw her best friend almost die, for God's sake."

"Exactly," Dec snapped, "and it could have been her!" He turned his glare on me, his blue eyes burning peculiarly hot. "This was your mother's nightmare, Téa. Because you're not simply oblivious to danger, you actively court it."

"How is this-" I started, but Jaden's arm was still around me and he tightened his fingers, warning me to let it drop. I clenched my teeth together. I didn't want to be fighting right now, but I was indignant that everyone was extrapolating this accident into something that could befall me. I wasn't a jockey; riding jumpers was far less dangerous.

I took a breath. "Are you going home or to Joanne's?" I asked Dec as civilly as I could. He usually spent time with his girlfriend on Saturdays.

"Home. Someone has to take care of the barn, I've barely seen Joanne in weeks. Gran and Catherine can't keep up with lessons on their own."

Guilt kicked me in the stomach. "I'm sorry about that," I murmured sincerely. "But... Dec, can I stay at Jaden's tonight? I want to come and see Ter in the morning." I asked permission anxiously, half-expecting him to say 'no' out of anger.

He gave a tired nod. "Okay."

It was dark when we got outside. Jaden and I were quiet in the car.

"Oh no — Julia!" I exclaimed suddenly. "I forgot to say bye to her."

"She left while you were in seeing Teri. She had to meet Al."

I scowled. "There's something weird about that relationship. Julia's never preferred to spend time with a boyfriend than with Teri and me, and she certainly wouldn't have left at such an emotional time."

He glanced at me. In the dashboard's glow, his angular face seemed severe. "Maybe it's the first time she's been this serious about someone. When your relationship is a priority, you learn to make concessions."

I covered my face with my hands. "Is it me, or is everything being turned back against me today?" My complaint came out muffled.

Jaden tugged one of my hands away and kept it in his. "You're right, now's not the time to talk about this." And since I agreed with the no talking part, I didn't ask what the 'this' referred to.

191

We trudged up the stairs, and I leaned on the wall while Jaden unlocked the door.

"Pizza?" he suggested. I shrugged, past caring. I collapsed on the couch, and when he was done calling he sat next to me and pulled my legs onto his lap. He began rubbing my feet.

"You know, Dec has a point," he said quietly. His eyes remained my feet. "Riding jumpers is dangerous."

"Says the polo player."

"*Ex*-polo player. I gave that up, remember?"

I nodded slowly. "Yes, you did, although you don't seem any happier for it. In fact, I've never seen you as stressed and unhappy as you've been lately."

He released my feet all at once. "How would you know, Téa? You've barely seen me in months!" he snapped.

"Yeah, and you sound *so* happy right now," I pointed out, irate.

He jumped up and took a long stride away from me, raking his hand through his hair.

"I'm planning for our future, dammit! I'm willing to-" The buzzer sounded. Jaden went to the door and paid for the pizza. He dropped it on the coffee table before glancing at me. I turned my face away, not wanting him to see my tears.

He sank onto the edge of the couch and gathered me into his arms. He pressed his face into my neck, one hand tangling into the hair on the back of my head. We didn't talk any more that night. We ate our pizza and went to bed, where there were no disagreements.

I met Julia at the hospital the next morning, and we went into Teri's room together. Her parents had stayed the night, but they'd gone home to shower and change.

"Thank goodness," Teri muttered. "They were stressing me out. My mom can't look at me without crying."

It looked as though Julia might do the same any minute, so I moved in front of her. "How do you feel?" I winced. "No, wait — that was a stupid question."

Teri peered at me. The bruises around her eyes had darkened overnight. "No, it's not. They're keeping me pretty doped up, so I don't feel as bad as you might think." She turned her head away from us and went on tonelessly. "The trainer called. The colt was put down. He broke both forelegs." Her breathing hitched. "I'm doing better than he is."

Julia and I made comforting noises. I walked around to the other side of the bed and took Teri's hand, being careful of the IV taped into the back.

"You know it's not your fault, right?" I murmured.

"Yeah," she mumbled listlessly. "But somehow that doesn't make me feel any better." We shared a look of deep sympathy. I knew exactly how guilty you could feel over the death of a horse.

We left her to rest after a short visit. "Oh my God," Julia said as soon as we were in the hall. She dug out a tissue and dabbed at her eyes. "Her face... she'll never look the same."

My jaw went slack. I stared at my friend and could not think of a single thing to say. Not only was Teri's recovery so much more important that it eclipsed her appearance altogether, it also plain didn't matter. Teri was a beautiful person, period. Her beauty came from her refusal to judge others, her steadfast helpfulness, and her self-deprecating humor. A change to her face wouldn't diminish her beauty one whit.

I cleared my throat. "Jules, remember when you first came to the barn and everyone stared at you all the time because of how you look?"

She chewed on her index nail pensively. "Not really. But I remember how no one could stop talking about how gorgeous Jaden was when he first arrived."

"You were the worst of all," I said. I felt my mouth quirk up at the memory, and Julia gave a wistful smile in response. "The thing is, Jules, when I look at Jaden now I don't see a gorgeous guy. I see the man that I love. Sure, how he looks is part of him, but I'll love him just as much in fifty years when he's stooped and grey. Or even bald." I held Julia's stunning grey gaze gently. "Teri will always be beautiful in the ways that matter."

"Of course she will! I didn't mean... I just feel so bad for her, that's all." Julia hung her head, her dark hair falling in a glossy curtain across her face. It was so unlike her usual confidence that it made me uncertain, almost like I was talking to a stranger instead of one of my closest friends.

"Is everything okay? How are your parents adjusting to the divorce?"

"All right, I guess. I haven't seen them much."

"Jules... maybe it's none of my business, but you seem to have gotten pretty involved pretty fast with Al. Are you okay? Are you happy?"

She tossed her head back and gave me a bright and completely false smile. "Yes. We're doing fine." I didn't buy it for a second, but I couldn't dig any deeper — I had to go home and make up for all the work that I'd missed.

I went to my room to change first

since I was still wearing the previous day's sundress. I checked my phone reflexively, wondering why I hadn't heard back from Seth yet. I tugged on shorts and a T-shirt before firing up my laptop and shooting him a short email. It read simply, "Call me now."

I was pensive as I wandered into the barn, but was snapped into alertness by anxious voices and the unmistakable sound of hooves thudding against wood. I hurried cautiously around the corner and was met by an odd sight.

Alan was leading Gracie, but she had planted her feet near the door. Her head was high, craned to look behind her for her baby. Smoothie was rooted uncertainly in the aisle, staring wide-eyed at the source of the ruckus — Rosy, in her stall. Rosy was a placid draft horse cross named for her strawberry roan color. She was built like a tank but was as gentle and caring a soul as you'd hope to find, not that you'd know it at the moment. She whinnied excitedly at Smoothie, then rose onto her hind legs and pressed her nose against the bars, snuffling loudly.

"Gracie won't budge without her kid," Alan called to me.

Gran marched in at that moment. "You take one side, I'll take the other," she said. She bent next to Smoothie and placed one arm around his hindquarters and the other on his chest. I did the same on my side, and we quickly steered Smoothie toward his mom. As soon as he saw her he sped to her side, and Gran and I let him go when we got outside. We watched the trio head for the pasture, Smoothie frolicking along the way.

"What was that about?" I turned to Gran.

She raised her hands, palms up. "Some horses get very excited around babies. Perhaps Rosy's already had a foal of her own, or perhaps she would very much like one."

"Maybe Gracie and Smoothie should just stay outside," I suggested.

"We'll talk to Stephanie about it," she agreed.

Alan came back, shaking his head. "I'd take him out the other door but I don't want the little tyke getting near the cars in the parking area."

At his age, Smoothie wasn't leading yet. If we wanted to take him somewhere, we simply brought his mother and he followed. I went inside and visited Rosy. She was still shooting hopeful looks in the direction of the door.

"You really like that little guy, huh?" I said, stroking her large neck. "Well, maybe one day you can have your own." Even as I said it, though, I wondered whether we'd be doing Rosy any favors by breeding her. Foals were usually weaned from their mothers at four to six months of age, although in the wild they nursed for a year or so. And fillies usually remained close to their mothers for life, living in the same herd. Maybe Rosy would be more hurt by having a baby taken away than by never having one at all.

I threw myself into work that week, trying to atone for my absences. I taught, I cleaned, I rode, and I organized a painting crew by trading lessons for labor. I bought paint using my prize money and started repainting the trim on the barn and shed. I drove into Toronto every second day to visit Teri and briefly see Jaden, and by week's end, my feeling of satisfaction was worth the aching muscles.

Monica and Neil arrived on Friday with their daughter, a bored-looking, gum-snapping fifteen-year-old. I had just finished hosing off Hades after riding him, and I held his leadrope while they patted him. The daughter gave me a cursory once-over, taking in my snarled hair and dirt-smudged clothes, then turned and wandered away. I can see why they rarely talk about her, I thought wryly. I reached out to pat Taffy, dangling in the usual shoulder bag. She, at least, greeted me excitedly regardless of my hair.

"I was talking to some other owners at the last show," Neil said as we walked Hades back to his stall. "It seems like everyone's gone to Vermont but us — how come?"

"We could go next year if you want." Vermont wasn't a show I normally considered because it was farther away and therefore more expensive.

"But what about now?" Monica asked. "Where's Hades going next?"

I hesitated. "There's the Orangeville International next week, and Angelstone the week after that. They're both a few hours away."

Neil rubbed his hands together. "Great, let's do it." I quailed at the thought of telling my family I was deserting them again, and I worried about leaving with Teri still in the hospital, but this was my future and I had made a commitment to the Donalds. I couldn't quit now.

I made sure to take care of every detail of work that evening and the next morning, leaving Dec and Gran virtually nothing to do. After washing my hands for lunch I sat down and peeked at Gran.

"What do you know about the Orangeville International?" I asked innocently. Dec's eyes narrowed.

"It's a fairly new show, but I've heard good things," Gran said.

"The prize money's good."

Dec stopped eating and put his fork down. "Out with it." The look on his face was not promising. Or rather, it promised things I didn't want.

I swallowed. "The Donalds want to go. I know you don't think me winning at shows benefits the barn, but I paid for the paint with my last winnings. When I get back I'll do the fences. And I'll buy more landscaping plants."

Dec examined his plate. "How long would you be gone?"

"Four days next week, and then five the week after that for Angelstone," I said with some trepidation. "But I'll bring Emma and Cameo to Angelstone with me."

He sighed and rubbed his temples. "We need to replace some light fixtures in the barn. Make sure you win."

He tilted his head sideways to catch my eye, and I smiled. "Okay." I went back to eating with renewed appetite.

"What's your brother been up to?" Dec asked, too casually. I normally kept everyone updated on Seth's doings.

The worry I'd been suppressing in order to deal with more pressing matters immediately bobbed to the surface and began to gnaw at me. "I don't know. I haven't heard from him for a while."

"I wouldn't worry. You know what Seth's like," Gran said reassuringly. "He's probably off on a little jaunt."

Jaden arrived that afternoon. I was debating how to tell him that I was leaving again, but first I had lessons to teach, and then I had to ride Cal, and when we snuck into the shed after feeding I didn't want to ruin the moment. Particularly since the moment involved his lips moving against mine and his hard body pressed against me.

"How come you haven't gone soft?" I asked when I had a second to breathe.

"Is that a trick question?" He laughed as blood rushed to my face.

"No, I mean... um, your *body*." I poked him in the stomach. "It's not like you spend your days in the saddle anymore but you're still stronger than I am."

"Let's hope I'm always stronger than you." He grinned. "There's a gym at the office. I went today, in fact. I need to maintain my strength so I can keep all those men away from you." He sat on the old trunk and patted the spot next to him, but I stayed on my feet. I rolled my eyes.

"What men? Jaden, no one but you even notices me."

"Oh, really. What about Alex?" He said the name as though it tasted bad. "I told you he was attracted to you, but no, you wouldn't hear it. You slept in his trailer!"

I suppressed a groan of frustration. "Jaden, when are you going to stop being jealous?"

He leaned forward and grabbed me around the waist with both hands. He pulled me between his long, jean-clad legs.

"Maybe when I've got a ring on your finger." His smile could only be described as roguish. "But I'm not making any promises."

"Jaden James Foster! This isn't a laughing matter." I planted my hands on my hips.

"Are you angry with me?" Jaden asked. The corners of his mouth were starting to curl upward.

"You do realize that prospect shouldn't amuse you, right?"

His smile only grew. "But you're adorable when you're angry."

"Ugh!" I tried to turn away, but he overpowered me easily and pulled me into his lap. I had just decided to forgive him when we heard Gran calling us in for dinner.

We were in the barn afterward, debating the merits of braving the mosquitoes for a twilight trail ride, when Brittney arrived.

"Where's Elise?" she demanded, glancing around. I shrugged; I hadn't seen Brittney's groom since morning. Brittney seemed to notice Jaden for the first time. She did a double-take before joining us, wearing a smile I'd never seen before.

"Why hello. I'm Brittney." She simpered, offering Jaden her hand. I felt my teeth snap together.

Jaden exuded charm as they shook hands. "I'm Jaden, Téa's boyfriend." He stressed the word *boyfriend*, and I felt a smirk twitch across my face.

Brittney stared first at him, then at me. Her shock was definitely insulting. "Well, well. So you're the one Alex was talking about." She was looking at Jaden with such undisguised acquisitiveness that I actually stepped closer to him. "The kissing cousin."

She turned to me, conspiratorial. "If I were you, I'd keep this one close. I mean, with all the stuff that's been happening to you at shows lately... is he coming to Orangeville? I heard you were going."

I stuttered, my fury at Brittney mixing with dread as Jaden turned a laser-like look on me.

"Excuse me?" His voice was like shards of glass. Before I could open my mouth to explain Elise rushed in, full of apologies which Brittney waved off airily. She was obviously in a fine mood.

Jaden gripped my upper arm and marched me outside. He hesitated for a second, then headed for the shed, pulling me with him. He propelled me inside, slammed the door, and turned on me.

"You promised me you were going to stay home for August!"

"I did not promise! I said I'd stay close by, and this is close. Sort of."

"Are you really going to argue semantics with me?" He took a quick step toward me, causing me to back up automatically. My temper sparked; I was mad at myself, mad at Jaden, and mad at the whole messy situation. I drew myself up and raised my chin defiantly.

"I'm not going to argue with you at all, Jaden, and you know why? Because I don't have to justify this to you! This is my career, and I-" My voice was rising before he abruptly cut it off.

"Your career? Then what about school, Téa? Why are you slogging through nine years of expensive education to be a vet if you're truly planning to ride for a living?" His jaw was hard, his eyes narrowed as if trying to stare through me to the truth.

"I... I'm in school because of you," I admitted crankily. "You and Dec. You can't very well have some ignorant shmuck for a girlfriend, and Dec didn't leave me much choice, anyway." I almost stamped my foot in frustration, so angry was I at having to make that admission.

He threw his hands up in the air. "That makes no sense! What about our future? I thought you *wanted* to be a vet. How can we have a life together when you're never here?"

"Why is it that *you* get to decide what kind of life we have?" I retorted hotly. "Plenty of people have lives on the show circuit."

"Not married people!" Jaden yelled.

"We're not married!" I screamed back. "And at this rate we never will be!"

He flinched and drew back from me, but I was too angry to try to make amends. He threw me a disbelieving, wounded look before turning and stalking out of the shed, leaving the door hanging open behind him. I shuffled over to the trunk and fell limply onto its hard lid. I buried my face in my shaking hands and tried to convince myself that I hadn't just seriously damaged the best thing in my life.

I spent the evening hiding in my room. Dec volunteered to do the night check, so the only time I emerged was to skulk to the bathroom, and I saw no sign of Jaden. He was playing polo the next day, and if he hadn't been I suspected he would have left.

Ten

I fed the horses by myself the next morning. I slogged back to the house slowly afterward, dragging my feet through the dirt and noticing all the potholes that needed filling — another job Seth had done. If only my brother were here, I thought wistfully, he'd fix everything. He'd crack jokes until everyone was laughing, until we all forgot to be angry with each other.

Jaden was in the kitchen with Dec. The sun streamed in behind them, making it hard to judge Jaden's expression, but it made no difference because he didn't turn his head or acknowledge me in any way as I darted for the coffeepot.

Dec's eyebrows rose. "Morning, honey." His look was questioning, but I did my best to keep my face impassive, despite my staccato heart.

"G'morning," I muttered. I buttered some toast and stood at the counter to eat it and drink my coffee. I had a good view of Jaden's rigid back for a few minutes before he got up. He came over, and I scooted out of the way as he dropped his dishes into the dishwasher without looking at me.

As soon as he left, Dec turned to me. "I take it you guys had a fight?"

I nodded miserably, wishing that my family didn't have to be involved like this, that Jaden and I could resolve our differences in private like normal couples. Then again, most of the nineteen-year-olds I knew still lived at home, so maybe it wasn't so weird.

Jaden avoided me until he went to the polo club, but I hardly noticed because my hours were stuffed to overflowing with work. The day was a scorcher, and I felt limp as a dishrag by the time I rode Cal late that afternoon. Although I noticed Jaden return, he didn't draw near. The wash stall was busy when I was done riding so I led Cal outside to hose him down. The air steamed under a hazy sky. Cal enjoyed his shower, drinking out of the hose and pushing his face repeatedly under the spray. I was almost done when Jaden strode by. His body was still tight with anger; he was wearing a sleeveless camel-colored shirt over the white jeans he played polo in. He didn't look my way — again — and I felt my temper rekindle. I quickly twisted the nozzle onto its hardest setting and aimed the hose at him.

The first blast hit him right in the head. He gave an inarticulate yell, but I braced my feet and kept the water on him. He didn't react the way I expected, though. Instead of dodging or trying to flee, he walked straight into the spray. I backed up, moving the jet up and down his body, but he was on me in a few strides. He seized my wrist and took the hose out of my hand.

"You're in for it now," he said grimly. He turned the hose on me.

"Aaah!" I shrieked and danced away but his steel grip was on my wrist, and I had the end of Cal's leadrope in my other hand so I couldn't escape. Cal tossed his head up and snorted. He liked water, but he'd never seen it used as a weapon before.

"Wait," I spluttered, unable to see, "Cal!"

When the assault stopped I heard giggling behind me and turned to see Catherine and several of my students looking on gleefully as I dripped everywhere.

"Can one of you girls take Cal?" Jaden asked. Catherine stepped forward, grinning as she took the sodden leadrope from me.

The minute my hands were free Jaden swooped down and heaved me onto his shoulder. I heard gasps from our entourage, but he ignored them and marched away.

"Put me down!" I demanded. This was exactly *not* the way I wanted to be seen by my students and employee. Jaden didn't slow. Water dripped onto his booted heels from my upside-down hair.

I reached down and smacked his solid butt with one hand. "Jaden! Put me down."

"Do that again and I'll double it on your small ass," he growled. We entered a shaded area and I was set unceremoniously on my feet. I barely had time to note that we were between the shed and the hedge that ran behind it before Jaden advanced on me. Startled, I backed into the wall. He stopped with barely an inch between our wet bodies. My eyes traveled from the shirt clinging to his muscled chest, up his corded neck, and over the droplets bejeweling his chin. His mouth, pressed into a firm line, made my insides tighten, and I tipped my head back to find his spiky lashes surrounding tawny eyes that burned straight into mine. I froze. I could feel his breath on my face, the heat from his body caressing me like fingers. A tremor passed through me.

"If I could get you alone for an hour I would make you pay for this in unimaginable ways," he breathed.

"A whole hour." I swallowed; I barely had breath to speak. "You must have a lot planned."

"You have no idea."

"We could go to our copse," I suggested.

He hesitated. "Not today."

I was struggling not to touch him, not to fling my arms around him and press myself into him. "Why not?"

"Do you realize that we resolve every disagreement by falling into bed?"

I was incredulous. "How is that a problem?" I bit my lip, staring at his mouth, and tried not to imagine it on my skin.

A shimmer of amusement crossed his expression. "Why do I feel we have a case of role reversal at play here?" He bent his head slowly, until it hung right next to mine, still without touching. "I can't believe you sprayed me in anger."

I was going to make a joke, but what came out of my mouth instead was, "I can't believe you fought me over following my dream." My sense of betrayal strangled my voice down to a whisper. "You told me once you never wanted to keep me down."

He pulled back a few inches, enough for me to meet his volcanic gaze. "I don't want to keep you down, Téa. I want to keep you close — I hope you can see the difference."

He leaned further away, and suddenly I couldn't stand the space between us. I reached for him, twining my hands behind his neck and plastering my wet body against his. His heat seared through our layers of clothing; I expected clouds of steam to rise around us at any moment. His mouth settled on mine with a groan and he kissed me ardently, holding my head in his hands. When he stopped he pressed his forehead against mine.

"Well, I can honestly say that I'm sorry to be going," I offered in a thready voice.

"We'll resume where we left off when you get back," he promised. He was referring to more than the kiss, of that I was sure.

I decided to bring Cal to Orangeville. I'd already spent more money than I'd planned on showing him that year, but it was the only way to keep him in training. Karen had been right in predicting that the furor over Hades' picture would be forgotten, and other than Alex's icy silence, the show was ideal. Hades won two classes, and I got home Sunday night in high spirits despite my tiredness. The next day I visited Teri, who was back at her parent's house and looking better, before taking the money I'd won and buying more paint. I spent two incredibly boring days painting fencing, sending Seth increasingly irate text messages, and counting down the minutes until I'd see Jaden. We'd talked while I was away but we hadn't discussed our fight, nor the fissure in our relationship, which seemed to crack wider and wider with every little bump we hit. It petrified me, and I'd dealt with the fear by ignoring it, but I knew we couldn't go on this way.

Jaden's car pulled into the driveway earlier than I'd expected, and I dropped my paintbrush and jogged over. He got out, loosening his tie, and froze at the sight of me.

"Hi," I said breathlessly.

His smile was like a sunrise. "I'd hug you, but... well, have you seen yourself?" I glanced down at my paint-smudged clothes.

"It's giving me ideas," Jaden said, his voice husky.

"Everything gives you ideas." I laughed before racing off to put away my supplies and have a shower. I bounded down the stairs, still toweling my hair, and found Jaden on the couch next to Dec, watching the news.

"I'm going to get some take-out." Jaden unfolded his lean body from the couch. "Come with me."

"How's work?" I asked as I buckled my seat belt. He'd been working late the previous few days. I was determined to maintain an interest in his work, no matter how boring his current job was compared to polo.

He grimaced. "As good as can be expected. I'm stuck inside all day doing meaningless paperwork."

"But isn't it challenging?"

"If you consider it challenging to build resistance to overwhelming tedium, then yes. I deal with office politics more than I'd like, but I suppose it's the same everywhere." Since I knew less than nothing about office politics, I refrained from comment. I told him about the show before moving on to barn gossip.

"Have you heard? Mateo and Summer broke up." Jennalyn had shared that tidbit.

"No, I hadn't. I've been out of the loop."

"Well, you know Mateo's handicap has gone up to six," I said. Jaden's expression tightened. The fact that Mateo's polo ranking was rising while Jaden's own was dropping surely rankled. "He wants to go to Argentina this fall, and spend the winter in Florida so he can hit all the big matches and keep boosting his ranking. I guess Summer wasn't ready to go with him."

Jaden nodded in understanding. "Summer has a very comfortable life here. I can't imagine her following Mateo around for the sake of his career."

I frowned. "I guess Mateo hoped that she would. He thought she loved him."

"I'm sure she does, in her own way. Not everyone is as brave as you are, Téa."

"I'm not brave," I said in a small voice. "I'm terrified... of losing you."

He reached over and gripped my hand. "That will never happen, querida. We'll figure out a way that works for us." There was a beat of silence. "And despite what you think, you're one of the most fearless people I know. Teri's accident hasn't even given you pause."

I studied the long-fingered hand in mine. I traced each one of his fingers, from the knuckle down to the nail, as I spoke.

"I'm just not afraid of the same things as most people." I swallowed hard, wondering how to explain without sounding either crazy or maudlin. My voice was very quiet when I began.

"My mom died when she was only thirty-five. She died after spending her whole adult life working to take care of me and my brother. She never got the chance to do all those things she was saving for 'someday', the things she'd do when we were grown up, when she had enough money, when she had the time... those things never happened." I cleared my throat. "I'm not afraid to die, Jaden, but I'm petrified to not really *live* while I have the chance."

I met his gaze carefully, feeling the sheen of tears over my eyes. His fingers tightened around mine, and his face was stunned and dismayed all at once.

"That's why all this talk about marriage and kids... it throws me for a loop," I admitted. "It's nowhere near where my head is at." Jaden's brows went up, but he didn't interrupt, so I bumbled along. "Think back a few years, Jaden. When you were eighteen, you left everything behind — your friends, your family, even your country — to chase your dream, and you did it. You kicked polo ass. No one and nothing can ever take that away from you. The confidence and happiness you derived from it are woven into your very being. And polo, I might point out, is probably a more dangerous sport than riding jumpers."

We were at the restaurant; he parked the car and turned to face me before answering. "You're right. But being afraid for your safety is so much worse than worrying about my own."

I nodded. I understood that part.

"And in any case, the more immediate issue is that we barely see each other." He rubbed the side of his face. "At least you'll be back in school soon. Our schedules are bound to sync up better then." I bit my lip. I'd been thinking seriously about quitting school, but now didn't seem like the time to mention it.

We were both quiet on the drive back, the smell of Chinese food filling the car and making my mouth water. After dinner Jaden helped me finish packing; I was leaving the following morning for the show, and since he had to work he couldn't stay overnight.

"We have unfinished business," I reminded him, running my hand down his chest and over his stomach, feeling the outline of his muscles under my fingers. I still couldn't believe how he'd left me hanging after the incident behind the shed.

He braided his fingers through my hair and pulled me close before whispering in my ear, "And it will remain unfinished until you return." And then he pulled me, indignant and frustrated, to his car to say goodbye.

Angelstone was only two hours away, but it wasn't close enough to go home every day so I stayed at a motel again. Getting a camper of my own would be a great idea, I mused as I checked in the next day.

The weather had cooled, and Tania got Hades ready for his first class while I walked the course with Karen. Brittney was on Karen's other side, pretending I didn't exist. She was riding George, the Nation's Cup winner, in the class, and I wondered how Hades would fare against a world-class jumper like him.

Not well, that's how. Hades and I had a disagreement over a distance — he saw it long, I wanted to go wide and put in another stride — and we ended up in that awkward in-between spot and knocked down a rail. I was surprised he didn't plow through the entire jump, considering, but it cost us the class. Tania gave me a look of sympathy as she took Hades, but Karen shook her head at me and frowned. I was pretty sure I'd be getting an earful from her later, but even that couldn't be as bad as watching Brittney go after me.

It's hard to have a big ego as a rider because horses are great equalizers. If you ride a variety of horses in a variety of situations, chances are good that you'll eat dirt regularly enough to keep you humble. But Brittney wasn't that kind of rider; although she was competing at a high level, she had ridden a succession of ultra-expensive, push-button horses. She was a decent rider, but she had a wildly inflated idea of her own skill. I saw her bring George into a combination way too slowly, and he lengthened stride gamely and got himself out of it without any help from Brittney. I turned away, shaking my head in disgust. She'd be in the ribbons without having done anything to earn it.

Neil fell into step with me as I headed back to the stables. "I was talking to another trainer," he said. I suppressed a groan. It wasn't considered diplomatic to talk to other people's clients but some trainers did it. And in all likelihood, the trainer full of free advice wanted Hades for him-or-herself.

"He said this bitless bridle business is nonsense at Hades' level," Neil went on. "He said you could've won that class if you'd had a bit."

"Neil, I tried half a dozen bits on Hades last year. He didn't go well in any of them," I reminded him.

I thought that was the end of it, but when we were alone later Karen seemed to agree.

"I'm just saying, don't be married to one type of tack. The classes you're riding in are going to get bigger and faster, and you'll be in more jump-offs. You may need something stronger than the bitless bridle, something with more precise control."

I hesitated. Karen was a good mentor, and in most things horse-related I took her word as law. She had proven time and again that she understood horses on a very deep level. If it weren't for her former substance abuse problems, I was certain that she would have reached the very pinnacle of our sport.

I chose my words carefully. "I don't know Karen, Hades really hated bits before. I don't want him to lose trust in me."

"He's not going to mistrust you based on one ride. Why not just give it a try?"

Out of respect for Karen's judgment, which was nearly always right, the next time I schooled Hades I chose a simple D-ring snaffle from Karen's collection. It was a mild bit, inoffensive to most horses. I saddled him myself, unclipped the lead rope, and slipped the reins over his head. As I raised the bridle Hades' eyes went wide. He'd obviously noticed, and he gave me a look that said it all.

Not this again! Haven't we been through this? Did I not make myself clear?

"Come on buddy, just try it... for me?" I coaxed his mouth open, gently raised the bit, and slipped the bridle over his ears, not an easy feat as he had raised his head in protest and he was much taller than me — his ears were out of my reach unless he deigned to lower his head.

"Come on, it won't be so bad, I promise." I adjusted all the straps to make him as comfortable as possible and led him to the perimeter of the schooling area, away from the other horses. I began warming up doing simple transitions and trotting circles, but Hades was tense, obviously unhappy. And the more I worked, the more unhappy he got. He was taking this personally. I sighed. I should have known. When he started grinding his teeth and whipping his tail from side to side I gave up. I slowed to a walk, dropped the reins and patted his shoulder.

"I'm sorry, big guy. You're right, we had a deal and I won't go back on it."

My conversations with Neil and Karen left me determined to prove myself, and Hades must have felt the same because we came in second in our next class. It was a two-star class, meaning it counted in the world rankings, and Neil was downright gleeful when he found me in the tackroom with Karen afterward. I was cross-legged on a tack trunk, slurping an iced coffee.

"Guess where the top horses are headed next? Spruce Meadows!" I'd never seen Neil so excited. "I want Hades there too. Monica entered him a month ago, hoping he'd qualify."

Karen and I exchanged a stunned look. "Spruce Meadows — you realize that's near Calgary, right? It's the other end of the country," I said.

"Hey, if you wanna run with the big dogs, you gotta go to the big dog park."

While I was trying to figure out what that meant, Karen spoke up. "When we go to Spruce Meadows it should be for the North American tournament, not the Masters. Hades isn't ready for international competition yet."

"Well, I think he'll do great," Neil blustered, puffing out his chest.

Karen gave me an exasperated look that said clearly, "Manage your client".

I turned to Neil. "We don't want to overface the horse so early in his career. We could ruin his confidence."

"His? Or his rider's?" Neil demanded, his face pugnacious.

I felt myself redden and stood up, hands fisted at my sides. "I have no problem riding him in the Masters. But don't expect him to perform like a seasoned veteran, because he isn't one."

"Excellent," Neil said, rubbing his hands together.

After Neil left Karen shook her head at me tiredly. "You need to disconnect that wire between your temper and your mouth, Téa."

I shrugged. "I know. But how could I pass up the chance to ride at Spruce Meadows?"

"Look, kid, you'll get there, but you're getting thrown in at the deep end this way." She sighed. "Well, it could be worse. I'm bringing other

208

clients, and we can enter Hades mostly in the Champions' Welcome classes."

"What's that?"

"They have a tournament right before the Masters, just to ease the international riders into it."

I gulped. "The international riders. Right."

Karen shot me a grin. "Hey, you wanted to experience Spruce Meadows. Buckle up."

Teri was the first person I told, when I went to her house the day after the show.

"Wow, Spruce Meadows. You have hit the big time." She grinned at me. Three weeks after the accident, the bruises had mostly faded from her face. Her nose was a bit bumpier than before, and her broken shoulder and ribs were still bandaged, but she could move around on her own. We were slouched on the flowered couch in her parent's small living room.

"I'm starting physio soon," she said.

"That's good." I paused as Teri's mom bustled in with smoothies for both of us.

"She doesn't think I eat enough so she packs these full of calories," Teri said, holding up her glass.

"And you both need them," Teri's mother stated tartly. She disappeared upstairs.

"By the time my body heals I'll be crazy from living at home again." Teri sighed.

"What are you going to do?"

She answered promptly, but of course, she'd had lots of time to consider the question. "I'm going back to school to be a nurse like I wanted before. I don't think I could race again, not after what happened."

"I guess you'll start in January?"

She nodded. The start of my own school year was just over a week away, but I'd be missing the first week if — when — I went to Spruce Meadows, and I hadn't broken the news to Dec yet.

I decided to take the bull by the horns when I got home. First I found Dec in the kitchen and handed over the money I'd won at Angelstone.

"We can replace all the light fixtures you want," I said.

Dec gave me a puzzled look. He counted the money, his brows climbing steadily, and then split the stack of bills in half and handed me one.

"Here. Keep some for yourself."

I shrugged. "I'll win more." I fidgeted, then went to the coffeemaker and started making coffee so I'd have something to do with my hands. "The Donalds want Hades to do the Spruce Meadows Masters," I said without looking at Dec. "It's a huge opportunity, and-"

"And it's in September," Dec interrupted. "You've got school."

I pushed the 'on' button and turned around. "Yes, but I'd only miss the first week, nothing much happens then." That wasn't strictly true, but I was confident I could catch up. I raised my eyes warily to Dec's face. I expected a gathering storm, but instead his expression was thoughtful.

He leaned back against the counter opposite me. "Téa, you need to start putting school first. This is your life we're talking about."

"But Dec, *riding* is my life," I said plaintively.

He came and stood before me. He wasn't angry; instead, he rested his large hands on my shoulders and looked at me while he spoke.

"Honey, you're still too young to have a sense of perspective about this. You don't fully understand how your choice of job will affect every aspect of your life — where you live, your health, the kinds of people you deal with every day. I'm doing this because I want what's best for you. I want you to get away from hard labor, to be able to take a vacation once in a while and not to always struggle for money."

Earnestness radiated from him like a halo. I swallowed. I'd expected a fight, something to rail against and defy, but I didn't know how to argue with this. Somehow this gentle, concerned version of Dec disarmed me more completely than the angry version ever could.

The coffeepot burbled behind me as he went on. "What happens at the next big show, or the one after that? Hades is worth a small fortune now; eventually, the Donalds will sell him or get a rider who can travel with him full-time."

I studied the white-tiled floor. "You know, I was thinking... things are going so well, maybe I could take a year off school."

He didn't respond right away, so I chanced looking at him.

"You drop out of school and I'll sell Cal so fast it'll make your head spin." Gone was the reasonable-sounding father making heartfelt speeches about my future. His face was hard and implacable, and I felt myself harden in response.

I'd never bothered to transfer Cal's papers from Dec's name into my own. A grave oversight, I realized in retrospect.

"Is that why you bought him, to use as leverage?" It was a mean thing to suggest, but my frustration was prodding me.

"You think I'm using him to control you? Téa, why do you think I'm keeping this entire barn? Joanne's been hounding me for months to move in with her, my siblings want me to sell so they can get their money, but I'm working my tail off in my second choice of business so we can continue to live here, all so that *you* can have stability and finish school."

I felt like I'd been punched in the gut. I stared at him with my mouth gaping open. "What... what about Gran?" I whispered finally. I desperately wanted someone else to be at least partly responsible for this burden.

Dec sighed. "Yes, Gran's happy that we're keeping the place. But she understands that we'll eventually need to sell. My argument to Peter and Penny is that I don't want to disrupt your life and income while you're in school. If you drop out, my argument goes out the window."

I deflated so far that I was surprised not to find myself pooling onto the floor. I nodded to Dec to show that I understood — I understood too well, now — and shuffled slowly upstairs to my bedroom. I fell forward onto the bed, hid my face in my arms, and lay without moving, my thoughts circling like lazy vultures.

It was hours later when Gran called up the stairs to ask me to join her for tea. Guilt made my tread heavy on the stairs. The teapot was already on the table, steaming. I sat across from Gran and tried to answer her questions about the show.

"Something on your mind, dear?" she asked after a minute.

I considered. Gran was probably the one person besides Dec who could give me some answers. "Why is Dec so hung up on me going to school? And why is he so willing to sell this place? You spent your life building this business and you raised three kids here."

Gran's brow furrowed in thought. "I'll try to explain. It may not be the only reason, mind, but a large part is his father's doing."

I started feeling uncomfortable — most of the stories I'd heard about Dec's dad, Jim Foster, weren't exactly complimentary. Gran topped up our teacups before she began.

"Jim had a difficult life. He was the only one of his siblings who wasn't well-educated: one of his brothers was a judge, the other a teacher, and his sister a physician. Their father demanded that all his children do well at school, but your Granddad was severely dyslexic. It wasn't understood in those days, and his father thrashed him regularly for doing poorly at school, thinking he wasn't applying himself."

I was staring at Gran, feeling bowled over with sudden understanding. My tea sat untouched, but now I wrapped my hands around the cup, needing the warmth.

"It was through sheer force of will that your Granddad rose through the ranks of the army," Gran remembered. "But he never overcame the stigma of being the uneducated one and he was determined that his children should outdo him. Partly, I suppose, as a matter of pride — in order to prove to his family that his children were bright enough to succeed." She paused, looking at me carefully. "Dec showed talent for riding from an early age, you know. I was very proud of him, but I knew his father wanted more for him, so I didn't interfere when he pushed him into university."

"But..." I hesitated, then went on quietly, not looking at her. "If Granddad knew how awful it was, why did he hit his own kids?"

Gran sighed. "It was the only way he knew. And you must remember, at the time it wasn't considered as improper as it is now. Why, even the schools used corporal punishment."

I nodded, feeling some consternation that I actually felt sympathy for Granddad.

She smiled slowly at me. "He would have liked you, Téa. He would have admired your hard work and perseverance."

That made me feel even stranger, but I sat with Gran and we finished our tea.

That evening I went to Jaden's. It was raining when I left, but my hair was still wet from the shower so I didn't mind. Large splotches dotted my baby-blue T-shirt and white shorts as I ran to my car. I tried to sort out my tangled mess of thoughts during the drive. I was quite anxious to get to one part of our 'unfinished business', and equally reluctant to tell Jaden that I'd be leaving the next day for another show.

I dashed up the steps to the second floor and let myself in. Jaden was sitting at the high counter that separated the kitchen from the living room, and at the sight of me he closed his laptop and padded over, his bare feet quiet on the dark wood floors. He was wearing faded cutoff jeans and nothing else. Without a word I slipped my arms around him and rested my face against his golden skin. He smelled of soap and aftershave, and when his arms closed around me every tightly wound worry within me eased. *This is what safety feels like*, I thought, my eyes closed.

A low chuckle vibrated through him. "You're all damp. And you smell good — like rain in a citrus grove."

I unwound myself long enough to take his hand and head for the bedroom. I stopped next to the bed and peeled my T-shirt off. His eyebrows crept up.

"I believe we left something unfinished," he remarked.

"We're taking care of that right now," I breathed, running my hands down his arms.

He caught my hands in his, stilling them. Amusement warred with desire in his eyes. "I was referring to our conversation. Once I sleep with you, what assurance do I have that you'll actually talk to me?"

I grinned and stepped forward, gluing my bare skin to his. "I guess you'll have to take your chances."

We lay in a tangle of sheets afterward, my head nestled on his shoulder. He held one of my hands against his chest and I felt the reassuring thump of his heart slow to its normal, steady rhythm.

"Doesn't staying home more often sound like a good idea?" he murmured.

"Right now, anything you say is going to sound good," I said, kissing his chest. "But how about you come on the road with me more often?"

His sigh ruffled my hair. "You know I can't, *querida*. My job is here."

"And *my* job takes me places."

"Please tell me we're not having a 'whose job is more important' argument," Jaden groaned. "I feel like my parents."

I shifted my head onto a pillow so I could look at him. "What do you mean?"

"We were supposed to temporarily move away once, but my mom's practice is here and she didn't want to leave her patients. She used to complain that my dad acted as though his job was more important than hers solely because he made more money."

"Oh. What did they do?"

"He ended up living in Hong Kong for eight months without us."

"It worked out, then."

He rolled onto his side to face me, his head pillowed on his arm, his face pensive. "I don't know... I think that time apart made us realize how much calmer life was without the constant threat of my dad's anger in the house. I think it made my mom see that we — and me in particular — would be happier without him."

I felt a sudden chill and pulled the sheet up to my chin. I'd never feel happier without Jaden.

"In any case, our issue isn't so much a question of *whose* job as it is *which* job. What career will you be choosing, Téa?" his voice was soft.

"Well, right now there's really only one," I hedged. One year of biology did not a vet make. I smoothed down the corner of the pillow as I spoke. "And my current career... well, it's taking me to Spruce Meadows," I hesitated. "In two days." I didn't look at him, but I felt him stiffen.

"You made plans to leave again without talking to me first?"

"You don't consult me when you make decisions about your job!"

"That's different — you *knew* we had things to resolve regarding your traveling." He rolled out of bed and yanked on his jeans. He jerked up the zipper while his eyes pinned me in place on the bed. "You can't build a relationship on unilateral decisions, Téa. What if I don't want you to go?"

"It's too late," I protested.

He planted his hands on his hips. "Come here," he demanded.

Incoherent anger swept over me. I shot to my feet and threw the pillow at him. Then I grabbed a shirt and marched out to the living room, leaving his perplexed, wrathful face behind.

I pulled the shirt on as I paced the living room. It turned out to be Jaden's and it hung halfway down to my knees. Frustration and fear and inexplicable rage were roiling around inside me, and I dropped onto the couch and put my face in my hands, my elbows on my knees. After a minute I heard Jaden move into the kitchen behind me and put the kettle on.

"Is it safe to come out yet?" he called.

"Venture forth at your own risk," I growled. It was muffled by my hands.

I felt him sink down next to me on the couch. "So, have you figured it out yet?"

"Hey, I don't do the psychoanalysis around here, remember? That's what I have you for."

"Nice that you've finally found a use for me," he said drily. I sighed and looked at him, finally. His expression was gentle.

"I had my hands on my hips," he said.

I frowned. "What does that have to do with anything?"

"Think, Téa. Picture Dec when he's angry."

"Oh, no," I groaned. "That's all it takes to set me off? I'm a freak." I'd been shocked by the sudden surge of anger I'd felt, anger that seemed out of proportion to our argument.

I met his eyes. "Sorry."

He reached for me, and I flowed into his arms with a sigh. "It probably wouldn't upset you under normal circumstances," he reassured me. "But things have been rather tense."

"I'm sorry about that, too," I admitted in a small voice. "But I don't know what to do about it."

He shifted so that he was facing me and took both my hands in his. "What do you want out of life, Téa? Don't think about it, just answer."

"I want to go to the Olympics," I said promptly. "And I want to be with you." I curled one leg under me.

He nodded slowly. "So I come second."

"What? No! It just... came out that way." But even as I protested, I wondered. I'd never been one of those little girls who dream about getting married. When I dreamt as a child, it was about how old I'd be when I made it to the Olympics (for the first time). I'd wonder how many Grand Prix horses I'd have, and what countries I would compete in each year. Love and marriage and kids — they never entered into that. Some part of my twelve-year-old brain had probably assumed I'd have a partner, but the relationships that were the main focus of my imaginings were the ones with my horses. And if I had fallen in love with anyone other than Jaden, that would probably still be the case. Only a love as all-consuming, intense, and larger-than-life as my passion for Jaden could have a hope of competing with my lifelong obsession with horses.

Jaden watched my eyes fill. I kept them open wide, willing the tears not to spill.

"Don't you think you'll want a family someday?" His voice was very soft.

I hesitated. "Growing up on the show circuit isn't a good life for a kid. They don't go to a regular school, don't have neighborhood friends, don't have a *home*. They grow up... I don't know, rootless. They exist as satellites of their parent's career."

"I don't mean now, you're far too young. I mean in ten or fifteen years."

When I looked at him blankly he frowned. "You think you'll still be showing then. Téa, how many riders stay in one piece long enough to compete at that level for that long?" I could tell his temper was beginning to flare.

"Ian Millar was on the Olympic team more than ten times," I reminded him. "Our sport has more longevity than most."

"He's the exception! God, Teri's barely out of the hospital. Are you truly so blind to the risk you're taking?"

"I could be a librarian and spend my days indoors, never taking any kind of chance, and get hit by a bus!" I burst out. "Sure, riding jumpers is riskier than some things, but nothing in life is completely safe."

He let go of my hands and closed his eyes. I watched his chest rise and fall as he worked to calm himself. I quickly wiped my tears so he wouldn't see. When he opened his eyes I was ready for him.

"Tell me something," he said. "If you achieve your goals, how many months a year would you be on the road?"

I wrapped my arms around myself. I tried to maintain eye contact with Jaden but, at the last minute, I chickened out and my head dropped forward. "About ten."

I heard his sudden intake of breath. "And you never felt it would be a good idea to discuss that with me?" he asked sharply. "I think I've been quite clear in my intentions. I want us to have a life together."

"Yes," I stammered, "I just didn't think... I mean, I didn't realize you'd want that so soon."

He gave me a disbelieving look. "I was in law school for three *years*. During all that time you watched me building a new life here, and you never thought to mention that you'd be elsewhere?"

"I thought you *knew*," I protested, not for the first time.

"How could I? In the two years we've been together you were always at the barn, until this summer. Now suddenly you're never there." His accusation was as cutting as his tone, and I turned away from him. I drew my knees up, pulled the large shirt over them, and buried my face in my arms.

I felt him rise. The kettle must have clicked off automatically while we spoke; I heard him turn it on again. It boiled quickly this time, and a minute later the aroma of French-pressed coffee stole into my nostrils. I heard the muffled thud as he placed mugs on the coffee table in front of me.

I looked up to find his face as dismayed as mine, though his wasn't wet. "What are we going to do?" I whispered.

He sat next to me and looked into his mug. "That's up to you."

Eleven

I didn't even remember driving home. My mind was like a hamster on a wheel, running through the same conversation over and over again. I wanted nothing more than to go cry myself to sleep, but I had another unpleasant conversation to face first.

I found Dec in his office. It wasn't my first choice of places to talk to him; it held too many memories of being taken to task for various misdemeanors and it made me feel like a child, rather than the assertive adult I needed to be now. He looked up from his laptop as I walked in.

"Dec." I stuck my hands in my pockets and willed myself to look him in the eye. "There's a van coming to pick up Hades in the morning." I faltered as he frowned. "To take him to Spruce Meadows," I finished.

The storm I'd expected that morning was clearly fast approaching.

"I would've told you earlier, but I just found out," I said quickly. That was true — Monica had called that afternoon with the details of our travel plans.

"You know very well that's not the problem," Dec growled. He stood up stalked around the large desk to face me. I resisted the urge to back up. "This morning when we talked, everything was already all set for you to leave." He was making a statement, not asking. I didn't say anything. "What will you do if I say no, Téa? If I put my foot down right now and say you're not going?"

I gulped. I'd had that very nightmare. If I didn't go I'd lose Hades, of course, because after spending that much money to get their horse to Calgary the Donalds would probably find another rider for him. And I'd lose all credibility. On the other hand, if I defied Dec, I could lose much more — my own horse, the approval of my only parent, maybe even, if he were mad enough, my home.

"Please don't," I pleaded in a whisper. I couldn't justify what I had done — at the very least, I should have given him more notice — so I didn't even try. I simply looked into his eyes and begged. "I'll stay in school. I'll get all As. I'll work hard in the barn. Just... please let me go to this one last show."

He scowled across the room for a minute while my heart raced and my palms sweated.

"You're making me the bad guy here for doing what I think is best for you. Your mom was always adamant that you get a good education, she didn't want you to end up stuck in a dead-end job like her..."

His voice droned on, saying "it's not safe" and "your mother wouldn't like it", but inside my head all I heard was *You're not good enough. You'll never be good enough.*

"Mom is *dead*," I burst out. "I can't live my life second-guessing what she would've wanted."

The second the words left my mouth I froze in fear. Dec's stricken look hardened quickly into one of resolve. He turned and marched to the door.

"Wait!" I ran and caught his arm but he wouldn't look at me. "I'm sorry. That was mean."

He glanced at me then. "Yes, it was." He pulled his arm away and left the room, leaving me feeling much worse than if he'd simply hit me as I'd half-expected.

I pressed the heels of my hands hard against my eyes. Was there anything else I could screw up today?

I went and did the bedtime check, slouching slowly around the barn as I took care of every possible detail. I was avoiding the house, but I knew I couldn't leave things as they were. A square of yellow light indicated that Dec was back in his office, and I took several deep breaths on my way through the cooling dark to the house.

I tapped quietly on the door before going in. Dec was working at his laptop. I swallowed hard before I walked around the desk, leaned over, and put my arms around him.

After a minute he patted my arm. "It's okay," he said.

I straightened up, keeping one hand on his shoulder. "It's just... I already have a dad trying to make all my decisions for me. To also consider mom's memory-"

I stopped as he looked swiftly up at me. It was the first time I'd ever called him my dad, at least in his presence, and the look on his face said

219

that he knew it. He smiled, and the blue of his eyes, like a shifting ocean current, went suddenly warm. He rolled his chair back to look at me fully; my hand fell away from his shoulder.

"I don't like how you handled this, Téa. You should have talked to me *before* the decision was made."

I nodded miserably.

"You're awfully young to be going halfway across the country by yourself," he muttered.

Relief washed over me so suddenly it nearly bowled me over, but I tried not to let it show. "I wouldn't be by myself, Karen's going too." The Donalds would be there as well, but since Dec didn't know them well they wouldn't count, to him. He wanted someone he could hold accountable for me.

He rubbed the back of his neck. "That's good. Karen knows Spruce."

I resisted the urge to cheer. "Does that mean... can I..."

He gusted out a sigh. "Yeah. You can go."

Hades left the next morning, bundled up for his ride on the luxury van that would deliver him to Spruce Meadows the following day. After a day and a half in transit, he'd have another day and a half to recover and acclimatize before his first class. Tania would be there to meet him and care for him until I arrived.

My relief over being allowed to go couldn't lift the weight of my conversation with Jaden, and I hadn't slept much the night before. My dejected air drew some questions, but I brushed them off. What could I say? *'Oh, just trying to decide between my lifelong dream and the love of my life'?* That was a tad melodramatic. There was only one person I could talk to when things were this sticky, so at lunchtime I went to my room and found the number of the stud farm where Seth was working. I'd called there once before but Seth had been out, and I'd left a message. He'd never returned the call, but I was prepared to forgive him for the chance to share my worries.

A woman answered the phone. Her Irish accent was almost incomprehensible; when I asked for Seth I couldn't understand her response.

I tried again. "I'm looking for Seth Everson?" I enunciated clearly, hoping she'd do the same.

"Ah, yes, the boy's moved on now ye see."

"Pardon me?"

"He's moved on. No longer employed here."

It took me a moment to remember to thank her. I put the phone down with a shaking hand and opened my laptop.

You are in SO MUCH TROUBLE. CALL ME!

I sent him the message using Facebook, email, and chat, though he wasn't online. Then I texted the same thing, feeling impotent and anxious. After a minute I lay down on my bed and closed my eyes. I took a few deep breaths and tried to quiet my nerves while I stretched out with my invisible senses. Sometimes, in times of crisis, Seth and I had been able to 'feel' each other, or at least, know that something was wrong. I didn't sense anything now, but neither was there a gaping hole anywhere and I felt sure there would be if something terrible had happened to him. I got up, disgruntled but calmer, to go back to work.

Sheer exhaustion helped me to sleep better that night. I hadn't talked to Jaden since our ill-fated conversation, and it was eating away at me, but I kept myself occupied. I had already bought myself a new raincoat, but if I was going to be riding on TV I figured I'd better dress the part. I went to the tack shop and bit the bullet. I bought myself new riding boots and two pairs of breeches. Thank goodness I had the jacket Jaden had bought me the year before, because as it was I spent more money than I'd ever spent on myself at one time. When I got home I finished packing and went to the barn to say bye to everyone. Excitement over my trip was running high, and all the hugs and squeals of delight couldn't help but raise my spirits somewhat.

"Good luck," Elise said shyly as I headed back outside.

I stopped and looked at her in surprise. "Thanks." To my immense relief, Brittney wasn't going to Spruce Meadows with us.

I went into the ring to say bye to Gran. She was teaching, her floppy sunhat perched at a jaunty angle.

"Take care of yourself," she said. "Will all your classes be televised?"

"I don't know, but check the Horse Junkies United website — if there's any video, they'll have it." I hesitated, feeling guilty. "I'm sorry about all the work I've been leaving, Gran."

"Oh, posh. I've missed teaching, and I didn't realize how much until this summer. You'd best go, your chauffeur is waiting."

I turned to see Kabir waving at me from behind the fence. He walked me to the house and helped get my bags out of my bedroom, but on our way through the living room Dec stepped out of his office.

"I'll take this." Kabir grabbed my suitcase away from me and went outside, and I went to say goodbye to Dec.

"Look, Téa, I know how things can get at these big shows. Your adrenaline gets going, there are parties, people are away from home and feeling adventurous..." He stopped and cleared his throat while I waited, puzzled. "What I'm saying is, be good. Be careful. Listen to Karen. And take this." He handed me a small piece of plastic; it took me a second to realize it was a credit card.

My eyes flew up to his face. I didn't know what to say.

"It's for emergencies," he explained gruffly. "I don't want you to have to rely on the Donalds if you need something."

I felt my throat tighten and my eyes fill with gratitude. "Thanks," I whispered.

He hugged me quickly before walking me out into the bright sun. He shook Kabir's hand. "It was nice having you around again, young man." Kabir had come over a few times during the summer, but he was headed back to California for school.

"So." Kabir grinned over at me once we were on the road.

"So, you and Ter looked pretty cozy the last time I saw you," I remarked. Kabir and Teri had been on the couch, and there seemed to be an awful lot of space on the cushions beside them.

"I have to do my part to make the poor girl feel better." He sobered. "It's awful, seeing her like that. And I'm leaving soon... we don't want to start anything, not when she's going through so much and I'll be away."

"But you would, otherwise?" I asked.

He nodded, and his dimples reappeared, like whirlpools in his milk-chocolate skin.

I met Karen at the airport; it was just us because the Donalds had taken an earlier plane so they could declare their horse before the deadline. It was only my second time on a plane, but to Karen the whole thing was commonplace and once the plane took off she promptly fell asleep. I was relieved because I had a lot to think about, on top of my nerves over the upcoming show, and I didn't think I'd be much use for conversation.

I tried to keep my mind off the giant question mark that was my future. I watched the movie and had some snacks, and the four-hour flight went by quickly. When we landed I dragged our luggage on a cart while Karen got her rental car. It annoyed me to no end that I wouldn't be old enough to rent a car for several years yet; it meant that I was stuck relying on taxis or lifts at every show that wasn't within driving distance.

Karen drove to the motel. It was dusk, and I craned my neck to keep my eyes on the Rocky Mountains, their snow-capped peaks gilded by the sun's last rays.

"Wow." I turned to Karen. "I'm really here." I felt a thrill of excitement that I'd felt only once before, when I'd traveled to Florida with Jaden. It was the thrill not only of new discoveries but also of complete and utter freedom.

We got to the motel in the dark. It was clean and welcoming, and after dumping my bags on my bed I washed my face and ran a brush through my hair because Karen wanted to go out to eat. We reached the elevator at the same time as a towering blond man. When the doors opened he politely allowed Karen and me to get in before following. I tried not to stare at him, but I couldn't help glancing up once in a while. I was just over five foot two inches tall, and this man was more than a foot taller than me. As we reached the ground floor his eyes slid over to me, and he smiled slightly. I smiled back before looking away quickly, embarrassed to have been caught staring.

We went to a nearby pita place. "That was one of the tallest people I've seen," I remarked as we sat down. "He had to be six five."

Karen smirked at me around her bite of overstuffed pita. "Did he look at all familiar?" she asked when she'd swallowed.

"Yeah, he did," I said thoughtfully.

"Maybe because it was Jo Van der Meer," she said drily.

I gasped. My pita fell onto my tray, spilling shredded lettuce. Jo Van der Meer was a Dutch jumper rider and the reigning world champion. His first name was pronounced "Yo", which I always found funny.

"Oh no, I was staring at him in the elevator. He's going to think I'm some kind of groupie," I moaned.

"Don't worry, I'm sure he's used to it."

I called Jaden before bed. I wanted to share my excitement, and I needed to hear his voice. I was afraid he wouldn't be as happy to hear from me, but I should have known better.

"*Corazon*," he answered warmly. "I miss you already."

The tight knot of uncertainty inside me slipped loose at his words. I felt a rush of love, followed by remorse. "Me too. I'm so sorry about the way we left things," I whispered. Karen was in the shower, but I was afraid my voice would crack if I spoke any louder.

"Don't worry about it now," he said. "Enjoy the experience, and please — be safe."

We had a quick breakfast at the motel early the next morning before heading to the showgrounds. I couldn't help gawking; I'd been to some nice facilities but Spruce Meadows outshone them all. Endless mowed green in all directions, opulent landscaping, and attractive red-roofed buildings were separated by strategically placed evergreens. In the distance, the Rocky Mountains sparkled, their white peaks vivid against the blue sky. I'd seen pictures of this place, of course, and watched countless tournaments on television, but neither of those had conveyed its sheer size or its sense of grandeur. I spun slowly around, absorbing the details.

"You'll have time to sight-see later," Karen said, taking my arm. "Let me show you the barns."

The stabling at Spruce wasn't housed in temporary tents like it was at most shows. Here, rows of long white barns housed visiting equine athletes in comfort. I followed Karen into a large barn and immediately spotted Hades. He stuck his nose between the bars and nickered when he saw me. It was an affectionate greeting, and I hurried to his side and made a fuss over him, realizing that the few days we'd spent apart must have worried him.

"He's been harder to handle than usual," Tania commented beside me. "I hope he'll settle down now that he's seen you." She wiped her hands on her jeans, which were already grass-stained and smeared with hoof oil. It was the sign of a good groom, I thought — she cared more about the horse's appearance than her own, and she talked about how he was feeling before mentioning anything about her own trip. I smiled, feeling lucky to have found her.

Hades had a class that afternoon; the jumps were on the small side for him, since I was using it primarily as a chance for him to look around. I met Monica and Neil for coffee first. Monica was aflutter with excitement, and they seemed to have met several other horse owners already, although I wasn't sure how. Rich person's radar, maybe.

"I hear that Irish horse is here," Neil commented. "The one that just sold for a million euros. I hope she'll be in one of Hades' classes."

I almost choked on my coffee. I was decidedly hoping she *wasn't*. I explored a bit afterward, visiting the tack shop, which was open year-round and housed in a building rather than a tent or truck, and wandering through the various buildings. My tour left me feeling quite insignificant, and I was happy to go back to the barn to help get Hades ready for his class. I noticed a security guard on my way in — not the first one I'd seen — and a small element of tension eased inside me. Hades was undoubtedly safe here.

We had lots of time before our class, so after Tania gave me a leg up I let Hades roam the grounds on our way to the distant warm-up ring. I was hoping it would calm him because he was acting very excitable. I didn't know whether it was the long trip or Alberta's crisp, thin air, but he snorted and jogged and generally acted like a cannon about to go off. We drew quite a few curious stares, which I did my best to ignore. I knew that I looked like a kid on a pony riding Hades, and his bad behavior was doubtless making people a bit nervous. It didn't help that I was already in awe of my surroundings and of the riding superstars all around me. Karen was waiting for me at the schooling ring. She tilted her head up to get a good look at us from under the brim of her cap.

"Well, it's a good thing we have time for some schooling," was her only comment. I worked at getting Hades to relax and soften, but every perfectly behaved horse that passed us only increased my sense of unworthiness.

"That's as good as he's gonna get," Karen said finally, after we'd jumped a fence in a reasonable manner a couple of times. I let Hades walk, staying away from the other riders as much as possible while I pondered what I was up against.

Seth and I had gotten riding lessons for our ninth birthday, something we'd spent years clamoring for. It had quickly become apparent that he was the more talented rider, physically speaking. He had strength and coordination I'll never enjoy. But what I did have — and I had it in spades — was fire. My passion for horses burned like a pyre, consuming every reasonable thing it encountered. The fact that my passion was expressed through riding jumpers was because my coach was one of Canada's best hunter/jumper trainers. Under different circumstances, I might have found myself eventing or doing dressage or riding reining horses — it was the *horses* that were my heart's center. And as Karen had pointed out, by some miracle horses seemed to love me too. That was my sole distinguishing characteristic, and it had gotten me to this point. Now, however, I'd be facing riders who not only had fantastically trained horses and bottomless pots of money, but also a burning drive to match my own.

When it was my turn to ride into the ring my heart thumped in a way it hadn't done in years. I put my leg on to ask Hades to canter and he decided to do a side-pass instead, snorting and moving sideways in an elevated, dramatic trot. I felt my face flame and asked again, much harder this time, and he burst forward into a wildly energetic canter. I focused on remembering my course; the height wasn't a challenge for Hades and we didn't have any rails down, but I wasn't proud of our performance and I hunched down in my saddle as we exited the ring. Normally Hades would relax now that he knew his job was over, but today his head stayed up and his step remained springy.

I decided to cool him off myself.

"What's going on with you, buddy? You're overdoing the drama a bit, you know." I patted his neck and lengthened my reins as he finally dropped his head and calmed down. I was heading back to the barn when Tania dashed up to us.

"You need to go back, you got tenth place!" I trotted back in amazement; it hadn't occurred to me that we would place in this elite company. Then again, not every show had ribbons to tenth place. Afterward, I helped Tania wash and groom Hades, and I was feeding him a final peppermint when Karen bustled in.

"Come on, let's get some dinner and get ready for the party."

"Party?" I gave her a blank look.

"Yes," she said in exasperation. "You know, the 'welcome to our show' party. Remember?"

The fact was, I rarely went to show parties. For the longest time I couldn't, because I was acting as instructor and groom and rider all at once, and those combined responsibilities left me little time or energy. The few times I'd gone, though, had been with my friends — Julia and Teri and occasionally Alex — and the thought of showing up after today's embarrassing ride was not tempting.

"I think I'll skip it," I said, closing Hades' stall.

"No, you won't," Karen said firmly. "You need to get out and mingle with these people. You were acting like someone was going to bite you today, and it's rubbing off on your horse."

The gathering was held in the main building. I found myself sitting rigidly at a round table next to Karen with several other trainers and riders. After dinner, Karen went to greet her many acquaintances while I sat and considered fleeing.

"You ride a magnificent horse." I looked up — way up — to find the towering Dutch rider, Jo, next to me. "But he is maybe a bit small for you, ya?" His smile was so playful that I laughed, and he joined in. I liked his accent, and he had a deep, pleasant voice.

"That was an interesting bridle you used today." Another man had joined us. "I'm Pietr." We shook hands as I introduced myself. Pietr turned out to be Hungarian, and he made quite the contrast with Jo; he was slender and not very tall for a man. He had murky green eyes and very short brown hair. He and Jo sat down and launched into an animated discussion of the relative merits of various equipment they'd tried. They both listened avidly as I explained my journey to the bitless bridle. I was pleasantly surprised by how open they seemed to trying different tack and training methods, something I had rarely found among my peers. Jo impressed me further by saying that he used natural, gentle horsemanship methods in training all his young horses.

We were comparing notes when a slim girl with glossy, shoulder-length brown hair joined us. "Hey, guys."

Jo and Pietr greeted her enthusiastically, and she turned curious brown eyes on me.

"Hi, I'm Téa," I introduced myself.

She stuck out her hand. "Sorrel." I knew who she was without the introduction. Although she was only a few years older than me, Sorrel Lang was already a household name among followers of our sport. She was the youngest person on the American Team, had rocked the World Championships, and was considered a safe bet for the next Olympics. She was also, it turned out, very down-to-earth, and she joined right in our training talk. I found myself having such a good time that when Karen came to find me shortly afterward I didn't want to leave.

"I will escort the young lady safely to the motel," Jo offered.

Karen gave Jo a speculative look, but she had greeted Pietr and Sorrel with familiarity, and she finally turned to me and said, "All right."

I blew out a breath of relief that she hadn't said anything embarrassing about being responsible for me, and hadn't told me to come home to bed as Dec would have. We got more drinks — I was having iced tea — and were soon laughing at Pietr's tale of being lost in the German countryside on his way to Aachen.

Shortly afterward I followed Jo's golden-blond hair through the semi-dark parking lot to a mid-size sedan. He folded his very long body into the driver's seat. It was just a regular car, I thought as I buckled my seat belt. Come to think of it, I wondered why he was staying at the same ordinary chain motel as me — surely a world champion rider could afford upscale accommodations? Monica and Neil were staying at a luxury hotel further away.

I plucked up my courage to ask him. "Do you always stay at this motel when you come to Spruce Meadows?"

"Ya," he said. "I like to be close to the horses." I smiled at him in the car's dim interior. I liked that, too.

I rode Hades in one small class the following day. He still wasn't himself, and although he'd settled down somewhat we ended up nowhere in the class.

"But on the plus side, I met two nice Portuguese riders today," I told Jaden on the phone that evening. I left out the fact that I'd also run into Alex, who had acted as though he didn't know me.

There were no classes scheduled for the next day, so when Pietr invited me to dinner with a group of his friends I was happy to agree. Karen came too, and we met up with Jo, Sorrel, and the Portuguese riders as well. By the evening's end I'd met so many international stars that I'd stopped feeling awed, and despite my lackluster performances so far, I began to appreciate simply being there.

I awoke Sunday to swollen grey skies. Hades' biggest class to date was that afternoon, and the rain started as Tania was tacking up. I was slouched on a tack trunk texting Jaden, who was planning to watch the streamed video of the class.

It's raining. R u sure u don't want to scratch?

Despite the format, his worry came through clearly. I shook my head in frustration as I texted back.

Jaden, the footing here is state of the art. They spent a gazillion $ on it. We'll be fine... but if ur nervous, u don't have to watch ;)

I left the phone in the tackroom before going outside. It beeped again but I didn't check it. I needed to focus on Hades; I didn't want Jaden's worry added to the burden of my own. I put the rain cover on my hat, then gratefully pulled on my new raincoat. It would protect my saddle from too much rain, at least until I had to take it off to go into the ring.

We had a short warm-up. The shower was turning into solid sheets of water now. Everything was slick; my reins slid through my gloves, and my new boots slipped on the rubber stirrup treads. Maybe the weather made him realize it was time to be serious because to my relief Hades seemed fully himself again.

At the in-gate, Karen grasped my boot and looked up at me, squinting against the rain. "Do you want to scratch? I'm surprised they haven't canceled the class." I wasn't surprised. The footing was grass and it held up quite well. Tania had screwed studs into Hades' shoes for extra purchase.

I shook my head, afraid that if I spoke she'd hear my teeth chattering. When my number was called I quickly stripped off my raincoat and handed it to Tania, shivering as cold water sluiced down my neck. There weren't many spectators, thanks to the weather, and the ring seemed unnaturally quiet as we picked up a canter.

"Go, Téa!" "You can do it!" I heard Pietr's voice among the chorus of yells from the sidelines and grinned as we headed to our first fence. Hades grunted as we cleared it; I felt the extra effort he had to expend because of the slippery ground. We kept going, taking it slowly through the downpour.

Hades was questioning me politely. *Should I lengthen stride? Are we turning here?* More incredibly, he acquiesced easily to my invisible responses. I realized that the conditions were making him nervous, too.

"Hang in there, boy, we're almost done," I murmured to reassure him.

We headed toward a straightforward oxer. I carefully measured our take-off distance, and I relaxed imperceptibly when I knew we would meet the fence perfectly. I felt Hades shift his weight backward, his massive hindquarters bunching to propel us... but as his neck rose beneath me I realized that something was wrong. We weren't going upward, we were sliding forward. There was a sudden splintering crash, a heavy blow, and then falling, falling, in seeming slow motion.

I blinked my eyes open to cold drops pelting my face.

"Don't move her!" Karen's authoritative voice snapped. I turned my head to see her kneeling next to me, her brown eyes wide with fear. It was an expression I'd never seen her wear before.

"That includes you, kid. Don't try to move," she ordered.

The sensation was returning to my body. "How's Hades?" I asked her anxiously.

"Don't worry about him for now."

I did a quick assessment while men's harried voices surrounded me, soon accompanied by thunking sounds as they cleared the fence away. I felt okay, other than my shoulder throbbing. I rolled onto my side and started pushing myself up.

"Hey!" I felt Karen's hands stop me at the same time as a cheer went up. I looked up to a sea of concerned faces; hard-core fans in the stands and my fellow riders and grooms at the in-gate.

"Karen, really, I'm fine," I assured her. I got to my feet, her hands now helping and supporting me. The cheer swelled again, louder this time, and I gave a little wave, blushing as I went to retrieve Hades. I took his reins from a nervous-looking ringman and led him forward a few tentative steps. His walk seemed normal. The shock of relief was so sharp that I wrapped shaking arms around his head.

"I'm sorry, buddy, I'm so sorry," I choked out.

Huh-huh-huh-huh. His response rumbled out from low in his chest, an unmistakable whicker of affection. I guess he'd been worried too.

I led Hades slowly out of the ring, waving away the hovering medics. Thank God he seemed to be sound. Tania took the reins from me, tears mingling with rain on her face, and I followed behind them so that I could watch Hades move from every angle.

By the time we'd made sure Hades wasn't injured and put him away, I had three frantic voicemails from Jaden.

"I'm fine," I said the instant he answered his phone.

"Do you own a dictionary?" His voice was shaking. "Because you clearly don't know what 'fine' means. You took twenty years off my life, Téa."

"Sorry. I guess you decided to watch after all."

"As if I'd miss it. You're just lucky Dec wasn't watching this time."

Cold fingers of dread clutched my insides. "Jaden, please don't let him see it," I pleaded. "Tell him the class was canceled or something."

There was silence for a moment. "I don't want to lie to him again," he said quietly. "Our relationship's been strained enough."

"I'm begging you, my love. Please."

I thought I heard a stifled groan. "All right."

We had two days to recover before the Masters Tournament started. Hades was massaged and hand-walked and was soon limber again. Fortunately, the motel had a pool and a hot tub, which helped my stiffness, if not my nerves. I'd had a bad end to the tournament that was supposed to help ease me into the biggest competition of my life, and I swatted away the niggling feeling that it was a sign that I didn't belong.

I had just done the official jog with Hades — where show officials checked the horses for soundness — when my phone rang. I answered distractedly, pushing Hades' nose away from my jacket pocket with my other hand.

"What's new, Sis?"

I stopped dead. Hades promptly began tugging at my pocket, trying to release the peppermints inside. Tania jogged over to take him and I handed him over without a word, ignoring her inquiring look.

"Well, are you going to talk to me? 'Cause you were pretty bossy about getting me to call you," Seth went on.

"Moo," I breathed. Then, much louder, "Where the hell have you been?"

"It's lovely to hear your voice too." My brother laughed, and despite myself, I broke into a grin. I turned the corner of the nearest building and leaned against the wall. It was quiet here, and I allowed myself a deep breath of relief.

"I've been worried about you," I chided. "And I don't have time for that, I'm at Spruce Meadows."

There was a gasp of surprise. "That's awesome! Things are going great for you."

I fell silent. But it was Seth at the other end of this invisible thread, my twin, the one who would understand even if I couldn't explain properly. So I told him about Teri's accident, and Dec wanting to sell our home, and my growing feeling of insecurity with the Donalds.

"What about Jaden?" he asked. It may have sounded random, but it wasn't. Seth knew me well.

My sigh seemed to come up all the way from my toes. "Jaden and I seem to want different things these days."

"Well, I can't do much about that, but I'll give you a hug to make you feel better," he offered.

Hope surged inside me. "You mean-"

"Yup. I'm heading home. I'll be there in a couple of days. Ol' Dec even sounded happy about it." I hadn't realized to what extent worry over Seth had been dragging me down, but I felt positively buoyant after our conversation.

Until the next day, that is. The reality of riding in my first truly international class struck me like ice water the next morning. I couldn't force myself to eat, so I only had coffee on my way to the barn. My face was rigid, and I gave terse answers to anyone who spoke to me. Puffy clouds graced a clear blue sky, and I loosened up marginally in the warm-up ring, but Hades lacked his usual swagger. I gave him an encouraging pat as Karen walked us to the in-gate.

I had worn my old boots. They were more comfortable, and at this point, I didn't think it mattered how I looked. It only mattered how I did.

I glanced down at Karen, expecting last-minute instructions, but instead, she met my eye and said, "You deserve to be here, kid. The only thing you lack is mileage, and that will come." It wouldn't come fast enough to help me now, but I appreciated the sentiment and gave her a weak smile. Then I looked up. The sky was above me, the earth was below me, and the fire was within me. It was time to fan the flames.

We walked in and began to canter. I allowed myself to be hypnotized by the steady *da-da-dum, da-da-dum* of Hades' feet, the rhythmic *whoosh* of each breath blown from his lungs. And this time, everything else fell away. It didn't matter where we were, it didn't matter that I was surrounded by elite riders whom I desperately wanted to impress — this time, I forgot anyone was even there. It was just Hades and me, jumping a fantastic course on a beautiful day, my heart pounding, my hands sweating, and my heart soaring as we flew as one being over each obstacle.

We walked out to cheers, and I dropped my reins and patted Hades enthusiastically with both hands. Tania was smiling from ear to ear as she took Hades.

When I jumped down Karen placed her hands on my shoulders. "That," she said solemnly, "was perfect."

It must have been because we won the class. I was so stunned that I stood rooted when it was time to collect my ribbon, and Karen had to shoo me into the ring.

Afterward, I stuffed Hades so full of peppermints that Tania scolded me, "You're going to give him colic!"

"You may need to get a bigger pony soon," Jo laughed. "It seems you are growing up. Soon all of us must be keeping our eyes on you."

"Congratulations." Sorrel flashed me a smile, and even though she'd won much bigger classes, it was sincere. "Let's go celebrate tonight."

I was glad I'd packed a little black dress. After dinner, I went to a bar with Pietr, Jo, Sorrel, the two Portuguese riders, and several people whose names I didn't remember. It was an upscale place, and the bouncer peered closely at my Ontario driver's license before staring at me.

"You don't look nineteen," he observed, his face dubious. I suppressed a flare of panic. Most of the others had already gone in, and I'd be mortified if I was turned away.

Jo was arriving, and he gave a questioning look as he stopped beside me.

"He thinks I'm too young to go in," I explained.

Jo draped a long arm around me. "This girl is a champion rider. She is old enough to go in a bar." I don't know whether it was Jo's words or his sheer size that convinced the bouncer, but he stepped aside to let us in.

"How old are you, then?" Jo asked as we made our way through the crowd. He had to speak loudly over the music.

"Nineteen," I said, laughing that he had championed my cause without even knowing. Sorrel waved us over, looking very trendy is a glittering blue halter top, and I was touched to see that she'd saved me a seat.

I had a great night. At home, I lived under Dec's strict rules, and in any case, I rarely had either the time or energy to go out. My life was very mundane. Now all of a sudden, glamorous international athletes were taking me to places that would have completely intimidated me had I been on my own. My newfound popularity and freedom were as intoxicating as the drinks. Under normal circumstances I rarely drank, but here, being toasted by some of the world's best riders, I didn't resist when my champagne glass was refilled over and over.

The next morning was brutal. Riders and grooms on the grounds gave knowing smiles as they took in my dark shades and mincing steps, and a few made good-natured jokes about my lack of staying power. My reception in the tackroom, though, was far less understanding.

"What the hell were you thinking?" Karen yelled, nearly causing me to clutch my head. "Do you have any idea what Dec would do if he caught you carousing without supervision? Do you want to get sent home?"

I shook my head carefully. "We were just celebrating, Karen. I didn't drink that much, honest."

"Yes, I can see that," she said sarcastically. "Care to take off your sunglasses?"

I sighed. "Look, Karen, I know you promised to watch over me, but I'm not a kid. So I went out and had a couple of drinks. It's not a felony."

She blew out her breath. "I'm not saying you didn't deserve to celebrate — just don't overdo it, okay?" Karen was a former alcoholic and never went to bars.

After reassuring Karen, I put on a hat and went to watch the morning's classes. I wasn't riding that day but I was at the grounds every day, trying to absorb as much as I could. Although at the moment, the thought of going back to bed was quite tempting.

"Hello." An accented voice broke into my reverie. "I've seen you often caring for your horse this week. Is this a habit of yours?"

I looked over to see a man leaning on the fence next to me. He looked distinguished, with silver hair and neat clothes that seemed rather dressy for a horse show. I felt a familiar crimp of embarrassment, remembering rich girls who had laughed at me when I couldn't afford a groom. *Things are different now,* I reminded myself, and gave this stranger the benefit of the doubt.

"No, Hades is special. Sometimes I groom him myself to read his mood. I can tell by the way he acts toward me whether he approves of what we've done that day," I explained.

The man nodded thoughtfully. "You seem to be always here, watching the other riders," he commented.

235

I shrugged. "They're some of the best in the world. I want to learn from them while I can."

He smiled at me. "That's quite wise for a girl your age. If you are ever in The Netherlands, come and see me." He handed me a card and strolled away, whistling.

I looked at the card. It had a name, address and foreign telephone number on it, and I pocketed it without further thought.

"What did Bert want?" Karen asked when I got back to the tackroom. "The grey-haired gentleman," she specified at my confused look.

"Nothing, he was just making conversation."

Karen grinned. "Do you know who he is?" Her smile widened when I shook my head. "He's the chef d'équipe for the Dutch national team. And he's known for having an eye for talent."

Jaden called right after I'd ridden Hades that afternoon. "What happened to your voice?"

I was hoarse from speaking over the music the night before. "I guess I overused it a bit," I said vaguely.

"How's your head?"

I hesitated, confused. "Fine, why wouldn't it be?"

"Hangovers are peculiar that way."

I sat on a trunk to unzip my half-chaps. "How..."

"I have my sources."

"Karen told you." I said flatly. I felt a prickle of irritation toward my mentor.

"Don't be angry with her, she's concerned. She thought you'd listen to me, although why she would think so is a mystery."

I finished pulling off my chaps and folded them on the trunk. ""I'm not doing anything you haven't done at polo tournaments — in fact, I'm way less wild than you were."

"There's a difference, Téa. You're a small, attractive girl; you're a lot more vulnerable than I was. Going to parties and getting drunk constitutes a greater risk for you. I'm not asking you not to celebrate, but please, be careful. For me." He was using his most compelling voice, and it was plenty compelling. When he pulled out all the stops like that, there was no way for me to refuse him. I think he knew it, too.

"I promise to be careful," I said dutifully.

"I can't believe it's come to this, but take Alex with you if you have to." I was so shocked by his suggestion that I didn't even mention that I doubted Alex would go anywhere with me.

Later that day Sorrel, to no one's surprise, won her first class at the Master's.

"Tonight, we celebrate *my* win." She grinned at me as she rode out of the ring. Well, it wasn't as though I had promised not to go out, I reasoned. Just that I'd be careful. And I would be.

I was quickly running out of clothes to wear to places other than the barn. My light blue summer dress would have to do, I decided, paired with a black wrap, the only one I'd brought. The dress was on the short side, but the bar we went to that night wasn't as fancy as the previous night's so I didn't feel out of place. I had one alcoholic drink and after that, I stuck to juice.

The music was loud, and we danced a lot, mostly as a group but pairing off occasionally. I was getting tired when Sorrel and I headed to the bar to refresh our drinks, but loud cheering caught our attention before we ordered. A circle of people were standing around a man who, as I watched, bent backward over the bar. The bartender poured a shot directly into his mouth, and then — I could hardly believe my eyes — someone lit it on fire. Blue flames shot up before the man closed his mouth and straightened with a flourish, his arms raised for the applause that followed. I saw that it was Miguel, one of the Portuguese riders I'd befriended.

"Miguel, you have hidden talents," Sorrel said admiringly. Miguel grinned and turned his large, soft brown eyes on me.

"It is easy. Would you like to try?" he offered.

"Oh, I don't know…" I said.

"It does not hurt," he assured me.

"I'll go first," Sorrel offered. Our new entourage cheered as she leaned back over the bar and opened her mouth for the shot. Miguel himself touched a match to the liquid, and with a gasp I watched the blue flames flare. It seemed more shocking now that it was Sorrel doing it.

"Now, close your mouth quickly," Miguel instructed. She did, then straightened up, grinning madly.

"That was awesome!" Sorrel exclaimed. She grabbed my arm. "Téa, you have to try it!"

I hesitated, but I didn't want to be a spoilsport, and I especially didn't want to set myself apart from this crowd. I was gratified at how easily I'd been accepted and I wasn't going to risk marring things.

I bent backward over the bar. From above my head the blond bartender plied her bottle.

"Ready?" Miguel appeared at the corner of my eye with a match. And just like that, blue flames filled my vision. I closed my mouth, wincing in expectation of heat, but I felt nothing but relief as I gulped down the alcohol, gasping at its potency.

Another cheer went up, and multiple hands patted me on the back. I looked up to find Jo watching with interest.

"How did you do that?" he asked. We explained, but it was easier to show him, so I demonstrated again. Then Sorrel went, then Jo tried, then it was my turn again... until, suddenly, the room spun. Miguel caught me as I swayed.

"This one needs to go home," he remarked.

I'd arrived with Sorrel, who wasn't ready to leave yet, and I needed to go. Not only was the room spinning but I felt decidedly sick. Without quite knowing how it happened I found myself being led outside by Jo. The cold night air felt good on my sweaty face, but my head didn't get much clearer. I groaned.

"Come, you will go to bed and you will feel better," Jo promised.

He had to pull over once so that I could throw up, to my intense embarrassment. After that, I felt marginally better, although I staggered as we entered the motel. Jo put an arm around me to steady me.

"My coach is going to kill me," I whimpered as we got in the elevator.

"Then you will stay in my room," he said, pulling me against his body.

Twelve

Morning came all too soon, and with it too much brightness, too much fury from Karen, and not enough coffee. Karen made some in the little coffee maker in our room while I got changed.

Her phone rang as I took another grateful sip of coffee. I could hear the angry buzz even before she held it away from her ear, and I tensed in apprehension. Karen held out the phone, her face pale. I took it reluctantly.

"Hi, Dec," I said with false cheerfulness.

Even though he was across the country, I winced repeatedly during the tirade he unleashed on me. Years of conditioning caused me to cower at that booming voice, but after a minute I made myself straighten mentally. I briefly considered reminding him that I was nineteen and legally entitled to drink anywhere in the country, but luckily thought better of it. I did want to go home eventually, after all.

My own cell rang shortly after I'd hung up with Dec.

"Ouch." The smile in Jaden's voice came through clearly despite the miles.

"Don't tell me you didn't enjoy that a little." I sighed.

"*Querida*, you know I could never *enjoy* your pain. But I do feel, in this one instance, it may be deserved."

"I know," I said quietly. "I was stupid. I got carried away." I shuddered to think what might have happened if someone less honorable than Jo had taken me home, and realized with panic that Jaden could never know how close I'd come to danger. I fuzzily recalled my reaction when Jo had offered to take me to his room.

I had stared at him, aghast. "No! I mean, thanks, but..."

He had laughed. "Just to sleep, I promise. You are so small, I would break you if we did more."

I tried to shake my head and immediately regretted it. "I have a boyfriend."

239

He hadn't seemed put out, and gallantly walked me to my door and helped me open it since I couldn't seem to get the card into the slot.

I came back to the present. "Who told Dec?" I spoke into the phone, but my eyes went to Karen. She shrugged.

"Don't you know?" Jaden sounded surprised.

"No." A throbbing pain was burgeoning behind my eyes.

"There's a picture of you leaning backward — in a very short dress, I might add — while a man pours alcohol straight from a bottle into your mouth." His voice was grim. "It's making the rounds online. There have been several comments about the show circuit's new party girl. You."

I was shocked into silence. Embarrassment that my family had seen the image, shame that I'd failed Jaden, and the vestiges of nausea combined to make me feel atrocious.

"Still there?" Jaden asked after a moment.

I swallowed back bile. "I... I'm sorry."

He let out a long breath. "Look, I've been there. You don't want to be the lone abstainer, and it's a heady feeling to be accepted into a group you admire. Combine that with legitimate reasons to celebrate and it's hard to resist."

Tears stung my eyes. Jaden being so understanding made me feel both better and, though it hardly seemed possible, worse.

"Yes," I sniffled.

"So *learn* from this experience. Even better, learn from Karen's experience."

"I can't believe there's a picture. I feel like I have no privacy anymore."

"It's only going to get worse as your reputation grows," Jaden warned. "Let's face it, Téa, it's not only your talent that's smoking hot. The press is naturally going to love you... and it doesn't hurt that you're giving them plenty of fodder, either. You need to stop this before it gets out of hand. Or do I have to fly out there to get my point across?"

"Why, is there a chance you could?" I exclaimed, instantly excited.

He chuckled. "That was meant as something of a threat, actually."

"Oh. Well, I promise to act suitably chastened when you get here. But please try to come. I miss you so much."

"I miss you too, baby."

I was surprised; it was an endearment he rarely used.

We stopped at a restaurant on our way to the show, where I sat and watched Karen eat breakfast while I drank more coffee.

"Did Dec put the fear of God into you?" she asked between bites. It was the fear of Dec, more like, but I nodded.

She slammed her hand on the table, making me jump and drop my cup, which luckily didn't spill.

"Well, you don't look scared enough! Do you know how many talented riders have ended their careers with the kinds of stupid stunts you've been pulling?"

I twisted my napkin, not meeting her gaze. Karen's own career had been severely limited by her drinking, and I realized with a sudden, sick shock that she might have been sitting right where I was at one time, listening to lectures and feeling irritated with people for overreacting.

I dropped the napkin and looked directly into her worried brown eyes. "I know, Karen. I'll be much more careful in the future. Really."

Hades didn't have a class that day, and I waited until late in the day to ride him, giving my headache time to subside. My phone beeped as I was riding back to the barn.

Look behind you.

Confused, I glanced over my shoulder. Then I spun Hades around and pushed him into a gallop. He had barely stopped before I threw myself down and into Jaden's arms.

"I can't believe you're here," I gasped when he finally let me go. Hades had backed up to the end of his reins as though distancing himself from our display. Jaden chuckled and patted him as we walked to the barn arm in arm.

I gave him a tour, introducing him proudly to everyone we met. Karen seemed relieved to see him.

"Um, I'm pretty tired," I told her. "I don't think I'll stay for the evening classes tonight."

She gave me a knowing smile. "Well, I'll be here for hours yet."

Jaden had rented a car, and we were at the motel room in minutes. I dropped my bag on the bed before facing him.

"Shall we get the unpleasantness over with first?" he asked, his face serious.

"What unpleasantness?"

"Have you forgotten the small matter of your excessive partying? Staying out until all hours worrying Karen to death? And my personal favorite, strange men pouring shots into your mouth?" he demanded.

I sighed and looked up at him. "If I say sorry and promise not to do it again, will the unpleasant part be over? 'Cause I haven't seen you naked in a really long time, and I'd like to get to that part as soon as possible." I ran my hands over his chest as I was talking; he caught my wrists. A smile was fighting to break through, but he controlled it.

"Are you trying to distract me from your punishment?" he asked with mock severity.

"Yes."

"It's working." The smile finally broke free, and I felt myself go weak in response. I never had been able to resist his smile. He pulled my wrists behind his back, drawing me against him, and my stomach quivered as his lips found mine.

The kiss stretched into timelessness. His hands moved leisurely over my body, and I hardly noticed how I found myself undressed and in bed. Our reunion was sweet, and after it I lay with my face tucked into the juncture of his neck and shoulder, breathing in his scent. I drew one leg over his body.

"I was afraid you'd be angrier," I confessed.

"It's not me you should worry about. Dec wanted me to read you the riot act when I got here. If you don't calm down, he's going to haul your little butt right back home."

I nodded against his skin and rested my palm on his chest.

Jaden stroked my hair silently for a moment. "There was another picture, Téa." His voice was strained. "A tall blond man had his arm around you, and you were... pressed against him."

I rolled away from him, my heart thumping. That someone had taken a picture of me with Jo at a time when I'd been so vulnerable made me angry. And scared.

"He brought me home when I was drunk," I admitted. I met his eyes directly, feeling an urgent need to convince him. "He was a perfect gentleman. I... needed help walking." Shame caused my face to flame, and I turned it into the pillow.

His quiet breaths sounded for a few minutes. "Okay," he murmured finally.

I raised myself onto an elbow. "Jaden, I'm so crazy about you, sometimes I feel like you should *know* how impossible it would be for me to look at another man. But maybe that's not a fair or reasonable assumption for me to make." I placed my hand on his cheek and looked him in the eye. "Just so we're clear — I adore you, Jaden Foster, and regardless of my sometimes inconsiderate and thoughtless antics, you have nothing to worry about. You're the only man that exists for me. I hope you know that."

He pulled me on top of him, then held my face in his hands and kissed me so thoroughly that we were soon rolling around the bed again. After the week I'd had, I was really going to be sore everywhere.

We had to be at the showgrounds early the next morning, but I left the bed reluctantly. I wanted to stay lost, submerged in the warm rich honey of Jaden's love. Despite everything that had happened, I felt a deep sense of contentment. When we were together, shelter was his arms around me and sustenance came from whispers passed in the dark. I was more at peace than I had been in weeks.

We walked to the barn hand in hand. My hair, still wet from the shower, was covered by my favorite light blue cap and I shivered as the occasional droplet rolled down my back. Sorrel came ambling down the path toward us, accompanied by two other American riders and Alex.

"Hey." Sorrel stopped and smiled at Jaden before sliding her eyes over to me. "I was wondering where you were last night." Her smile turned sly.

"Sorrel, this is my boyfriend Jaden," I introduced them.

They were shaking hands when Alex spoke. "Your *cousin*, you mean."

Sorrel gave me a brows-raised look, but I was staring at Alex. The scorn in his voice hurt, and I couldn't believe he was being so spiteful.

"Step-cousin," I specified. I was about to say more when Alex's eyes widened and he backed up half a step. My hand automatically shot out and grabbed Jaden's arm. When I looked at his face I could see why Alex might've found his expression alarming.

"Look, Alex, I'm sorry we haven't talked about-" I began.

"Whatever. You should try dating someone who isn't a relative," Alex spat. He marched down the path, leaving Sorrel and her friends shifting uncomfortably.

I crossed my arms over my chest. I genuinely liked Sorrel, and lord knew I wanted to fit in here, but I was well and truly fed up of this happening.

"There's no blood relation between Jaden and me," I said firmly. "Alex... well, he wanted more from me than I could give."

Sorrel shook her head. "Jealousy makes people crazy."

After they'd gone Jaden examined my face. "Do you want me to beat him up for you?"

I frowned at him. "If I said yes you'd do it, wouldn't you?"

"The way he's hurt you? I'd do it quite happily," he said, grim.

I slumped. "I don't want to hurt Alex. I just wish he didn't want to hurt me," I whispered.

We went on our way. I held Jaden's hand tightly, keeping my head down so my cap covered my face. Jaden pulled me to a stop and chucked me gently under the chin.

"Chin up. We have nothing to be ashamed of." His fervor gave me the strength to keep my head high.

I checked in with Tania and Hades and was about to set off in search of Karen when Jaden caught my shoulder.

"I have work to do," he confessed. "Do I have time before your class?"

"Sure, I only ride at eleven."

I had a brief meeting with the Donalds and got some more coffee before strolling back to the barn. The day was bright but not hot. Conditions would be perfect in the ring, I thought. Tania and Hades were at the paved entrance to the barn, and Hades stretched out his nose to noisily sniff my coffee.

"That's not for you." I laughed, holding it out of his reach.

"Can you hold him for a sec?" Tania handed me the leadrope. Hades reached for my coffee again, and I turned my back to him to shield it. A sudden shove sent me flying forward.

"Ow!" I landed on my hands and knees, my right hand crushing the cup and resting in a puddle of hot coffee.

Tania came running. "What happened? Are you okay?" She grabbed Hades as I pulled myself to my feet.

"He pushed me." I gave him an exasperated look, but my hand was throbbing. "I think I burned my hand."

"Quick, go run it under cold water."

I did, but when I tried to twist it under the stream a sharp pain shot through my wrist. I swore quietly and kept it under the water a bit longer. I tried moving my wrist again; this time the pain was worse. I rejoined Tania, cradling my dripping wrist with my hand.

"Is it better?" she asked worriedly.

"I think I strained something. What do we have in the way of bandages?"

I was wrapping my wrist in Vetrap when Karen and Jo came in together.

"What happened?" she exclaimed.

"I fell," I muttered.

"How bad is it? Can you move it?" She and Jo both watched my hand expectantly.

I moved my hand carefully up and down a bit. "I just wrapped it tightly," I said by way of excuse.

Karen narrowed her eyes at me. "Move it from side to side."

I gritted my teeth and bent my hand to the outside, but when I tried to bend it toward my thumb I gasped.

"That's it, you're going to the hospital," she said.

"I can't, my class is in two hours," I protested. I looked up at Jo, hoping for support, but he shook his head.

"You must do as your trainer says," he advised me. "I can take you, I ride only tomorrow."

I gave Karen a despairing look. She had another client riding that morning or I was sure she'd be dragging me off herself.

"Fine," I muttered. I fumbled for my phone and dialed awkwardly with my left hand, but Jaden didn't answer. I decided not to leave him a message until I had a better idea of what was wrong — no need to panic him unnecessarily.

Jo kept up a cheerful conversation on our way to the hospital and settled in patiently to wait with me.

245

"I'm going to miss my class," I moaned. It was the biggest class I'd ridden in to date, and after all the money the Donalds had spent getting here I was sure they'd be upset if I had to scratch.

"It is part of our sport," Jo reminded me. "People are injured, horses are injured — we are not machines."

It wasn't a long wait, but I'd already called the Donalds and told them to scratch Hades from the class when the X-rays came back. To my disgust, they showed a fractured wrist bone. I was sitting in a small room waiting for a cast when Jaden rushed in.

"Karen told me where to find you," he said. I got up and hugged him with one arm, and he held me gingerly. I could feel the exact moment his eyes lit on Jo. I pulled away in time to see recognition register.

I put my good hand on his arm, which was hard with tension. "Jaden, this is Jo. He was kind enough to drive me when I couldn't reach you."

Jo gave an open smile, and after a second's hesitation on Jaden's part, they shook hands. It was odd to see Jaden look up to someone.

"Thank you," he said sincerely.

Jo wished me luck and said he'd see me back at the barn. As soon as he left, I turned to Jaden.

"It's a coincidence," I started to say.

He laid his hands gently on my upper arms. "*Querida*, I know," he murmured.

I stopped, startled. "You're not upset?"

"I've been doing a lot of thinking, and you're right. It's time I got over my insecurities. I trust you, and if you tell me that I have nothing to worry about, then I won't worry." His eyes held me as tenderly as his hands. "I'm willing to change for the sake of our relationship."

I had a feeling my mouth was hanging open unattractively when the casting technician bustled in and got to work. She had to pause as a coughing fit shook my body.

"Maybe you should get that cough looked at while you're here," she said cheerfully, finishing up.

"I'm okay," I said, though my voice was so hoarse I hardly recognized it.

Jaden led me by the hand to the parking lot, and I inspected my new cast as we went. I'd opted for fiberglass because it would be impossible for me to keep a plaster cast dry while working in the barn. It was a pretty blue color and felt quite light compared to the other cast I'd had.

"At least it's not serious," I commented as we got to the car. "I can still ride."

Jaden spun to face me. "What? No."

I looked at him in surprise. "Jaden, we came all the way here. My biggest class is tomorrow, and I'm fine now that I have the cast. I can even manage with one hand if I have to."

"I said no," he said sharply. I flinched at his tone — I couldn't help it — but the look I gave him was furious.

"You can't forbid me from riding."

A storm cloud passed over his face. His hand scrubbed over his hair and he glared at me, but I held his stare. He exhaled loudly.

"I know," he said finally, "much as I'd like to. But we do need to talk about it."

I tried to cross my arms, but the cast made it awkward. "So talk," I said.

"You're worried about one class at one show, but you need to start taking the longer view when it comes to your health. You're going to be living in that body for a long time — you don't want to spend the next sixty years in pain, or worse, with impaired function, all because of a short-sighted decision you made as a teenager."

"Don't call me a teenager."

"You are a teenager."

I took a deep breath and gave him a level look. "Okay. Then stop saying it as though it's an insult."

He had the good grace to look abashed and moved his hand to cover to my cheek. The warmth of his touch was enough to dissolve my ire, and I turned my head and kissed his palm.

We got in the car, and I let Jaden find his way back to the main road before I spoke again.

"The thing is, Neil keeps talking about how much other jumpers are worth. I don't know how much longer they'll keep Hades." It was the first time I'd voiced that particular fear aloud. "And if I can't ride him,

247

what if they find someone who will? Now that he's rideable, they could put any half-decent rider on him and he'd do great."

"Maybe, but he's only rideable because of you." He gave me a thoughtful glance from behind the wheel. "Have you ever thought that maybe your particular talent lies in training, *querida*?"

I frowned at him. "Why can't I be good at both?" I thought I was, personally.

"You can, but if you focused on training, you wouldn't need to spend all your time traveling."

I answered slowly, dismayed that the conversation had come back to this. "I'd at least like to see how far I can make it."

"And where would that leave us?" he asked impatiently. "One of the reasons I left professional polo was because I couldn't put down roots anywhere, and now my girlfriend is doing the same thing? Do you expect me to sit at home waiting for you?"

My cast lay in my lap. I traced the edge with one finger. "What happened to you, my love? Where's the boy who was always laughing, always so sure of our future?"

"He grew up," he said with finality.

"You sound like your father," I said bitterly, and watched him wince. I hadn't meant it hurtfully, but that didn't stop it from injuring him all the same.

We didn't speak another word until we got to the barn. My arrival was met with exclamations; everywhere I walked, riders, grooms, and officials commiserated with me on my bad luck, but the only reaction I cared about was the Donalds'. They hurried into the barn after I texted them, and Monica's hand went to her mouth at the sight of my cast. Neil frowned.

Jaden was a stiff sentry beside me. I shot him a glare. I wanted more than anything to tell the Donalds that I'd still ride their horse, but at the last minute I realized that a messy personal fight with my boyfriend would not give a good impression — and a fight was bound to ensue.

"I broke my wrist," I said. My dismay came through clearly despite the raspiness of my voice. "I'm sorry, but I can't ride tomorrow."

"You can't ride for six weeks," Jaden gritted beside me. I fought a childish urge to kick him.

Neil gave a start. "Six weeks? That means we'll miss most of the indoor shows."

I wanted to assure him that I'd be recovered enough to ride, even if the cast was still on, but I realized with plunging certainty that even if that were true, Dec would never let me miss more school for those shows.

I understood, suddenly and viscerally, Hades' objection to bits. I was sick of being reined in too. I wanted to find my stride, to seek the absolute limits of my abilities — and then push a little further. To see how fast and high and far I could go if given the chance.

But it wasn't going to happen. Dec was convinced he knew what was best for me, and it involved choosing safety — physical, psychological and financial — over risk. Jaden had put himself in harm's way for me, emotionally and physically, and all he wanted was for us to build a life together, a life I knew most women would give their left arm for. Jaden and Dec loved me. They were my family. If I went against them, what did that say about me? Dec and I had come such a long way, and Jaden had sacrificed so much for me. A normal person would be happy with what I had, I told myself. But clearly 'normal' didn't describe me because my feelings bore no resemblance to happiness.

I gritted my teeth and looked first at Neil, then Monica. "I'm sorry," I repeated. "Accidents happen in our sport." They left, not hiding their disappointment. It looked as though Jaden was going to speak, but I turned away from him and went to Hades' stall. He examined my cast with interest before checking my pockets.

"I don't have anything for you." I had nothing to offer anyone right now.

The somber mood lasted through the next day. We watched Jo win the final class of the show, with Sorrel a close second, and even though I hadn't been entered I found myself calculating what the rider's share of the one million dollars in prize money would be.

Jaden and I were on separate flights home, and I was actually relieved. Tania drove me home from the airport in the middle of the night. I woke up late, showered, and wandered downstairs as Seth emerged from the kitchen. He loped over and grabbed me in a hug before holding me at arm's length.

"Looks like it was about time you came back," he noted, taking in my cast and the dark smudges under my eyes.

"It's about time *I* got back?" I meant to make a joke but found myself choked by sudden ire. "I've been here the whole time, working while you've been gallivanting," I said loudly.

"Oh, that's rich!" he snapped back. "Last year you were gone half the time while I was stuck here teaching up-downers and dodging Dec's temper! Why are you the only one allowed to leave?!"

"You didn't just leave, Seth! You — you disappeared! I was worried sick about you, do you have any idea what that's like?"

"Oh please," he scoffed, "you know damn well you'd know if anything bad had happened to me."

"And a fat lot of good it would've done me since I didn't know where you were!" I screeched.

He shrugged carelessly. "Well, I'm fine, so it doesn't matter."

"Aargh!" I swung my palm up, intending to connect with his thick skull, but he ducked and gave me a shove, using my own momentum to send me sprawling onto the couch.

"Pick on someone your own size, squirt, or you're gonna get hurt," he said grimly.

In answer, I launched myself off the couch at him. I only got in one glancing blow to his body before he caught my arms, and I struggled wildly, incoherent with anger. Almost instinctively I jerked my knee up. It found its mark; Seth dropped like a stone. I followed almost as quickly, falling to my knees beside him.

"Seth! Are you okay?" His groan made it plain that he wasn't. "I'm so sorry." I hovered uselessly, smoothing his hair, until his face regained some color and he sat up.

"When did you start fighting so dirty?" he panted. "Is that Jaden's doing?"

"I don't know where that came from." I grinned suddenly. "D'you wanna hit me back?" It was an offer from our childhood, used when we didn't want grownups involved in our squabbles.

"Do I ever," he muttered. He got up and hauled me to my feet by my good hand. His dark blue eyes found mine, which were suddenly wet.

"Aw, c'mon Sis, you know I wouldn't," he grumbled, pretending to misunderstand.

"It's just... I don't even know why we're fighting. I missed you so much, Moo." I hiccupped.

He sighed and went over to the couch. We sat looking in opposite directions, more uncomfortable with each other than we'd ever been.

When he finally spoke his voice was quiet. "You know why I had to go. I don't regret it; it might be as much of the world as I'll ever see. You're going to travel, whether with Jaden or because you're jumping the big sticks. And one day you'll be at the Olympics, and I'll be sitting in this same living room, on this same couch, watching you."

I gave a strangled whimper and fell against his dear, comforting body, at once so familiar yet also somehow new. He hugged me back, silent, until I pulled away.

"You really believe in me," I whispered.

"'Course I do. I got the looks, you got the ambition." He grinned.

Seth helped me make coffee and told me about his travels while I ate cereal carefully with my left hand. Despite my sore throat and wrist, I felt better now that I'd seen my brother, and I kept my eyes on him as I chewed.

I'd already missed my morning class and rushed off to school as soon as I'd eaten. I was four days behind and spent my break at the bookstore buying textbooks. I put them on the credit card Dec had given me, where they would join charges for my fiberglass cast and, I was afraid, a few drinks at the bar.

I did my best to settle back into a routine, but it was hard when I couldn't ride, or write very well. Hades got back two days after I did and I arranged for Karen to ride him while I convalesced. I recorded my lectures, and Chuck and Shannon were in some of my classes and made copies of their notes for me. I tried to keep busy because my phone conversations with Jaden held an undercurrent of strain, and I was at a complete loss as to how to relieve it. Or maybe I knew, and simply wouldn't acknowledge the option.

At least Seth's return made me feel as though life was normal again. He resumed teaching lessons, which took some of the pressure off Dec and made life at home more pleasant. Gran, like me, was happy simply to have him back.

By Saturday I was looking forward to spending a day in the barn, and I strolled in to hear whistling. When we had first moved to the farm Dec used to whistle all the time, these complicated tunes that Seth and I used to try to twist our tongues around but could never manage to duplicate. Since my mother's death, I'd hardly heard a note escape his lips. I was surprised at how nostalgic it made me to hear those tunes floating down the aisles again. I wasn't the only one glad to have Seth back.

My first lesson turned out to be a small child riding for the first time.

"You're supposed to take all the beginners, Seth," I complained.

He gave me a half-shrug and lazy smile. "Would you rather fix the tractor?"

"Oh, fine," I grumbled, brushing past him in a huff. Seth was mechanically inclined, which came in very useful with the farm machinery. I, on the other hand, was useless in those situations.

My student was a tiny thing with candy-floss white hair. I put Chocolate Chip on the crossties and started showing her how to groom.

"Is Chip a daddy pony?" she asked.

"No, he's a gelding. He's a boy, but he can't be a daddy," I responded absently, adjusting the curry comb to fit her small hand.

"Why can't he be a daddy?"

"Um, well, because he can't have babies," I floundered. I wasn't about to get into the details of gelding — castration in horses — with a six-year-old.

"Well, 'course not," she scoffed. "Only mommies can have a baby in their tummy. Everyone knows *that*." She was regarding me with suspicion, as though doubtful that anyone not aware of this basic fact of biology could possibly teach her anything.

"You're right!" I agreed quickly. "If you want, after your lesson I can show you a baby horse, okay?"

"Oooh, yes," she squealed. I let out a relieved breath that my ruse had worked. I headed for the tackroom and found Seth doubled over. At the sight of me, the guffaws broke free.

"When it comes time for the birds and bees talk with your kids, better let Jaden handle it," he snorted between laughs. I shoved him, but I was frowning as I got Chip's tack. When I was finished teaching I found Seth dumping bags of grain into the feed bin.

"What you said earlier... why do you assume I'll have kids?" I asked.

He folded the empty feedbag as he answered. "I don't know. I know you've never been keen on the idea, but I thought, since you were with Jaden — well, he wants kids, doesn't he?"

I nodded slowly.

"And you still don't," he guessed. "Well, aren't you in a pickle." His words were light, but his face showed his concern.

"He told me that if we never have kids he'd still be happy, as long as he has me. But I can tell he's hoping I'll change my mind, and what if I don't? What if fifteen years from now I still don't want children?" I asked miserably.

"What makes you think you won't?"

"It doesn't interest me, and how unfair would it be to bring a child into the world when they're at the bottom of your priority list? I'm not sure I'd be a good mother even if I wanted a child more than anything. As it is... well, until I have the same passion for raising kids as I do for riding, I don't think it would be fair to do it. I mean, think of mom."

My mother was born in Sweden fifteen years after her only sister. She was more than an unplanned pregnancy; she always felt like an unwelcome intrusion into the orderly lives of parents who were already middle-aged. Her father died when she was ten, and when her mother suggested that Elina go live with an aunt in Canada, she was happy to go — she was adventurous by nature anyway, and she was old enough by then to realize she might find greater acceptance elsewhere. It turned out to be a good move, her childless aunt doted on her and they grew very close. Although our great-aunt passed away when Seth and I were only four, she was the closest thing we'd had to a grandmother until we met Gran.

I'd seen firsthand the kinds of scars that being an unwanted child had left on my mother. In fact, I'd often felt that she'd had Seth and me largely because she was desperate for a family, even though she'd been too young and ill-equipped to raise us.

"I think you'd do just fine as a mom," Seth said, "but why are you even thinking about it if it's not something you want?"

"Because Jaden wants it," I whispered. "He'd be a great dad, and if I deprive him of something so monumental I'm afraid he'll grow to resent it."

I planned to bring the subject up the next day but discarded the idea when Jaden arrived distracted and moody.

"What's wrong?" I croaked. My voice hadn't improved.

He frowned at me. "You should be in bed, not in the barn."

I shrugged. "Can't. Teaching."

"No you're not," he said. He wrapped an arm around my shoulders and set off through the barn until he found Dec.

"Téa's too sick to be teaching," he said heatedly. "Can't someone else take over?"

"I'll call Gran," Dec said. He gave me an exasperated look. "Haven't you been to the doctor yet? You said you'd go this week."

"I'll go tomorrow," I promised.

"And now you're going to rest." Jaden steered me toward the house. I wanted to protest, but in truth, it felt good to have his arm around me and feel nothing but concern emanating from him.

"I'll make you some tea and you can spend the day in bed or on the couch," he said as he sat me down in the kitchen.

"I hate being sick," I grumbled. "I don't like being fussed over."

To my surprise, he grinned. He turned the kettle on before sitting and taking my uncasted hand.

"What happened when you got sick when you were little?"

I shrugged. "The after-school care people got ticked off." His wince made me sigh. "Jaden, my mom was trying to support two kids while working retail. We were taken care of by the daycare when we were small, and after-school care later on, but that was expensive so by the time my mom and Dec got married we were already latch-key kids. There wasn't ever anyone waiting for us with cookies — that's not my life." I hesitated. "That's why moving here was so great. For the first time, we got to come *home* after school, like other kids did."

I changed into sweats while Jaden made the tea, and he spent the afternoon on the couch with me, watching TV. The frown he'd arrived with disappeared, and I felt his tension gradually leak away as I snuggled against him.

"Why were you upset earlier?" I asked tentatively, not wanting to disrupt our peace.

He stroked my arm absently. My head was against his shoulder so I couldn't see his expression, but I felt his chest rise with the deep breath he took.

"My mother wants me to go to Argentina," he began.

"What? Why?" I pulled away and sat upright, staring into his face. This was far from what I'd been expecting.

He grimaced. "My uncle Emiliano broke his leg. He's the one who breeds polo ponies, remember? The one I got Kermit from. His family is having a hard time managing the ranch without him. I've tried to explain to my mom that I can't go, but you know how she is about family. She feels I have an obligation."

"You can't go because of work?" I asked carefully.

His eyes went swiftly to mine. "Of course I don't want to leave you either, but I need ten months of articling in order to be called to the bar next June. And in any case, there's no way my firm would give me that much time off."

We went back to watching TV, but my mind wasn't on the screen.

Jaden went into law because he wanted to make the world a more equitable place. It was a noble ideal and not one that I could argue with on any level. But I couldn't help but feel that he'd been a far happier person when he played polo for a living. I was beginning to think he could do more good in the world as a happy, fulfilled polo player than as a discontented, frustrated lawyer.

"Don't you miss polo?" I blurted.

"Yes," he admitted.

"I already miss riding like crazy, and it's only been a week."

"You made an incredible leap forward this year. You can afford to take the time to heal."

"I suppose," I acknowledged grudgingly. "Although Spruce didn't go quite as I'd hoped."

Jaden turned off the TV and studied me. "I thought you'd be thrilled with how well you did at Spruce Meadows."

"It's not that I'm unhappy, but I can't help feeling that I could have done better. I feel as though..." I hesitated, tasting the flavor of my emotions and trying to identify the elusive, niggling sensation that had been keeping me up nights. "I feel as though I choked, almost. As if I could've done even better but I was blocked somehow." I raised my eyes to find him watching me thoughtfully. "Does that make any sense?"

He nodded slowly. "I know polo players who have gone through the same thing. Sometimes you hit a ceiling in your performance and you need help to break through. A good sports psychologist can do that."

I rolled my eyes and was about to object, but Jaden covered my mouth with his hand, grinning.

"Be quiet and listen for a minute. I'm not suggesting therapy."

I raised my eyebrows since that was the only response I could give. His golden-brown eyes were laughing, and I felt myself go soft all of a sudden. This was the old Jaden, *my* Jaden, the warm, kind, good-humored man I loved. I was glad I'd decided to confide in him; I missed this sense of closeness. My warm feelings must have shown because he leaned in and kissed my forehead. He kept his hand over my mouth, though.

"There are psychologists who specialize in this, who work with athletes."

I pulled his hand away. "Have you ever gone to one?"

"Nope. Never needed to." His cocky grin made me laugh. I couldn't remember the last time I'd seen it, and I supposed nothing about his current job made him feel that way.

"I love you, Jaden," I said.

He pulled me tight against him. "I love you too," he murmured into my hair. But it was followed by a sigh, and I felt my insides clench.

I went to the clinic at school the next day and ended up on antibiotics because it seemed I had a throat infection. I was still feeling lousy the day after that, and Seth stopped me in the main aisle of the barn as I was going to teach after school.

"You'd better let me take your group," he said, sliding an arm around me.

I was peripherally aware of someone approaching but paid no attention until an overly saccharine voice said, "Why, Seth! What are you doing here?" Brittney's expression turned sour as her gaze moved to me. "I thought you had a boyfriend."

I snickered hoarsely. "Seth's my brother."

For a moment she looked genuinely shocked. Then she recovered herself and gave a harsh laugh. "Yeah, right. You look nothing alike."

I shrugged. "Maybe not, but he's still my brother. My twin, in fact."

Her wide eyes went to Seth's face.

"What are you doing here, Brittney?" he demanded. He was obviously far less happy with their reunion than she was.

"I board my horses here. Didn't you know?"

Seth steered me abruptly toward the arena's viewing lounge and hustled me inside.

"Do you know who that is?" he asked. I obviously didn't, and he went on. "That's the girl who posted those pictures, the ones that broke me and Julia up!"

I gasped. "But... it can't be." I tried to recall the girl from the pictures, but all I could remember was that she had long, straight blond hair — I remembered how it had blended in with Seth's own pale locks. The Brittney in the barn had short, curly red hair, but of course, hair could be easily changed.

Seth started pacing. "Julia's gonna freak. She hasn't been here since I got back, and this is not the way I pictured seeing her again."

"She has a new boyfriend," I reminded him. "Maybe she won't care. And anyway, if she hasn't guessed, do you have to tell her?" It would only hurt her to know.

He gave me a bleak look. "Have you gotten to know Brittney at all?"

I had a sinking feeling. Brittney wasn't exactly the soul of discretion.

The very next afternoon Julia appeared with the inevitable Al in tow. I had texted her to let her know that Seth was back; I hadn't wanted it to be a shock since they both had unresolved feelings about each other. When Seth came in, leading a pony and herding a child in front of him, Julia swept past regally with her head held high and barely acknowledged him. He gave me a confused look, and I returned a small shrug. Al was leaning against the wall, texting and looking bored.

When Julia started grooming Jasmine Al looked up. "I'm going to wait in the car," he said. "You won't be long, will you?"

"Of course not, sweetie. I'll just ride her a little bit," Julia reassured him quickly.

I frowned at her. "Why do you bring him to the barn when he's always rushing you?"

She flipped her long hair over her shoulder. "He likes to come. He worries about me otherwise."

I regarded her in puzzlement. "Jules, I've hardly seen you without him in months. And you've only seen Ter twice since the accident. We'd like to hang out with *you* once in a while."

She turned to me, her face flushed with surprising anger. "He *loves* me. He bought me this diamond bracelet." She held up her arm; stones winked on her wrist. "And he's taking me to Venice soon. I'm finally doing the kinds of romantic things your brother would never think of."

"That's all you want? Someone who can buy you stuff?" Seth's voice was quiet as he stepped around the corner.

"You wouldn't understand," Julia spat at him, "Al is a man, not a boy."

"I'm man enough not to have to buy my women," Seth retorted.

Julia threw the brush at him; it sailed over his shoulder and hit Brittney square in the chest.

"Hey!" She scowled at Julia. Her expression became calculating as her eyes moved from my friend's flushed face to Seth, standing with his fists clenched and his eyes still locked on Julia.

"Well, well." To my shock, Brittney picked up the brush and strutted over to Julia to give it back. "You must be the girlfriend."

"*Ex*-girlfriend," Julia hissed.

Brittney waved a hand carelessly. "That's quite a large club, isn't it? I'm a member myself." Seth blinked in shock and turned to Brittney in time with Julia's exclamation.

"No she isn't-" Seth began.

Julia turned on him savagely. "You lied to me!"

"We dated last fall," Brittney interjected. Things went downhill from there; Seth angrily denounced Brittney, Julia yelled at Seth, and

Brittney raised her voice for no reason that I could see. I went to stand with my brother just as a loud voice cut across the noise.

"Enough!" Dec strode into the sudden silence, his face already reddening with anger. "What's going on here?"

Julia thinned her lips but didn't say anything. I shared a quick look with Seth, enough to tell me I should speak, but Brittney piped up before I could.

"I don't know what happened," she said in a quavering voice. "I was only trying to talk to Julia and your son started *screaming* at me." Her eyes welled with tears.

I rolled my eyes, but Dec was glowering at us. "You two, in the house."

Seth and I had just gotten drinks in the kitchen when Dec stomped in. He stood with his hands on his hips, framed by the doorway.

"You didn't buy that whole act, did you?" Seth asked tiredly. He leaned back against the counter.

"No, but that's irrelevant. Your romantic entanglements are creating problems in the barn, son, and you'd better fix them."

Thirteen

It was a tense week. Dec had refused to accept Seth's solution of ejecting Brittney from the barn, and we were faced with her gloating face almost daily. My workload at school was already heavy, and I found myself truly resenting school for the first time. I was too physically fit to comfortably sit still for long periods, and I plain didn't want to be there — I wanted to be at the next show, I wanted to be riding, I wanted to do what I knew, in the deepest core of my being, I was born to do. Instead, I swallowed back my desires, and they writhed in my belly like a nest of snakes. Not the cuddly, nice kind of snakes, either.

I decided I might as well work on those aspects of my sport that I could, and made an appointment with the sport psychologist Jaden had recommended. Her office was in a house, and on arriving I found myself in a pleasant, plant-filled waiting area. A sign instructed me to wait so I perched on the edge of a chair. It was a comfortable chair, upholstered in cheerful yellow, but I couldn't relax into it.

A woman with shoulder-length chestnut hair came into the room. She held out her hand and I rose nervously to shake it.

"I'm Susan," she said simply. Not 'Dr. Orfield', as I would have expected. She was of average height and looked as though she kept in shape. I followed her into another sunlit room. She gestured me into a blue plaid armchair and sat in a matching one, angled toward me. I clasped my hands together.

"Tell me a little bit about yourself," she invited, smiling. I began hesitantly, not sure what she wanted to know, but as Susan nodded encouragement and asked the occasional question I loosened up. By the session's end, I found myself talking about my riding with enthusiasm.

Teri came to visit the next day, but it was apparent from her careful movements that she was still a long way from healed. All in all, when Seth asked me to go out with him that weekend I was very tempted to accept, but sadly I knew I couldn't.

"But Kabir's flying up for the weekend and I haven't seen him in eight months. Kyle's coming too. Come on, it'll be fun."

"I'm sure it will, but I promised Jaden no more parties for a while."

He shrugged. "So don't tell him."

"That won't work," I tried to explain. "He'd know, he always knows when I'm hiding something. And he hates it." It was probably the thing he hated most, in fact.

"I think our dear cousin's got some control issues, Sis. And what about me?"

"What about you?"

"We haven't been out together in ages. I need to get out and kill some stress, and I'd like my sister to be with me. Think of it as celebrating my triumphant return." He gave me his best boyish smile. I sighed. I couldn't refuse Seth, not when I knew he needed me.

I wondered how best to break the news to Jaden, and when he phoned to say he was working late on Saturday I took the coward's way out. I lied.

"Don't worry about it, I'll go to Teri's. Maybe I can see you Sunday?"

The regret in his voice was sincere. "I promise to reserve next weekend entirely for you."

I spent Saturday teaching and doing homework, which took a long time to do with a cast. Seth and Kabir had gone out for dinner with Kyle, and around ten o'clock I drove my own car into the city to meet them.

The party was barely outside the downtown core, in an industrial-looking building. The guys were waiting for me on the sidewalk, Kyle rocking his hipster look, Kabir his new California punk, and Seth his usual messy surfer-boy self. After exchanging hugs we plunged into the dark, loud space. The music was thumping, the people had that edgy city style, and I found myself having a good time dancing with my brother and my old friends.

I remembered my promise to Jaden, though, and only had a few drinks. As a result, I got tired long before the boys did, but when I suggested leaving they raised a chorus of protests and convinced me to stay. Kabir grabbed me and pulled me into a dance, Seth got me a drink, and I kept going until my feet were sore. What felt like hours later I went to sit on a ratty old couch in a corner to rest, and I was thinking that it was time to head home when Seth came to find me.

He flopped down next to me. "Hey, we got invited to an after-party!" He was flushed, his eyes glassy in his sweaty face. I hesitated. I didn't want to mar Seth's night, not when he was so obviously enjoying himself, but I didn't have it in me to go to another party. I just wanted to go home and sleep.

"You know what, bro, I'm pretty tired, but you go ahead. The guys are going with you, right?"

He focused fuzzily on me. "Are you okay?"

"Sure. Just tired. I don't want to be a buzzkill but I'm not up for more partying."

Kyle staggered over and blinked down owlishly at us. "Seth, we gotta go, the cab's waiting for us."

"You sure you're okay?" Seth asked me. "Can you drive?"

"Yup, I'm good. Go ahead, Seth. Have a good time."

He hugged me quickly and got up to follow Kyle outside. I found my black hoodie in the corner of the couch and pulled it on, slipping my thumbs through the holes in the sleeves so that my hands were covered. I shuffled through the exit; the sky arced above me in the gradated grays of pre-dawn, blending smoothly into the charcoal tones of the city below it. I wondered what time it was. I was wearing a short skirt, and the wind slipped like cold fish around my bare legs. I pulled my hood over my head and walked the block to my car as briskly as I could. I fished the car keys out of my little shoulder bag as I rounded the corner, then stopped in confusion. I looked down the street, then turned and checked behind me. No car. I craned my neck to read the street sign above me. Yes, this was definitely where I'd parked — I was entirely sober, and I clearly remembered this spot. I looked around again and saw the graffiti-covered mailbox I'd parked next to. I felt a flutter of panic, which rippled out in ever-increasing waves from my core as I noticed the short orange sign on the sidewalk. A towing company. One of those temporary signs that they toss down when parking is disallowed in a place where it's usually fine. I stood dumbly for a minute before heading back toward the party, my heart thumping. My cell phone and wallet were both in my purse, which was in my car. Seth hadn't brought his cell either; we hadn't wanted to lose them. There was no one at the door anymore. The bouncer must have joined the festivities. I stepped into the welcome warmth and leaned against the wall in the semi-dark entrance to try to think. I was too tired for problem-solving; my thoughts felt muddy and slow. I didn't know anyone here. I had no phone, only five dollars cash, and no way to get home. It occurred to me that I should have gotten the towing company information — maybe I could retrieve my car since my bank card was in my purse. I hurried back, ignoring the three homeless men sleeping on grates along the way. A car slowed down next to me, the window rolling down.

"Hey, do you need a ride?" A middle-aged man with greasy long hair leaned out the window.

"No thanks," I said tightly. I shoved my hands into my pockets and walked faster.

I spent a minute with the orange sign, committing the number to memory, before rushing back to the relative safety and warmth of the party. I wandered around the dark room, looking for a familiar face in the thinning crowd.

I spotted a girl that Seth had befriended earlier. "Do you have a phone I could borrow? My car got towed." I could have cried with relief when she produced a cell phone, and I dialed the number I'd been repeating like a mantra since leaving the cursed orange sign. My relief all leaked out my feet, though, when an indifferent electronic voice informed me that office hours were weekdays from eight to six. I checked the phone; it was five-twenty a.m. on Sunday morning. I hedged and agonized, but there was no way around it. I'd have to call Jaden. I went to the somewhat quieter entrance hall and pushed the numbers with trembling fingers.

I almost wished he wouldn't answer, but on the third ring I heard a click, then his sleepy voice was in my ear, intimate, familiar, and making my heart pound.

"Hey, it's me." I tried hard to sound normal.

"Téa... is everything all right?" He sounded immediately more alert.

I didn't bother with too many details. I just asked him to pick me up and gave him the name of the nearest street corner, since I didn't know the exact address.

He didn't hesitate. "I'll be there as soon as I can. Are you okay? Are you safe?" He was worried, but I knew that worry would convert to rage in a flash when the situation became clear to him.

"Yes," I whispered.

After returning the phone I went and paced the cold street corner. I divided my time between heartily wishing I'd never gone to the party, berating myself for not noticing the no-parking sign, and trying to control my sick, cold dread of Jaden's reaction. This was the last thing our relationship needed right now.

"Hey, beautiful, why don't you come join me?"

I glanced up to see a man in his twenties staring at me from across the street. I shook my head quickly.

"Come on, don't worry — that's my truck right over there," he persuaded, hitching his thumb at a pickup. "I'll take you anywhere you want to go." He started crossing the street towards me. He looked normal enough, but something felt off and I turned and hurried back toward the party, my shoulders hunched. I heard footsteps behind me and broke into a trot just as a car screeched to a halt next to me. I was about to bolt when I realized it was Jaden's; he must have broken speed records to get there that fast. I halted as he ran around the hood of his car. I followed his gaze down the street but the other man had vanished. Jaden stared down at me. I thought he was about to grab me and wished he would; I desperately wanted the comfort of his touch, although I knew I didn't deserve it.

"Get in the car." He was breathing hard.

When I didn't move he took my arm and pulled, yanking the door open with his other hand.

"Wait," I pleaded. I met his gaze, burning like a brushfire. "I... I know you're really mad right now," I said haltingly, "but could you just hold me for a minute?" My eyes drifted downward. They hadn't gotten far when I felt his arms enfold me. He pressed me hard against his body, hard enough to almost still the tremors running through me.

"I'm going to kill you," he muttered into my hair.

I nodded mutely against his chest. He squeezed me tighter, until my bones creaked, but I didn't make a sound.

He drove too fast, and without saying a word. I couldn't help thinking about the other time I'd gone out like this. Jaden had driven me home then too, after carrying me bodily from the party. There had been a lot more yelling on that drive, but his face bore the same resemblance to livid granite. I hadn't known him as well back then, and there was an instant when I'd actually wondered if he would get violent. And although I knew now that he wouldn't hurt me I was more afraid this time, because this time, I had so much more to lose.

The minute we stepped inside the loft he wheeled to face me with his arms crossed over his chest.

"Start talking."

"Please, Jaden, don't do this," I whispered. "Don't turn this into a fight."

"Pardon me?" he said. He edged closer, and I saw that dangerous muscle jumping in his jaw. "I can't imagine what you would have to fight about, Téa — you're in the wrong and you know it. You were caught red-handed, engaging in something you know full well you shouldn't have been doing."

I felt the familiar *whoosh* inside me as my temper broke free of its tenuous restraints. My voice shook with the effort not to yell. "I'm a grown woman, Jaden, and I make my own decisions. Yes, I knew you wouldn't like it-"

"Not to mention that you promised-" he broke in.

"But it was my risk to take-"

"Risking your life does not only affect you!" he thundered.

I froze, watching him struggle to control himself. My feelings of guilt only made me more defensive, but I tried to explain the night's events calmly. Which almost worked, until I got to the part about Seth leaving.

"Just wait 'til I get my hands on him," Jaden snarled. "I can't believe he left you alone! What was he thinking?"

"I told him to go, don't go dragging him into this!"

"How can I not? He's the reason you took this insane chance!"

"He's my *brother*, Jaden," I snapped, "and he had a hard week."

"And you thought going out and getting drunk was the answer?" he asked, scathing.

"I was showing him some support without judging his choices. You might want to try that sometime." My retort snapped like a dry branch.

He glared at me through slitted eyes. "Maybe there's a reason you got smacked around so much, Téa," he spat. "Maybe you need to learn the hard way."

I recoiled. We'd had fights before, but neither of us had ever resorted to this — to saying something downright mean to the other. I could see regret already coloring his face, but I didn't want to be the pathetic, wounded one. I turned and stalked to the bedroom. I was almost surprised that he didn't stop me, but he didn't make a move. I fell onto the bed and hid my face in my hands; now that I was alone my tears flowed fast and hot. I kept quiet, though. I didn't want him to know how much he'd hurt me. For the first time ever I wanted to leave Jaden's house, but even if I could get there, showing up at home at this hour and obviously distressed was bound to raise questions, and I wasn't prepared to answer any.

I wondered suddenly whether Jaden was also wishing I wasn't here. Doubt settled onto my chest like an elephant. I considered going and talking to him, but he'd been so angry... I couldn't bear to be wounded again so soon if he hadn't calmed down yet. I changed for bed, stifling the occasional sob, and crawled under the covers. I was lying awake, shivering, when he let himself quietly into the room. I stayed curled in a tight ball and pretended to sleep as he got in beside me. He didn't say anything, didn't turn my way. I might as well not have been there, for all the notice he took of me. I felt a jagged blade dragging through my heart; I almost convulsed from the pain and fell asleep with silent tears coursing down my face.

When I awoke his arm was around me, his body warm against mine, spooning me. I froze; he must have still been sleeping. I was afraid to wake him, afraid to feel him pull away again.

"Are you awake?" he whispered.

I slipped my hand into his before nodding. He kissed my hair, and I turned, burying my face in his neck and pulling myself against his body.

He held me tightly, the fact that he didn't murmur words of comfort a clear indication of how upset he still was, too.

"Jaden, please, next time... don't do that. Anything but that," I said when I could speak. My face was still hidden against him.

"Do you think I said those things on purpose, Téa? That I meant to hurt you so badly?" Regret roughened his voice. "I'd do anything to take those words back."

"It's not so much what you said," I whispered. "It's that you ignored me for so long afterward. I was afraid you didn't want me here."

He pushed me away from his body and took my face between his hands.

"I always want you here, *querida*. Even when I'm angry, even when I can't quite bring myself to speak yet, I still want you near. Don't ever doubt that." His eyes bored into mine, glowing with passionate sincerity. I gave a tiny nod and he released me.

It was almost midday; we hadn't slept for long but I had to get back to the barn. Fortunately, I kept a few clothes at Jaden's, and I pulled them on silently, brooding. Even though we'd made up somewhat, I still felt an empty, cold space between us. We barely spoke during the drive.

"I'll come in and help you answer questions," Jaden said quietly as he pulled up in front of the shed. We walked to the house without touching.

Dec's eyebrows shot up at the sight of Jaden coming in with me, then drew together quickly as he turned to face me. "I thought you were going out with friends yesterday?"

"I did," I answered quickly, wondering what explanation Seth had offered for my absence, "but I had car trouble this morning, so I called Jaden." That was the cover story Jaden had planned.

"I'm having my mechanic look at it," Jaden assured Dec.

Dec looked doubtful.

"I was out with my own friends last night," Jaden assured him with a rakish grin, "until far too late. I could use some coffee."

Dec shook his head, but I could see the beginnings of the indulgent smile he seemed to reserve only for Jaden. They headed into the kitchen and I heaved a relieved breath as I climbed the stairs to change. The sounds of arguing made me hurry back down when I was done, a loud bang nearly making me trip on the final step. I raced into the kitchen to see Jaden scowling at Seth, the muscles in his arms standing out in sharp relief. My heart jumped into my throat.

"Jaden!" I yelped.

He didn't answer, but turned his face slightly away from me, releasing Seth from his fierce glare. Seth came over and gave me a semi-nervous grin.

"Don't worry, Sis. Loverboy here was just expressing his concern for your welfare. Very tenderly, of course."

I glanced over at Jaden. He was standing in profile to me, his head hanging and hands fisted at his sides.

"What was that bang?"

"Jaden slipped and had to catch himself on the table," Seth said blandly.

The corner of Jaden's mouth twitched up, and he looked around slowly to lock eyes with Seth. A look of understanding passed between them as he loped over to us.

"I'm glad you're both safe," he said softly. "But you were lucky. Both of you." He turned his stare on me; I dropped my gaze quickly before walking him to the door.

"See you later," he said simply. He didn't touch me, didn't even meet my eyes before he drove away. That alone hurt more than anything Dec could have inflicted.

I taught a lesson that afternoon. I'm sure I sounded like the zombie instructor from hell, and my students shot me weird looks, but I didn't care. Dec refused to let me skip dinner so I endured the torture of trying to act normal. The instant it was over I hid in my bedroom. I sat, dropped my head into my hands, and pondered my idiocy. I'd gone out and done something that I knew Jaden would hate, with the people that would bother him the most: my ex-boyfriend and the guy who'd had a crush on me for six years. What was wrong with me? I loved Jaden, loved him with every fiber of my being. Why hadn't I realized what this would do to him?

Maybe Jaden was wondering the same thing because, other than a quick text to let me know he'd gotten my car and was having it delivered, I didn't hear from him all week. I only texted him twice and apologized both times, but my panic grew with each passing day. What if I'd pushed him past his breaking point? Being with me was no picnic — our family blamed him, his mother disapproved, and I constantly worried him. What if he'd decided I wasn't worth it? While it would be utter hypocrisy to blame him if he had, the mere thought was enough to freeze the breath in my lungs. By Friday I couldn't take it anymore. He didn't answer my call, but I had my car back. I drove to his place.

He was home, though I'd been prepared to wait. He let me in and stood with his arms crossed in the hallway. He said nothing while the tears pooled silently in my eyes.

"Jaden, please... forgive me," I managed finally.

He stared hard into my eyes. "You want to be forgiven? Then tell me the truth. All of it."

"I-I told you already," I stammered. "Seth begged me to go. And I know I sort of lied to you, but..." my voice got quiet. I didn't realize that I had turned away until Jaden put his hand to my face and pulled it around again. I dragged my eyes back up to his.

"Why didn't you tell me you were going?" His voice was a knife edge, and I felt it slice inside me.

"I didn't want to fight," I whispered.

"Yes, thank God we dodged that bullet," he said acidly. "Who was with you?"

"I told you, Seth, Kabir, and Kyle." I had to strain to maintain eye contact as I said their names; I could see Jaden flinch inside.

"No one else?"

My eyes widened as I clued in. "Is that what this is really about, Jaden? I thought you said you trusted me." Anger was sparking dangerously in my belly.

"This is about you acting like a child, Téa. Adults talk things out, they don't sneak around doing stupid things, hoping not to get caught."

"Fine," I spat, "the next time I plan to do something stupid I'll let you know in advance."

For several endless seconds, nothing moved. And then Jaden turned and put his fist through the wall.

I jumped, my pulse drumrolling in my ears. I stayed very still as he jerked his hand free and disappeared into the bathroom without looking at me. I coached myself through a few steadying breaths before going to stand in the doorway. He was running water over a split knuckle, the blood swirling down the drain in slick scarlet ribbons. I got a towel from the linen closet behind me, dark blue so the stains wouldn't show, and offered it to him without finding his face. He took it with his cut hand, and with the other reached for me but stopped halfway.

"Téa... you know I'd rather die than hurt you, right?" His voice was ragged.

"Do you think it hurts any less because the blow wasn't aimed at me?" I murmured. "That watching you hurt yourself is somehow less painful?"

The smallest of sounds escaped him, and I flung my arms around him, cursing myself for telling the truth. "I'm sorry," I whispered against his shirt. "I didn't mean it."

"Yes, you did." He said bleakly. I trembled from the effort as I dragged my eyes unwillingly to his face.

I saw it then. Under the anger in his eyes lay the hurt, like a raw wound inside him. I felt it spear right through my gut, leaving me breathless. I hadn't trusted him. I had excluded him. I had lied to him. And I had hurt him. Tears flowed hot down my face, but they couldn't wash away the stain of deceit on my soul.

"It was a mistake." I could barely whisper the words. Tentatively, I kissed his neck, his jaw, his cheek... I hesitated, wondering whether he'd pull away if I touched his lips, and afraid I would die if he did. But his hand went to the back of my head, his mouth came down forcefully on mine, and we dropped ungracefully down to the floor, only managing to get halfway undressed before melding our bodies together. The wooden planks were hard, and before long Jaden rolled us over, pulling me on top of him. I knew he was using his body to cushion me against the floor's hardness, and this small act of kindness, of protection, was at once so typical and so unexpected, given his anger, that it almost caused my tears to fall again. I focused on making love to him instead, desperate to demonstrate with my body what I couldn't adequately express with words.

We rested for a while afterward. When I tried to shift off him — not wanting to press him against the floor — his arms tightened around me, holding me in place. I raised my head to look into his eyes. We didn't speak, but got up and moved to the bed.

I perched on the edge and stared at the wood floor. When I glanced up Jaden's eyes were on me. He looked devastated but made no move to touch me. In fact, he didn't move at all, as though he was afraid of spooking me. I turned slowly and put my palm to his cheek. He closed his eyes tightly.

"I feel like a brute," he whispered hoarsely.

"No." My hands moved to his, and I gripped them tightly. "Jaden, all you've ever done is protect me."

He opened his eyes then. "I spent so many years swearing I would be nothing like my father. But I saw it in your eyes, Téa. You were afraid of me. I'm no better than he is."

"That's ridiculous," I said sharply. "Sure, I jumped — I was surprised. And I was surprised precisely because it's so *unlike* you, my love." I hesitated, watching doubt flicker in his eyes. "I don't know what's happened with us," I said honestly. "I know you're unhappy, and probably a lot of that is my fault." I hung my head. "You can't blame yourself for snapping when I keep pushing you past your limit."

"I don't have a limit when it comes to you, Téa," he said fiercely. "The very fact that we're together is proof of that." He took my face in his hands and made me look at him. "My dissatisfaction is not with you. If you still want to be with me, we'll make this work. We'll do whatever it takes." His eyes burned into mine, scorching me with their resolve.

I placed my hand over his. I swallowed. And then I said the words that I could barely stand to think.

"I think you should go to Argentina." My voice cracked on the word 'go'.

His eyes widened, and slowly he straightened, dropping his hands from my face. I felt suddenly cold.

"Is this... do you feel we need time apart?" He looked away from me as he said it, as though afraid of what he'd see.

"No, that's not why," I stammered, trying clumsily to explain. "You're not happy right now, with me, with our relationship, with your new career." The way he winced at the word "career" confirmed my suspicion. I went on quietly. "I think it would be good for you to get away from everything and do something you love for a while."

He ran his fingers slowly through his hair. "I'll probably lose my job."

"Do you care?"

He seemed to consider it seriously for a moment. "Not as much as I should."

"It'll make your mother happy."

When he looked at me this time his eyes were haunted. "I don't know if I can do it. I don't know if I can leave you."

Hearing the words 'leave you' coming out of his mouth nearly made me gasp, but the tears pricking the backs of my eyelids were from relief that he felt that way.

"The only way I can stand it is knowing it will help you."

I trudged through the following day in a funk. Not riding always made me irritable, and I vacillated wildly between confidence that I'd done the right thing and a dark dread of losing Jaden.

He arrived after dinner that evening and announced his plans to Dec. He spent Sunday morning helping me, and in the afternoon he went to the polo club to visit his horses and friends. He strode back into the barn as we were feeding that evening.

"Seth! Why are you letting your sister carry hay bales? Come on man, be a gentleman," he admonished.

"Since when do I have to be a gentleman with my own sister?" Seth grumbled. "She's always managed those bales just fine, you know."

"Well, she shouldn't have to," Jaden retorted. His tone could have cut glass. "She's only got one good arm, she's going to hurt herself."

Seth had just finished telling me the same thing, but instead of saying so he dropped his bale and sauntered slowly over to face Jaden, frowning.

"You know, if Téa's got a problem with what I'm doing, you can bet that she'll let me know," he said slowly.

I felt Jaden tense beside me. A glimpse of his face showed his jaw muscle bunching; I felt suddenly breathless with something akin to fear.

"Jaden, don't," I pleaded. I put my hand on his chest and his eyes slanted down at me. His expression had barely begun to ease when Seth reached out and plucked me away; my brother tucked me into his side and wrapped an arm around me.

"Seriously, Sis? You're actually worried?" His eyes twinkled — of course, Seth would have plainly recognized the fear on my face.

I hesitated.

"I just want to remind this joker that I've been looking out for you since long before he arrived on the scene." He gave Jaden a challenging look.

My eyes moved to Jaden, who gave me a reassuring nod. I was starting to feel annoyed with both of them. I pulled away from Seth and crossed my arms, scowling.

"Okay, let's get something straight. You two are my absolute favorite people in the known universe. So you are not allowed to argue. Ever."

Seth snorted. "Since when do I take orders from you, half-pint?"

"Since always," I said in surprise.

"Yeah, but only because it's not worth arguing with you," Seth muttered. He picked up the haybale as he and Jaden shared a grin. I allowed myself to breathe again now that they were back to their usual easygoing camaraderie.

When we were done feeding I pulled Jaden up to the loft. "You can't fight with Seth, Jaden, you just can't."

His arms closed around me. "No one's fighting, *mi amor*. I'm worried about what will happen when I'm gone, I don't want you doing so much heavy work. You have a large presence, Téa; it tends to make people forget how small you actually are."

Time accelerated impossibly fast, and in what seemed like seconds Friday arrived, and with it Jaden, to say goodbye.

He hugged Gran and Seth before turning to shake Dec's hand. "Don't let Téa ride until the cast comes off," he exhorted.

273

Dec clapped him on the shoulder, his other hand still holding Jaden's. "Don't worry about anything here, son. Have a safe trip."

Jaden's eyes found mine. Without exchanging a word we headed for the shed, and once there we clung to each other silently, cemented by our mutual dismay. Finally, he took my face in his hands and leaned his forehead on mine, and I breathed in his scent, committing it to memory.

"The bond we have can't be affected by distance or time," he murmured. "But promise me you'll take care of yourself."

"Don't worry about me," I said. "You'll come back to find me as impossible as ever." But the part that echoed in my head was *you'll come back.*

I didn't go to the airport. He left in the middle of the night, and in any case, I didn't think either of us could have made it through the parting. I listlessly pulled on a jacket before trudging out to the barn the next morning. The sky was colorless. Fall was early, and yellow and orange leaves fluttered to the ground, every downward spiral drawing me with it. Yet the first day wasn't as bad as I'd imagined — we'd spent days apart before, after all, so I simply shut my mind down and functioned on autopilot. But the next day was worse, and the one after that, nearing unbearable.

Teri was well enough to meet me at a coffee shop that evening, and she did her best to stay off the topic of Jaden.

"Julia came to see me," she said. "Did you know she's thinking of moving Jasmine out?"

I gasped. "What? No! Why would she do that?" Not only was Julia a close friend, but Jasmine had boarded with us for five years, as long as Julia had owned her.

"It's Al's idea, apparently." The distaste in her voice was apparent.

"You don't like him either?"

"No, but I can't put my finger on why. He's pleasant enough."

"I'll tell you why, it's because we don't recognize Julia anymore since she's been with him," I said bitterly.

I called Julia as soon as I got home. "We've been friends for years, and now you're going to move your horse based on the say-so of some guy you met a few months ago? He doesn't even like Jasmine!"

"I don't want to move her either," she said uncertainly, "but Al-"

"Never mind Al! He's not good for you, Jules. There's something off about him." I should probably have kept that judgment to myself because her voice was much cooler as she said goodbye.

I dragged myself through another week. Friday afternoon Seth found me sitting on the house's front steps. The weather had warmed again, and the yellowing leaves seemed out of place in the balmy air.

"Where's Cal?" Seth looked around as though expecting Cal to pop out of a bush.

I gave him a strange look. "In the barn. Why?"

"I don't know. I just kind of expected you to be with him on such a nice day. I remember you hanging with Blaze a lot more."

I bristled. "Well, I'm not thirteen anymore. I have more responsibilities now, I can't be playing with a colt all day."

I got up and hurried into the house. I didn't know whether to cry or scream, but Seth had hit a nerve. It was true, I'd spent every possible minute with Blaze when he was young, but with Cal, I just didn't feel like it. Something about his presence disquieted me. It wasn't one of those comfortable friendships where you can just 'be' together; with Cal it took effort. But I couldn't tell anyone that Cal wasn't perfect. Dec had spent a lot of money on him, money we could ill afford, and now it was up to me to make it work. I'd always been good at training 'babies' — young horses who were learning the ropes — but lately I'd been petrified that my first real failure would be with my own horse.

I woke up the next day determined to make some progress with Cal. Seth had been riding him since I couldn't, and the two of them got along famously. I could barely stand to watch other people ride all weekend, so when the barn quieted on Sunday I took Cal out and started grooming him, struggling a bit with the currycomb in my casted right hand. Stephanie walked in carrying her own grooming tools. I wondered whether she should; she looked as though she could give birth at any moment. Cal immediately thrust his nose out, looking for attention.

"You're not going to ride, are you?" Stephanie asked, casting a suspicious eye on my tack.

"Well, yeah," I admitted. "The wrist doesn't hurt."

"That's because not many nerves run through the scaphoid bone, but it's the bone with the highest risk of necrosis when it's fractured," she informed me.

"And that's bad?" I guessed.

"It means bone death," she said shortly. "Really, Téa, don't you know better than to ride with a cast?"

I huffed my breath out in frustration. I hated that Jaden was right about this. I reluctantly assured Stephanie I wouldn't ride, thinking that at least I trusted her not to say anything to Dec. Cal clearly expected something more than simple grooming though, and on impulse, I decided to free-jump him. I hadn't done it since he was two, when his gangly coltish body had put me in mind of a hopping spider.

I brought him into the empty indoor arena and let him trot around to warm up. Then I set up two fences along one wall, small ones, to give him an idea of what to expect. Standing in the middle of the ring, I urged him into a canter and watched him leap unnecessarily high over the hurdles. I sighed; I wasn't sure whether he was genuinely nervous about touching the jumps or whether this was just more of Cal's singular flair for drama, but either way, it wasn't ideal. He stopped in a corner and looked at me inquisitively.

"Yeah, we're doing it again," I told him. I raised the jumps to about three and a half feet and made sure he could fit two strides in between. He seemed to be waiting for my signal, and as soon as I headed toward him he burst into a gallop and careened toward the verticals.

"Whoa, easy," I coaxed worriedly as he exploded over them. I let him go over once more at a less breakneck pace, then asked him to stop. He pranced sideways, snorting, and watched me with shining eyes. He was already breaking into a sweat and he'd hardly done anything.

"Some jumper you are," I muttered as I raised the fences again.

He started off way too fast again, but as he rounded the corner and saw the increased size he drew back, balancing himself and bouncing lightly over each fence with catlike grace. My jaw dropped. He'd never jumped anything of this size before — the fences were over four feet — but his form had been perfect. In fact, he was jumping much better than I'd ever seen him. I stared at him, now rooting in the arena dirt with his nose.

"Okay, buddy, let's see what you can really do." I raised the rails as high as they could go, filled in some of the empty space with more poles, and made the second jump an oxer. I was pushing him, and I wasn't at all sure that he would jump it, but I wanted to see his reaction. I saw the surprise in his eyes as he came around the corner, but he didn't stop. Instead, he carefully rounded his body over each fence, snapping his legs up tightly, and I could have sworn he was smiling. As he landed a swell of whoops and whistles rolled toward us from the arena door, and I turned to see Seth and Stephanie. Seth went over to Cal and patted him enthusiastically, grinning hugely at me all the while.

"Looks like you two might have to learn to get along."

Cal's latent talent certainly raised my spirits, but they crashed right back down when Alan burst in the door at 6:45 the next morning.

"There's a flood in the barn," he said tersely before turning and dashing back out. Seth ran to the base of the staircase.

"Dec, we need you!" he yelled upstairs. We ran outside.

The barn was a mess. Shavings and manure floated in an inch of water, covering the aisles, and the smell of urine hung heavy in the air. Normally the wood shavings absorbed most of the odor but I supposed the wetness had released it. I sensed the horses' anxiety as I splashed down the aisle, and realized we couldn't even calm them down by feeding them because we couldn't put hay down in the dirty, wet stalls.

A muttered oath signaled Dec's arrival. We turned out as many horses as possible and fed them outside, leaving the unfed horses to stamp wetly and whinny in frustration. Then we gathered every cleaning implement in the barn and got to work. It was hard going; the sodden shavings were heavy and we had to empty every stall out entirely, which was much more work than usual since we normally only removed the manure and wet spots. I worked by holding the shovel's handle in my left hand and balancing the shaft against my cast and after a couple of hours my arms, shoulders, and back were aching. I belatedly remembered I had a test that day but there was no way I was going to school before the mess was cleaned up, especially since Dec was anxious to put it to rights before any boarders arrived.

As stalls were emptied, we put horses in them and fed them. We were about halfway through when a sudden clank and yell made me run out of the stall I was cleaning.

"What is it?" I asked Alan. Dec's towering temper was causing us to avoid him as much as possible.

"The conveyer's broken," Alan said with a sigh. "I think we burned out the motor."

I groaned. The muck we were piling into wheelbarrows was trundled to a conveyer, which dumped it on top of the manure pile. If the conveyer was broken we'd have to rig planks and wheel the heavy loads up manually, which would take forever.

Dec's expression darkened even further at the news, but we talked him into taking a break before we tackled the new plank set-up. A good thing too, because even I was starving — I was surprised Seth was still standing.

We got back to work after a hasty meal and lots of coffee.

"Cheer up, li'l brother, we're halfway done," I said as I pulled on my lone glove. I was already feeling relieved at the prospect of finishing. I should have known better. Dec's bellow echoed through the barn and I ran to the storeroom see what new calamity awaited us.

I trailed slowly after Dec as he marched back into the aisle.

"Seth, did you forget something?" Dec's voice wasn't loud, but his hands-on-hips stance made it clear trouble was brewing.

Seth stepped out of a stall and shot me a look.

"We're out of shavings," I said quietly. "I would've ordered them-"

"It wasn't your responsibility!" Dec burst out. "It was Seth's, and I'd be very interested in hearing why it wasn't done!"

"Take it easy, Dec," Alan urged, dropping a hand on Seth's shoulder. Alan had known our family for a long time, and he'd seen Dec manhandle us more than once.

Dec ignored him. "Come here, boy," he ordered.

I was still reluctant to approach Dec when he was mad, but Seth threw Alan a quick smile and strode up to Dec easily.

He looked him in the eye. "C'mon, Dec. I'm good, but I'm not psychic — I couldn't have predicted we'd have a flood. I was going to order the shavings tomorrow, and if it weren't for the waterworks that would've been fine."

I gaped at my brother as though I'd never seen him before. More than anything, this small exchange showed me the extent of the changes that his trip had wrought. Seth really had found himself.

Dec rubbed the back of his neck before giving a curt nod. He turned to me. "Téa, take my truck and go to the feed store while we finish up here. Buy as many bags of shavings as you can fit into the truck to tide us over."

By the time we were done it was the horses' dinnertime. I was exhausted down to my last muscle fiber and my fondest wish in life was to sleep, but I had a lesson to teach that night. My left hand was so sore I had trouble holding my fork. We had leftovers since no one had had time to cook. The hot shower I had that night was the best thing I'd ever felt, but before I could crawl into bed Dec called us downstairs.

I was surprised to find Gran in the kitchen too. She placed cups of tea in front of Seth and me as we sat down.

"I hear you've had a trying day. I wish someone had rung me," she commented.

"We were rushing the whole time," I explained. "And we didn't think... I mean..." I paused.

Gran smiled. "I could have fed you and the horses, at least. I'm not quite useless yet, you know."

"I never understood why you moved away from the barn, Gran," Seth said. He had always loved having her around.

"It seemed the right thing to do when Dec and your mother were married. Every new married couple needs some space and privacy."

"We did talk about building another house at the time," Dec said.

Seth brightened. "Why don't we do that now? I think it's a great idea."

"Now's not the time for us to be building," Dec said with a significant look at Gran.

Seth and I exchanged a look.

"Today's emergency underlies a few things," Dec began in what I imagined was his 'official meeting voice' when he was at work. "First of all, the barn's getting old. The pipes need to be replaced or we're going to be facing more situations like today's."

I sagged at the very prospect. The flood had been traced to a broken pipe in the horses' automatic waterbowl system, which meant we'd be watering half the horses by hand with buckets until it could be fixed.

"You've done a good job of sprucing the place up, Téa, and with Seth finishing the paint job on the fences," he hesitated and glanced over at Gran, but her eyes were on her folded hands, resting on the table.

Dec seemed to gather himself. "It's a good time to put the place up for sale."

It took me a second to realize the sound I'd heard came from me.

"But... I thought you weren't going to sell at least until we were done school," Seth protested. Hectic spots of red on his pale cheeks highlighted his agitation.

"You're not *in* school," Dec pointed out. He looked into his tea. "My brother and sister have been pressuring me, and there isn't really a good reason to resist. And in any case, it may take a long time to sell."

I stood up. I felt as though all the elements of my life were whirling around me, out of control and dizzying. "If we sell, then what the hell have the last ten years been for?" I yelled.

The look Dec gave me was weary. "They were for you to grow up."

I swallowed back a sob and raced upstairs. A minute later Seth joined me; he sprawled backward on my bed and I stopped my pacing to slump next to him, one leg folded beneath me.

Seth crossed his arms behind his head and I noticed his biceps bulge. He'd returned from Europe thinner than when he'd left, but was quickly regaining the muscles he'd lost.

"Way to keep the doors of communication open, Sis," he commented wryly.

"I'm tired, give me a break." I scrubbed my hand over my face. "What do you think about this whole thing?"

He thought about it for a long minute, his blond brows pulled down in concentration. "I think that maybe we don't get much of a say," he said finally.

I gave a tiny nod. I'd been feeling the same way. "Do you get the feeling that Dec's been biding his time until he could get out of here?" I felt as miserable as I had the first time I'd entertained the thought.

"Nah, it's not that bad. He loves being the boss of this place, but maybe he's ready to move on. Maybe Joanne's leaning on him, too."

"I wonder how Gran feels about it," I mused.

He nudged me with his knee. "If it weren't for your dramatic exit you could've asked her. But I don't think she wants to sell — I mean, she built this business from the ground up."

"I know, right? What is wrong with this family?!"

He grinned. "You want an itemized list?"

I studied him carefully. "How do you feel now that you're back? Do you feel like you're more a part of the family, or less?"

"You're wondering whether we have a right to fight for this place."

I nodded. "The lease is valid as long as one of Granddad's descendants runs the place. But Jaden said that Uncle Peter could fight us over that." I clutched my damp hair. "Is it worth fighting to keep a family business if it ends up alienating the family? They obviously feel we don't have the right to it."

"Gran does," Seth pointed out. "And so does Dec; he just doesn't want us to have this life. He gave me the speech again just the other day, about what a hard way this is to make a living. I guess now I know why."

I understood Dec's concerns. Working with horses isn't a job, it's an all-consuming lifestyle. Some aspects of it are tough — winter, for instance. Around February of every year I started dreaming about nice cozy indoor jobs, jobs without frozen water buckets and frozen fingers. I always worked weekends, but on the other hand, I was free to go places during the week when they were less crowded. I had a certain flexibility and control over what I did. And beyond all of that, I loved being with the horses. I loved the little things like tucking in the barn at night or being able to kiss a velvety nose whenever I wanted, and I loved the big things, that deep sense of connection, the way a horse's majesty could still, after all these years, leave me breathless. I'd grown up with this life. But at the moment, I didn't see how I could possibly keep it.

Fourteen

I shuffled mindlessly through school the next day. I recognized the symptoms I'd suffered after Blaze's death two years before, and with a sense of panic realized I'd have to fight to stay afloat. The last time I'd been this depressed, Jaden had saved me, but that wasn't going to happen this time. And in a way, I didn't want it to. I wanted to pull myself up by my own bootstraps. I needed to find *myself* in all of this, before Jaden and I had any chance of succeeding as a couple. I wanted to be strong. If only I didn't feel so wretched, it would be a lot easier. My sore throat was finally gone, and my voice was back, but my appetite wasn't. That wasn't a surprise though, since my stomach was usually quick to react to stress.

Mid-morning on Saturday I was setting up a course in the main ring when a strange car pulled in. Two kids shot out, followed more slowly by a middle-aged woman. She stood there for a moment, looking all around her with a small smile. I felt a roll of uneasiness and wondered whether Dec had told anyone of his plans to sell, but at that moment Gran stepped outside, dusting her hands on her pants.

"Kate!" the woman exclaimed. She hurried over to Gran and hugged her before waving her children over. Gran caught my eye, smiling widely, and beckoned me over as well.

The children dashed off as soon as they'd been introduced, and Gran turned to me. "I'd like you to meet Charlotte."

"I learned to ride here thirty-five years ago." Charlotte spoke with animation. "I must have ridden here for what, ten years?" she inquired of Gran, who nodded. "I was so happy when we moved back to the area. Now my kids can learn to love horses in the same place that I did."

I went to help Seth round up his new students while Charlotte went to the house to have tea with Gran. Gran walked her out after the kids' lesson, and they hugged again before Charlotte wrangled her kids into the car.

"She was one of my first serious students," Gran commented as the car bumped down the driveway. "And she was the first to join the Pony Club I started. That's when the business began to flourish, you know, when I opened the first local Pony Club branch."

"I didn't know that." I glanced over at Seth; I didn't need to speak my thoughts aloud.

He faced Gran. "You've given your whole life to this place, Gran. Do you really want to sell it?"

She seemed to deflate suddenly, looking smaller and older than I'd ever seen her. "I'd like for my children to be happy and get along peaceably, and it appears that selling is the only way to achieve that." She reached up and brushed Seth's hair out of his eyes; he was frowning. "I don't feel it's fair to you children, if that's what you're wondering. I would rather have given you the choice of keeping it."

I didn't know whether Gran's declaration made me feel better or worse, and when Teri came over the next day we discussed it at length, sitting at the picnic table in the shade of an old oak. She had started riding again and seemed as recovered as was possible after her ordeal.

"Do you regret becoming a jockey?" I asked her quietly.

"Not as much as I would have regretted not ever trying. When I'm an old granny I'll still have those memories, and I'm going to be a better nurse because of everything that happened."

I understood her perfectly; I had always thought I'd rather live a short, passionate life than a long, indifferent one.

"Would you have done anything differently if someone you loved had begged you to?" I wondered.

"It's hard to say," she said slowly. "I've never loved anyone the way you love Jaden."

Which was exactly why this was so hard, I thought. Jaden's absence had left a ball of ice growing in my chest, and although we texted almost every day, the distance between us was more than physical. Every night I sat down and wrote him an email, an email I almost never sent. That night was no different.

Your scent is in all my dreams.

It may have been maudlin, but it was the closest I could get to him.

My spirits rose marginally the following week because the cast was due to come off. I went to the hospital in Guelph between classes and sat through the usual wait for X-rays before seeing the orthopedist.

He shook his head. "There's a slight shadow on your X-ray. You'd better keep the cast on for another two weeks to be safe."

I stomped back to school, alternately miserable and furious, but mid-terms had begun and I eventually resigned myself to studying. The week dragged by, and on Monday morning I was sorely tempted to ditch school, but I forced myself back there and trudged into my Mammalian Physiology lab. Charlie was already set up at our bench.

"Don't you look chipper this morning." He grinned as I slumped into the seat next to him.

I rested my head on my folded arms until Professor Morty started to speak. He was a wiry man with steel-grey hair and a surprisingly deep voice.

"As you know, in this course we've undertaken a detailed study of the physiology of the nervous, endocrine, reproductive, cardiovascular and digestive systems. We will examine each system in the lab as we cover the corresponding material in lectures. To that end, today we will begin our dissection of fetal pigs. One person from each table can come up and collect your specimen."

Charlie glanced at me, smirked, and went to get our pig. He came back bearing a silver tray with a little pink body on it, and we listened to Professor Morty's directions on how to properly cut it open.

Charlie handed me the scalpel. "Ladies first."

I swallowed. I wasn't squeamish in the least, and I'd seen death before. I'd once held a dying mare's head in my lap, and I'd watched my own mother disappear before my eyes. And when you work with animals, you deal with body fluids on a daily basis. So why was I hesitating?

I shook myself and began the incision. It was hard to figure out how much pressure to use; I didn't want to cut too deep or the underlying tissues would be damaged, but cutting a millimeter at a time would take all day. The skin over the thorax split open, revealing tiny fibers and smooth membrane. I dropped the scalpel and ran to the bathroom, barely making it into a stall before throwing up. One of the teaching assistants came in as I was rinsing my mouth.

"Are you okay?" she asked. There was a smile hiding behind her concern. "Don't worry, we get a few every semester."

I shook my head. "It's not like that. I mean, it's not because of the dissection. I think I'm coming down with something."

"Uh-huh," she said, unconvinced.

The smell of formaldehyde hit me like a solid thing when I walked back into the lab, and my face reddened as scattered snickers trailed me.

"You okay?" The concern in Charlie's eyes was real, and his face betrayed no hint of his usual joking manner. "I can take over if you want."

"Yeah, thanks," I said faintly. I still felt like gagging, and class seemed very long. I tried to stay away from the piglet as much as possible.

I rushed outside as soon as the lab was over and gulped in huge lungfuls of the late October air. I felt better almost immediately.

"How about a nice ham sandwich for lunch?" Charlie came up next to me.

"Only if you're buying."

I ended up eating a bagel, which seemed to settle my stomach a bit. It was just as well that I still couldn't ride, though, because I was out of sorts for the rest of the day. I taught one lesson, studied a bit, and fell into bed exhausted.

Apparently, I didn't look much better when I staggered into the kitchen the next morning.

"Don't tell me you're getting sick again." Dec perused my face carefully.

"I think I'm just tired." I grabbed some coffee and headed out the door. Other than the tiredness, I was okay for the rest of the day — until I came home and saw Hades being ridden by a stranger.

I shot out of my car and ran to the ring. "Hey! What the hell do you think you're doing?" I yelled as I slipped between the fence boards. When he turned toward me I staggered to a stop. The man on Hades was Paul Baker, a favorite for Canada's next Olympic team. My heart sank like a stone.

"Téa!" Monica called in a singsong voice. "Have you met Paul? He was good enough to agree to tackle Hades until you're up to riding again."

My eyes narrowed. Paul was a well-known professional; he wouldn't be riding a horse without charging a hefty fee. And he wasn't likely to give that income up once my wrist was healed.

He hopped off Hades and held out his hand. "Téa, right? I remember you from the Royal last year. That was some ride."

I couldn't help being flattered and felt my scowl ease as I shook hands awkwardly with my left hand. His was big and completely engulfed mine; Paul was a tall man.

"Don't worry, dear, it's only temporary," Monica assured me brightly. I doubted it, though. Even with the delay, my cast would be off well before the Royal. I could have ridden Hades there. I heard the details Monica gave me through a fog and took refuge in the house as soon as I could. I was alone, and paced around aimlessly while ignoring the tears that fell by my feet.

"Dammit, Jaden," I growled as I grabbed the phone. I'd done things his way and look where it had gotten me. Exactly where I'd been afraid of ending up — without a jumper to ride, again. Jaden didn't answer, but I left him an angry message telling him exactly what I thought of his anti-riding edict. Then I went out to the barn and tacked up Cal.

Jaden called that night. "Nice to hear from you," he said wryly.

I took a deep breath. Now that I'd heard his voice, smooth and warm, I was suddenly a lot less angry.

"Hades is moving out." My own voice was tight.

There was a pause. "*Querida*, I'm so sorry," he breathed. "Why?"

"*Why?*" My outrage returned in a rush of flames. "Because you told me not to ride, that's why! And because I was stupid enough to listen to you! I rode Cal today and I was fine, totally fine!"

"You did what?" His voice went suddenly cold. I could feel its edge sliding against my skin.

"You heard me," I said quietly. "I'm through being a good little girl and taking orders from everyone. It's my career and my life at stake here."

The silence on the phone was louder than my voice had been. "Your life is more important to me than my own, Téa."

"My life as it relates to yours, you mean!" I shouted.

We didn't say much more. I hung up still angry; Jaden, for his part, sounded more shocked than anything. But what had he expected? I was losing everything.

Two days later I was beginning to feel like tiredness was my perpetual state. I watched enviously as Seth assembled a large breakfast for himself.

"Want some?' he offered through a mouthful of waffles.

My stomach twisted at the thought of eating. "No thanks."

He finished chewing and examined me with concern. "You don't look so good. Maybe you should go to the doctor's."

"I'm okay." I yawned sleepily. However, as the morning progressed I felt increasingly strange, so when I had a break between classes I went to the clinic at school and spoke to the nurse. She was a motherly-looking woman in lavender scrubs.

"There's a flu bug going around," she said as she stuck a thermometer under my tongue. "Don't worry, dear, we'll have you right as rain in no time."

Afterward, I went and sat on an outdoor bench, gulping the crisp air in an effort to clear the haze from my head. It didn't work, though, and I drove home in a kind of stupor. When I shuffled into the house Seth looked at me curiously. His gaze quickly shifted to alarm.

"What's wrong?"

I gestured weakly to the stairs and he followed me to my room. I collapsed into the chair and stared at him as he perched on the bedside.

"Did you go to the clinic today?" he prompted.

I nodded dumbly.

"And? What's wrong with you?"

I swallowed loudly. "I have any-time-of-day sickness," I whispered.

"What kind of bogus disease is that?" He laughed. "Sounds like an excuse to get out of work to me."

I cleared my throat but could still hardly get my voice above a whisper. "Well, some people refer to it as morning sickness." His face went slack with shock. His mouth fell open. It would have been comical if it weren't so serious.

"But... but..."

"I know."

He leaned forward and took my hand. It felt icy in his warm grip.

"How could this happen." I was still whispering.

"Well, we had this talk with mom, but I'll walk you through it again. When a man and a woman love each other very much-"

I would've hit him, but I was too tired. "No, I mean — we used birth control. We were careful, we-"

Seth slapped his hands over his ears. "T.M.I., Sis!"

I felt myself dissolving.

"Hey, hey, don't cry," he soothed. He pulled me from the chair and sat me next to him on the bed. He got me a tissue before wrapping his arm around me. "It'll be all right."

But I didn't believe him. Nothing would ever be right again.

Although I was tired, now that I knew the reason for it I couldn't sleep. I lay in bed rigid with fear. I tried to think rationally about the situation but found I couldn't, and I finally gave up in frustration. I ran my hands over my breasts; they were swollen and sore, but I'd attributed that to my impending period. I slid my hands down further to my flat abdomen. It didn't feel any different than usual. I certainly couldn't detect the presence of a potential *person* in there. Ugh. The thought made me shudder. I'd always found the idea of pregnancy distasteful.

School the next day was entirely a waste of time. When I got home Seth was feeding hay and I picked up a bale to start feeding the school horses.

"Hey, put that down." Seth strode over quickly, frowning. I dropped the bale, startled.

"You shouldn't be lifting that," he went on.

"Seth!" I hissed, looking wildly around us.

"No one heard," he murmured, moving closer. "And anyway, they'll look at your arm." As though I needed any further reminders that I was falling apart. I sat heavily on the bale.

"Let me finish and we'll go talk," he promised.

I went to the house to dump my things in the meantime, feeling queasy and useless. Seth came and found me in my room. He straddled my desk chair and rested his arms along the back.

"Have you thought about what you want?" His eyes were grave.

"What I want is to turn back the clock and have this never happen. I want to never know what it feels like to be pregnant, but it's too late for that."

"So you don't want to be pregnant," he said slowly.

"Of course not." I dropped my head into my hands. It felt like it weighed a hundred pounds.

"Are you going to end the pregnancy?" His voice was strangely quiet.

I peered up at him. Strands of my hair drew dark lines across his face. "Oh, how I wish it were that simple. Jaden wants kids, Seth. If I do that, will I ever be able to look him in the eye again?"

"Well, it's not like you have to decide today," he said.

"The sooner the better, though. I feel like a ticking time bomb."

He started biting his thumbnail. I resisted the urge to pull his hand away.

"Don't you want to talk to Jaden about this?"

I felt the sharp twist of guilt. It was a question I'd grappled with half the night. "Not yet," I murmured. "If I tell him now, I know what will happen, and I'm not ready for it."

Seth's blue bottle-glass eyes searched mine. "What will happen?"

"When Jaden finds out, he'll come home, insist on marrying me, and my life as I know it will be over. My choices will all be taken away from me. No riding jumpers, no Olympics, no traveling to shows."

My brother's face was serious. "Would that be so horrible? You love him."

I groaned in misery and buried my face back in my hands. "Yes, I love him. But thinking of that life makes me feel like I'm drowning in molasses."

He reached out and patted my shoulder.

"Besides," I went on, "did you know that if you get married before the age of twenty, you have almost an eighty percent chance of ending up divorced?"

Seth made a huffing sound. "You and your research, Sis. Do you really think you and Jaden will end up as a statistic?"

I raised my face and frowned at him. "No, but neither does any other nineteen-year-old in love. That's the point. Statistically, the older you are when you get married, the likelier you are to stay that way. The same goes for kids — the longer people wait, the happier they are with their decision."

"So it's a numbers game to you?"

"No." I sagged. "But it's all happening so fast. I guess I'm trying to wrap my head around it. What if I can never ride the same way after having a baby? What if my body changes? Remember how mom's tailbone used to ache whenever she sat for too long?" My mother had broken her tailbone while delivering Seth and me — not an unusual occurrence, apparently.

A look of alarm crossed his face. "Um, maybe you should talk to Teri about that... or, you know, some other girl."

I smiled weakly at him. "You're such a guy." My smile faded. "But I can't tell anyone else before I tell Jaden. It wouldn't be fair."

The only ray of light was that Dec was leaving on a trip the following morning, a cruise arranged by Joanne. He left in a flurry of last-minute instructions, looking harassed rather than like someone on their way to their first vacation in years. My nerves were stretched as tight as piano wires, but at least I wouldn't have to hide that fact in my own home.

I debated discussing my situation with Susan later that day, and I still hadn't decided by the time I got to my session.

Susan started off differently this time. "Tell me the first word that comes to mind when you think of Dec."

I thought for a second. "Intransigent."

She smiled gently. "That's a good word, but was it really the first one that came to you?"

"No," I said quietly. "It was 'disapproval'."

She nodded, unsurprised. "Dec is the only father you've ever known, and he's the only parent you've got left. A part of you wants his approval and love, wants to make him happy. And since you know that he doesn't approve of your choice of riding as a career, you may be subconsciously holding yourself back. You don't feel free to give it your absolute best."

I sat and absorbed her opinion. It didn't shock me, which made me think there was probably a kernel of truth to it. Finally, I faced her, dejected.

"How do I get past it?" I asked.

"It's natural to want our parents' approval, and it's a difficult thing to let go of. But in your case, you haven't even stated your intention to go against your dad's wishes — you're still on the fence. You're trying to pursue your dream halfway while still making him proud, and you have to ask yourself if you think that will work out for you. If you can't do it halfway, are you willing to live your life according to his expectations? If not, are you willing to deal with his displeasure and possible alienation?"

I felt myself slump. She was right. It wasn't in my nature to do things halfway, and yet I'd fallen into that trap and not even seen it close around me.

I returned to school still submerged in the revelations of the counseling session. As I searched out a washroom I recognized a girl from one of my classes heading the same way. She went into the stall next to mine, and I was washing my hands when she came out. Her eyes met mine in the mirror; she must have seen the slight double-take I did. She'd gone in wearing a head covering, one of those religious things that covered everything but her face, and a long flowing skirt. But she had emerged shaking free her glorious, shiny black hair. Instead of the ankle-length skirt she'd come in with, she was wearing shorts. I was trying to be discreet in my glances but she must have noticed.

"Yes," she said. "I change out of them every day when I get here."

"Why do you wear them at all then?" I asked shyly. "Does your family expect you to?"

She nodded. "We're Muslims, it's our custom."

I got a piece of paper off the roll and dried my hands thoughtfully. I didn't want to pry, and I was worried about offending her, but I was also raging with curiosity.

When I looked up she was watching me with a confident, open smile. I smiled back.

"Would they be angry if they knew?" I asked, probably more bluntly than I should have.

She shook her head slowly. "No. They'd be heartbroken," she said.

"I understand," I said softly. And I did. I shuffled slowly to class, thinking about the crazy things I was doing in order to maintain harmony in my own family. For Dec- I stopped in my tracks; someone bumped into me before the stream of students parted to go around me. Dec wasn't really the one I was compromising myself for, I realized suddenly. It was Jaden. It was for Jaden that I wasn't riding, for Jaden that I was still in school, for Jaden that I was considering changing not only my body but the course of my entire future.

Every time I bent to someone else's will, every small concession I made, took me a bit further away from who I was. At this rate, I was afraid that I'd wake up one morning and not even recognize myself — and by then, the person that Jaden had fallen in love with would be gone.

I sat through an agonizingly long lecture before driving home. The first nip of fall was in the air, and I breathed in the fresh air gratefully as I tugged my backpack out of the car. It helped quell my nausea.

Seth motioned me over to the barn. "I need help turning out Gracie and Smoothie."

The colt was learning to lead now, although we still relied on his instinct to follow his mother. I clipped on his leadrope and we followed Gracie and Seth. Once outside, however, Smoothie balked. He pulled backward on his halter, his little nose in the air, acting every bit the independence-seeking toddler he was.

"Here, let me," Seth said calmly. He took the long cotton leadrope out of my hand and, in one fluid motion, flipped it over the colt's body. The leadrope now ran along the foal's off side and around his rump; Seth had one hand near the halter and the other on the lead's end.

"Come on, little guy. You need to stay with your mama," he encouraged. With Seth on one side and pressure from the leadrope on the other two, the only way for the foal to move was forward. He tucked his bum under and scooted forward a few steps before raising his head and prancing the rest of the way to Gracie's side. Obviously, he was trying to give the impression that coming along had been his own idea. We got to the paddock, and Seth and I unclipped our leadropes simultaneously and watched mother and son trot off together.

"Pretty smooth, bro," I said appreciatively. "You picked up a few tricks while you were away."

He smiled at me. "I guess. I really liked working with the babies in Ireland."

I nodded thoughtfully. It made perfect sense now that I thought about it; Seth's sweet nature and patience were perfectly suited to working with youngsters.

"In fact, I realized that I truly enjoy working with horses in general. Which sucks since we'll be out of a barn soon. Not to mention a home."

On that sad note, we went inside.

Gran was supposed to be staying with us while Dec was gone, but after dinner, she surprised us. "I think you two are old enough to handle things on your own, don't you?"

Seth and I shared a relieved glance. "Absolutely," he assured her.

"Thank God," I groaned after she'd left. "Now I don't have to pretend. I'm going to bed. Oh, and I'm not going to school tomorrow either."

"Aren't you worried about Cal?" I'd told Seth about Dec's threat.

"He said he'd sell him if I quit. He didn't say anything about flunking out."

After a solid twelve hours of sleep I felt halfway human again, and after some coffee and toast, I made my way slowly to the barn. One of the boarders drew me aside as soon as I'd stepped inside.

"I need to post-date my board check this month. It's only by a week or so. That's not a problem, is it?" I tried to recall whether Dec had said anything about this situation. He probably had — he'd spouted off at length about seemingly everything — but my slow brain couldn't find it.

"Um, sure, I guess that's fine," I told her.

Five minutes later it was Alan. "The feed store says there's none of our regular supplement in stock. What other brand do you want?"

By the day's end, Seth was almost as exhausted as me. When Dec was around, the business ran like clockwork. The vet, farrier, osteopath, equine dentist, and other specialists were regularly scheduled. Feed, supplements, and bedding were re-stocked on time. Hay was grown, cut, baled and stored. The arena and rings were dragged and watered to even out the footing and keep down dust. The tractor and conveyor were maintained, buildings repaired, and grounds kept looking presentable. Money was collected; bills and employees were paid. Although I was peripherally involved with many of these things, I had never realized how much work went into making them happen.

The cast came off at last. My wrist was stiff, and I threw myself into physiotherapy with determination. Stephanie had finally had her baby — a girl — but once she was back at work I planned to get osteopathic treatments as well. In the meantime I was overjoyed to be able to ride again. Dec was due home in two days, and I was still frozen with indecision about my situation.

"You've got to decide soon," Seth pointed out that night.

"I know. I've got a doctor's appointment tomorrow, will you come with me?"

He nodded solemnly.

"It's a preliminary visit," I said to his unvoiced question. "They'll only ask questions, I think."

That night I had a dream. I saw a small, laughing, golden-haired child. My heart gave a loving lurch as I recognized Jaden from his childhood photos. There was someone else, though, on the periphery... I couldn't see her clearly, but somehow I knew it was a girl, the way you just know things in dreams. She was around the same age as the boy, with straight brown hair. Jaden's sister, I assumed. When I struggled to wakefulness the tendrils of the dream still held me. It couldn't have been Lexie in my dream, I realized sleepily, because Jaden's sister was four years older than him and had curly hair. Suddenly I felt as if all the air was being sucked out the room. The children in my dream — those were *mine*. I supposed my subconscious had provided two children because, as a twin, I could no more imagine life without a sibling than life without limbs.

At the appointment, they did an ultrasound. I found myself lying on my back with my jeans pushed down past my hips and my shirt pulled up, hating how vulnerable I felt.

"Why do I have to do this?" I griped.

"We need to determine how far the pregnancy's progressed," the ultrasound tech said. She sounded bored, like she'd given the same answer a hundred times that day.

Seth took my hand. "Behave yourself, Sparky, and I'll buy you an ice cream after."

"And I'll puke it up."

My skin shrank away from the cold blue gel the technician squirted onto my abdomen. She moved a bulbous instrument through the gel, pressing it firmly against my muscles.

She straightened suddenly. "Oh."

"Oh, what?" I asked. "What does 'oh' mean?"

"Don't worry, the doctor will tell you everything you need to know."

We were both quiet as Seth drove us home afterward. "Dec's coming home tomorrow, and you can't hide this much longer." We shared a wondering look. The whole pregnancy seemed so much more real since our experience that afternoon.

Dec came home in a fine mood, other than groaning about all the food on board the cruise ship and how much weight he'd gained.

His gaze raked over me. "You could stand to go on a cruise."

I went cold. I knew I wasn't looking my best; my hard-won muscle mass was fast disappearing and the constant nausea had left me gaunt and pale. According to the doctor, I was nine weeks pregnant. I didn't know how long it would take before it began to show in obvious ways.

"He knows something's up," Seth warned me during the bedtime check. We were alone; Dec had gone to bed early.

I stopped suddenly and leaned back against a stall, wishing I'd worn something warmer than the long-sleeved T-shirt I had on. I hugged myself.

"I can't do this," I said in a strangled voice.

Seth came and lounged next to me. His pale lashes cast soft shadows across his cheekbones in the dim light. "Which 'this' would that be?"

"Either. Both. I don't know." I covered my face with my hands. "I don't want this pregnancy. I don't want the life it will doom me to. But it's a part of Jaden, something he wants so badly… and I don't think I can let go of that."

He slipped a brotherly arm around me. "Either way, I'm here for you. I'll pick up all your marbles if you lose'em. And maybe Jaden won't react the way you think he will."

"Maybe." I'd hardly talked to Jaden over the past few weeks. He'd sent me a small gift for my birthday, a cup engraved with a horse and a kind of perforated spoon used to drink *maté*, an Argentinean tea. We texted and emailed every few days, but our correspondence was strained by the weight of all we were leaving unsaid. I saw the occasional picture or video of him online. In addition to helping at his uncle's ranch, he was also riding in matches again, and was playing with all of his old ferocity.

Although what I'd told my brother was true, there was another element to my newfound ambivalence. Since my dream, the pregnancy had felt different to me, as though the child inside me was living so close to my heart that he was leaving his handprints on it.

The following afternoon was grey and threatened rain. I decided to ride Cal in the indoor arena, where we were alone except for Seth. As soon as I picked up a trot my stomach roiled violently, and Cal dropped to a walk without me even asking him to. We walked along the wall until my nausea subsided, and then I pushed Cal into a trot again. I ignored my rising gorge, but we only managed to get down one long side of the arena before Cal halted.

Seth ambled over, frowning. "What's wrong with him?"

"I have no idea," I said, exasperated. I took a deep breath, closed my eyes, and willed myself to relax despite ongoing threats from my stomach to reject its meager contents. I became aware of my body, stilled my mind, and gently, even timidly, opened my heart to Cal's feelings. This was dangerous for me now, of course. I expected at any moment to be devastated by the crushing weight of my own anguish, but it didn't come. Instead, I felt something akin to concern. I pushed the feeling aside impatiently; of course I was concerned about Cal, but my feelings weren't the ones I wanted to examine right now. I tried again and felt that flickering, transient awareness of an emotion that wasn't mine. I gasped and slid to the ground, trembling.

"What is it?" Seth demanded.

I didn't answer, but stood in front of Cal and looked into his soulful, long-lashed eyes — eyes that were alight with not only love, but worry. I fell against his neck, crying. I felt Seth's hand on my back as I darkened Cal's neck with my tears, my arms around him.

"He... he feels me," I hiccupped when I could speak. "I was trying to feel him, and he was feeling *me*. The worry, the concern — he's mirroring my emotions back at me." I clutched Cal harder, sobbing afresh as a further realization burst upon me. "All this time, the resistance, the fear, the oversensitivity, it wasn't him. It was me, all along. *I* was shutting *him* out."

The magnitude of my discovery was overwhelming. I put Cal away and patted and spoke to him for a long time before heading for the house. My mind was abuzz; if I could be mistaken about something so basic, what else had I been wrong about? More than anything, I wanted to share my discovery with Jaden, and I felt again the sudden fierce ache for his presence that always left me shaken and weak. I could call him, I supposed, but I was afraid that he would know something was wrong and that I would end up revealing my pregnancy. He was too good at reading me. Even from a distance, my tone of voice might give me away, but the desire to feel his voice in my ear was seductive.

I got up to my room and picked up the phone. I put it down. Picked it up and found his number. Dropped the phone again. Terrific. Now I was developing obsessive-compulsive disorder on top of everything else. I decided not to risk it and sent him a text instead, explaining that I'd had a breakthrough with Cal.

I lay awake thinking about it that night. I realized that I was more cautious and reserved with Cal than I had been with Blaze, because I'd been hurt so deeply that it was terrifying to risk that sort of attachment again. I was excited by my discovery, but also sad for the time we'd wasted, and for the sadness Cal must have felt because of me. And it made me wonder, had I made a similar mistake with Jaden?

In the face of male anger, the only response I knew was withdrawal. I'd learned early on to make myself scarce until things were calm again, but that wasn't a useful response to someone who loved me. When Jaden had been upset I hadn't encouraged conversation — quite the opposite. I'd kept my distance and waited for him to work things out for himself. It might not have been too damaging in the case of his job, but when it came to our relationship my withdrawal was slowly suffocating us.

Sleep came far too late, but when it did it was peaceful. I had resolved to call Jaden and tell him everything.

The next day was busy, and I decided to wait until evening to make my fateful call because I was sure we'd need time to work through things. But all day at school I felt a new sense of calm, and even hope.

I was alone in the barn that afternoon when I heard footsteps.

"Oh, hey Al," I said, glancing up in confusion. I froze. Julia's boyfriend was moving slowly down the aisle, the soft tap of his dress shoes marking his progress. He looked as sleek as ever in a narrow olive-green suit. Even the long gun he carried looked sleek. He held it casually by the barrel, and I stared at it uncomprehendingly for a minute. Then I shook myself and took a step forward.

"What are you doing here?"

He stopped. "This doesn't concern you, Téa. Why don't you go into the house? I'll only be a minute." His dark eyes were feverish, his olive skin flushed. He turned away, and with a sudden flash of insight, I knew where he was going, and why. I took four long strides and planted myself in front of Jasmine's stall.

He didn't change expression as he came to stand before me, but he shifted the butt of the gun into his right hand. I heard something click and assumed it was the safety.

"You'll have to move," he said casually.

My heart was thumping and I crossed my arms over my chest to muffle it. "I can't do that." I swallowed; my voice was scratchy and rough.

Al sighed. "Really, Téa, there's no need to make this difficult. It's only a horse."

I heard Jazzy snuffling through the bars behind me. Her warm breath ruffled my hair. I wanted to scream at her to get back, but I was afraid to be distracted for even a second. My mind worked frantically. What do you say to a deranged person with a gun? For once, I wished I'd watched more of those police shows that Seth loved, for surely I would have picked up some tips and not felt as completely useless as I did right now. I made sure to look right into Al's eyes.

"Whatever's going on, Al, it's between you and Julia. Why don't I call her? We can all sit down and talk," I persuaded softly. His eyes narrowed at the mention of Julia's name.

"Get out of the way," he commanded again. His voice was harsher this time, and he dropped the barrel of the gun downward so that it pointed at my chest. I felt my entire body curl inward, as though it was trying to present as small a target as possible. I shook my head. I wanted to tell him he'd have to go through me first, but I doubted I could speak. I didn't feel afraid, though. Just numb.

Al started to shift position when another voice spoke.

"Easy, now.

I started as Al whirled around to point the gun at Dec, who stood barely six feet away from us. I felt shock that he had been able to sneak so close, but no relief — there were simply more of us in danger now. Dec's eyes flickered over to me for a millisecond.

"Téa, why don't you let Al and I discuss this man to man," he suggested in a low voice.

I began to turn and Al looked at me. I saw the flare of victory in his eyes, and I knew exactly what he would do. The instant I was out of the way, he would shoot Jasmine. I stopped dead.

"Téa," Dec gritted through clenched teeth, "Go. Now."

"I'm sorry, but I'm staying here," I said quietly.

Al moved toward me, and Dec lunged. He grabbed the barrel of the gun in one hand and Al's thin neck with the other. A deafening bang made me jump backward; I slammed into the stall, my head cracking against the bars. I saw stars for a second and blinked rapidly, while all around me horses snorted and kicked in fear.

Fifteen

I blinked to clear my head.

A clang sounded next to me as Dec shoved Al face-first against the stall. With his other hand, Dec held out the rifle to me.

"Hold this."

I took it gingerly, surprised to find that death felt smooth and oily.

"Struggle and I'll beat you senseless," Dec snapped. He twisted Al's arms behind his back and frogmarched him towards the tackroom. I was still rooted to the spot a minute later when they returned. Dec shoved Al into an empty stall and wrapped a chain around the bars, then fiddled with the lock he'd gotten.

The lock clicked into place. Dec was breathing heavily, and as he turned slowly to face me I saw how white his face was. He reached out and very carefully took the gun out of my hands. He laid it on the floor. Then he straightened up, grabbed my arms, and gave me one quick, hard shake.

"If you *ever*-" He choked suddenly and pulled me against him, holding me tightly. To my surprise, I was happy to be there — the fear that had been absent earlier was rushing into me and I felt weak and shaky.

After a minute he let me go, and with a last glare at our prisoner he picked up the gun and led the way into the house. I sat at the table petting Blue while Dec called the police, but I was growing increasingly worried. I dashed to my room and got my phone, tried dialing. When I got no answer I rushed back downstairs while trying Seth.

"Seth! Thank God," I blurted when he answered. "Look, we have to find Julia. I don't have time to explain, but I think she might be in trouble. I'll call her parents, you try her friends, okay?"

Seth paused for one confused second before agreeing. I left a rather frantic message on Julia's mom's answering machine before realizing I didn't have her dad's new number. Dec came into the living room as I was searching for their cell numbers, the phone shaking in my hands.

"What's the matter?" His face was drawn.

"It's-" I swallowed. "If he wanted to hurt Jasmine... what if he hurt Julia, too?" My voice cracked; my hormones were amplifying my emotions, and I felt as through any second I might burst into a million jittery pieces.

His eyes widened. "Okay. Keep trying to reach her." He headed for the door but stopped when I followed him.

"Stay here," he ordered. "You too," he added, looking down at Blue.

"But... where are you going?"

"To ask our inmate about Julia," he said grimly.

"Then I'm-"

He cut me off. "No, Téa. I want your word that you'll stay in the house." He looked worried.

At my nod, he left quickly. I scrolled through my contacts while pacing and called everyone who remotely knew Julia. I still hadn't found her by the time the police showed up. I opened the front door to find two officers, and man and a woman. They were a matched set, both tall and brown-haired, hers pulled into a tight bun.

"We got a report of an incident with a firearm?" the male cop asked. I nodded, feeling a sudden panic. I didn't know exactly what Dec was up to in the barn, but I strongly suspected he wouldn't want witnesses. Particularly uniformed ones. I opened the door wider.

"Do you need to go out, Blue?" I stared at her, willing her to understand. She slipped past the officers' legs and I relaxed somewhat. She would find Dec first; like most Australian Cattle dogs, she was absolutely devoted that way.

"He's in the barn." I led the way slowly and spoke loudly as soon as we stepped inside. "It's this way."

Dec came forward calmly to speak with the police. He looked unruffled, but when I moved toward the stall he stopped me with a hand on my shoulder. We went back into the house to give our statements. Seth came home as we were finishing; I jumped up at his entrance.

"Did you find her?" I pleaded.

He shook his head and eyed the police warily. "What's going on?"

The afternoon's events came tumbling out, but when Dec accompanied the police outside I stopped talking and ran into his office. From there, Seth and I could see the parking area and the barn through a small bay window. We watched the officers escort Al to the squad car, and even from a distance, I could see the red stain of blood around his mouth. One of his eyes seemed swollen, too. I gave a shudder and turned. I was still sitting on the window's small bench when Dec strode in.

He gave me an appraising look and I felt my gaze slide away from his. I was afraid he'd be angry that I was spying, and I stood as he came over, but he simply put an arm around me.

"I had to, Téa," he said gently. I looked up at him; his expression was concerned. "I don't think he knows where Julia is, and I don't think he hurt her. Okay?"

I nodded. Suddenly I went limp and my knees turned to water. Dec grabbed me and led me to the couch, supporting most of my weight.

"Seth, get her some water."

I drank most of the water and was feeling almost human again when Julia burst in, wild-eyed.

"I just heard... omigod... are you all right?"

Seth stalked over to face her. "This wouldn't have happened if you had listened to your friends. You owe my sister a huge apology." He gave her a blistering look before stalking out.

Julia flashed a nervous glance my way. "He's kind of hot when he gets all forceful like that, isn't he?"

I shrugged irritably. As far as I was concerned, the words 'hot' and 'Seth' didn't even belong in the same sentence. She seemed to deflate then and came to sit next to me.

"I'm so sorry, Téa," she said quietly. "I broke up with Al yesterday, and he flipped out." Her head was hanging, and she looked over at me imploringly. "I can never thank you enough for what you did. Never."

She shifted on the couch so that she was facing me, and when I tried to smile she hugged me tightly. I squeezed her back. "I've missed you, Jules."

"Me, too," she sniffled. "I've been so stupid. You and Ter were right." Her voice was subdued.

"We'll give you a pass for this one," I said, and together we went to hug our horses.

I went to bed early, but Seth barged into my room before I fell asleep. He dropped onto the edge of my bed and stared at me, his eyes like sapphires.

"You're an idiot," he announced.

"Yeah, thanks for the newsflash. Now can I get some sleep?" I said, cranky.

"No!" he yelled. I jumped a bit but tried to hide it by sitting up in bed and staring him down.

"Get a grip," I said. "Everyone's fine."

"But you almost weren't, Sis! And you're responsible for more than just yourself now. What about my niece or-"

"Shut up!" I hissed, terrified that Dec would overhear. Then I saw his face, and the genuine fear there, and my head dropped down heavily. "Sorry," I muttered, picking at a thread on my comforter. "You're right, I should've been more careful. But tell me, Seth, what would you have done?" I looked up at him pleadingly, and he sighed.

"I don't know."

I lay awake after Seth left, his words echoing in my head. He was right, I thought with a pang. I had to start being more responsible.

I slept uneasily, tormented by fragments of guilty dreams. I only threw up once while getting ready for school, which seemed promising. I was already outside when my phone rang, and my heart pounded when I saw who the caller was.

"Hello?"

He was yelling, of course. He kept it up for quite a while, and I listened quietly, feeling only a trifle pathetic that I was so happy to be hearing his voice, regardless of the circumstances.

"Did you call just to yell at me?" I asked finally, when I thought he was done.

"Essentially, yes. You should thank your lucky stars that I'm not standing in front of you right now, Téa." His voice was rough with emotion.

There was a long silence. "I'll never feel lucky for that," I whispered.

He groaned. "I want you to swear to me, swear by all that is holy, that you will stay out of mortal danger until I come home."

"And when will that be?" I asked quietly.

"The World Cup runs into December, and I've committed to playing in it." He sighed. "Probably after that."

That night was Dec's turn. I'd been at school all day, and Gran had spent all of dinnertime haranguing me about my lack of sense. It had been a relief to come upstairs, and now this. He knocked quietly, and I stood up and steeled myself before telling him to come in. He didn't come close, just stood there watching me with an inscrutable expression until I began to get uncomfortable.

I lost patience first. "Okay, I know you didn't get the chance to yell at me properly yesterday. So, go ahead." I crossed my arms tightly and stared at the poster of Hickstead on my wall.

"I think Gran did quite a fine job of covering the bases, don't you?"

My eyes flew back to his face. One corner of his mouth was lifted, like he was trying not to smile.

I sank into the chair. "Yeah, she was pretty thorough."

Dec went and sat on the bed. He gave me another peculiar look. "Téa, I know you've had a hard time lately. You've been sick a lot, and missing Jaden and Hades... and, well, you're not..." I watched in confusion as he fumbled for words. I'd never seen Dec act like this. He straightened up suddenly and looked right at me. "Are you suicidal?"

"What?" I stared at him in amazement. "No! Dec, he was going to hurt *Jasmine*. An innocent horse. And Julia's one of my best friends."

"You and Julia have barely spoken in months." He regarded me with suspicion.

I threw up my hands. "That doesn't stop her being my friend, does it?"

His face softened, and he patted my shoulder on his way out. "No, it doesn't."

I'd almost interrupted Jaden's tirade that morning to tell him the big news, but good sense had for once intervened. I decided to have a shower, go over what I would say, and call him. I went to the bathroom and started undressing while mentally rehearsing my speech. I had just pulled my shirt over my head when I felt a sharp pain in my abdomen and doubled over, gasping. The pain eased, and I was straightening up when I felt a rush of wetness between my legs.

I yanked down my jeans. My underwear was covered in blood. "No, oh no, no," I mewled. My abdomen cramped again, and I started tugging my clothes back on while yanking open the bathroom door.

"Seth!" I yelled. No answer.

I tottered carefully to my bedroom, one hand over my belly, and found my phone.

Find me upstairs NOW, I texted quickly. Then I got clean clothes and a hygienic pad, tossed my bloodied ones in the hamper, and lay down. Seth barreled in seconds later.

"I need to go to the hospital," I groaned.

He helped me down the stairs, and we were almost at the front door when Dec walked through it. I quickly moved my hands upward.

"Stomach pains," I gasped. "Seth's taking me to the hospital."

Dec's face clouded with concern. "I'll come too."

I shook my head quickly. "It's okay, someone has to stay. We'll call you."

I kept my feet up on the dash during the drive, although I doubted it would help. Seth sped toward the hospital, throwing occasional apprehensive glances my way. If he thought it was strange that I was suddenly trying to hold on to the pregnancy, he didn't say so.

My case wasn't a priority and it was hours before a doctor confirmed my fears.

"You've had a miscarriage," he said kindly. He was an elderly man with a halo of white hair. "There's no more heartbeat or detectable signs of the fetus, but the ultrasound shows bits of tissue remaining, so we're going to do a D&C to be safe."

I'd have to be anesthetized, the doctor explained, although the procedure itself would only take fifteen minutes.

I dragged my eyes over to Seth's. "You should go home. It'll be hours before I can leave."

"You're in no shape to order me around, Sparky. I'll call Dec and tell him we'll both be home tomorrow. Or rather, later today."

I didn't argue. I was more grateful than I could say for his presence.

The first thing I did upon regaining consciousness was to throw up, which I thought was grossly unfair under the circumstances. Seth supported me by the elbow as we emerged, blinking, into the early-morning light. His face was slack and grey from lack of sleep, and I could only imagine how I looked.

Bad, if Dec's reaction was anything to go by. We gave him the food poisoning story we'd concocted and both went up to bed. Dec brought me a glass of water and hesitated by the edge of my bed. It was as close to hovering as he'd ever come.

"I should've gone with you," he reproached himself.

"I'll be fine, Dec. Just give me a couple of days." The world was spinning around me, and I didn't think I could stay conscious for much longer.

He patted my arm gingerly and left. As soon as I was alone, hot tears sprang from my eyes and ran down my temples. My brain was fuzzy, and my body felt empty, so *empty*, and the only person who could possibly make me feel whole again was over five thousand miles away. On impulse, I got up and opened my laptop. I wrote him a short, passionate, despairing email, and finally surrendered to sleep.

I woke up after dinnertime, had some clear broth that Gran had thoughtfully left for me, and went right back to sleep. I felt better the following morning. The bleeding was still fairly heavy, but it was Saturday so I got dressed, found coffee and headed outside to teach.

The tackroom was full. Gran was there, along with Catherine, Seth, and Dec, all busily divvying up my lessons.

"I'm not dead, you know," I said wryly.

Gran bustled over, scanning my face anxiously. "You don't look well, dear. Why don't you rest for another day?"

I shook my head almost frantically. The last thing I wanted was to be imprisoned in the house with my guilt all day. "I'm fine. I want to work."

After some haggling, I was finally allotted a few lessons to teach. I debated riding, but even if I managed to sneak by everybody, my ongoing cramps would have made it impossible. I hung around the barn doing odd jobs, feeling dejected and useless, but eventually, I had to admit to tiredness and go to the house. I started making dinner. I was a very indifferent cook, but it kept me busy, which was my only goal.

Seth came in as I was chopping carrots. He went to the fridge and gulped down three glasses of apple juice before coming to rest his hip against the counter next to me.

"How are you feeling?"

I shrugged, almost slicing my fingertip. "Okay."

He took the knife out of my hand and laid it on the cutting board. "Don't even try that on me."

I faced him, suddenly angry. "You want to know how I feel? I feel like crap. I ache and I'm bleeding and I'm still goddam nauseous. But it happened for a reason because when I was standing in front of that gun, I didn't even think about the fact that I was pregnant. Didn't even *remember*. What kind of horrible mother would I have made?"

Seth scowled at me. "You think you had a miscarriage because for one minute, in an ultra-stressful situation, you forgot you were a few weeks pregnant?" he scoffed.

"Sure, if you say it like *that* it sounds stupid," I said irritably.

He flipped his shaggy hair out of his eyes and leaned forward so that our gazes were level. "The doctor said it was a real common thing, remember? It wasn't anything you did." His voice had gone soft. I wanted to believe him, but it was hard. Especially when the miscarriage felt as much like a reprieve as a loss.

Gran stayed for dinner, and she and Dec did most of the talking. I excused myself as soon as I could and tried to distract myself with a paperback in my bedroom. I was contemplating another early bedtime when Dec called me.

"Téa, can you come down here for a minute?" His voice sounded strange.

I trudged down the stairs but stopped in surprise at the bottom. "Aunt Paloma." I faltered. "Hi."

Dec patted the couch next to him; I obediently went and sat beside him before giving him an inquiring look.

"Did something happen with you and Jaden? Is something wrong?" he asked hesitantly.

I dropped my eyes to the ground. What could I say? That everything was wrong? That I hadn't done a single thing right since being lucky enough to have the most wonderful man in the world fall in love with me?

"Why?" I asked a question since I couldn't figure out an answer that wouldn't sound trite.

"My brother called me," Aunt Paloma said quietly. "He said that Jaden disappeared for a whole day, and that when he came back it was obvious he'd been in a fight."

I inhaled sharply as my eyes raced to find hers; my heart was already slamming against my ribs. "Is he okay?" I demanded.

She nodded. "Yes, but his uncle couldn't get any kind of explanation out of him. Emiliano said he got the impression it had to do with... well, with a girlfriend." She uttered the word slowly, carefully, as though it didn't feel right in her mouth. Which it probably didn't.

I stared unseeingly at the floor. Could there be another girl? The thought made me want to vomit, and I shoved it away. No, I had to believe this was about me. I tried to remember the last time I'd talked to him, what I'd said. A chill began to creep through me. I'd sent him an email, I remembered suddenly, when I was drugged-out and upset. I wracked my brain to remember what I'd written. Every word was a separate claw, tearing at me.

You left, and now something awful's happened, and I'm afraid nothing will ever be the same between us. I didn't mean for it to happen, Jaden. I'm sorry.

That was the gist of the message I'd sent.

Damn, damn, damn. My eyes were filling with tears, which I struggled to contain. My now-clear brain knew all too well how Jaden would have interpreted that email — it sounded as though I had cheated on him. Why had I gone and sent that stupid message? I jumped up.

"Where are you going?" Dec's hand on my arm stopped me.

"I have to call him," I said hoarsely.

"Why don't you explain to us what's going on first?" Aunt Paloma asked. She appeared on the verge of anger, her dark eyes throwing sparks.

I pleaded with Dec. "I can't. Not now, please."

He nodded slowly, releasing my arm. The expression on his face made it clear that I'd have to talk later, but I'd deal with it then.

"Sorry, Aunt Paloma," I said hurriedly.

I ran upstairs. I called his Argentina cell number; his Spanish message came on almost right away. Even across the thousands of miles that separated us, the warmth of his tone made my insides melt.

"Jaden, it's me." I hesitated, unsure. "That message wasn't what you thought." My voice broke even though I was speaking hardly above a whisper. "Please call me. Please."

I tried viciously to suppress the sobs that were tearing through my chest. You don't have the right to cry over this, I told myself savagely. You should suffer the pain of it, as Jaden so obviously is.

There was a soft knock at my door. Too soft to be Dec.

"Yes?" I straightened up, hurriedly wiping away tears with my sleeve.

Aunt Paloma came in. She hesitated by the door for a minute before coming to sit by me on the bed. She wasn't close, but it was the first time in a long time that she'd sought me out.

"Jaden told me that you're the one who convinced him to go help his uncle. I wanted to tell you that I'm grateful."

I hadn't done it for her. I shrugged, feeling ungracious but not quite managing to care.

"Can I ask why you did it?" Her voice was soft but compelling. There was a lot of his mother in Jaden.

I looked into her face for the first time. "You saw him this summer, he was miserable. And I remembered, after Blaze died... well, falling in love with Jaden saved my sanity, but it wasn't until I began riding jumpers again that I found any real joy, you know? I thought playing polo might do that for him."

She nodded slowly. A small, sad smile curved the corners of her mouth. "You have great trust in each other."

I hesitated, but I had nothing to lose. "If by that you mean I trust Jaden to be faithful, then yes."

She seemed startled by my directness. "The Foster men, for all their issues, are a faithful lot. I was referring to the fact that long-term separation can be hard on even a seasoned relationship."

"Look, Aunt Paloma, I'm not naïve. I realize that he may find that life without me is more peaceful than a life spent putting up with my impulsiveness and my ambitious dreams. And if he does, well, I'll learn to accept that. It may just about kill me, but above all else I want him to be happy."

Tenderness stole over her features, and she leaned forward and enfolded me in her arms. She was soft and smelled like vanilla, and it had been so long since I'd been held like this, in an embrace so maternal, that my tears spilled forth despite all my attempts to control them.

"He's my own son, and it's taken me two years to come to the realization that his happiness is more important than my limiting beliefs," Aunt Paloma murmured. She released me and leaned back to find my face. "I hope you can forgive me for taking so long to reach the right conclusion."

I took her hand. "There's nothing to forgive. We're all just doing the best we can."

Jaden didn't call back that night. There wasn't much of a time difference so I knew that wasn't the reason. The realization that he didn't want to talk to me was almost intolerable, and I lay awake all night, staring into blackness. How would he react when he found out the truth? That I'd been pregnant and hadn't even been careful enough to stay that way, after giving him my word that I'd take care of myself? I could only imagine how betrayed he would feel.

I stumbled to the bathroom for a shower the next morning. The reflection in the mirror looked positively haggard. I had just wrapped a towel around my dripping hair when my phone rang. I ran to my room, and my hand shook when I saw Jaden's name.

"I'm so glad you called," I stammered. "My love, I'm-"

"Save the apologies," he said harshly. I doubled over, choking back sobs. I pictured his face; I knew how it would look when his voice was hard like that — as though it was carved from granite.

"It's not what you think," I whispered.

"It never is." He hung up.

I had school the next day. It seemed completely pointless to go, but at least at school, I could stare numbly into space without anyone commenting on it. Days passed, even though I was only dimly aware of them. The Royal Agricultural Winter Fair was running and my friends tried to convince me to go, but in the face of my steadfast refusal they compromised and came over to watch it on TV. Julia sat on one side of me, Teri on the other, and Seth sprawled his lanky body over the loveseat.

I'd been avoiding so much as a passing thought of Hades. I hadn't wanted to hear news, gossip, or updates on his progress. Everyone around me knew it was a forbidden topic. But we were watching an international class, so I wasn't shocked when he came on the screen. What did shock me was the manner of his entry.

Paul Baker was unquestionably a better physical match for Hades, but someone had apparently forgotten to tell Hades that. He rocketed into the ring practically breathing fire, his nostrils as red as blood, dripping sweat although he hadn't even started his round yet. I sat bolt upright.

"What the hell does he have in his mouth?" I yelled. Hades was wearing a brutal-looking bit, and the way he was jerking his nose up with every stride made it clear that he hated it. Of course, anything that actually injured the horse would get the rider disqualified, but there was no visible injury, just Hades' obvious distress. I dug my nails into my palms as he started his round. He was fighting Paul's hands, but Paul was implacable, keeping Hades going with his spurs. My heart lodged in my throat as they jumped the first line; as they rounded the corner Hades tossed his head up dramatically, almost hitting Paul in the face. Paul brought his whip down, and Hades predictably went ballistic. He flung his head up and bounded sideways, knocking Paul into the boards. When Paul tried to force him forward Hades reared. There was a sea of shocked faces in the background — this was the type of behavior almost never seen at shows, and certainly not in a class of this caliber. As soon as Hades' front hooves hit the ground, Paul

311

signaled his withdrawal from the class. It was the first smart move I'd seen him make.

I shot to my feet. I felt as though I'd been hit with a blast of cold air, clearing the miasma of confused emotion that had been plaguing me for weeks and leaving me shaking with rage.

"Téa, wait-"

I stomped upstairs for my phone. I called Monica and left her a message stressing that what I'd just seen was abuse and that if they didn't do something about it, I would report them. To whom I'd report them I wasn't sure, but I was determined to get Hades away from that monster.

Seeing my former partner like that was the last straw, but my fury snapped me out of the self-pitying stupor I'd been wallowing in. I had lost Hades, I had lost a pregnancy, and I was probably going to lose my home, but there were some things I would fight to keep.

After Teri and Julia left I called Jaden. He didn't answer, but I left him a message, hoping he would hear the earnestness in my voice.

"I know you're upset, but you're upset for the wrong reasons. I need to talk to you. You probably won't like some of the things I have to tell you but above all, I want to say that I love you. I love you, Jaden."

My newfound determination was sorely tested when I didn't hear back from him the next day, and I went to bed wondering what more I could do. I was loading the breakfast dishes into the dishwasher the following morning when I heard voices; when Dec called me I strolled into the living room wiping my hands on a dishtowel. As I looked up I stumbled to a stop, the dishtowel fluttering to the ground.

Jaden was standing in the entrance.

He was wearing a thick cream-colored sweater and faded jeans, and sported more stubble than I was used to seeing. He looked like he'd just stepped off the Pampas. My heart beat painfully in my chest, and my mouth was too full of all the things I couldn't say for me to make a sound.

Dec looked back and forth between us. "Well, ah, I'll just leave you-"

"It's all right, Dec. I think Téa and I will go for a ride," Jaden said. His eyes moved to me. They were hard, almost challenging, and I felt heat where they touched me.

I took Seth's horse Winter since I could easily ride him bareback with a halter. Jaden rode Dec's horse, Beau. We didn't speak as we got underway. I shivered in my long-sleeved shirt, as I'd been too shocked to put on a jacket. My stolen glances at Jaden showed that he wasn't even looking at me. He moved Beau into a jog, and we rode in silence to our copse. Once the horses were tied he sank to the ground and rested his arm on one bent knee. I lowered myself shakily into the grass. I was at an angle to him, not quite next to him but not facing him either.

I started trembling from more than cold, and I was reminded of the old days, before we were together, when we couldn't touch because we couldn't admit our love for one another. Oh, how simple those days now seemed.

"You wanted to talk," he said, his voice low. "Go ahead."

But all my carefully thought-out words had fled at the sight of him. Every electron in my cells seemed to vibrate to the pitch of his body. My trembling increased as I heard him shift closer. He was sitting beside me now. My throat was so tight that my voice was hoarse when I forced myself to speak.

"Aren't you even going to touch me, Jaden?"

I felt him go very still.

"I wasn't sure you would want me to."

I looked at him then. I was frowning. In what weird parallel dimension would I not want Jaden's touch?

"Why?" I whispered. His eyes searched mine, his expression moving from hard to hopeful. I started to reach for him, and his hands closed around my face, his mouth crushed mine, and we fell together into the long, leaf-strewn grass. His lips worked urgently against mine as his body covered me. I clutched him to me with all of my might; I wanted to hold him so close that nothing could ever come between us.

I ripped my mouth away from his only long enough to whisper one word. "Please."

He knew what I wanted. He always knew. He yanked my pants down in one motion; I barely had a chance to register the cool air brushing my skin before he was pushing into me, flooding me with his heat.

It was over in minutes, and he lay still, blanketing me with his body. I kept my arms wrapped around him, holding him in place. He was leaner than I'd ever seen him, not thin exactly — he still had too much muscle mass for that — but he'd definitely lost weight. I turned my face so that my cheek rested against his stubbled one.

"Did I hurt you?" he muttered.

"No," I whispered. And if he had, I wouldn't have cared, so desperate had I been to feel his body against mine.

Suddenly I stiffened. I wasn't supposed to be doing this yet — there was a danger of infection or something. In the heat of the moment, I'd forgotten. Jaden misread my tension and started to move off me.

"No," I pleaded, tightening my hold. I was loath to put any distance between us now.

He sighed a hot breath onto my neck. "We're doing it again. Having sex instead of talking."

"We'll talk," I murmured. I slid my hands up and down his back under his sweater, feeling the ridges of his ribs. Now that he was here, so close, I was growing reluctant to have that conversation, afraid of the judgment I was sure I'd find in his eyes.

His belly rumbled loudly against mine. "You're hungry," I said. Just call me Captain Obvious. "Why don't we eat something first."

Jaden's look said he knew I was stalling, but he helped me up and we straightened our clothes, and it occurred to me that maybe he was stalling, too. We pointed our horses toward home without speaking. I could feel the marks of his palms seared onto my skin, but I didn't fool myself into thinking everything was fine because we'd made love. We'd always had a frighteningly strong physical attraction, but in real life, it turned out that wasn't enough.

We were dismounting by the barn when Seth ambled out. "Dec wants to see you pronto," he told me, taking hold of Winter. "Something about a post-dated check."

I gave Jaden an apologetic shrug and trudged to the house. By the time Dec had finished lecturing me on how the post-dated check had been returned by the bank and all the problems it had caused him, Jaden still wasn't in the house. A twinge of worry made me step out onto the porch. I spotted him right away, having an animated conversation with Seth near the barn. I was too far away to hear the words, but the way they braced themselves made me realize it was an argument.

All of a sudden Seth took a swing at Jaden, and I burst into a run, my heart lodged in my throat. Jaden blocked the blow easily, of course, but Seth didn't stop there. His fists were flying, trying in vain to get through Jaden's practiced defenses.

"Seth! Cut it out!" I was close enough to hear Jaden's exclamation. And then one of Seth's punches landed, and in the instant it hit Jaden's face I saw his expression shift, grow feral and dangerous.

"No!" I cried, sprinting as fast as I could. I'd seen that expression before, the one time I'd seen Jaden fight. Jaden was a trained fighter, powerful and fast. He could annihilate Seth in seconds. Jaden's arm drew back as I flung myself at him, wrapping my arms and legs around his body. The impact sent him staggering backward, but he didn't fall and his arms seemed to close around me automatically.

"Don't," I sobbed, "Don't hit Seth, please, don't."

His arms tightened around me, and he hid his face in my hair. He was breathing hard.

"That's enough now, settle down," Dec snapped behind me.

Jaden put me down and I turned to see Dec pinning Seth's arms tightly behind him. As soon as Seth stopped struggling Dec gave him a shove in the direction of the house.

"Get inside," Dec growled.

As Seth stumbled forward I ran and linked my arm through his.

"You too." I heard Dec bark behind me.

"Sorry, Dec, but I don't answer to you."

I spun around, my heart rate shooting back up.

Dec stepped into Jaden's space. "You really think you don't answer to me? After you date my daughter? When you were about to take a swing at Seth? You're like a son to me Jaden, but you'd better get your butt into that house or so help me-"

315

The sound of my whimper drew Jaden's glance, and I reached out to him. He came and took my hand and we walked to the house together, my other arm still entwined with Seth's.

We all sat stiffly at the table, Jaden next to me and Seth across from me, next to Dec.

"What the hell's going on, Seth?" Jaden demanded. "I think of you as a brother. Why don't you try talking to me before punching me in the head?"

Seth didn't say anything, his expression stony. His eyes flickered to me. I gave a tiny shake of my head, my expression pleading. He turned his face away as Jaden shifted the full force of his attention to me.

"Téa?" His voice was quiet, but I could detect anger licking the edges. I didn't look at him; instead, my gaze found Dec's, who shook his head at me.

"I don't know what's going on, honey. But one way or another, I don't want to see any more fighting."

I nodded, studying the tabletop. When I lifted my eyes to Jaden I noticed how exhausted he looked. He'd probably come straight from the airport. "You look like you could use some sleep," I murmured. "Can I come over to your place later?"

"Sure," he said uncertainly. He stood to go, giving Seth one last perplexed look. Seth, for his part, was beginning to look embarrassed.

As soon as Jaden left, Dec turned on Seth. "And you! Jaden could've destroyed you if he'd wanted to! Stand up."

Seth rose warily. Dec grabbed his arm and pulled him roughly away from the table. "Make a fist. Not like that," Dec snapped, "you'll break your thumb that way." He rearranged Seth's fingers so his thumb wasn't inside. "Now take a swing at me."

Seth shot me a panicked glance and I rose worriedly. If Dec was planning on hitting back, things were going to get ugly very fast. Was this his way of teaching Seth a lesson?

"Listen, son," Dec said more quietly, "I don't want you to fight. But if you're going to do it, I want you to know the basics so that you don't wind up badly hurt."

Seth relaxed. The swing he launched at Dec still had a tentative quality, and Dec blocked it easily. He was positioning Seth and giving him tips when I went upstairs.

I thought about the evening ahead, my heart thumping madly against my ribs. To everything, there is a time — and mine had come.

I did my best to distract myself with work that afternoon.

"Were you trying to kill yourself this morning?" I demanded when Seth came into the barn.

He gave me a tired look. "Jaden said you looked terrible and demanded to know why I hadn't made you take better care of yourself."

"Oh." Given that Seth had been through the wringer with me, I could see why he'd lost it.

In late afternoon I had a long shower to try to relax, which was wasted when I got caught in rush-hour traffic on my way into the city. I knocked on Jaden's door instead of letting myself in with my key, wondering even as I did so why I felt so reserved. He answered the door right away. He was wearing jeans and a blue T-shirt that was soft and faded from washing. I stepped inside, hugging my arms around myself. He made no move to touch me but led the way to the tan leather couch.

I studied his face as we sat. It had always been sharply planed, but there were new hollows in his cheeks, and the smudges under his eyes were proof he hadn't slept much. His hair was long, and he brushed it out of his face impatiently as his amber-flecked gaze fixed on me. I tensed. His eyes were hard as jewels, and they searched mine with that peculiar intensity that was so much a part of him.

"You need to tell me what's going on."

I turned my face away, knowing as I did so that he would see it as a sign of guilt. My breath was coming fast. The next few words could change the way he looked at me forever.

"I... we shouldn't have done what we did today." It wasn't how I'd planned to start this conversation, but those were the words that emerged when I opened my mouth.

"I see." He said it quietly, but his tone could have cut glass. "Because there's someone else."

I shook my head. Still without looking at him, I dug a folded paper out of my pocket and handed it to him. He unfolded it slowly, but when he looked from the black and white image back to me his expression was blank. His face was at an angle, a lock of hair falling over one eye, and my hand ached to reach out and smooth it back for him.

"It's an ultrasound picture," I whispered. "I... I was pregnant."

The paper made a soft rattle as his hands began to shake. All the hardness slid away from his face, leaving it unguarded and vulnerable. His eyes went wide as he shifted to face me. His mouth was open, but he didn't say anything for a minute.

He finally managed a single, hoarse word. "Were?"

I felt tears flood my eyes and I nodded carefully, willing them not to spill.

He swallowed hard. "So... did you..."

"I had a miscarriage just over a week ago. When I sent you that email I was still woozy from the anesthetic at the hospital." I pushed the explanation through my own tight throat.

"Pregnant," he said slowly, as if testing the word on his tongue. He stared at the ground. "And at what point were you planning to tell me?"

I hesitated. "If you came back, I wanted it to be because you wanted to, Jaden, not because of some misplaced sense of obligation."

His head snapped up then, and his eyes burned into mine. "*Misplaced?*"

I flinched. All of a sudden his arms were around me; he crushed me to him and murmured into my hair. "I'm sorry, *querida*, I'm so very, very sorry."

My eyes overflowed. I buried my face in his soft shirt as a tentative hope flowered inside me.

"Why are *you* sorry?" I whispered.

"That you went through all of that on your own," he said, as though it were obvious. His arms were still around me, one hand smoothing my hair as he spoke.

"Well, *I'm* sorry I didn't tell you sooner. I wanted to. My first impulse when I found out was to call you. But I was afraid you'd drop everything and come back and marry me, and I didn't know what I wanted. I felt trapped. Then I felt so guilty for not telling you that it got harder and harder... and I was about to do it when I had the miscarriage." Now that I'd begun explaining it was as though a dam had burst, and the words tumbled out pell-mell.

He drew away and took my face gently with both hands. "*Querida.* Yes, I'd like to have a child someday. But I'd never force you into a decision like that. It's your body; it was always your choice. You could have told me."

I searched his eyes. They held nothing but a golden, glowing sincerity.

"I let you believe I'd cheated on you." I was determined to get everything out into the open at once. "And when you came back, you looked so... hard. As though you'd never forgive me."

He sighed and dropped his hands from my face. I reached for one of them and entwined our fingers in my lap.

"Téa, do you know how much I had to scramble to get here from Argentina in one day? I forfeited tens of thousands of dollars by missing the World Cup, in addition to angering several people. My uncle's cast is off but he still needs help. That look on my face was determination — I was determined to prove to you that whoever you'd met, he couldn't be as good a match for you as I am."

I gazed at him in wonder. "You... you still want to be with me?"

"I was never trying to escape you. I left to *protect* you. I was angry all the time, I was making you miserable, and I lost my temper and hit something right in front of you. Given your history, that was inexcusable."

I considered. "Given *our* history, that was almost unavoidable. Everyone has family-related baggage, my love. And since we share a family, we happen to have matching luggage. But I'm willing to work through it if you are."

His eyes blazed. "We're meant to be together, Téa — that's the one thing in life I'm still utterly certain of."

It was my turn to hold his face in my hands. I shifted onto my knees and pressed my lips against his, trying to pour all the love I felt for him into his body. He fell back against the couch, and after a minute I pulled away reluctantly.

"Do you know that old proverb?" I asked. "'A fish may love a bird, but where will they live?' We're faced with the same issues we had before you left. Except for one." I looked at him shyly. "It may not come soon, but when the time does come for us to have children, I know I can do it."

Jaden straightened up beside me. He ran one hand slowly down my back, and his expression was softer than I'd ever seen it. "You're not the only one whose perspective has changed. I shouldn't have tried to talk you out of riding for a living. It was selfish. I didn't want to be without you, didn't want to worry for your safety, or about what would happen if you took this big career gamble and didn't make it. I thought being older than you granted me some measure of greater wisdom, but I was wrong. Playing polo again these past few months has been a revelation. I feel like I've come alive again."

I faced him, tucking one leg under me, and seized both his hands. I was grinning. "I'm so glad to hear you say that, because I have a plan."

"Of course you do." He grinned back.

His look of amusement turned to surprise and then, finally, to pride as I outlined my plan.

"Did you come up with all this on your way over here?" he asked. He looked slightly awed.

"I've been thinking about it for weeks," I confided, "but I didn't think you'd agree." I picked up the ultrasound picture from where it had fallen on the floor. "And if I hadn't had a miscarriage... well, my plans might have been different."

He laid a hand tenderly across my abdomen. "How are you now?"

I thought about it. Physically I was fine, and that was probably what he meant. "I guess I'm grieving for them," I finally murmured. Utter silence followed. I looked up. Jaden's face was bloodless, and I stroked it in concern.

"*Them*?" His voice was a strangled whisper.

I held his hands, and his fingers clutched mine convulsively. "Yes," I said quietly. "Them. I was pregnant with twins."

Sixteen

I bounded down the stairs the next morning with more energy than I'd had in months.

"I take it things went well yesterday." Dec smiled. I hadn't seen him when I'd come in the night before.

"Yup." I poured myself coffee and glanced over at Seth. "Do you want to go for a hack after school?" It was getting a bit cold for trail rides, but I needed to speak to my brother privately.

"Maybe," he said, non-committal.

"Why, afraid I'll out-ride you like always?"

He snorted.

"Yeah, that's a convincing comeback." I laughed at him.

Dec and Seth both stared like they'd never heard me laugh before, but then, I supposed it had been a long time. I left them sitting in surprise and zoomed off to school, where fortunately Chuck and Shannon were willing to help me catch up on the material I'd missed. After class, I went to see Julia. She was back at her mom's, and she looked like her old self when she opened the door.

"What's the closest thing you've got to a power suit?" I asked.

She grabbed my arm and tugged me toward her bedroom. "I have just the thing."

I smiled sideways at her. "I'm glad you're back, Jules."

"Me too. You need me to be your fashion sense."

"Well, if I had to have good taste in only one thing, I'm glad it was in friends."

When I got home I went straight to the barn.

"Ready?" I asked Seth. I gave him a significant look. At his nod, I went to get Cal.

As I stepped onto the shavings he turned to me with a low nicker, his large eyes luminous with the same joy that I felt swelling within my own chest. He blew a soft breath against my cheek as I slipped on his bridle, and I kissed the edge of his satiny nostril before leading him outside. Cal was always touching me now. When we walked his nose was pressed against my arm, when we stood he leaned against me, when I turned him out he stayed at the gate watching me walk away. The contact filled us both up, and I knew down to my bones that we'd be this way from this point on. I hopped on him quickly and joined Seth outside.

We didn't speak until we were out of sight of the barn. Seth clapped Winter on the neck before turning to me. "You want to tell me what's going on?"

I outlined my plan. His eyebrows crept up as I spoke, and he offered a few suggestions of his own. By the time we got back from our ride he was grinning from ear to ear. "Do you think they'll go for it?"

"Just do your part to convince Gran, and I'll do the rest," I promised.

The next morning I put on the plum-colored suit that Julia had lent me. The skirt was a bit long on me, so I pulled it higher on my waist.

"Big presentation at school," I said in response to Dec's expression when I came downstairs. It was a flimsy excuse, since no one wore suits in a science program, but he didn't question it.

I didn't go to school. Instead, I headed into the city and met Jaden. I parked in a lot to save time and found him at our prearranged meeting place in front of his dad's office building.

"Nice suit," he said, bending to kiss me quickly.

"Same to you." He'd always looked impressive dressed up, but I'd come to realize that I preferred seeing him in his everyday riding clothes because that was who he really was.

Uncle Peter himself greeted us in the reception area, and he led us through an open area filled with cubicles and down a hallway to his office. Jaden was a bit taller than his father, though Uncle Peter was heavier set, I noticed as he turned around. He didn't sit down, so neither did we.

"So," he said, spreading his hands wide. "To what do I owe the pleasure?"

"Téa, would you like to explain your proposition?" Jaden asked. He gave me an encouraging nod.

I drew myself up to my full height, which probably wasn't impressive but did make me feel better, and outlined my plan. Uncle Peter's face went from incredulous to angry to suspicious, but eventually, thanks to Jaden's persuasive talents, it settled on acceptance. He shook hands with each of us as we left, and I thought his eyes held grudging admiration as they met mine.

I spent the next few days tying up the last details. Then one night after dinner, with my heart thumping, I told Dec I needed to talk to him.

We went into the living room, and he looked mildly surprised when Jaden and Gran entered the room. They settled on the couch next to Seth, and I sat next to Dec on the loveseat. His blue eyes slid sideways to meet mine, holding what may have been a warning.

"What's this about?" Clearly, his suspicions had been aroused.

I put my hand on his. "Have you ever wondered what your life would have been like if you'd followed your heart?" I asked him softly. His brows drew together but I plowed on. "If you'd ridden horses for a living, and made Gran proud that you were following in her footsteps? If you'd met amazing riders from other countries, and traveled around the world, and maybe even gone to the Olympics?"

"Maybe I wondered," Dec allowed. "But it made no difference. I had a duty to my family to stay here and help out, and to educate myself and better our lives as much as possible." The implication was clear that I should do the same.

I took a deep breath. "For a long time now, I've been trying to please other people — you, Jaden, even Seth." I glanced over at Seth; he didn't look surprised. "But not only am I not making you happy, I'm making myself miserable. I want to live my passion, Dec. I want to be *me* to the fullest because if I don't fill myself up first, I'll have nothing to give to anyone else. Not to my family, not to my work," I met Jaden's eyes. "And not even to my future children." I lowered my gaze to the floor; despite my conviction, I couldn't look at anyone now. "I want to follow my dreams wherever they take me. So... I'm leaving." I paused, swallowing hard. I heard Dec's intake of breath but he didn't say anything. I went on.

"I'm finishing out the semester and in January I'm going to Florida." I risked a sideways glance at Dec; his eyes were glacial, his mouth pressed into a flat line. Somehow, instead of making me cower, it prompted me to sit up and face him. "But that's not all. We know you've been tied to this place and that you might be ready to move on, so someone else is taking over."

"You can't do that," Dec interrupted impatiently, "my dad's will-"

"States that only one of his descendants can carry on," Jaden interjected smoothly. "And I qualify. I'm taking over the lease."

Dec's look of shock was almost comical. His mouth dropped open, and he went pale. I was beginning to worry when Gran spoke up.

"And don't worry about your brother and sister, Declan. You — and they — will be paid the fair market value of the property. It will be purchased so we can end this silly lease business for good."

Dec launched to his feet and started pacing. "This is ridiculous!" he shot at me.

"It isn't," Seth assured him. "We're just doing a lousy job of explaining it." He grinned at me. "That's your cue, Sis. Explain away."

I took a deep breath. "Okay. Jaden, Seth and I are buying the property. We put Jaden's name on the current lease to convince his dad that if he didn't agree to sell to us, we'd get the place anyway and he'd have nothing to show for it."

Dec's brows shot up, but he didn't interrupt.

"Jaden's selling his loft to cover the down payment and after that, we'll make monthly installments. Jaden's going back to polo." I found his eyes, beaming love at me from across the room, and smiled. "We'll both stay at his friend Michele's in Florida until spring, and then we'll come back here for the summer. Eventually, we may spend our summers in Europe; Jaden can play in England while I follow the Global Champions Tour."

"What about in the fall?" Dec asked, frowning.

I hesitated, and Jaden smoothly took over. "Téa will go to the big indoor shows and I'll go to Argentina. We'll be apart for about two months every year, but we've learned we can cope with that. And we can be here for a month every winter, including the holidays," Jaden explained.

Dec rubbed the back of his neck. He'd stopped pacing, but he was still standing and staring down at all of us. "If you two are gone, who's going to run the place?"

"I am, with Gran's help," Seth said. He grinned over at Gran. "We've always made a great team, and Gran's going to sell her house and move back in here." Gran beamed. She had leaped at the chance to continue her life's work, and she'd been touched that we wanted her involvement.

"And Jaden and I are going to build a second house on the property," I added.

Dec threw up his hands, palms outward. "Hold it! All this talk of buying and building — where's all the money going to come from?"

"Well, Jaden will be playing polo, which pays awfully well. As for me, the Donalds called me last week. They wanted me to take Hades back and I told them I'd do it if they signed a two-year contract, which they did. I also got a position as assistant trainer with Sasha Reznikov in Florida."

Gran's eyes went wide. "I didn't know that. However did you manage?" Sasha Reznikov was a well-known former Olympian, a tall blonde with a reputation as a fierce competitor.

"Karen introduced us, and the chef d'équipe of the Dutch team put in a good word for me." I grinned, still in a state of minor shock over my good fortune.

Dec's hard gaze returned to me. I turned away from it, suddenly nervous.

"You're quitting school?" he demanded.

"I'll take a few online courses, but basically, yes. And if you choose to sell Cal, that's your prerogative. But please, Dec-" My voice hitched, and I took a breath to steady it. I raised my eyes to the pale blue discs that had so often denied me the things I wanted most. "Sell him to me," I whispered. "I'll make payments every month, as much as I can."

Dec looked away, frowning. "Let me see if I've got this straight. You three kids are buying the business. Seth and Gran are going to run it, and Téa and Jaden will pitch in when they're around?"

"This will be my training base," I supplied.

"What about me?" Dec asked quietly.

My eyes went wide, and for a minute I floundered, wondering what to say.

"You can be as involved as you like. We just thought... I mean, we know you've wanted to focus more on your consulting business, and if you ever marry Joanne..." I trailed off, feeling a sick sense that I'd somehow made Dec feel supplanted in his own home.

He marched over to the loveseat. "Do you remember me telling you that you'd never make it in this business?" he rumbled. I nodded miserably. "I said you didn't have what it takes, that you weren't tough enough."

He was staring down at me, and I stood, forcing myself to hold his gaze no matter how humiliated I felt. This was my life, and I was finally going to live it as I saw fit, but I didn't bother to argue with Dec. He had made his feelings abundantly clear.

He put his hands on my shoulders. "I was wrong," he muttered.

I gaped at him. Tears sprang to my eyes, making me want to scream with frustration — it was just the kind of reaction Dec would scoff at. I felt a goofy grin form at that thought, and I threw my arms around my father.

"For the record, I wouldn't sell Cal," he murmured as he hugged me back. "He was a gift. He's yours." He drew back and looked around. "The people in this room are proof that we don't have to repeat our parent's mistakes. This family is a far sight better than it used to be, thanks to you kids."

Jaden came over and slung an arm around me, and I thought I could get used to the proud smile he bestowed on me.

Dec sat next to Seth. "Listen, son, we should talk about the courses you'll have to take in order to manage this place. You'll need bookkeeping and marketing-"

"And animal husbandry," Seth interjected. "I plan to start a breeding program."

Jaden's arm moved me outside. I closed the screen door gently and we stood on the porch, looking out over the land that had been his ancestors', and that would form the foundation for our future. I wrapped my arms around his waist and he rubbed my arm, warding off the chill although I hardly felt it next to the heat of his hard body.

"Do you know how proud I am of you?" He spoke quietly. "You were the driving force behind all of this, and you've changed all of our lives for the better. You've never once given up on the things you care about, and I'm honored to count myself among them." He cupped his warm hand to my cheek for a moment, and then, slowly, he sank downward. I reached for him in concern, and he gathered my hands between both of his.

"Jaden..." I gazed at him in confusion, and it slowly dawned on me that he was kneeling. On one knee. His honey-drop eyes were molten, making it impossible to look away.

"I realized a few things while I was away," he said. "I realized that wherever you are is home to me. That the first person I want to share my joys and sorrows with is you. That I can no longer even imagine a life without you. And that I love you more than I ever thought it was possible to love another person. Téa Everson, will you marry me?"

Shock stole my breath, and for a long moment I simply stood and trembled.

Finally, I managed to open my mouth. "Yes. Of course, yes."

Those stupid tears were back, and as Jaden rose to his feet he wiped one away with his thumb before cradling my face in his hands.

"I'm sorry I don't have a ring," he murmured. "I wasn't actually planning to do this now. I didn't want to rush you."

"The wedding can wait until we both feel the time is right," I said, looping my arms around him. I felt a new sense of calm and certainty about the future. "Would you want me to change my name?" I asked. Everson was my mother's name, after all.

His face was radiant as his eyes burned into mine. "It makes no difference what your name is, *querida*. As long as you're mine."

"Forever," I agreed as I smiled against his lips.

ABOUT THE AUTHOR

When she's not hiking up the sides of active volcanoes in the company of stray dogs, M. Garzon likes to take time to appreciate the fierce beauty of the natural world around her. She used to ride horses for a living, which was fantastic, but now considers herself extremely lucky to be a writer. She shares her home with two kids and too many rescue animals.

Please keep in touch at www.mgarzon.ca or on Facebook, Twitter, or Instagram

87732929R00188

Made in the USA
Middletown, DE
05 September 2018